THE EXILE CARPET

Dreamscapes

E. R. Blake

ISBN: 1537143654
ISBN 13: 9781537143651
Library of Congress Control Number: 2016913702
CreateSpace Independent Publishing Platform
North Charleston, South Carolina

For three priestesses, a white witch and a guardian.

1

*D*awn's brilliance fractured a misty gray sky. Cold radiated from a leaded glass window, sending tingles through her body. Glancing down at a string of sapphire beads in her hand, she whispered a tiny prayer for forgiveness and strength while the beads pressed into her delicate skin. Graceful fingers found their end, where a golden crescent dangled from a blue tassel. Dressing auspiciously in black for the day's events, her ladies in waiting had been dismissed the night before, to spare the embarrassment of their witness to her arrest. Her last moments of solitude were broken by a creaking sound in the wall. Three men of the Clan Donnachaidh, disguised as palace guards, silently crept through a hidden door. Peering across the surrounding hills one last time, geese dotted the sky with the morning light reflecting off their feathers. She spun around. "My Lords, I am grateful for your arrival to such a hasty summons."

"Majesty, we are honored to assist you," the first man declared, bowing deeply.

She approached them slowly, looking each one of them in the eye. "Your chieftain informed you of what is to come in the days ahead?" They nodded. "Then you know what is required once you secure the artifact?"

The man dared to interrupt. "I am afraid your instructions are vague. We are unsure to whom we are to relinquish your treasure."

The woman approached a small writing desk gracing the other side of the room. From its top drawer she retrieved a small envelope with a royal seal in red wax. *"Give this letter to your chieftain. It holds the name and location of the priestess who is to receive the article. It is imperative that they reach her by the time I am imprisoned. Should you fail in your task, the legitimacy of your family will be at stake."*

Bowing his head, he placed the letter inside the pocket of his coat. She gestured for him to accompany her to the wardrobe next to the window, where the other two clansmen stood guard. A large object was removed from the wardrobe, housed within a red velvet bag. Looking down at the rich color of the fabric, he inquired if this was the same object he had heard legends about as a young child.

"You hold the Exile Carpet. I have been its guardian since adolescence, as my mother instructed. She protected it before me, as all the women in my family have for generations. Its survival is vital, even if mine is not," she remarked with a tremble in her voice.

"May I view the piece? I have only heard it described from the memory of those who have been fortunate enough to do so," the man requested.

She insisted it be spread out onto the bed, so that the other men could view it as well. The man untied the golden cord that held the fabric over the carpet and removed it from its housing. Gently exposing the intricate nature of the woven textile, its colors were vibrant against the stark-white backdrop of bed linens. Four unique heads, consisting of three females and one male, floated peaceably among ocean waves in a crescent-shaped vessel. Above them an identical moon decorated the sky, as a dove guided them toward a distant shore. The edges of the carpet were beginning to unravel—a clear threat to its existence, should it be handled improperly. A surprising wave of grief swept over him as he glanced at the woman standing at the opposite side of the bed.

"May I be so bold as to ask a question?" he asked reluctantly. She silently nodded her permission. Summoning his courage, he tried not to offend her. *"What threat can a carpet pose to those outside this room?"*

Hiding her hands within the folds of her skirt, she fingered the crescent before speaking. It served as a symbol of education and brought great comfort during times of trial. *"The Exile Carpet is confirmation that four refugees fled the Holy Land, following Christ's crucifixion. It is tangible evidence that hope endures among all turmoil, be it great or small, and is the missing puzzle piece* required for a chosen priestess to awaken the masters and restore this earth to the balance that has been lost."

The man stared at her. His encounters with her had always been brief, but he had never heard her speak in enigmatic phrases. It would be one of his main topics of conversation with the chieftain once the Exile Carpet had been safely delivered. "Majesty, we will complete what has been instructed," he stated, diverting his eyes from her piercing gaze.

Heavy footsteps echoed in the hall. She instructed the men to quickly place the carpet back in its satchel. The woman hurried them back through the wall just as the lock turned on the bedroom door. Three palace guards violated her sanctuary. The woman rolled her shoulders back, pursing her lips at their intrusion.

"Mary, Queen of Scots," the captain of the guard barked.

Annoyed at his casual tone, the woman replied, "You know that to be true, sir."

"By the order of Her Royal Majesty, the Queen of England, I hereby arrest you for the act of high treason against the Crown. Do you plead guilt or innocence?"

Choosing her words carefully, Mary paused. "I know not of guilt or innocence. It seems in this instance that it does not matter if I am either. I am sentenced and punished as a criminal simply for inhabiting the skin on my back."

The captain walked menacingly toward her, halting inches from her face. "I can charge you with other crimes, should you fail to cooperate, Your Majesty," he said, sneering.

The foul stench of undigested meat and ale lingered on his breath.

"If you feel compelled to do so, sir, I cannot stop you. However, since I retain the title of 'Majesty,' you should resist the urge to be anything other than a gentleman."

His palm flew through the air, meeting her delicate cheek with a brute force, knocking her to the ground. Crumpling into a ball, she raised a trembling hand to her cheek and choked back hot tears. She wouldn't give him the satisfaction of being vulnerable before him. She wouldn't allow any of them to know that they penetrated the safeguards of her mind. She slowly stood up to face the guards. The captain delivered a second blow to her body. This time his *fist met her abdomen with such a tremendous pain that she feared she would lose consciousness. She once again fell to the floor. Two guards hoisted her up to her feet, dragging her across the room. She glanced at the captain before crossing the threshold. His smug smile hung in the silence and confirmed that her confinement would prove to be more torturous than solitary. He would make her feel pain out of sheer pleasure until she no longer felt anything at all.*

"Take a good look around you, Majesty. This is the last time you'll see this opulence. But I assure you that your accommodations in the tower have fresh straw from the horse stables." He signaled for the guards to let him pass her in the doorway. "Hopefully the day your head rolls, the sun will peek out of the clouds. It's a bit nicer when the sun is shining." His cruel laughter echoed as he drove his fist into her stomach for the second time.

2

The vision of the guard's blow rippled through each nerve, forcing Tamara to fold in half. The teacup in her hand tumbled toward the ground. Shattering glass disrupted the morning's silence, as tiny shards scattered across a wooden floor. Since the sun had not fully appeared, the task of retrieving the pieces seemed impossible. As she tried, a speck of glass found her bare foot, forcing her to cry out. She didn't need more pain: not now, *not ever.*

Tamara held onto the kitchen counter, her strength waning as her pale-pink skin faded to a ghostly appearance. The tile of the counter felt icy, confirming the return of a fever. She would have to use her last bit of strength wisely if she wanted permission to ever leave her bedroom again.

The sun's first rays peeked over the horizon, filtering through a multitude of woven baskets. Lifting her head, she marveled at its arrival. She loved this part of the day. The numerous baskets were collected from flea markets, garage sales, and bargain stores by her Gammie. She had a story for each and every one of them.

"Maybe a basket story will make my brain feel normal again." The deep throbbing in her head wouldn't allow relief.

With a small burst of courage, she reached for a well-worn farm table to aid in her departure. Left hand found the wood first, then the right. She needed her legs to work. They were often dependent on the support of crutches, or worse yet, "the chair." The mere thought of her dependence on a wheelchair filled her with rage, giving her the push she needed to get to the door. "I can make it this time." She took a weak step. Pain shot through her toes from a piece of glass. It would have to wait until she got back into bed. Luckily, her bedroom had been moved down to the first floor, a few feet from the main staircase.

As a young girl, Tamara ran up and down those stairs at a break-neck pace. Beneath her fingers, the elaborate mahogany carvings breathed a life of their own. Up and down and up and down she would go until her ribs felt as if they would burst. This grand stair-case, as well as the rest of the house, felt magical.

"I can't see the staircase!" she declared in the doorway of the din-ing room. "Damn this useless body!"

Three solid steps brought the warmth of an antique rug. Her plan was to make it to the table, the door jam, the staircase, and finally the salvation of her bed. She threw her hands in front of her for the sup-port of the dining room table. Looking up from this vantage point, she viewed Gammie's prize possession: a woven carpet bearing the heads of four individuals, a boat, a moon, and a shoreline.

The museum-quality display case lit the carpet from above. No lon-ger in pristine condition, it could still be considered a stunning piece of art. Over centuries, it had lost a bit of its form, but the center weav-ing remained intact. This morning's vision had included a woman named Mary, who handed the same carpet to three men. She felt the pain Mary endured at the hand of her captors. The pain had pulled her from Mary's world and back into reality. And, like Mary, Tamara had run out of time.

"You think you could tell me about the freaking carpet now, Gammie?" she shrieked at the case. *Don't do that; don't get mad. Mad doesn't help.* With her fever, a chill seeped into her bones. Even her flannel nightgown offered little resistance to this new intruder.

Three more unstable steps, and her fingers met the rounded top of the banister. Looking up at the second floor landing, the new day's sunlight flooded an enormous stained glass window. A single red rose reflected from its center into a yellow halo of light. The figure of a woman dressed in white appeared. She was the same one from her dream, as well as one of the faces in the carpet.

"Mary?" she shouted into the dark. The figure made no reply. "Mary, do you have a message for me?"

Violent pain returned to her abdomen. "Not now!" she yelled. "She has something to tell me!" Light engulfed the glass. Mary dissolved into penetrating sunbeams. "No!" she cried. "I need to know why this is happening!"

The pain was so great, it made the room spin. *Is this how your life ends?* she wondered. Without warning, anger kept deep within broke free and reached the surface with an eruption. She reached over to grasp a silver candlestick from the hall table. Years of pent-up frustration, torment, and confinement boiled over. She was an outcast, a freak, someone whom no one but family wanted to be around. Since her mysterious illness, their eyes turned from pity to fear. She despised it all.

She became a monster screaming for vengeance. Without a sacrificial lamb, she spun around, hurtling the candlestick into the dining room. Her entire body fell onto the wood floor with a thud, causing strength to retreat and pain to return.

The candlestick smashed through the glass case, releasing the carpet. Free of its protective enclosure, the carpet sprang to life. Woven heads broke free from the yarn. The illumination of colored yarn created intricate patterns in the air above her. Four heads spun into a high-speed blur, culminating in a burst of brilliant light. They sparkled around her, leaving vapor trails in the night.

Unable to fight the encroaching darkness engulfing her mind, she surrendered to the loss of consciousness. Her head was the last to hit the floor while her mother rushed to her aid, shouting her name as if in slow motion. In the darkness, her mind took hold. The elusive figure of Mary manifested with outstretched arms to cradle the young girl before shadow seized its claim.

Her last thought was clear. "At least I won't die alone," she whispered.

3

D r. Mitchell Brody strode toward Tamara's bedside with the confidence of a man wiser than his years. His most recent professional honor had come the previous month, when he was named top in his field internationally. He found it both exhilarating and humbling. Once accolades flooded his e-mail, the pressure for success became paramount. To his dismay, the practice of medicine had become more about numbers than actual care. He excelled at the intimate relationships with his patients, combining their battle for survival with his sheer determination. The result was a team atmosphere during their fight for life. This battle was powerful motivation during endless hospital nights without sleep.

He was met by a group of women huddled around Tamara's bedside, whispering prayers with arms outstretched along the length of her body. Tamara's mother, Lillian, sat close to the group, looking as calm as she had the first time she met him at the age of seven. The women completed their intentions and silently exited the room.

Dr. Brody teased his patient, stating, "I see your mother has you settled."

"She's a beacon of efficiency," Tamara snapped.

He stepped over to her mother, noticing the subtle anxiety she exhibited by twirling her wedding around her finger.

"It's been too long," Mitch admitted, gently covering her moving hands with his own. Tamara watched their exchange, noticing a piece of jewelry gracing Dr. Brody's finger. The glimmer of gold on his right hand stood out in stark contrast to his navy scrub pants.

"I had to read about your new accomplishment from a magazine article rather than receiving a personal phone call. Too busy to pick up the phone?" Lillian scolded.

Only Lillian could discipline him on the same level as his own mother. "I should have called. I had every intention, but the awards ceremony was a complete surprise, and then there were the obligatory press interviews. Believe me, it was not intentional."

Lillian rolled her eyes at his pitiful excuse. "Yeah, yeah, Brody."

He chuckled and withdrew his hands. She managed to hold onto them a few seconds longer to reveal the ring. "Your father would be proud. Is it his, or have you finally obtained your own?" Smiling, Lillian added, "I am slightly disappointed that it isn't a wedding band."

Mitch blushed. "A wedding band? I can't remember to call an old friend when I achieve one of the highest honors of my career, and you want me married? I am afraid Tamara will be walking down the aisle before I do," he admitted, winking at his patient.

Tamara noticed the curious markings etched on the ring. The piece of jewelry became an accidental heirloom following a dark day during his adolescence. Presented as a token of affection upon graduation from medical school, it had graced his finger since that spring day.

He quickly changed the subject.

"A nasty situation has developed." Skimming over the medical chart, he continued, "I was hoping we wouldn't reach this level before figuring out the best course of action."

Lillian read the notes over his shoulder. "Still no answers?"

"I searched every database, asked colleagues with experience in this type of case, and not one of us has found anything that solves

Tamara's circumstance," he announced. "I'm afraid the latest results of her labs show we no longer have time to waste."

"Surely we haven't tried everyone, Mitch!" Lillian suggested.

"Uh, hello…could someone please talk to me, since it is *my* body we are discussing?" Tamara was frustrated with the way they casually spoke as if she wasn't there.

Looking at her frail frame, Mitch took a deep breath. He attempted to formulate the right words without scaring her. He needed them to believe that she could survive, to mentally defeat the disease before the rest of her body had the opportunity to succeed. Hope was the human body's greatest weapon against disease. Too many times he informed patients of what he believed would be the prognosis only to have them deteriorate because they believed survival wasn't an option. Tamara needed to stay positive to heal. He couldn't waltz into this with his normal arrogance. He had to think, plan, and execute exactly what was needed without wasting a single minute on theories. His obligation to her far surpassed average medical ethics.

Tamara sensed his stress. Since the moment her parents requested him to be the specialist on her case, she looked into his eyes for a signal that he possessed more human attributes than medical jargon. Today, she saw fear.

Mitch walked toward Tamara with the chart, pulling a second chair over to her bedside. "You deserve to know the truth. I haven't known how to communicate it to you without fear being your first response. If your mother approves, I am ready to speak with you now." Lillian nodded her head, granting permission. Pausing before he began, the breath in his lungs seemed to harden like concrete. "Due to the angle of the impact from the car accident two years ago, the left side of your body suffered the highest level of trauma. The initial surgery immediately following the accident revealed that all was repairable, except your left kidney, which was the reason for its removal."

"I know all that," Tamara sneered. "I lived through it."

"Let's cover all the facts up to this point, OK?" he requested calmly. "Be patient with me."

Tamara blocked his stare by closing her eyes. "Go ahead."

Clearing his throat, he continued, "Once we removed the kidney, we were confident you would recover normal function with little disruption. We truly believed that your remaining kidney could function without any problems. Its failure six months ago combined with the deterioration of other organs left us baffled."

"Failure" was a word Tamara had grown accustomed to. It followed her like a new puppy. She desperately wanted this ordeal to be over. Months of painful dialysis taught her that life wasn't fair. Being ill was not any type of normal. Illness doesn't allow normal; it only allows you the life of a hostage in your own body. Originally when they told her that dialysis was not working, she completely surrendered. She accepted that she was destined to die young, to not reach the same milestones as her peers. She felt fortunate to have survived the accident, but with the news of her body failing, she felt like the victim of a cruel karmic joke. Being young, she felt immortal. But this illness made her taste her mortality and robbed her of youth.

Her mother's perspective was different. Instead of giving up, she fought harder. She did not accept failure when it came to her only child. She demanded the best of the best in what she referred to as, "The fight of her life."

Dialysis left Tamara too weak to fight as hard as her mother expected. All she craved was sleep. In her dreams she was free to do anything, go anywhere, and eat anything she desired. This newfound freedom became an addiction to escape the dismal reality of her illness. During this deep dream state her visions had become not only more frequent but accepted as her new "normal."

Lillian's search for a physician resulted in endless phone calls across the nation. None were the right fit. While most had experience in one arena, they lacked the ability to handle multisystem organ failure. Most feared failure would result in a negative mark on their reputation.

One of her closest friends told her that the right person was under her nose. Dr. Mitchell Brody was a close family friend, who often accompanied his father, a brilliant physician in his own time, to her home for visits. Mitch combined the gentleness of his father with a quiet tenacity. Lillian was sure he had inherited his persistent nature from his mother, a member of the woman's group that met monthly at Lillian's family home. If anyone could save Lillian's child, it would be Mitchell Brody.

The waiting list of patients requesting his expertise was shy of two years, but for this family, he would make exceptions. Three weeks passed without any new information. Two more weeks passed before a course of treatment was solidified. The option to acquire a kidney donor was paramount, and dialysis would continue, along with controversial medications recently cleared by the FDA. Tamara's name was put onto every conceivable donor list, and the critical waiting had begun. That was four months ago.

Tamara opened her eyes, hearing Dr. Brody say, "That brings us to today."

"Your rare blood type makes the donor match difficult, add to that the compounding issues, and I am stumped." He leaned forward, placing his elbows upon his knees. "How often are you having episodes?"

Ignoring this intrusion, Tamara turned her head to the wall.

"Three to four a day. An increase from one or two," Lillian answered.

"When did they increase?" Mitch asked.

"About a month ago. Do you think they are related to the organ failure?"

"I don't know, but it's worth considering. Anything at this point is worth considering," Mitch conceded.

Raising her voice, Lillian took aim. "Are you telling me that there isn't anyone in the whole wide world who can provide a match or who is bright enough to solve the puzzle of the other failing organs?"

Finding the courage to look at her, Mitch sighed. "For today, no one matches. We tried every database in the world."

Standing to face him, Lillian recognized the defeat in his posture. "We aren't done fighting, Mitch! There has to be another way! Failure is not something I will ever accept. I *won't* accept it."

Shaking his head, he asked, "What would you have me do?"

"Keep looking until we find a match!" Lillian pleaded.

Keeping his calm, Mitch repeated their enemy of time, adding that he couldn't determine how much of it they had left before Tamara went into full failure. Walking slowly to the window, Lillian peeked through the blinds. A flood of jealousy swept over her as she watched people come and go without the undue stress of losing their child. Missing the carefree toddler days with Tamara, she recalled the way her child preferred the role of peace keeper between other children and never challenged parental boundaries. Raising her head toward the sky, Lillian watched the light diminish with the setting sun. The last rays followed the top of the great half dome, vanishing in a blink of an eye, leaving the sky a dark-blue hue. Offering a silent prayer to the universe for the life of her daughter, she faced her old friend with a sigh of exasperation. "Do you remember what we discussed last time?"

Mitch's eyes widened at the magnitude of her question. He had known this day would come for the past week, but he didn't want to accept that they had reached the point of desperation. "We can manage her care without going to those lengths."

"You just admitted that you are unable to manage her care without the aid of others," Lillian repeated. "Did I misunderstand any of that?"

Mitch avoided eye contact, sensing her anger at his lack of resolution. "I didn't think you were seriously proposing that topic as a credible solution."

Tapping her fingers against her upper arm, Lillian's lips pursed. "When it comes to the life of my daughter, I am dead serious. We have exhausted all resources at our disposal. I cannot allow my baby to be taken without a fight." Looking over at Tamara, her mouth loosened into a warm smile. "She was born for greatness, and it is my obligation to make sure she reaches her destiny." She looked down at the ring gracing Mitch's finger. "By the looks of the oath on your finger, it has become your obligation as well."

Mitch twirled the piece of jewelry around his finger. "I'll make the necessary arrangements," he whispered. "The contact needs to be personal. I would need to leave in the morning. To be honest, I'm not entirely comfortable leaving her without proper monitoring."

Lillian walked over to her old friend as he continued his focus on the ring. With a gentle touch to his chin, she lifted his face up to eye level. "I have tremendous confidence in your abilities and judgment. No matter what may happen, you must remember your strength." As she spoke these words to him, Mitch looked deep into her eyes. There was nothing he wouldn't do for her or her family.

"When you two are done with your inspirational exchange, would you kindly take me home? If I have to die, it won't be in this institution," Tamara insisted.

With the spell broken, Mitch faced Tamara. "I will sign orders for home care if you promise to follow every medical order without question or attitude."

Tamara nodded enthusiastically. She would agree to anything to get out of the hospital.

"I will sign your discharge upon completion of blood work tomorrow morning." He rose from his chair and slowly walked toward the door. Looking back at Tamara, Mitch teased, "I know how you love tests."

Lillian met Mitch at the door. "I'm not sure how long I will be away," he warned.

Placing a hand on his shoulder, Lillian answered, "It will take as long as it is meant to."

"We don't have that luxury," Mitch reminded her.

"I know I'm flip-flopping here, but I have faith in the hands of the Master. He is a man of quiet peace. During times like these, we need to remember that hope remains," Lillian confided.

Mitch sighed. He never possessed a large quantity of faith. His career consisted of facts and figures with absolutes mixed in for good measure. Medicine was all about results; spiritual faith had nothing to do with it. Grasping the door handle, he knew his path, and no matter what the end result, he had to move forward. "I know a suitable replacement."

"Wellington, perhaps?" Lillian remarked.

Stepping into the hall, Mitch laughed. "I'm sure it won't be a surprise. Tell me where to meet this master of yours."

Lillian brushed a stray hair from Tamara's forehead, silently continuing her prayers for a miracle. Her faith would now need to shift to a man she had never met and to a promise he had made at Tamara's birth. Would she be able to hand her daughter over when the time came, or would she falter, deferring to her motherly instinct of protection? Her brain formed the words before her heart told it to stop. "London."

4

aylight dripped heavy fog as her red car turned onto the familiar tree-lined street. Guilt created a shade of doubt. Upon accepting this assignment, she was asked if directions would be needed. Not wanting to tip her hand, she accepted the mapped location. She could find her way to the house during a blinding rainstorm in the dark. She had been such a frequent visitor during her childhood that she often referred to it as her family's second home. Speculation floated within social circles about her father's participation in an extramarital affair, given the amount of time he spent alone at the house. During his meetings with the other men, she remained in the library, reading about distant lands. Wondering if the same books still occupied the shelves, she parked in front of a large black lamppost.

She took great pains not to look at the house before approaching. The rearview mirror reflected her pristine appearance as she smoothed her hair one last time. She expected nothing short of perfection in all aspects of her life, with little patience for those who didn't share the same opinion. Perfection was the ultimate definition of dedication. However, this attitude meant the majority of her time was spent either alone or at work, where people tended to shy away from her as well. The ringing of her cell phone was a reminder that solitude would need to be abandoned for an increased volume of phone calls.

"Have you been updated?" a gruff male voice questioned.

She responded quickly. "Sure."

"Are you being coy, or do I not have your undivided attention?"

"I was making sure no one was watching me while we spoke," she choked out.

"Your directions are simple. Perform the duties of nurse without deviating from the medication. The liquid in each vial will ensure our success as well as her demise." he paused, while huge lumps formed in her throat. "It is imperative that she does not fulfill her destiny."

The guilt in the pit of her stomach grew as he continued. "I have waited for their defeat for the last twenty years, which is why I agreed to your demands. Your tainted reputation is your greatest qualification. I don't require a saint. I prefer the sinner."

He laughed effortlessly at his scheming. "Dr. Brody will be out of the country, unable to oversee her progress. This current development will allow you to remain invisible as long as he stays away. They will never know what horrors await until they are laid at their feet."

She squeaked out a question. "What about Dr. Brody's medical replacement? Surely you don't assume that he would leave her unattended while snooping around for a miracle."

"Not even a blip on my radar."

"What about the contacts he makes while there? Shouldn't we stay on top of who he speaks to?" she asked nervously.

The man sighed out of boredom. "If Dr. Brody is your intended target for a personal vendetta, then you do so without any of my resources at your disposal."

Irritated by his tone, she snapped, "I know my job."

"You are not to question my authority, but to act solely on the directions I give you. Dr. Brody will flush out the Master *and* the Professor. Once exposed, I will see to their elimination, which includes Dr. Brody."

She stammered. "Yes, sir."

"Once you are apprised of the orders Brody left, you will report to me. At that time, I will give you the next set of instructions."

With a sharp click, the voice was gone. She knew her part, and she knew her role, but most importantly, she knew the family. She checked her scrubs to ensure they were wrinkle free, and then she peeked into a duffle bag sitting on the passenger seat, confirming that the vials were secure. Finally, she looked up at the house.

The Victorian architecture stood out from the rest of the historical homes on the street. The stone foundation was visible up to the wraparound porch, which welcomed visitors with hanging baskets full of flowers. Three wooden rocking chairs nestled between pristine white columns. Reminiscing about her mother's monthly meetings, she glanced up at the tower on the third floor with its massive floor-to-ceiling windows. The house's fresh coat of tan paint was highlighted by the stark-white trim and the red hue of the roof. Flowers lined the front walk, making the fog less gloomy, their bright pinks, purples, and reds peeking through the mist.

The weathered double front door held bronze fixtures and a bee-shaped doorknocker. Her fingers curved around the cold metal, giving it three hard raps. No other sound than the wind through the trees was audible. Not seeing movement within the house, she used the bee once more to announce her arrival. Anger bubbled inside for being made to wait, resulting in three stronger knocks that rattled the door.

Turning sharply on her heels, she began to walk back to her car just as the massive door creaked open. The outline of a disheveled woman stood in the darkened doorway. She remained silent, waiting for her visitor to speak first. The young nurse stepped closer. "I have been assigned to Tamara's home care. I was told the agency confirmed the arrangements."

The woman remained motionless. Her brown tailored trousers were severely wrinkled, appearing as though they had been slept in, while her green cardigan sweater hid a beloved diamond pendant. Breaking their awkward silence, the woman gave her a small smile. "You look so much like your father, Daphne! Give me a hug!"

Daphne felt uncomfortable being touched by anyone, especially this woman. She pulled away first, looking into the blue eyes of her new employer. "I wasn't sure if you would be comfortable with me caring for Tamara."

"Other than her doctor, there's no one else I trust more."

Daphne smirked as she walked toward the opening of the front door. "I never dreamed that you would enter the nursing field, considering your passion for glamour dolls as a child," Lillian teased. "Do you remember?"

Without hesitating, Daphne answered. "The only dolls I have now are my patients. And they are quite real."

A flush of embarrassment found Lillian's cheeks. "I don't think we need to go over the guidelines of this case as long as the doctor's office already discussed them with you. Let's get you settled." Daphne brushed past her into the foyer. Lillian looked outside to see the junkyard car. "Would you like to park in the driveway?"

Daphne couldn't resist the opportunity to shoot a little venom. "I didn't think you would want anyone associating that heap of scrap with this house." The look of shame on Lillian's face reflected that the intended target had been hit. "Besides, at the curb, it won't block deliveries. Easier for everyone, don't you think?" Lillian said nothing as she closed the door behind them.

From further down the street, he watched the women disappear into the house. Replacing the binoculars in his hand with a cell phone, his attention now turned to an interruption of poorly timed conversations. Snatching his sunglasses off the dashboard, his nails left a mark on the smooth leather. "What details are you micromanaging today?"

"There is no need for petty insults. I am not responsible for the mundane activity of your present assignment. Your expertise will come shortly."

Switching the phone into speaker mode, he threw it onto the dashboard. "Nothing to report," he snarled.

"Continue your observations, and make sure your replacement is briefed thoroughly before your departure to London. The council will take possession of the journals within the next few days. As for the Exile Carpet and the girl, their destruction will follow the handoff."

"And the nurse? Is she my warm-up before the doctor?"

"Not unless she steps out of line. The completion of the planetary alignment will occur before the girl has any opportunity to reach the temple. Once the Exile Carpet and the journals have been destroyed, humanity will no longer require her."

"This can be finished tonight," the man admitted.

"Not until Brody fulfills his purpose."

Frustrated by the lack of activity, he focused his gaze upon the windows of the house. The military-style binoculars could permeate anything within a ten-mile radius, rendering its occupants fully visible to prying eyes. Directing the lenses toward the first floor, he continued his mundane vigil.

The foyer was darkened with the day's gloom. Daphne trailed her hand along a round table in the center, which held a vase of dying roses. To her right, she squinted at the only brightness in the house. It danced through dust particles, traveling through the dining room from the carpet's display case. She was told that the girl and the carpet went hand in hand. To harm just one would be insufficient. Both needed to be eliminated. She was only given instructions for the girl, but after seeing the carpet, its destruction would be easier.

Her excitement rose with the anticipation of administering the contents of the first vile. Clutching the duffle bag a little tighter, a small surge of adrenaline ran through her veins. She could hardly believe that her moment of glory had arrived. She felt like a kid in a candy store with a fistful of cash.

"Tamara's room has been moved downstairs to the library to accommodate the machinery, hospital bed, and wheelchair. This way, she has access to the first floor in the wheelchair and feels somewhat normal during her recovery. All of the equipment was delivered this morning," Lillian stated, waking Daphne from her haze.

Before opening the doors to the library, she turned to face Daphne. "Let's settle some issues before they have the opportunity to arise. First off, you are not to upset her in any way. Second, you are not to discuss her case with anyone. We need to be discreet with her care, her illness, and her condition. Third and finally, you are not to ask questions about this house or anyone in it, or to question my judgment. I will be discussing the daily situation directly with Dr. Brody, which means that there will be no need for the two of us to confer about his orders. You will receive medical guidance from Dr. Brody and everything else from me. Is that clear?"

Daphne felt an intense rage welling up inside. She was a trained professional who didn't appreciate her abilities being second-guessed by anyone, least of all an arrogant idiot like Lillian. She calmed her temper before answering. "Lillian, we are all here for Tamara. I will follow any directions I am given by the people who know her best."

Convinced of her sincerity, Lillian opened the double doors. Compared to the rest of the house, the room was warm and comfortable. From the large marble fireplace, a fire provided a hypnotic effect. The oak mantle held small figurines of men in kilts, hunting dogs, and an antique clock. Above it, an heirloom artwork had been replaced with a flat-screen television. This had been Daphne's favorite room as a child; except she remembered a massive desk and chair next to the fireplace. The books were housed according to color in floor-to-ceiling bookcases specifically designed for the house, with rare editions encased behind glass doors for protection. A hospital bed replaced the familiar furnishings she loved. The only feminine touch came from flowered curtains framing the windows.

Daphne started to walk toward the machines to check Tamara's vitals, but Lillian grabbed her arm. "Wait," she whispered. "They gave her medication to help her sleep before we left the hospital, and she just drifted off. Please don't bother her."

Daphne glanced down at her arm and then up to Lillian's face. "It's my job to make sure her IV is done properly and the meds are administered correctly. I *have* done this before, Lillian."

Hearing the warning in Daphne's tone, Lillian released her arm. She rolled her shoulders back and planted her feet firmly on the floor. "Sorry to overrule you so soon, but you will leave her be. I brought you here to show you where she is staying and nothing more." Daphne's lips pursed. Lillian tried a lighter tone accompanied by a small smile. "In the end, we're all on the same team."

Daphne looked at her with disgust. *Don't tip your hand too quickly,* she told herself. *She'll soon find out who's really in charge.* Daphne regained her composure and her most sincere smile. "Mothers are always right. Rest *really* is the best medicine. Let's catch up while she sleeps. Got any tea?"

The two women turned away from Tamara's sleeping form and exited the room. Before crossing the threshold into the living room, Daphne turned to look at her young charge. A smirk appeared as she realized that this "special" child was now at her mercy.

"Coming, Daph?"

Slowly closing the door behind her, Daphne answered sweetly, "Absolutely, Lillian. Lead the way."

5

A black cab sped along the rain-soaked streets of London. His late arrival into Heathrow Airport created a panic to find last-minute accommodations. Luckily, a cancellation enabled him to confirm a reservation for the next couple of days. Dr. Brody wondered what his meeting with the Master would entail; he was curious if he would surrender the answer to Tamara's condition. Given her medical anomalies, he hoped the trip would be brief, but he secretly wished he would be afforded the opportunity to stay a few more days. To him, London was one of the most fascinating cities in the world. Modern-day architecture mingled with historical landmarks in a quiet symbiosis. The rain twinkled inside puddles on the street, causing the pavement to come alive. Turning from the window, he asked the driver, "Will the rain let up tomorrow?"

"Bloody unlikely. You're in the land of rain, sir," the driver answered, glancing at his passenger through the rearview mirror.

More rain might delay his trip, and he longed to get time away for light sightseeing before returning home. Lillian assured him that the Master was available, even on short notice, but the uncertainty was a concern. He preferred structure, and the notion of flying by the seat of his pants set him on edge. When the driver arrived at the valet stand at the Ritz Hotel, a familiar face greeted him.

"Back so soon, sir?"

Mitch couldn't help but smile. "Good to see you again, John. A pressing matter, I am afraid," Mitch added more seriously.

"Very good, sir," John answered while holding an umbrella above the door.

Walking to the entrance, Dr. Brody felt the brush of a hand upon the top of his hip. Cautious, he quickly spun around. He saw the cab with the engine running at the curb and John holding the large navy umbrella above his head. Nothing seemed out of the ordinary.

"Is there a problem, sir?" John asked.

Mitch lied. "Just checking to see if the rain was letting up."

"Not in the last few seconds, sir. But you never can tell."

Dr. Brody smiled. If he was going to convince people that he knew what he was doing, he would have to stop acting like an amateur. He extended his right hand toward John, passing him a twenty-pound note. "Thanks, John. I can always count on you."

"That you can, sir. Have a nice stay."

Mitch frequently arranged for accommodations at the Ritz whenever his personal or professional life brought him to London. With so much recent travel, it felt more like a second home. He felt the need to surround himself with comfort and familiarity as he journeyed into an unknown abyss. After the necessary paperwork, he requested all calls be blocked to his room, with a few noted exceptions, and a rental car in the morning. Stepping toward the elevator, he made a visual sweep of the lobby for anything out of the ordinary. He couldn't think of anyone off the top of his head who could jeopardize the importance of this trip. Or was there someone? To air on the side of caution, he decided to pay more attention to details he would normally disregard.

Room 3313 was considered a standard room in the hotel, comprising a small sitting area and bedroom with an attached bath. His first task was to confirm his plans with Lillian. After leaving a message on her voice mail, his body succumbed to jet lag. Drifting off quickly, one last thought lingered. Tomorrow, the challenge would begin.

After a restful night, Mitch threw back the curtains to embrace the new day. His morning routine usually began with a jog, a steam shower, and an update of patients before rounds. This trip was a nice distraction from the grind of everyday life, but the day ahead felt daunting. He wasn't sure why he had volunteered for this, but the pesky little voice in the back of his head spoke before he had a chance to think about it. It was more logical to be in the United States with Tamara at this critical time, but he refused to back down.

Sauntering toward the bathroom, his feet gathered electricity from the plush carpet; the shock ran through his fingertips when he turned the metal handle of the shower. Steam rose to the top of the glass stall, swirling into clouds of rich moisture. He jumped in to feel the high-pressure massage from the shower head as he made a mental list of the day's events. Thinking the day would be more like a treasure hunt than business, he allowed his mind to wander. Feeling the ache of his muscles under the water, he wondered if the cost of the hunt would be worth the life of a young girl. As a boy he adored hearing heroic tales with great quests. A powerful force repeatedly drew him to the British Isles, speaking to his soul that it was his true home rather than merely a tourist destination.

Finally relaxed, he grabbed a warm towel off the bar at the far end of the bathroom. Wrapping it around his waist, he wiped steam from the mirror as the phone rang. Rushing to pick up the receiver, he waited for the caller to speak first.

A soft spoken voice came through the phone. "I am calling for Dr. Mitchell Brody. Are you at liberty to confirm your identity?"

"A man's character is his fate," Mitch answered.

"I assume you have been given the proper greeting for the location of your meeting?"

"I have it written somewhere."

"I suggest you memorize it and dispose of the paper with flame. We do not desire for the information to fall into the wrong hands."

"Don't you think that is a little dramatic?" Mitch asked.

"Not when you have witnessed the horrors that I have on this earth." He paused. "Write down what is needed for your appointment carefully, for I will not repeat any of it. If you miss any portion of the information, you will be lost." Mitch scribbled as fast as his fingers would fly. "Are we clear, Dr. Brody?"

"Crystal."

"My duty is complete. It was nice to speak with you. We have heard a great deal regarding your accomplishments. Best of luck in your endeavors."

Mitch concluded their dialogue politely. "The pleasure was mine." Hanging up the phone, he heard the strange man whisper, "God be with you, Mitch."

A renewed sense of energy allowed him to dress quickly. The call spurred a rush of adrenaline that he normally felt after saving a patient's life. He jammed a few personal items into a small bag, grabbed his Blackberry, and headed for the door. The change of clothing he packed was a precaution in case he didn't return this evening. He pondered the challenges that lay ahead as he breached the threshold into the unknown of the day.

Once in the lobby, a female staff member stood behind the glittering marble reception desk. "Early start today, Dr. Brody?"

With a smile, Mitch responded, "No rest for the wicked, Bridget."

"I don't think you could ever be wicked, Dr. Brody," she suggested with a wink. "Unless you wanted to be."

He hated to admit that he enjoyed their flirtation, but he never took it beyond that. He was searching for something much more than a one-night stand. "Bridget, I requested a rental car. I'm sure it's ready and waiting."

Her eyes pleaded with him for more. "Oh yes, sir, ready and waiting."

"Please hold my room through the end of the week." Stepping away from the desk, he felt her eyes following him. He hastened his pace across the lobby to retrieve his car, surprised not to see John manning the valet desk. He made a mental note at the oddity of his absence.

The Audi's dark-navy paint shone brightly from the lights of the valet desk, making it appear jet black. Stepping into the car on the right side made him laugh. The other side of the road he could deal with, but driving on the other side of the car was a different story. The engine roared as he steered into the bustle of the London streets. He sped past shops and cafés beginning to open for the day and noticed shopkeepers wiping off chairs that had been sitting outside overnight. Mitch loved the fast pace of this city. Its harmony and welcoming people made him feel as if he were a part of the history. Moving deftly through the streets, he began to lose himself in questions, life revelations, and daydreams. An angry car horn jarred him back to reality. The destination was in an unfamiliar part of London, but given the vast expanse of the city, there were lots of areas he had not seen. Today he headed for a prestigious suburb.

Notting Hill was not always considered posh. Before 1870 it was lush farmland, but during the nineteenth century it morphed into a grand Victorian suburb, with Portobello Road selling its wares and antique finds. All classes mingled among its streets on a regular basis, especially for the yearly carnival. The historic Georgian row houses shared common walls with fortunate homeowners who held special keys to unlock hidden gardens. The location surprised Mitch when he wrote it down. Why would his appointment be so readily accessible to the masses living in this area? Why not somewhere remote? Sometimes hiding in the open could be the best camouflage.

Row upon row of stark-white homes greeted him as he searched for the address. The only distinguishing characteristic of each house seemed to be the vibrant colors painted on the front doors. He came upon the house number that matched his memory. He parked along the curb and turned to look at the front of the home. His hands began to sweat, and he rubbed them along his pant legs to dry them off. He stepped nervously toward the door, lifting his hand to grasp the bronze doorknocker in the shape of a dove. He felt his heartbeat slow down as he knocked three times. No one bothered answering the door, so he used the knocker to repeat the motion. Without a response a second time, concern surfaced that he had the wrong address. He attempted one last time, letting the knocker fall three more times against the bright-red door. Turning away, he was confused as to what to do next. He wasn't told what to do if no one was present for the appointment.

The door silently slid open. In the doorway appeared an older man wearing a stiff black suit, his white hair neatly combed. His posture was straight and proper, giving the impression that he had more strength in his muscles than imagined at first glance. "May I assist you?"

Mitch answered quickly, afraid to hesitate. "I have an appointment."

"I was not made aware of any visitors on today's schedule."

"I was given this address specifically."

"You were *told* to come here?" he probed.

"My name is Mitchell Brody, and I have a scheduled appointment."

The older man stepped back into the house. "If you were given no other directions than to show yourself upon this doorstep, then you are most assuredly mistaken. If you will excuse me, I have more pressing matters."

Before the man closed the door completely, Mitch recalled the additional instructions that Lillian had shared. Mitch lunged for door and grabbed the edge with his right hand. "Wait! May we start over? I'm not really myself this morning."

The older man looked down at Mitch's hand. Noticing the ring on his finger, he spoke against his better judgment. "Your identity must be confirmed before going any further, for few people fall asleep as one person and awake as another."

Gathering a deep breath, Mitch repeated the phrase Lillian had taught him. "Aristotle believed all men by nature desire knowledge."

The older man cut him off before he had the chance to make another mistake. "You are expected, Dr. Brody. However, we have had some unexpected events. I have been instructed to apologize for the inconvenience and request that your appointment be scheduled for another time."

The news was frustrating. "Will it be today?" Mitch asked.

"The individual you seek is available this afternoon and into the evening." Extending his gloved hand toward Mitch, he placed a scrap of paper into his hand. "You will find all of the information you need here."

Mitch graciously took it from him, looking at its elegant cursive writing. "I'm unfamiliar with the different sections of London. I don't recognize this address. Is this close by?"

"No, sir. Your appointment is in Scotland."

6

Tamara floated into consciousness. Since being discharged from the hospital, her dreams were filled with fuzzy images singed in black. Question after question swirled about whether or not her body was indeed shutting down or the effects were caused by the new medicine. Either way, she was positive that she had never felt like this before. Days passed like hours with a new uncertainty playing tricks with her mind. Her room was kept dark to allow the maximum amount of rest during a twenty-four-hour period. The fireplace generated continuous heat. During brief moments of consciousness, she glimpsed her mother crying by the fire or a smirk from Daphne while she forced foul liquid down her throat. If anyone else visited her, she would never know.

Heavy footsteps on the hardwood floor caused creaks and groans, signaling a visitor's approach. Tamara was pleasantly surprised to see that rather than Daphne, Uncle Earl stood before her bed. Without an actual blood relation to bind them, Earl had been promoted to the role of "Uncle" because of his long-standing relationship with the family.

"Sleeping Beauty has awakened! Too bad I'm not your prince," he teased.

She returned his smile with as much energy as she could muster. "Uncle Earl!" she whispered. "I'm no beauty. Besides, you protect me better than any make-believe prince on a smelly old horse."

A quiet laugh escaped his lips as he pulled a chair up beside her bed. "Mind if I stay awhile?" he asked.

"I'm glad you're not the nurse. She sneaks around and hums skin-crawling melodies without cracking a smile. I know Mom trusts her, but I think she is creepy with a capital *C*."

Earl made himself more comfortable. "I haven't had the pleasure of meeting her yet." Like he had so many times before, his simple statement instantly put her at ease. He possessed a quiet gentleness that made anyone feel safe. Now in his midsixties, he had taken a liking to wearing black suits with crisp white shirts. The only adornment was the vividly colored tie that changed daily. His oval face held blue eyes that matched photos of ocean tides she had seen in travel magazines. Her fondest memories of Uncle Earl were playing with him in the back garden of this very house. He would spin her around until she felt as if she were really flying. Closing her eyes and extending her arms out from her body, he convinced her that she was riding on the back of a giant dragon. In her mind, it was more than make-believe; it was a superb reality. "What's the news on the western front, kiddo? What does Super Doc say?" Earl questioned.

"Ask Zombie Nurse. All I do is sleep, eat, sleep, go to the bathroom with someone's help, sleep, and did I mention sleep?" Tamara whined.

Earl sympathetically nodded. "We're full of piss and vinegar tonight, huh?"

"Oh, I'm vigorous, all right. I can barely raise my head, and my whole body feels like a lump of concrete."

"Could it be the new medicine?"

"Could be that I'm doomed."

"I don't believe that."

"I do. I've always been the outsider. This sucks, Uncle Earl. I'm the weakest person on the planet," Tamara admitted.

Earl rolled his eyes. "Wow! I didn't know I was crashing a pity party!" Tamara rolled away from his gaze. "You're stronger than you think, and being an outsider can be a blessing. From my view, you can be yourself without the fear of rejection or having to conform to someone else's perception. Many well-known people have been social outcasts, including members of your own family."

Tamara expressed a giant sigh. "Can't you join my wallow in the mud?"

"Sorry, kiddo, not in my job description," he replied. Attempting to change her mood, he pulled a white handkerchief from his coat pocket and waved it back and forth. "What do you say we call a truce and I attempt to take your mind off things?"

She was never good at staying mad at him. "What are you proposing?"

He teased her with a smirk. "Have any good dreams lately?"

Lately her dreams had become far too realistic, as if she were personally experiencing each event. When her dreams began at a young age, Earl had been the one with whom she could share them without judgment. He would sit and document each one carefully in a green leather journal that he kept hidden among other books in his own library. Each accounting that he transcribed would be discussed at great length using his passion for ancient history. It was a special time they shared together as she grew up, and now she questioned whether or not he would be interested in hearing about these new dreams. "Are you sure?"

"Always." He paused before bringing up a sensitive topic, tapping his pen on the journal to a silent rhythm. "I spoke to a colleague at the university about the possibility of publishing the dream journals."

"Make them public?" Tamara asked, horrified at the thought.

"That's the general idea," Earl remarked, keeping his eyes locked onto the pen. "It would be a tremendous achievement for the academic world to hear accounts of alternative versions that leave holes in their documentation."

"Who would ever take me seriously?" Tamara whispered.

Halting the cadence of his pen, he could tell that her confidence had been shaken. "Do you believe I could place you in a situation that would make you anything less than successful?" She shook her head silently. "There are others who are hungry for information only *you* can give them. Would you deprive the world of important facts simply because you are afraid of some imaginary assumption from unknown people?"

Tamara remained quiet, refusing to respond before she had a chance to think. She opened her mouth to plead for more time when Earl interrupted.

"You can't remain locked up in a protective case like that carpet in the dining room for the rest of your days. There must be a point when you break the glass, take a risk, and breathe the air of freedom," he commanded.

Tamara shot him a look of intrigue for mentioning the artifact hanging in the dining room. It had been a bone of contention between members of her family for years. When her questions were left unanswered, she took it upon herself to find the answers. She tried library searches through racks and racks of books, along with endless hours on the Internet without success. Only her Gammie could tell her the story of the carpet, and she died without a single discussion occurring between them. "Tell me about the carpet, and I will tell you the dream."

A sharp intake of breath forced Earl to cough. He made a mistake in mentioning the carpet. Lillian requested that he not speak about it until Tamara came of age. Yet there he sat at the brink of divulging information in the selfish attempt to gain her permission to publish their journals. "It represents the fortitude of the human spirit. The faces shown in that weaving are some of the bravest people I have ever had the privilege to study. It is a shame for you to think of it as some dusty museum piece."

Tamara manufactured a deep sigh. "That still doesn't answer any of my questions."

"The timing isn't right for me to tell you all you want or need to know. It is for your mother to tell you, not me." He saw sadness on her face with the refusal of her request. He gave in a little. "The three women have been at the center of controversy for centuries. They are shown traveling to a land far from the persecution of their homeland. However, the most interesting aspect of their appearance in the weaving is that they are all family."

Tamara paid more attention at his mention of family. "Am I related to them?"

Earl smiled, recognizing her longing for the connection of her own personal history. "In a manner of speaking." Tamara openly questioned him about her family during childhood, but never seemed distraught at the prospect of not knowing anything. He cherished the ability to watch her grow, surrounded by people she had given family titles to, but who lacked a genetic link. It continually amazed him that as a little girl she never questioned her environment. She merely accepted that the people she trusted told her the truth. "How about we get back to the dream before you get too tired!" he suggested, seeing fatigue set in her eyes. Earl didn't want to be accused of jeopardizing her health by pushing too hard.

Satisfied with the tidbit of information regarding the carpet for the time being, Tamara prepared to tell him her latest dream. He settled into the old comfortable armchair, cleared his throat, and pressed pen to paper. She opened her mouth to allow the words freedom.

Two men sat along a riverbank, tossing stones into the calm water while chuckling at each other's attempt to disturb the current. The edges of their white robes were soiled from the meeting of water and earth. At first glance, any visitor would mistake them as identical without closer inspection. Twins were a rarity, suggesting the suspicion of demonic possession even at the time of their birth. Standing to throw a pebble into the river, one man named Jesus noticed the position of the sun in the sky. Footsteps in the distance alerted him to the interruption of their privacy. The man's brother, James, stood up quickly in response to the intrusion.

"Do you have questions?" Jesus asked.

James paused, tossing a stone up and down in his hand. "You are confident I am the one to do this?" he asked, throwing his stone into the water.

"I have remained awake many nights wondering if there was another way, but have been unable to find one. I do not act alone in this decision," Jesus confessed.

"Who assisted with the decision?" James asked.

Jesus looked down at the water. Ripples from the stones had reached the shore, and small waves encircled his toes. "The elders. They consulted with me many times to ensure that all went according to plan. They have complete faith in your abilities."

"Will the women be told the details?" James asked, looking at his twin brother.

Stepping naturally into his appointed role as a leader, Jesus gently placed his right hand on James's shoulder to calm his brother's obvious doubts. "They have been informed of their roles. Each will perform as expected." James's nerves showed signs of stress as Jesus presented him with a scroll. "If you are unsure, we will find another way." James took the papyrus, holding it with his left hand. Jesus had taken the time to write it personally, without guidance from any of the elders. "Take this to the priestess who resides at the location I have written at the bottom. It is too great a risk for me to be seen after today." He whispered the last sentence as a look of sadness crossed his usually confident face.

James could count on one hand the number of times he had seen a look of distress on his brother's face. "I will not betray you, brother. But I must ask you one last time if you do not think it should be me who stands in your stead with the Romans."

Jesus's dark-brown eyes welled with tears. "You are the one who must continue this path, not me. If you are lost, then the teachings are destroyed, and my sacrifice will be of little consequence."

A tear rolled down Jesus's cheek as they embraced. "I'm sorry you must carry this burden on my behalf, but I would never trust anyone other than you to protect me." He released his hold on the man. Placing his hand on James's chest, just above his heart, he whispered, "We share the same blood. You know me better than any person on this earth." James lowered his head while Jesus issued a warning. "I have been informed that your role in this game we play will be as torturous as the one they intend for me. As you carry the timber to the hill for my punishment, you shall be tortured while I hide in the crowd. I shall replace you at the right moment. The guard, who professes his affection for our sister, Ruth, has pledged his aid to our family in decreasing both of our *suffering." He brushed another tear from his cheek. "It brings me overwhelming grief to know that you will have pain imposed upon you."*

James took his brother's hand gently in his own, turning it over to reveal the shape of a star beneath the skin of his palm. "Am I closer to you than Mary?" he teased, dodging the serious nature of their dialogue.

Laughter broke the tension. "I would not use those words in her presence, but in some regards, you are." Jesus winked, holding a finger to his lips, indicating an additional secret. He turned his brother's hand over to reveal an identical star. He guided him to pay close attention to the instructions that would be given to him by the priestess upon delivery of the scroll. "The herbs they give you will enable your body to feel less pain during the ordeal. Do not disregard their knowledge."

Nodding, James heard footsteps approaching closer. He asked one final question. "Will you take the same precautions that I am allowed?"

Jesus bowed his head. "I have received the herbs from the female disciples that walk with Mary." Ten feet away, the bushes signaled a disturbance to their privacy. Signaling for his brother to leave the area before being seen, he whispered into James's ear that after the punishment, his body would be moved. His recovery would take place with the monks of the highest peaks, where the completion of his enlightened transformation would occur. James looked startled, but instead of questioning further, he grasped the scroll tightly and ran off, bound for the location written on the papyrus. Once inside the safety of the tall brush a few feet from the water's edge, he paused for a final glance at Jesus, who stood staring up at the sky. James made a small prayer of protection for the coming days as he caught sight of the first members of the meeting. Jesus greeted them with outstretched arms and a wide smile.

"Brothers, sit, and we shall continue. I realize you have questions that need to be addressed."

Furiously writing to keep up with Tamara's vivid description, Earl completed his dictation of the last few sentences. She was correct in one aspect; her dreams had become much more fascinating.

"I have a pressing question about this one," Tamara announced. "If this could be a true event, then why didn't anyone write about it or teach it?"

Instead of attending regular Sunday services, her family chose a path of spiritual enlightenment over dogma. She hadn't realized what that meant other than she wasn't obligated to attend church functions, which according to the few friends she had, was a benefit.

Earl replied cautiously. "I don't believe I'm qualified to answer. I studied a bit of theology through the years, but not enough to substantiate an answer, other than personal theory."

"Which is what, exactly?" Tamara pressed.

"I prefer to think of Jesus as a master teacher who spread a special message in order for humankind to move forward," Earl stated casually. "There have been other teachers through the ages who presented lessons in different ways. Their messages weren't recognized until long after their passing, but they *were* teachers, nonetheless."

"Did the Romans murder him?" Tamara asked.

Earl smirked. Tamara had a tendency to get straight to the point without consideration for any gray area. Issues fell into two categories: black or white. "It wasn't the Romans, dear girl. You forget one important group in power at the time of his teaching. The temple priests. Jesus was the snag in their plan of control. He threatened their very existence with his progressive theories of love and forgiveness. They needed to perpetuate the mask of the vengeful deity who punished those who didn't follow their lead."

Tamara disliked when Earl danced around the meat of a story. He liked to lecture as if back in his classroom rather than hold a casual conversation. "Then why isn't that in the history books?"

"The priests are mentioned, along with their dislike for Jesus's followers. The accounts of manipulation to rid themselves of Jesus's annoyance are not widely known. A few documents have surfaced from the black markets that tell a story similar to what you have seen," Earl stated. Tamara smiled at his casual mention of the black market. "I have colleagues with connections to that disreputable business," he answered. "A man came to the university to meet a friend of mine. He brought photographs of an ancient text dealing with the crucifixion of Christ, and I was allowed to sneak a peek before he disappeared with what I can only presume were fake identification documents."

Crossing her arms against her chest, Tamara asked, "Did the ancient text name the men who condemned him?"

"Not entirely," Earl stated. He explained that the photographs were of an incomplete text with the final pages being held for a larger sum by another buyer. "The pages indicated that two meetings took place in the presence of the Roman governor, Pontius Pilate. The first meeting was between him and the priests who abhorred Jesus. They falsified his crimes to warrant a capital offense of death."

Tamara gasped.

"The second and incomplete account was a meeting between Pilate and Joseph of Arimathea, the uncle of Mary, who requested to take his remains following the crucifixion. Allegedly, Pilate confided in Joseph that he didn't feel comfortable handing down the sentence, but had extreme pressure to do so. Joseph was able to convince Pilate to have the punishment take place on his property, along with the burial."

Tamara rolled her eyes. "You didn't answer my question."

Earl paused before opening his mouth to satisfy her need for direct answers. "I was privy only to a portion of the text, and I was unable to finish translating it before it was taken away."

Tamara slid further into her bed. A sharp pain crossed her abdomen, causing a wince from the sensation. Earl noticed her immediate change in demeanor and expressed concern for her pain level. Tamara waved her hand, signaling for him to ignore her expression and continue. Earl made a quick notation inside the journal reminding him to ask Lillian about Tamara's medical status in greater detail.

"The Dead Sea Scrolls opened a world of information that might have been lost if a farmer had not come across them in a cave. The Apocrypha holds a wealth of wisdom authored by men *and* women that was not added to the Bible, yet the authors all reiterate the message of love that Jesus openly preached."

Tamara opened her eyes as the pain dulled. "Was his death common?"

"No," Earl said and sighed. "Roman punishments varied with the crime." Tamara's brow wrinkled with confusion. "There isn't a whole lot of evidence to support the myriad of theories, but the most common is that it was a way for the priests to make a public example out of him to the general population."

Opening the journal to a page close to the front, Earl quickly read a dream from a few years ago. When he finished, he asked if she remembered it. The details of the dream were fuzzy, but she did remember. The faces of the individuals involved had been out of focus, and the only thing she saw was the recurrence of a man's head being severed from his body by the blade of a large sword. "Do you remember who we thought the man was?" Earl asked.

"No," she lied, as the pain from her stomach increased and traveled down to the tips of her toes, causing a moan to slip from her lips.

Earl couldn't help but notice her obvious discomfort and knew she couldn't take much more before needing additional pain medication. "Can you hold on for one more thought?" he asked. Tamara closed her eyes to block out the intensifying pain. "The man was John the Baptist, and he was beheaded for crimes that, just like Jesus, came unfairly. The major difference between the two men was that, unlike Jesus, John had a trial before being condemned to death. His beheading was a more common punishment for individuals who were spiritually enlightened. By chopping off their heads, the accusers gained the ability to control the incarnation of their souls, since they believed that the head housed the soul."

Tamara looked baffled.

Earl beamed. He appreciated her inquisitive mind during the struggle for a healthy body. "If we look closely at the information presented, it seems as though the important factor is *not* his death, but rather the existence of a twin brother." He glanced at his watch, noticing that hours had passed since the start of their conversation. He was late.

Tamara noticed his change of focus. "Do you have to be somewhere?"

Covering the timepiece with his sleeve, Earl replied, "I can spare all the time in the world for you."

"Time is slipping away faster than her health," a voice sneered from behind.

Earl and Tamara glanced toward the door to see Daphne leaning against the threshold. She held a syringe in one hand with a vile of clear fluid in the other. She silently slithered toward the bed, making Tamara's skin crawl. Daphne checked the IV pump and adjusted the settings to a higher dose of pain medication. Shooting a venomous look toward Earl, she announced that visiting hours were over, adding that if Earl wished to see her again, he would need to limit his time.

"Dr. Brody would not want you to be worn out when he returns," she warned, touching Tamara's feverish forehead with the back of her hand. "Judging from the amount of perspiration, you've been in pain for a while. I took the liberty of increasing your pain meds, but I don't want to have to continue along this route if you're not going to follow directions."

Earl watched Daphne insert the syringe of medication into the IV while Tamara objected. He felt an urge to speak up on her behalf, but held his tongue.

"No more meds, Daphne. They make me so drowsy. Can we skip one dose so I could feel a little normal?" Tamara pleaded.

"Normal?" Daphne laughed. "You want normal? It would take ten lifetimes for you to be considered normal, and no amount of medication could ever correct it that quickly." Tamara's eyes widened at the snide comment. Changing gears, Daphne suggested, "You can direct all complaints to Dr. Brody. If you don't appreciate my presence, then I can leave, and you can feel as normal as you want. But you will be facing death."

Glaring at Tamara with stone eyes, Daphne placed the vile of clear fluid toward Tamara's mouth. "Down the hatch, Princess."

Standing up in horror at Daphne's bedside manner, Earl bent over to kiss Tamara on the forehead. Deciding not to rock the boat at that exact moment, he would sneak out with his dignity intact. He had lost track of time, and there was a possibility that he was late for his evening engagement. He walked through the bathroom door, turning to take a final look at his young friend. She lay in her large hospital bed with a pleading in her eyes that broke his heart. He winked, whispering that he would be back soon, and slipped through the door. He had a hard time watching her be ill. He never thought she would look this opaque and frail. He saw Lillian standing before him with her usual warm, welcoming smile.

"Have a nice visit, Earl?" she whispered.

Spinning around to confirm their privacy, he whispered, "She's worse than I thought. Are you certain Dr. Brody knows what he is doing?"

Lillian's smile faded. "I have faith in Mitch's abilities. He has never given me any cause for doubt. We will continue our prayers of thanksgiving for her continued presence in our lives and remain confident that she will overcome this trial." Her statement sounded as if she were trying to convince herself.

Earl changed topics. "Tamara expressed that she doesn't like her nurse, and after the spectacle I just witnessed in the treatment of your daughter, I would say her concern has merit."

Lillian snickered in disbelief. "You don't recognize Daphne? She was practically raised in this house. I see no reason *not* to trust her." She looked toward the closed door. "I am sure she was just being stern so Tamara wouldn't get away with not taking her medicine. I told her to force her if she had to." She added with a smirk, "Tamara doesn't like to be told to do anything."

"Point taken...thank you," he said, walking past her toward the secret stair behind the kitchen pantry. The door led to a meeting he was late for. He silently promised to look in on Tamara one last time before heading home. Whether or not Lillian trusted Daphne, Tamara did not, and that distrust raised a warning. Something about Daphne didn't add up.

7

The last twenty-four hours raced through Mitch's mind as he navigated the A9, heading north. The rain had finally subsided, allowing glimmers of sun to peek through the dark clouds. Mitch Brody had never been able to stop his mind from racing, always thinking toward solutions. He insisted on pondering the infinite number of possibilities that could contain the correct answer. In medical school, he didn't have any difficulty, since his patients didn't include breathing people. With his practice, he felt he needed to emotionally detach himself from his patients, but the task proved difficult with his heart permanently attached to his sleeve. This trip was a prime example. It seemed unnecessary, when all the details could have been managed through phone calls and inquiries. Yet something in his bones led him here, telling him to make the extra effort. "I'm an idiot!" he muttered.

Deciding to give in to the self-inflicted mental torture of thinking, he shut the radio off and welcomed the silence. Whizzing by a Little Chef restaurant, its bright lights beckoning hungry travelers, Mitch smiled at a memory of a visit to this same area with his father when he was a child.

He was ten years old. To him, a vacation involved theme parks and junk food, not educational activities and meetings. He liked seeing the castles with their shiny suits of armor, but resented that he was left alone for hours with a history book while his father conducted a business meeting. The fault lay with his mother. She felt the trip abroad would be a bonding experience for them both. His father was not a man who enjoyed playing catch, climbing trees, or being silly. A doctor in his heart and his career, he demanded a standard of excellence, prioritizing education in a person's life over family. He ran himself ragged with patient care, and sacrificed personal time to remain at the hospital. In that regard, Mitch and his father were identical. In retrospect, Mitch realized that the trip had set his future into motion.

Pulling up to Stirling Castle for his father's appointment, Mitch wasn't clear about who the men were, but they were nice, older men who each gave him a strong handshake. They arrived early, due to his father's affinity for being on time. Mitch looked at his father in the driver's seat, who gazed up at the castle in reverence.

"Dad?"

"Yes."

"Have you been here before?" Mitch asked.

"Twice," his father replied.

"Lately?"

"No, not since your sister was born."

"Why?"

"I haven't needed to be."

"Why now?"

His father abruptly changed the subject. "How about you crack open your Latin workbook and bring that with you? I would like to see more proficiency with verbs by the conclusion of the meeting."

Mitch hung his head. His father could always be counted on to turn any communication into an exercise in what he thought Mitch should be doing. He hardly ever gave a direct answer to a question, choosing to create more questions instead.

"I'll get the book."

Hearing the frustration in his son's voice, his father turned to face his young son. A small smile appeared as he watched his son remove the Latin workbook. He had raised a dutiful son—a boy who would grow up into a fine, educated man. Unfortunately, his son would need more than basic obedience to become the man he wanted him to become.

"Mitch," his father began in a soft voice rarely heard. "I haven't always spoken to you concerning matters other than your education, and I feel I've let you down in that regard, but I've tried to give you the necessary tools to be greater than you ever dreamed. My aspiration for you is to achieve everything you were born for, and situations may arise in your life where the answers you seek can't be found in a book." Mitch looked confused. "There will be things you just feel are right. I have been remiss in teaching you about feelings, but I see the time has come."

Mitch looked at his father, and for an instant he didn't recognize the look on his face. It was almost sad. "Now you sound like Mom."

His father smiled. "Your mom is a brilliant woman in many regards. You should listen to her."

Mitch answered sarcastically. "How am I supposed to know what I was born to do?"

"It is a passion that drives you, that makes you want to be better. It's your heart's song. It is…" As his father started to finish his sentence, a black Mercedes station wagon drove along the gravel entrance to the castle. His father looked at the driver and adjusted his burgundy tie.

"Dad?"

"Not now, Mitch. The men are arriving. Let me finish this quickly: your passion will drive you throughout your life, but it is the dedication you give to it that provides the fuel. You need to be a man who is loyal and true to your passion. When you feel defeated, you need to continue moving. Failure is a natural process for you to discover a new way to reach the same goal." His son stared at him with a blank expression. "Do you understand, Mitch?"

"Sure, Dad," he whispered.

"Grab your books. I expect verbs to be known by the time we are finished. If they've been learned correctly, we can order dessert at dinner," his father remarked, stepping out of the car.

Rain splashed the windshield, returning Mitch to his present location. At the time, he hadn't considered his father's lecture as anything other than nonsense. But he did grow up with the heavy expectation of being faster and greater than anyone else in his class. He knew from an early age that medicine was his passion, but it never propelled him forward in the manner in which his father described. As a much-needed break from the frustration of those early years, he tried to find a radio station that would allow his mind to wander. A familiar tune wafted through the speakers. Only one person came to mind when he heard the song. Pressing speed dial on his phone, he waited for an answer.

"Graham Cracker!" he shouted. "I'm listening to our college party song." Turning up the volume, Mitch asked, "Remember this one?" Silence filled the phone line. "Cracker? Can you hear me?"

"I can hear you. What do you want?"

Mitch chuckled. "Offended or sleeping?"

"Stop using the joke, man. You've been calling me Cracker since high school, and it gets less amusing the older we get. I was sleeping," Graham snarled.

"Sorry to wake you, but it's a term of endearment," Mitch reminded him.

"I get the pleasure of pulling an all-night marathon monitoring a patient. Where the hell are you?"

"I need some help, and you're the first person I thought of, but I'm on the road. Ah, crap, the weather is starting to turn ugly. Maybe I should call you back later," Mitch suggested.

"*You* wake *me* up, and then casually suggest calling back? Those are brass ones, my friend. I'll be rounding in three hours; after which I'll be really asleep. Tell me now, or forget it!" Graham shouted.

"I need to be able to concentrate on what I'm telling you. Driving doesn't help," Mitch begged.

"Tell me now!" Graham screamed through the phone.

In the medical profession, sleep was a luxury. When you were in charge of critical patients demanding round-the-clock care, an hour of sleep was golden. Mitch understood the frustration in Graham's voice. He summed up the day's events quickly.

"Let me get this straight. You flew to the UK on a goose chase, when you could have made a few phone calls and hopped on the Internet?" Graham responded, irritated by Mitch's hasty decisions.

Mitch took a deep breath and shook his head. His old friend could be counted on to take the path of least resistance in most situations. "I knew you would say that. You're not hearing what I'm telling you. I can't be glib and make phone calls. I have an obligation to this family."

"You have an obligation with every family! Come on, Brody, you're confusing personal history with professional ethics. How many doctors would be doing what you're doing?" Graham suggested.

Mitch sighed. "That's just it. No one would."

"OK, then why are you?"

"Quite honestly, I don't know. I just have a feeling I have to do this, and my father told me to follow my feelings."

"You never believed that crap before, so why are you starting now?" Graham asked. Mitch's silence gave him the only answer he needed. "Tell you what, since I am the most stellar friend on the face of this planet, I will make some phone calls, hop on the Internet, and see what I can come up with. So, let me round, get some shut eye at home, and get back to you later."

Smiling broadly, Mitch replied, "I can always count on you, brother."

Graham snickered. "Sucker to the core. I'm assuming I need to call some of the elders, since you're in their neck of the woods?"

Mitch laughed. "You read my mind, but do me a favor and hold off until I meet the Master."

Graham laughed harder. "They always said we shared the same brain in medical school, why mess with tradition? Since I'm now awake, I'll go round on your patient. I'll call you later and return the favor of waking you up."

"She's not in the hospital. I sent her home for care. It was her mother's wish before I left," Mitch replied nervously.

Graham shouted. "Are you nuts? You just handed her daughter a death sentence!"

"Tell me something I don't know."

"Fine, you don't need a lecture. Where are you now?"

"No idea."

"Perfect, Brody, just perfect."

The line went dead. Mitch knew he had taken a gamble by involving Graham. Regardless of his promise to not discuss the details of his journey, he still needed an ally. If anyone knew how to help him out of a jam, it would be Graham. As an added safety precaution, Mitch felt the need for someone to know where he was going. There was no comfort zone in being out on a limb alone.

The address directed him to a country inn in the Highlands of Scotland. The lights from the stark-white building cast a welcoming glow from the front doorway onto the gravel car park. The gray slate roof of the two-story building contrasted with dark-green ivy that grew along its edges. To the right of the double-door entrance, a large glass window exposed a glowing fireplace in a softly lit room. It was cozy, quaint, and homey.

Slamming the car door, Mitch heard its echo surround him. Other than that, the night was silent. Above, millions of stars shone brightly as the galaxy awoke to greet him. Somehow, in the country, he felt small when the night sky loomed above his head in all its glory. Acutely aware of his own footsteps on the gravel, he made his way toward the entrance. Even though he knew it was silly, he listened for any additional footsteps.

Entering the inn, he immediately felt its warmth permeate the cells of his tired body. Sumptuous smells of lamb and venison from the dinner service lingered in the air. The foyer was tastefully decorated in soft-green wallpaper with paintings of the Scottish Highlands in gilded frames. Behind a wooden reception counter, an older gentleman stood in a moss-green sport coat, his silver glasses clinging to the tip of his nose. He was surveying the day's receipts as Mitch approached him respectfully.

"Welcome to the Killiecrankie Hotel, sir. How may I be of assistance?" the gentleman asked without raising his head.

"I think I have a reservation," Mitch choked out.

The gentleman's accent punctuated each question mark as he spoke without looking up from his jumble of paperwork. "Not sure, eh? And how is that?"

Mitch responded nervously. "I have a scheduled appointment at this address, but I'm not sure if a reservation was made. The last name is Brody."

"Hmmm," the gentleman said, shuffling papers around the desk. "Brody, you say?"

"Yes. Dr. Mitch Brody."

Upon hearing the full name, the gentleman looked up to view his latest guest. He looked Mitch over carefully through the glasses that had slid even farther down his nose. "Well, of course you are Dr. Brody! I have your room ready. Let me show you to your accommodations!" he exclaimed.

Slipping out from behind the desk, Mitch saw that his crisp tan trousers were accessorized with black leather cowboy boots. This vision resulted in a chuckle while he followed the man through a small corridor toward the staircase. Before ascending the stairs, Mitch caught a glimpse of a Tina Turner picture on the wall. Reacting to the eccentric nature of the picture hanging amid nature prints, he laughed a little too loudly. "Something humorous?"

Mitch gulped. "I haven't seen a picture of Tina Turner in a while. It took me by surprise."

"She is magnificent, isn't she? You must be a fellow fan," the gentleman gushed.

Mitch agreed. "You're right. There's no one like her."

The gentleman continued his tour of the inn, explaining that two common bathrooms occupied the second floor. He proudly mentioned that his wife had personally chosen the décor for each room. Mitch turned the doorknob to his room as the gentleman cleared his throat. Embarrassed, Mitch searched his pocket for a tip. "No, sir, a tip is not necessary. Before you retire, I must relay a message. Tomorrow morning, you are to meet a distinguished man by the name of Duncan on the bridge in the Pass at ten o'clock, sharp. I would advise you not to be late, sir. Duncan detests tardiness."

Mitch's eyes widened at the man's puzzling message. "What is the Pass?"

The gentleman descended down the stairway, shouting backward. "I'll give you directions in the morning, after a thorough spot of breakfast. We have an excellent kitchen staff, and your meal will be splendid. Sleep tight."

Without even switching on a light in his room, he dropped his bag on the floor and threw himself onto the bed. The thick duvet allowed sleep to instantly envelop him.

Mitch rubbed the sleep from his eyes as he checked the time on the clock. Eight o'clock. Wow, an entire night of sleep without interruption! It was heaven to his brain, but since his body was used to much less sleep, his bones and muscles felt heavy. Looking around the room, he surveyed his surroundings in the morning light. The gentleman from last night had been correct; the room was tastefully decorated with coordinating patterns and fabrics. It reminded him of something his mother used to say: "A woman's touch is always noticeable." He was sure she meant that men couldn't decorate if left to their own devices, preferring to have beer kegs as furniture, with posters of half-naked women on the walls. Deep down he knew she was right.

Mitch could see the charm of this hotel. It was the kind of place that made you feel like a houseguest rather than a patron. The morning smells surpassed the dinner service, conjuring visions of a full Scottish meal with strong coffee. Nothing would top a piping hot mug of Highland coffee. He turned the corner, expecting to see the man from last night keeping watch at his post. Instead, an attractive woman with brown hair, in a matching floral skirt and shirt, stood guard. She spoke softly to a patron booking an additional night's stay and nodded to Mitch as he walked by. He thought she must be the man's spouse. He silently nicknamed her "The Decorator" in his mind.

Freshly pressed white linens covered each table of the dining room, giving it the intimate feeling of a small café. The buffet along the far wall held coffee, scones, and a choice of hot or cold cereals. He hardly had time to sit down before a young woman approached him. Dressed for a tennis match, her messy blond ponytail swayed from side to side.

"Dr. Brody?"

"Yes," He gulped, surprised by her charisma.

"Mummy sent me to give you the directions to the Pass. This is the fastest way down there. If I were you, I'd leave now. Dunc doesn't like to be kept waiting." She threw the paper on the table in front of him and spun around to leave.

"Wait! Do you know Duncan?"

Looking over her shoulder, she shot him a smug smile. "Doesn't everybody?"

He watched her throw a kiss to the woman behind the desk and run out the front door. He hoped he would be able to stay at the hotel on a real vacation sometime in the future. There was a feeling about this place that he liked. Grabbing a scone from the buffet, as suggested, he walked into the foyer. The directions showed that the walk wasn't too far from the hotel.

In the day's new light, he viewed the beauty of his environment. The Highlands afforded the most vivid colors anywhere, highlighting nature in all its finery. The emerald color of the surrounding hills sparkled as mists rolled across them. Trees were alive with birds and wisps of wind. Flowers filled each tiny nook of soil as if someone had walked by with a pocketful of seeds. He could see why legends came alive with this type of backdrop, and he wondered how people could question their validity.

Making his way to the small visitor center, he read the sign marking its location. "Killiecrankie Visitor Center and Soldier's Leap," he read aloud. "See, *this* is history."

Soldier's Leap became famous during the battle for Scottish independence. An individual soldier attempting to flee English soldiers made a daring leap over an expanse of the river. Seeing the distance was too wide for a successful jump, the English soldiers became cocky, expecting an easy prisoner. Miraculously, his chance at escape proved successful, and their prisoner was lost.

Mitch followed the directions to the bridge just past Soldier's Leap. Stopping in the middle afforded him a breathtaking view of the river. Fishermen waded in the shallows, trying their luck. A red fox drank from the bank before scurrying quickly back into the brush. The river's fog crept toward the bridge as the heavens accompanied it with a dotting of rain. Mitch turned up his jacket collar, wishing he had remembered to bring a hat.

Rain made him nervous. It brought memories of the night his world shattered. He was sixteen, learning to drive, and looking forward to touring colleges with his father. His father's idea was not only to tour the campuses, but to secure Mitch's placement with an early admission. "Never leave until tomorrow what you can accomplish today," was the phrase he would repeat tirelessly. Sitting in his room listening to rain pelt his window, he sorted through his baseball card collection when headlights turned into the driveway. Rushing to the top of the stairs, he watched two police officers enter the house. His mother and sister stood with the officers, a look of horror on his sister's face. His mother sobbed quietly as her knees gave way, and she collapsed onto the wooden floor. Mitch scrambled down the stairs two at a time to help his mother. Gulping back tears, his sister ran to him and threw her arms around his neck.

"What is it? What happened!" he shouted.

His sister remained glued to his body as he looked into her tear-soaked eyes. "Daddy is dead!" she wailed.

Disbelief ravaged his brain. Dragging his sister along, he approached the second officer. The officer explained that his father had been involved in an accident at a nearby school. He was dropping off a letter of recommendation for a student's college application to the office when a vehicle struck him while he walked across the parking lot. A Good Samaritan witness called emergency services, but unfortunately, his father died en route to the hospital. Mitch cautiously approached his mother, who lay in a heap on the floor. Looking at the officers, he announced, "I'll take it from here." His arms wrapped around both his sister and mother, and the broken family wandered in a trance into the kitchen.

"Too young to be the man of the house, if you ask me," one of the officers whispered.

"No shit," Mitch thought, unaware of footsteps on the bridge. He was starting to recall the days following his father's death as a voice dragged him from the past.

"Dr. Mitchell Brody?"

Turning into the fog surrounding the bridge, Mitch made out a person's faint outline. Beyond that, he could tell nothing more until they stood face-to-face.

"Dr. Brody?" the voice asked again.

"Yes," he replied.

"Oh, good! Thought I got the wrong chap again. People are always mucking about on the bridge, and you never know who you come across in this weather."

"Come closer so I can see you," Mitch suggested.

Mitch felt the wooden beams vibrate below him. Looking down at the wood, two black leather cowboy boots emerged from the mist. With eyes full of surprise, he opened his mouth to speak, but no words came.

"I'm Duncan." The man smiled brightly. "Are you seriously shocked? Hearing of your intellect, I assumed that you would have it all figured out by now. Pity." Duncan replaced his smile with a smirk. "You really didn't have the foggiest notion it was me you were meeting last night? Peculiar indeed."

Mitch choked back words he desperately wanted to utter, but instead decided manners should rule out. "I didn't really think about it at all. I guess I'm just going with the flow since every time I think I'm right, I am completely wrong. This whole journey is one big ball of confusion."

Duncan looked at Mitch. "You look like your father," he admitted with grief in his voice. "Don't look so shocked, my boy. Why do you think I was asked to meet you if I hadn't known your father?" He walked toward the railing of the bridge, holding the cold metal tightly, as he watched the fisherman below catch their first trophy. As if lost in prayer, he glanced toward the clouds disappearing into the sky. Mitch was bewildered as to how he knew about his father or his family. He knew his father traveled for his job, but he never mentioned any names. Why all the damn secrets? What the hell was it about his job that the man needed this many secrets? After what seemed like an eternity, Duncan took a deep breath and sighed. "I met you on a trip with your father when you were younger. I thought at the time that he was grooming you to one day replace himself. Although in this day and age, girls have begun apprenticing their fathers, which tends to surprise me at how brilliant they prove to be. Not that girls aren't intelligent, you know. But this tradition has been maintained by male heirs. Funny how it's more natural with the female heirs." Duncan laughed.

Nothing this man said made sense to Mitch, and he felt the need to get this information session moving along at a faster pace. "Would you mind telling me what I need to know so I can be on my way? I don't have a whole lot of time to play with here." Mitch's frustration grew by the second, while Duncan's calm demeanor never faltered.

"Oh, yes, we're always in such a hurry, aren't we? I know about your patient; I know about your time frame. No need to get your knickers in a twist, son. I imagined that you might have your father's patience and fortitude. The emotional reminder was an expected one, to be sure. There is a bench on the other side of the bridge. Why don't we use it?" Duncan asked, moving away.

The two men walked in silence across the bridge to the other side. The cry of a hawk, desperate and shrill, brought him back to the present. Once they reached the metal bench, they sat as if in the pews of a church, rigid backs, legs straight out in front of them, and both impatient to hear what the other had to say. The combination of the black leather cowboy boots and his quirkiness made Mitch feel at ease in the man's presence. The feeling was trust. He was beginning to see his father as an adult, with responsibilities beyond his career; it was a very new version of the image he had known in his youth. Duncan seemed to be a man who didn't give up secrets easily, which was probably what his father liked most. His father surrounded himself with people who possessed integrity, responsibility, and honesty. Duncan possessed all of these characteristics. The man's demeanor, oddly, created admiration in Mitch.

Breaking the silence, Mitch posed an uncomfortable question. "You mentioned my father's death. Are you insinuating that my father's death was *not* an accident?"

"My statement is without any insinuation," Duncan stated bluntly.

"Wait a minute," Mitch stammered. "There was an investigation, the driver was cleared, and the police were unable to prove fault. How do you call it anything *but* an accident?"

"Sometimes things are not as they seem. What you see is often what others wish you to see. But it doesn't mean it is the truth. Truth is subjective to the person who hears the information."

Mitch wiped his brow. This conversation made him feel more worn out than jet lag.

"I realize this has been a trip of great confusion for you, and I'm not here to add to that. I am merely here to teach you. There will be other individuals who will do the same, though not with my particular flair, before you return to the colonies. This trip you were sent on is a journey of discovery—not only for your patient's future, but for your own. Remember one important thing: people who know too much are in danger. Your father was, you are, and now the young girl sits atop the list."

"Danger?" Mitch asked, astonished. "Over a young girl's medical condition? That's impossible. The only danger is if I am unable to figure out what is causing her illness."

Duncan paused a moment before asking a basic question. "Do you believe in magic, Dr. Brody?"

Mitch stood up to leave, but instead turned to face his "teacher" one last time. He was finished with all the crazy talk, the insane idea of coming here in the first place, and intended to go home. Graham was correct; he could make phone calls and use the Internet to get the job done just as efficiently. Before he could speak, Duncan repeated his question.

"Do you believe in magic, Dr. Brody?"

"Only on Halloween when kids knock on my door asking for candy. In my line of work I don't use magic, sir. I use science," Mitch shot back.

"Well said, but have you have never witnessed a miracle?" Duncan probed.

"I've witnessed unforeseen survival against medical advisement, but I wouldn't classify it as a miracle. I have to work in a world of facts and reality. Not hocus pocus."

Duncan laughed. "Hocus pocus, huh? Haven't heard that retort in a while. What will you say next? That the colonies still hold witch trials? Wouldn't be surprised. Poor girls."

Mitch stood to leave, unable to deal with the ghosts of his past, and unwilling to repair the tender bandage healing his father's memory.

"Sorry, old man. Don't flee quite yet." He patted the metal seat with his left hand. "Why did you become a doctor of medicine?"

Mitch was reluctant to sit back down. He hadn't been required to answer that question since his interview for admission to medical school. When he answered it then, he was full of hope that he could make a difference, and he was confident in his abilities. Only during the last few years had doubt crept in with some cases that hadn't turned out the way he hoped, or promised. Only with Tamara had he begun to fear that he could no longer heal anyone. "I'm a doctor because I want to give people hope. I want them to survive, to have the quality of life they imagined."

"Sounds a bit one-sided. You are talking about what *you* can do, not what the *two* of you can achieve together. Any illness is a team effort, Mitch. The patient's body and soul combine with your knowledge and instincts to create a positive direction toward healing," Duncan stated.

"It isn't one-sided; it's a way to help that's positive. If doctors didn't heal, would there even be humanity at all?" Mitch argued.

Duncan stroked his chin. "Interesting point. If people ceased to exist because you weren't present to heal them, is there humanity? Rather a lovely philosophy essay, I think. Your concern is for humanity's continuance based solely on the body's chemical makeup, yet you don't believe in humanity's ability to experience magical properties. You are, no doubt, intelligent, Mitch, and your knowledge is extensive, but you need more. Sit back down and allow me to tell you a story." Mitch accepted that he wouldn't be allowed to leave any time soon. His father would have wanted him to sit. So he sat with a deliberate thud.

"There is a point in any struggle, be it life, or death, when faith, or instinct as you called it, enters the mix. A time existed in the history of this nation when man and magic walked hand in hand, when people looked to their elders as a source of knowledge and eternal wisdom. In so doing, they created enemies who did not think in the same fashion. In reality, they lacked the vision to see past their own insecurities, taking the information their elders imparted as gospel truth. It was this drive for power and control over people that led them to conquer other nations and increase their power base. They prefer to step on the meek to inherit the earth.

"History is the story written though the passionate cycles of humanity. It is written by the conquerors, the rulers, if you will, of nations that have bullied their way into infamy. History is rarely written by the quiet ones living their destinies in peace. We only hear their voices when by chance they rise up. They are the mystical ones.

"At the time of this struggle for power and control of land, members of one faction believed that their way of life should not have to be destroyed for the benefit of strangers. Instead of running away and accepting defeat, they rose up and spoke out, drawing together a small group of followers. Now, their army was nowhere near the size of the invading forces, and they had no weaponry. They were simple country men who left their homes to defend their land, not unlike your colonies." Duncan winked and continued his tale.

"They fought the invading army through every terrain this land had to offer. They fought valiantly until they witnessed too many of their countrymen dying at the hands of the enemy. Hope was stretched thin that they could defend their own land, let alone their homes. The night before a huge battle, they gathered and waited. They watched the larger army advance closer to the battlefield with their weapons, and yet at dusk, they stoked their campfires and bunked down for the night, unsure if this was their last sunset. In that moment, faith took over. The solitary fight within each soldier was lost to the faith of the group. They knew that if they would fail, then at least they failed together. And if they succeeded, then victory would taste even sweeter. They slept, waited for daybreak, and prayed for a miracle.

"Peace precedes a battle, a calmness that manifests. Maybe it's from men whispering individual prayers that they will be able to lay eyes on family again. Or maybe it's the quiet before the storm. Whatever the reason, the day broke quiet and somber. The fog rose, as it did every morning in that area, as campfires were snuffed out and men on both sides prepared for the day that lay ahead. The enemy began to advance while the smaller army watched with hearts pounding along with the drumbeats. They didn't know how they would defeat such an army, but they felt in their hearts they had to try.

"As if by magic, the small band of men beheld a wondrous sight coming from within the mist at the right side of their forces. Hundreds of men on horseback rode toward them, joining their ranks. The fighting commenced. The smaller army did prevail, and because of the horsemen, the battle was won. It was a turning point, not only for the army, but also for the country." Duncan concluded his story and smiled. Mitch wrinkled his brow and looked more confused.

"Nice story, but what does that have to do with anything we were just talking about?" Mitch asked.

"It has to do with everything, dear boy! Don't you see the point of the story? Don't you understand what I am trying to tell you?" Duncan sputtered.

"Uh, clearly I don't. I just told you that." For the first time Mitch saw frustration on Duncan's face. He saw the weight of responsibility upon the gentleman and felt compassion for what the man was trying to accomplish. Instead of continuing to argue, he decided to listen.

"You young people don't read between the lines. If we don't give you the answers in front of your face, you fail to look for yourselves. Nothing but generations of lazy people. The core of this story speaks of faith."

Faith and religion were not things Mitch was comfortable with. He never discussed them, and he didn't like it when people brought up their own religious beliefs at work. He voiced his opinion to Duncan and waited for the inevitable backlash that followed his rehearsed remarks.

"All that statement tells me is that you don't comprehend faith," Duncan replied.

"What is faith?" Mitch asked.

"Faith, dear boy, is when your head stops and your soul takes over."

Mitch felt frazzled. His head never stopped. It was the reason for his lack of sleep, his drive, his ambition, and his professional accomplishments. He never experienced the sensation of something else starting. That was completely foreign. Unsure of what to believe anymore, this statement challenged everything he stood for.

Sensing the internal struggle within his young pupil, Duncan stood up from the bench. He turned to face Mitch, who sat with his head in his hands. Duncan felt sorry for the young man. He had so much to learn, with so many of the upcoming lessons challenging his very core.

He remembered the days of his own enlightenment and the excitement that followed. When he was able to realize what it all meant, he felt like shouting from the rooftops. He hoped that this young man would feel the same. Deep down, however, he feared he wouldn't. "Come with me. Let's see what speaks to your soul." Duncan started to walk back across the bridge.

Knowing he had to follow, Mitch stood up. "Where are we going?" he asked.

"To show you something miraculous."

8

The questions compounded upon each other as Mitch walked back to the hotel. If Tamara perished, her death, like that of his father, would haunt him. Each defeat, either personal or professional, shouted insecurities. Each one knowing exactly which button to push. He was desperate to try anything to regain his confidence. To solve the problem and win the battle, he had to make Tamara better. Failure was not an option. Reaching the gravel drive of the hotel, the two men paused to gather their thoughts before addressing each other.

Duncan seemed tired after their walk and conversation on the bridge. His strength and vitality at their initial meeting had diminished. "My car or yours?" he asked. Mitch thought for a second, choosing to defer the driving to someone who knew where in the hell they were going. "Very well, then. My car is round back. Follow me."

Venturing to the rear of the hotel offered Mitch the opportunity to capture the beauty of its unique location. Set far enough off the highway to muffle sound, its stark-white walls contrasted sharply against a backdrop of Highland green. Blooming flowers daring to creep up the side of the building exploded in pinks, yellows, and blues. Their combined fragrances reminded him of his grandmother's garden. She had been his only ally in the fight against his father's rigid structure.

But this day was crisp as the sun scattered light through the clouds. If not for this little excursion, he would have enjoyed a hike in the local mountains to explore the countryside.

A modest two-story home occupied the space behind the hotel. An entryway and windows were decorated in the same fashion as the larger building in front of it. Two caramel Cocker Spaniels wagged their tails anxiously in the adjacent kennel. Duncan patted their heads with great affection as he turned his attention to a black Mercedes parked inside the nearby carport. Mitch walked to the passenger side, looking at the doggies. He could tell they were well loved, if not slightly spoiled.

"Wonderful things, aren't they? Dogs, I mean. They can tell whatever mood you're in and accommodate their behavior to match. Brilliant beasts, just brilliant," Duncan said, praising them. "My Augustus and Niro are the best in the nation, if I do say so myself."

"Augustus and Niro?" Mitch asked.

"Strong names for strong boys. Can't just name them Fido or Duke, can you? Would be madness," Duncan stated.

"I'm surprised one of them isn't named Turner," Mitch teased.

Bursting into laughter, Duncan backed out of the carport. Aside from his light-hearted comment, Mitch was afraid to speak.

When Duncan agreed to the meeting, he assumed it would go better than it had. Starting from scratch could prove to be frustrating and overwhelming for all parties involved. As he moved forward with Mitch, he needed to remember that a flood of information would be disastrous. His saving grace would come once they reached their final destination. At that location, he would not be the only one convincing the young man to remain in-country.

Mitch broke the tension by posing a less-than-serious question. "Do you plan on telling me where we are going, or should I assume that you will dump my body somewhere along a country road?"

"Finally, a sense of humor!" Duncan exclaimed. "I knew you had one in there somewhere. We are traveling to a museum in a nearby town. Seems you are a visual learner, so I assumed it would be advantageous if I showed you what we had discussed on the bridge."

Mitch nodded. "I have a tendency to play out situations. Kind of like watching a movie."

Duncan had never met a young man with more idiosyncrasies. He could be rough, intelligent, impatient, courageous, and loyal in one breath. Yet, he didn't know what he would passionately defend if given the opportunity. He seemed more like the politician, consistent in his ability to tell people what he felt they needed to hear rather than fight for truth. An intriguing contradiction. When he met him as a boy, Duncan saw the fire in his eyes for education. He was reminded of Mitch's father in his carriage and charisma. Now, the man in front of him seemed lost, devoid of the passion he once possessed. This man had seen too much loss, and Duncan wondered if there was anyone Mitch confided in during times of doubt or crisis.

Removing his cell phone, Mitch casually remarked, "I need to check how things are going in the States."

Duncan nodded his head. Mitch's ability to make a phone call while in Duncan's presence calmed his fears concerning the man's ability to trust. It would be Duncan's first task to make sure the doctor met only trustworthy people. Mitch redialed the last number on his phone. It rang without any type of answer. He hung up and dialed once more. Maybe he was being ignored. It wouldn't be the first time.

"Don't hang up; I'm here!" Graham shouted.

"Why are you shouting?" Mitch asked.

"Force of habit. I was trying to find the phone when I heard it ring, thinking it might be you. I didn't want you to hang up, since your tendency is a lack of patience," Graham replied.

Mitch laughed at his friend's intimate knowledge of his personality quirks. People used to joke that if the men never married, they should consider marrying each other because they argued like a couple. Staff at the hospital often referred to each of them as "the wife" whenever they joined forces on a case. The running joke got old fast. "I'm on my way to God knows where, and I need you to check on

Tamara. Think you could run over to the house, survey the situation, and give me some updates?"

"Way ahead of you. I am already on my way. I knew you would need information, and seeing as how I am the next best thing to you, possibly better, I thought I would check things out for myself. Can't let you have all the glory."

A laugh escaped Mitch's lips at Graham's response.

"I made a phone call to our friend's office in Austria. They requested records be sent to the office for a consultation, but judging by the tone of our conversation, they might be able to help with new treatment ideas. As her primary physician, you need to release a copy of her records." Graham ended with, "Let's get this done."

Mitch knew better than to challenge his old friend. "Thanks, Graham. You're a lifesaver."

The appreciation threw Graham for a loop. In all their years of friendship, there had been jokes and sarcasm, but never sincere gratitude. "You sound weird. Are you having some sort of midlife crisis?" Graham asked.

"Just a lot on my plate."

"Are you dying?"

Mitch paused. Truthfully, he wanted to confide everything to Graham, but didn't feel he could do it in front of Duncan. "Be the hero, clean up my mess, and I'll call you later."

"That's more like it. Who's the home-care nurse? Should I pour on the old Wellington charm?"

"You can try, but it's Daphne."

Graham paused. "Daphne? Yeah, you aren't messed up at all with this case."

"Keep me posted, and act like I'm there," Mitch suggested.

Graham burst out into laughter. "I'll do one better and act like me."

Mitch clicked the phone off and gazed at it sadly. He felt detached from the people in his life over the last few years. He was unable to connect with anyone and had begun to act like a hermit in his townhouse and his practice. He even isolated himself from Graham. These days he spent more time reflecting on his past decisions as a gauge for his future. He questioned every choice he had ever made. In his mind, each critical juncture was a test. And now, he wondered if he failed. He saw women on the street who reminded him of someone from his past. Someone he should have grown old with, but let slip through his fingers without a fight. Her face flashed before him just as Duncan announced their arrival.

"Where are we?" Mitch asked.

Duncan exited the car. "The village of Blair Atholl. A quick jaunt from the hotel makes it the ideal day-trip for the adventure seeker or castle enthusiast." He smirked.

Surrounded by lush greenery, the Clan Donnachaidh museum was a tidy whitewashed building with an impressive memorial statue of a piper on the lawn. Had it not been for the carpark and tea shoppe attached, it could have been mistaken for a private residence.

Attached to the outside wall of the building, a carving of the family's crest had been handcrafted from a single piece of stone. Mitch couldn't help but marvel at the craftsmanship and talent of the completed work. Over years of being outside, weather had worn the stone into a striking piece of artwork. Next to the carving stood a man scowling. The combination of his patched woolen jacket and wind-blown hair made him look disheveled.

"You get me out of bed early on my day off? Duncan, you have no respect for me whatsoever. I might have had my own plans for the day."

Duncan scoffed. "You never have plans. Besides, there isn't a lady in the county who would take you on, you old fool."

"You never know. I think it's you who scares them off. Must be the stench."

"That is the stench of superior scotch. Ladies who recognize the odor would only be of exceptional quality and breeding."

Mitch recognized the man's voice from the phone call at the Ritz. The gentleman turned and extended his hand.

"Duncan can be a rude old bugger. The name's Stewart. Don't let the banter fool you. Dunc and I go way back. It's all in good fun, boy."

Mitch was surprised at the warmth of his fingers with such a cold breeze blowing. The look on his face caused Stewart to ask if anything was wrong. Mitch narrowed his eyes at the man. "Did you call me with instructions to go to Notting Hill?"

Stewart smiled, raising his arms above his head in a gesture of surrender. "Guilty! I was told to give you the address of a meeting Duncan had with some of our senior members, but it fell through when accusations from the Professor came down the pipeline that our inner circle had been breached. I asked the butler to send you to Scotland to meet Duncan at the hotel."

Duncan interjected before Stewart had any more opportunities to stick his foot in his mouth. "There isn't any need to go into a lengthy discussion about that matter. There will be plenty of time for questions at a later date."

Stewart rolled his eyes at Duncan's lecture. "We are here to present you with our truth. Is that right, Dunc?"

"Visual aids only. The boy is already processing his own thoughts. No pushing will be required," Duncan replied.

"Nothing like the last minute for Dunc to call, but I am prepared no matter how late the hour."

They entered the building as the two older men continued their argument about nothing. Their friendship reminded him of the one he shared with Graham. An indescribable loyalty existed between the two, despite their joking and teasing.

Walking past display cases filled with ancient artifacts, tartans, pottery, and photos, Mitch was fascinated by the surrounding history. Two extra-large cases stood beneath the portrait of a stern faced woman dressed in black with cascading curls of ginger peeking out beneath a starched white cap. The two men stopped by one of the cases on the left, motioning for Mitch to join them. Inside, a crystal sphere was cushioned on a pillow of deep, red velvet.

"You brought me here to show me a crystal ball! What's next, backroom fortune readings by an overdressed gypsy?" Mitch teased.

"You said he was stubborn," Stewart commented.

"Would we really bring you here for hocus pocus? Open your eyes and listen," Duncan demanded. "Take it away, Stew."

Stewart grimaced at Duncan, took a deep breath, and began his lesson. "Families in Scotland are referred to as clans, with a chieftain as head. He is in charge of all major decisions: marriage ties, feuds with neighboring clans, and with which clans to align. Your clan defines who you are, broadcasting to the world what you stand for, where you belong, and often what you believe. The major ruling houses of Europe all have familial ties by either blood or marriage. This keeps the power base intact."

Duncan grunted. "Good God, man, get on with it! If I knew you were going to give a bloody dissertation, I would have told him all this myself."

Giving Duncan a sideways glance, Stewart continued. "In ancient Israel, during the period of Solomon's Temple, a clan system existed there as well. Back then they were referred to as tribes. Each one was known by different talents. They went through a migration process once the temple was destroyed. The system of lineage, spirituality, and government was changing, so tribes knew that their survival and way of life depended upon change. One tribe in particular, the Dan, migrated to this region."

"The Dan Tribe?" Mitch answered sarcastically.

Stewart hardly noticed, announcing enthusiastically, "That's right! The Tribe of Dan. We had a system of spiritual clans with priestly classes almost identical in nature to their heritage, confirming their decision to move. With the exception of the climate, of course."

Duncan interrupted. "You see, Mitch, the mystics they traveled to meet here knew their secrets of spirituality. The druids were the medicine men and women of the area, acting as consultants to the high kings. The Tribe of Dan brought their culture to the druids in order to safeguard their lineage."

Mitch raised his voice. "Why are we having a history lesson?"

Duncan sighed. "My boy, the ones with power and money write the books. The meek, who serve the humanity of this earth, are the defeated and downtrodden. When you discover *their* secrets, the answers to your questions will be achieved."

Mitch scuffed his shoe on top of the polished floor, purposefully leaving a mark. His juvenile defiance made him feel in control. He immediately felt guilty and apologized to Duncan.

"No need to apologize. Frustration is a human emotion not easily remedied. Everyone falls prey to its tricks of seduction, and more often than not perform in a less-dignified manner because of it. However, it is what we do with our frustration that catapults us toward greatness. A cool head prevails when all rational thought becomes a victim to frustration's tightening grip." He pointed to the portrait of a lady above their heads. "Princess Mary, or as she is more widely recognized, Mary, Queen of Scots, is the perfect example of frustration. One of her first memories as a child was being told that she didn't matter; yet her existence threatened the power base of this entire country. She was born to a life of privilege, which was stolen by a queen who convinced herself that Mary was her destruction. There were few confidantes in her life whom she could trust. As a result, false accusations were lobbied, creating a civil war of loyalists to Queen Elizabeth and to Mary. Those trustworthy people were the chieftains of the Donacciah Clan, the heads of the Robertson family. They guarded her, helping her escape capture by moving her to various safe locations. Their oath to her service remained steadfast."

Mitch's attention was achieved.

"The night before Mary was taken to the Tower of London to face execution at the hand of her queen, she summoned the chieftains to her apartments at Holyrood House. Once there, she made one final request."

Mitch now clung to every word while Duncan paused dramatically. "They entered her chamber the morning after her arrest through a secret passageway. Mary handed them a parchment with specific instructions to deliver an artifact. She presented this to them along with the instruments you see in the case to the right of her portrait." Duncan pointed to two small harps lying on crushed blue velvet. "These were her last personal possessions, aside from the crucifix and rosary shown in the portrait, that were not destroyed after her arrest. It is rumored that the harps emit a peculiar tone, which when played correctly, unlock ancient stone monuments around Scotland."

As Mitch gazed at the dainty harps with gilded edges, he could imagine Mary's slender fingers brushing the strings. The songs meant to soothe frayed nerves during hours of solitude.

"You mentioned an artifact. Is it the crystal ball?"

"No, the artifact she surrendered is the most precious. We refer to it as the Exile Carpet. It has been passed down through generations to an individual who has been prepared to guard its legacy. It is a lifetime commitment."

Pointing to a crest, identical to the one on the outside of the building, Duncan added, "This family's history of guarding secrets is known only within the inner sanctum of the organizations they have served."

"Who was the recipient of the Exile Carpet?" Mitch asked.

"A woman educated in the realm of those spiritual arts and next in line, should Mary succumb to her tormentors. It has to always be a woman, due to women's unique connections with the spiritual realm," Duncan casually stated. "The Exile Carpet has remained hidden with her family since the time of Mary's death."

"With guidance, of course," Stewart added. "The Professor is our current hope for unlocking the secrets held within the threads of the Exile Carpet."

Mitch looked confused at the amount of players being thrown onto the game board. "Is he someone I will be meeting?"

"Oh, no, the Professor must be kept away from the public. He is close to solving the riddle. He must remain hidden within his sanctuary to complete the translation of the inscription embroidered into the Exile Carpet."

Duncan kicked Stewart's shoe. Sensing his old friend's frustration, Stewart once again took the lead. "Mitch, look at this stone, a perfect quartz crystal without any marks. It has a legacy for possessing magical healing properties. Dipped into water three times, any recipient could be healed from illness. The manner in which it was discovered is equally impressive."

Mitch crossed his arms. "Continue."

"Duncan told you the story of a battle. That was the Battle of Bannockburn. The British outnumbered the Scots, and there was no way on God's green earth that the Scots would prove victorious. One of their commanders, Robert the Bruce, was aware of their situation, and yet he hoped his men would be courageous enough against the enemy.

The morning of the battle, a clan member awoke from a disturbing dream. He had dreamt of a young woman in a white cloak directing him to an area close to the battlefield where a weapon of great power was hidden. Confused, he dug where instructed and discovered a silver box. As the top swung open, a tingling sensation shot through his body. Inside lay this stone glowing in the morning's light. Rushing to the battlefield, he asked to speak with Robert the Bruce. Upon seeing the stone, Bruce's spirits lifted as he too felt its magic. When they took the field, Bruce surveyed his small number of forces, continuing to pray for a miracle. In that moment, the mysterious men on horseback arrived through the fog. They came to assist a family to whom they had sworn allegiance. The horsemen were Templars. The army commander, Robert the Bruce, was a family member of the Donacciah Clan. Or, as we have pointed out in straightforward terms, The Tribe of Dan."

Mitch shook his head to make sense of it all. "You are telling me that this museum and this stone are of the ancient Tribe of Dan?"

"Catch on quick, do you?" Stewart quipped.

"Provided all of this is true, what does this magic rock have to do with what I am searching for?" Mitch ordered.

"What are you searching for?" Duncan asked.

"I'm not entirely sure. But I am sure that a life hangs in the balance, and I have no time to waste. Although at the moment, that is all I seem to be doing," Mitch admitted.

It was apparent that Duncan did not receive his remark well. Stewart stepped in before an argument ensued. "This stone is part of the path to enlightenment. During the time of early Egypt, India, China, and Sumeria, groups of alchemists were surrounded by stones, both natural and synthesized, which were ascribed with the properties of transforming a base metal into pure gold, thus transforming a human into a god or goddess. The most popular stone, known as the Philosopher's Stone, literally translates as the 'Stone of the Heavens.' It is the physical evidence of the phrase 'God is the Rock,' which was used as a code for those who held the knowledge of the alchemists. It holds magical properties for the one who knows how to use it correctly." Mitch continued to look confused. "After the alchemical process, a white-gold powder is produced and consumed by a human initiate. The powder reacts with human genes to elevate to the divine level."

"Those men created a hallucinogenic state where they convinced themselves they were speaking to God?" Mitch asked. "Sounds like cult behavior to me."

Stewart cast a look in Duncan's direction. "You know, Mitch, it seems to me you need time to process all of this. How about a drink? Clear your head. Get a good night's sleep. I know a great place where you can do both."

"Brilliant!" Duncan exclaimed. "I'll drive so we can get there faster. Mitch can make any necessary phone calls while we inform him about tomorrow's adventure."

Still perplexed by the mangled information without any clear definitions of truth, Mitch asked, "Tomorrow's adventure?" He wasn't sure how many more history lessons he could manage. He was sent here to rendezvous with Duncan in order to secure a route to Tamara's cure. But so far, all he had managed was to be given historical stories from two gentlemen whose sanity was beginning to come into question.

Duncan smirked. "Tomorrow you meet The Three. They are much clearer than we are—and much more fun."

"The what?" Mitch questioned, preferring to go along with their charade in the hopes that these new individuals would get him back on a track that included answers to his core dilemma of Tamara.

Duncan walked ahead as Stewart turned off the lights in the cases. "That is what I said. Just 'The Three.'"

9

Returning to the hotel brought a welcome relief after his exhausting day. Dusk settled around the grounds while a wonderful variety of fragrances from the dinner service filled the air. Walking into the lobby with Duncan and Stewart, Mitch surveyed the jovial patrons and wondered if they, too, knew the secrets that had been imparted to him. If they shared the same knowledge, how on earth did they go about their daily lives? He preferred absolutes rather than theories. It occurred to him that to question the absolute carried the potential of increased complications in one's life. That was something most people tended to avoid.

The three men sauntered into the bar. Tartan-covered walls kept the room cozy with scenes from the Highlands hanging in various areas. The fire provided a comforting protection against the emerging damp of night. Guests laughed over drinks, as Duncan and Stewart made their way to a corner table near the hearth. Mitch watched the same woman who had tended the reception desk in the morning fill patron's glasses behind the bar. She waltzed over to the table, her long skirt swaying with the movement of her hips, and placed a bottle of old Scottish whiskey in front of them.

"Thanks, love," Stewart remarked. "Nothing like a fine drink to take the chill out of your bones."

"Always a chill to bones as old as yours," Duncan mocked, pouring the whisky and signaling Mitch to join them.

"Don't let him fool you, Mitch; Duncan has discovered the fountain of youth. Tell me, was it the sale of your soul to vampires that keeps you vibrant?" Stewart quipped.

Duncan raised his amber-filled glass. "I believe it is the combination of the love of a good woman and a fine Scottish tonic, aged to perfection, such as this in my hand, that keeps me going."

"I'll drink to that!" Stewart toasted. "Even if you are older than that bottle of hundred-year-old whisky."

The two friends laughed heartily. The continuous amount of jesting could be mistaken for competitive dislike, but their underlying loyalty stood strong against people's assumptions. Viewing their friendship reminded Mitch to call Graham.

"Excuse me; I have a phone call to make."

Duncan looked up from his third glass of whisky. "Take your time, son. We'll keep a dram or two for you. You've earned it today."

Mitch found a quiet nook beneath the stairs. He dialed Graham's cell number and was routed straight to voice mail. Odd and very unlike Graham. He decided to try again, opting for an attempt later if Graham didn't answer.

"Speak."

"Graham? Are you all right?"

"I'm in the middle of something."

"What's her name?"

"Funny. What do you want?"

"What's the update?" Mitch pushed.

"I won't candy coat it. She had another episode last night, which according to Lillian has lasted longer than the others. I watched her while it happened. Have you ever done that? Kind of creepy, but fascinating. Anyway, her vitals are off the charts, and not in a good way. This leads me to believe that there is an unidentified problem that we're missing. Her body isn't reacting to the meds, and the mystery issue is causing every organ to rapidly begin the descent toward shutting down. I changed some of her doses to see what we get by morning, but I have to be honest, if there isn't improvement overnight, I'm admitting her. I don't care what her parents say," Graham reported.

Mitch panicked. Not responding to meds? Graham was right; there was something he was missing. He certainly wasn't finding it in Scotland, and he felt the urgency to return stateside.

"Mitch, you still there?"

Mitch let out a deep sigh. "Yeah, go ahead."

"Listen, I can't hang on the phone. I want to watch the nurse administer Tamara's next dosage in two minutes. She's been acting a little weird, and I've got a funny feeling in the pit of my stomach."

Mitch laughed out loud. "You always have a funny feeling with Daphne. You've had it since sophomore year. It's called a crush, remember?"

"No, man, this is different. There is a coldness to her that I'm not comfortable with. Even Tamara mentioned her behavior is odd."

"Don't misread professionalism for distance. Just because a woman doesn't fall into your arms doesn't mean she's cold. It means she's doing her job," Mitch scolded.

Graham's tone turned stern. "In regards to *our* patient, I'll stay and monitor her overnight. The on-duty resident will take my patients at the hospital. I'll call you in the morning with the next plan of attack. You OK with that?"

"I trust you with my life."

"Yeah, but do you trust me with hers?" Graham whispered as he switched off his phone.

Mitch held the phone in his shaking hand as a wave of nausea overtook him. How could he miss something? He was meticulous, even anal-retentive, preferring to have all the information before making a decision. Did he not run the correct chemistry panels? Deciding to retrace his steps over his notes later that evening, he would get the latest vitals from Graham in the morning and maybe an answer would appear. Hoping the two old friends in the bar might have loosened their reserves with whisky, Mitch returned to the corner table in the bar.

"Everything OK?" Duncan asked.

"It isn't anything you two can help me out with. Unless you are world-renowned doctors in disguise," Mitch snapped.

"Actually," Stewart stammered, "I *am* a doctor. I received my PhD from St. Andrews. Maybe I could be of assistance."

"Oh, piss off, you old codger! He would only ask for your help if he wanted to bore the patient to death. He means a medical doctor, not a doctor of useless crap," Duncan quipped.

"I thought you needed the useless crap from me in order to educate our young friend here," Stewart remarked.

Duncan nodded. "Quite right, a million apologies. Take a sip, Mitch. It will clear your head and right the wrongs." Against his better judgment, Mitch complied, if only to get it over with so he could retire to his room. The tense muscles in his shoulders relaxed, bringing about welcome relief. "Better already. Do you have any questions about today?'

"Yeah, about a billion, but I guess in a bigger, broader picture, it all makes sense. I just don't have the same background in history that you do. It's a little hard," Mitch admitted.

"You don't need a historical background to receive information." Duncan rubbed his head while glancing at his wife. She shot a small smile over to him and continued her work. "You can read a book and let it sink in, deciding to believe the written word or not. Did anything sound believable?" Duncan asked.

"No doubt it's believable. But I trust tangible things. If I can see it and touch it, then I can deal with it. You can't fight a ghost," Mitch stated casually.

His remark sent Stewart rocketing from of his chair. "Indeed you can! Haven't you ever looked at people? I mean, really looked at them? Every day is a combat with ghosts. They fight against being better, stronger, faster, making more money, and being better looking. No one else creates that mental battle; only they do."

"And why do they do that?" Mitch asked.

Stewart pointed to his heart. "Because they don't know who they are in here. They don't want to know; it's too scary. The answer is to numb themselves with careers, big houses, designer clothes, and even churches, thinking that all the wrongs will magically turn right. When in reality, it never does. Only their deathbed brings clarity."

Duncan nodded. "Too true, too true. Know thyself. The kingdom of heaven is deep within, and whoever knows himself shall find it. All the answers that people seek are as simple as that one phrase." He raised his glass in salute without taking his eyes off Mitch.

Mitch's wit cut through the two men like a knife. "It's that simple, huh? Well then, let's gather all the shrinks of the world into one room, have one giant cry session, and everyone's problems will be solved."

Stewart stood up again. "This isn't a joke; its universal law! Don't disregard ancient teachings with your bravado! You don't know it all, and I would say after meeting you that your knowledge is primitive at best!" The activity in the bar halted abruptly as all eyes focused on Stewart. Duncan motioned for him to sit back down. As he did, the activity in the room resumed. "I'm sorry, Dunc," Stewart whined. "This kid gets me all heated up."

Mitch set his glass on the table. "I didn't mean any disrespect. I haven't had as much time for my brain to absorb this as you have. I need to put all the pieces together quickly so this trip can end."

Duncan glanced from Stewart to Mitch. "Your journey is just beginning. Let your prejudices dissolve, and allow yourself to open up. At that point, you will learn and grow." Duncan paused long enough to finish the liquid in his glass. "Has there ever been a person in your life who you surrendered all your defenses to?" he asked.

Mitch smiled slightly. "There is a colleague of mine. He knows me better than anyone."

Stewart frowned. "He means a female, meathead. Have you ever had *that* kind of relationship?"

Mitch searched his memory for a member of the female persuasion who truly knew him. His mother was the obvious choice. Mothers knew every detail about their children, loving them unconditionally. He had dated unsuccessfully through his life with nothing that he could define as core-shaking love. Nurses had tried to set him up with their friends who were searching for a doctor to marry, but he wasn't interested in one-night stands. Sure, he had dreams of a home with children, but had never found a person who would be willing to put up with his insane schedule. "No one earth-shattering, if that is what you are getting at."

"Are you queer, then, with this chap of yours?" Stewart asked. "No judgment. We need to know if you have ever had feelings for anyone other than yourself."

Mitch's jaw dropped. "I have feelings! I have so many, in fact, that they get in the way of patient care! I care too much for each and every one, and that is how I wind up in situations like this! No, I am not queer with the chap, as you put it. I…" Mitch stopped himself midsentence as the image of a girl popped into his head.

They met while he was in medical school and she was completing her dissertation in ancient history. They bumped into each other one night in the library after the rest of the students had gone home. Being friends with the research librarian afforded "after hours" luxuries few students were permitted. She sat in the middle of the room with books scattered around her table, brown hair tucked back into a messy ponytail, scribbling furiously into a worn-out notebook. He watched her for a few minutes before she started gathering her belongings to leave. He mustered up the courage to approach her. Their connection was immediate. To Mitch, it came so easy; and their relationship progressed rapidly. They shared the same passion, drive, and work ethic for their fields of study as well as career paths. In his final year of med school, he decided to propose. He purchased the ring, set a plan with Graham's help, and prepared for his life to change. He knew that years of medical residency and fellowship would not scare her off, and his confidence soared as the day of his proposal dawned.

The night was magic. After their candlelit dinner, a walk around the lake holding hands produced a multitude of stars in the heavens, presenting the perfect moment. They sat on an iron park bench as Mitch reached for the ring box. Before he had a chance to pose the important question, she excitedly announced a recent offer to lead an archaeological dig site in the Middle East after graduation. The opportunity was too great to miss, she explained, feeling that if anyone would understand what this meant to her career, it was Mitch. Leaving the ring in his pocket, he silently took her home and let nature run its course. Mitch never saw her again. He heard tidbits about her life from old school friends, but refused to contact her. He remained emotionally devastated. Relaying his story of unrequited love made the men nod their heads in mutual understanding.

"And no one has been able to fill her shoes?" Stewart inquired.

"Deep down I compare anyone I meet to her," Mitch confided.

Duncan's eyes were beginning to look a little glassy. "I knew you were a deep individual. We just had to get to the bottom of it. You are quite a guy."

Mitch looked at the empty whisky bottle. "I think we should call it a night, guys. I'm beat."

"Not so soon," Duncan replied. "You will meet your teachers in the lobby tomorrow promptly at eight a.m. The Three don't like to be kept waiting. Annoying sometimes, if you ask me. Stewart and I have other business, but you can always contact us if you have questions or concerns. We are happy to help a brother."

"A brother?" Mitch asked, baffled at his reference to fraternity.

Duncan smiled, holding up his hand. "We three wear the same ring." On his right ring finger sat the accessory that also graced Mitch's finger.

"I should have known." Mitch chuckled. "By the way, why do you call them 'The Three'?"

"'Cause there are three of them," Stewart mumbled.

Duncan watched the room empty of its patrons. Two people lingered at the bar, but he didn't feel they were any threat. "Along this journey, you will be given teachers in various shapes and sizes. Some are experts in their field, while others advanced as teachers based upon personal experience. Each teacher will bestow an object of importance pertaining to the lesson. Keep all the objects close, and share them with no one."

"What are the objects?" Mitch asked.

"Too hard to explain now. It will all make sense in the end. No doubt about that. Now, what lesson did you learn from us?" Duncan queried.

Mitch thought for a moment. "I learned about a battle, a family, and a magic stone."

Duncan squinted his eyes out of both frustration and an alcoholic haze. "You learned that faith, magic, and belief go hand in hand. You learned that there are secrets and lines of families that reach back to our most ancient records, with living relatives today. These families are important in what they have given to the world, not just because of who they are." He paused while reaching into his pants pocket. In his hand he held an object slightly larger than a golf ball.

"This blue stone is made from a mineral called Lapis Lazuli. The ancients believed that different minerals held properties for healing and spiritual work. This stone is given to you as part of your journey, but it will also give you the spiritual energy that you require. Keep it close and listen."

"Listen to it?" Mitch squeaked.

"Yes, listen," Duncan snapped. "The Three will show you how to do that. I got my stone ages ago, and it has never failed me." He leaned over and whispered, "Mine is green."

Mitch was too tired to pose any further questions. He reached out, feeling the hard surface of the stone along with the warmth from its hiding place. For a brief second, he thought it vibrated in his hand. One final question popped into his mind as he turned to leave. "Hey, whatever happened to that Robert guy after the battle?"

Stewart looked up with sleep-filled eyes. "What always happens when you go against a substantial foe? At that time the Roman Catholic Church controlled the majority of the European monarchies, except Scotland. Because of Robert the Bruce's connection with the Templars, and his reluctance to pledge allegiance to the Pope, he and his family were excommunicated."

"Is that a good or a bad thing?" Mitch inquired.

Stewart smiled. "When your journey is complete, you will be able to tell me."

Mitch laughed while retreating to his room with a drunken stagger.

Stewart watched the young man grab the banister tightly, trying not to fall while he quickly entered the shadows of the hallway. His eyes perked up at the rapid questions being thrown his way by a bar patron in the dark. Answers were brief and to the point before he stumbled away. Light from a cell phone keypad interrupted the dark.

"The doctor is in place."

10

It had been years since Mitch dreamt. Something about the Highland air transformed him into a different person. Now, scenes of knights on horseback, soldiers, and royal persons clothed in rich robes were vibrant. Being relaxed in his surroundings made time slip through his fingers quicker than he preferred, causing him to run late for the day's adventure.

Going downstairs to the dining room, a beautiful distraction met him at the door. The same young woman who had given him instructions for his first meeting with Duncan leaned against the doorway of the dining room. Casually dressed in jeans and brown hiking boots, her green barn coat held a crescent moon pin on the lapel. Her arms were folded across her chest, expressing annoyance at his casual attitude toward punctuality. "Having a bit of a lie-in?"

Mitch was flustered with her accusation of languid behavior. "Sorry, I lost track of time. Miss…"

"Call me Pip. The parentals gave me a formal name, but I'm not a formal person. Know what I mean?"

"My father was traditional too."

"Ready, then? We've got a schedule to keep, and the others are in the car. They aren't good at waiting," Pip announced.

She grasped Mitch's elbow, leading him toward the front door. Before leaving, she shouted to the woman behind the reception desk. "See you later, Mummy! Love you!"

The woman smiled. "Careful up there, Pip!"

Mitch stared at the blond beauty with only one thought. "Duncan is your father?"

She smirked. "Stewart was right. You do catch on quick."

A silver Range Rover idled in the parking lot with two identical brown-haired women seated in the back. Their argument seemed heated, as their voices could be heard from outside the car. Pip opened the driver's side door, releasing loud music that tore at the serenity of the morning air. "You two going to argue all morning, or are we going to be professional?" she asked, slipping behind the wheel.

The argument halted abruptly when Mitch entered the vehicle. Each woman wore her brown hair differently, one being shoulder length and the other falling just below her ears. They were dressed in identical jeans with sweaters of coordinating colors. Pinned to each sweater, a gold crescent moon glimmered in the sunlight.

"I'm Mitch."

Shifting the car into drive, Pip remarked, "Girls, this is our assignment for the day. Assignment, meet the girls. And before you ask, yes, they are twins. The one on the left is Gillian, and Genevieve is on the right."

Mitch smiled as the twins said a quiet hello, noticing that each one had the most beautiful eyes he had ever seen. Gillian's eyes were deep blue; while Genevieve's were an incandescent green. "You're taking me to The Three?"

"The Three?" Gillian laughed. "Who said that?"

"Duncan. He said I was to meet The Three," Mitch stated.

Genevieve sighed. "Was he with Stewart? Those two have a flair for the dramatic. Shame they never went into acting; they would have been brilliant."

Pip laughed. "Yeah, Daddy seems to bring mystery into everything he does. He also tends to talk around things before getting to the point. The Three, though? That is hilarious."

"Then what are we doing?" Mitch asked.

Gillian leaned forward to touch Mitch's shoulder. "You're in a car with three women."

Mitch spun back to look at her. "*You* guys are The Three!"

Pip was the first to reply. "In the flesh. There are more of us, but they tend to send the three of *us* out on more assignments. I guess after yesterday with those two old goats, they figured another day with them would wig you out. So, we get the daunting task of teaching you the next lesson. And from what I hear, you aren't a very willing pupil."

Mitch knew better than to argue with three women in the same car, so he watched the countryside zoom by. Stone walls strewn with moss marked the division of property as they ran the length of the road. Each home added to the beauty of the area, with tidy front gardens overflowing with seasonal foliage. Families walked and biked along trails of green toward the village, while farmers managed their flocks of sheep in the fields with well-trained dogs and hearty waves. Passing through the town center of Blair Atholl, they turned onto a dirt road that ascended into the mountains. After two miles of banging around, the Range Rover slowed down to pass a sheep farm on the right-hand side.

Pip yelled into the backseat. "Hey, guys! Remember this place?"

Gillian laughed first. "Yeah, what did Dunc call it? Retaliation?"

Genevieve leaned across her sister. "Oh God, I was sore for weeks. And those poor sheep. I think I nicked more than I sheared."

Mitch watched Pip laugh. He was interested and almost surprised by quick feelings that she was the type of person he could befriend—someone whose natural energy could lift a person's spirit, making everything instantly better. "Sheep?" Mitch asked.

Pip explained their antics. "The summer we were twelve, we had a mischievous streak that continually landed at Dunc's feet. He got tired of us being underfoot at the hotel, playing pranks. So one day when we managed to take it a little too far, he brought us out here. He demanded that we dress up in the new clothes we purchased during a trip to Perth. Dropping us off in the afternoon, he told the farmer to bring us home when our task was complete. We had no clue what we were in for." All three girls began to snicker.

"He dropped you off at a sheep farm? What did you do to deserve such punishment?"

Pip confessed. "We put rubber dog muck in the men's WC."

Gillian added, "Placed rubber sick on top of the bar, and played tennis outside against the dining-room wall during a full dinner rush."

"The final straw was playing around with squirt guns and shooting Dunc," Genevieve said amid renewed laughter.

"He was dressed for the dinner crowd, and we hosed him down. He looked at us and asked us if we knew what the word 'retaliation' meant. When we replied that we didn't, he said we would learn," Pip concluded.

Leaning forward in her seat, Gillian interrupted. "He made arrangements with the farmer for us to help out with the shearing. He had heard that the farmer was looking for extra hands during the season, and Dunc saw a prime opportunity to teach us the meaning of the word."

"Plus, I think he liked us being gone for the day." Pip couldn't help herself from laughing through her words.

Gillian leaned back, and Genevieve leaned forward to capture Mitch's attention. Her floral scent reminded him of wildflowers.

Genevieve chuckled. "We were perfect angels the rest of the summer. In fact, if I remember correctly, didn't we just walk the dogs to stay out of the way?"

"That's right!" Pip squealed. "I almost forgot about that. We walked those poor pups three times a day!"

Gillian's laugh was infectious. "We logged eighty-six kilometers that summer!"

Everyone erupted in laughter. Mitch was genuinely enjoying his three lively companions. As they climbed higher into the mountainous area, he couldn't help but join in on the laughter from other stories of their youthful summers. He was envious of the ease with which they moved from one story to the next, almost of one mind.

The hillsides were full of blooming heather. Shades of purple and white engulfed them, making the vibrant green of the hills dull in comparison. The scenery and conviviality were calming to the point where Mitch's eyelids became heavy. Just as they were about to close, he felt the car come to a stop.

"We're here!" Pip announced.

The women piled out of the car, while Mitch stretched. They had climbed the dirt road to a makeshift parking lot at the base of a hill. Stepping out of the car, he realized that the peak was much higher than a hill. The girls all stood at the back of the car, with the rear door open, helping each other with backpacks. Genevieve held out a fourth pack. "Ready?" she asked.

"Ready for what?"

Clutching the pack tightly, she walked toward him. "Ready for the climb, of course. It isn't that hard, but we each have some provisions. I packed this one for you."

"Provisions?" he asked, slipping the pack onto his back.

"Bottled water, snacks for the top, and the necessary materials for your lesson."

The three women headed for the paths leading to the top. Mitch watched them begin to ascend without him, wondering what he had gotten himself into. His brain processed the moment. He should have paid more attention to the location of the sheep farm in case he needed to go for help. Before concern mounted, he decided to go with the flow. He began to walk the path. Following Genevieve in a steady stride, she motioned for him to pick up his pace.

As he crested the peak, Mitch bent over to catch his breath. The women had set a brisk pace. He hadn't worked out in six months, and the change in altitude made his lungs struggle with the crisp air. Surveying his new environment, he noticed that the three women each took a different location at the top. Pip stood to his right, looking over the valley, Gillian was to his left and Genevieve stood in front of him. From where Mitch was, the four of them resembled the four points of a compass. Mitch walked toward a tall stone monument occupying the space between them. Walking around to the face of it, he noticed that time and weather had taken their toll. The engraved markings, that at one time must have been prominent, were eroding. He used a finger to trace the shapes within the well-weathered grooves.

Witnessing his interest in the stone, Pip approached Mitch. "Welcome to your lesson," she stated casually, removing a water bottle from her pack.

Mitch patted it firmly with his palm. "This rock is my lesson?"

"It's an important part. The pressure is on for you to understand what we teach. If not, it will screw up any hopes of you comprehending the rest." She finished the entire bottle in a single breath. "Did you remember to bring the stone Dunc gave you?" Reaching into his pocket, Mitch reluctantly handed it to Pip.

"Don't give it to me." She motioned for the others to join her. "It has to keep your energy. Place the stone in the palm of your right hand and don't let go. We'll do the rest."

Placing their packs on the ground, they began to remove objects from inside. Genevieve lit a small white candle, placing it at the base of the monument. Gillian removed a leather-bound book and placed it at the base, while Pip placed a medium-sized bowl alongside the other objects. In unison, they removed the crescent moons from their clothing, wrapped themselves in white muslin cloaks, securing them with the pins, and removed their shoes. The cloaks whipped around their bare ankles in the wind.

"I don't think Dunc is the only one with a flair for the dramatic," Mitch suggested.

Pip laughed. "OK, it runs in the family. But this isn't drama; it's business."

Gillian stepped away from the group. "We belong to a spiritual group that believes in the power of women. We follow the same belief structure as our ancestors, who were enlightened through the Masters. We wear white as a symbol of purity, cleansing, and protection. White is a powerful mantle when worn properly."

Genevieve pushed past her sister. "We believe in a balance of opposites and harmony. You can't have good without bad, cold without hot, male without female. We make our prayers for blessings to the laws of the universe and the Mother Goddess, who works with the earth. We are in tune with nature and its creatures. This is why we remove our shoes from this place of piety. The ground that is walked upon by the anointed feet of females creates a cleansing of the earth, and the space is energized."

Mitch looked at Pip, who smiled proudly at her friends. She resembled her father when she smiled. The twins stood on either side of the monument. Pip was standing as the apex of a triangle with Mitch seated before her.

"I know we sound mad, but here is what they are trying to say. The people who lived thousands of years ago were more advanced than we could ever hope to be. They knew things that we have yet to master. I'm not talking about civilization or technology, but rather spirituality. Those people knew themselves, what they believed in, and how to work within their community for the betterment of all humankind. They lived a life of grace and blessings, something we as civilized people have lost. We have lost sight of the supreme deity that is necessary for ourselves as well as for our planet."

Mitch scowled as he sat on the moss-strewn ground. "Is this some earth-friendly, environmental lecture? You don't need to get me to the top of a mountain to make me use my own shopping bags rather than the plastic ones."

Pip laughed at his frustration. "Cheeky! Open your mind, funny man, and listen! Really listen! For thousands of years, the balance between male and female has been corrupted. Following the time of Jesus, when Christianity was getting its start, men decided that women were unequal in the eyes of their church. They suppressed them, called them witches, and banned their writings from the final version of the Bible. And in doing so, they threw the whole energy alignment out of whack. Women have been trying to reclaim their acceptance in spiritual positions ever since."

Gillian motioned for Mitch to remain seated. "Are you confused?" she asked gently. Mitch nodded. Handing him a bottle of water, she addressed him in a motherly tone. "Let's all take a deep breath, calm down, and restart. I think I can make this simpler." Again Mitch nodded as he took a sip from the bottle. "All creatures, human beings included, are made up of energy. Energy is what gives us our link to the divine spark. This energy can be either positive or negative, depending upon the individual or the situation. Have you ever met someone who rubbed you the wrong way, and instead of staying around them, you fled, giving them the title of 'negative'?"

"Sure," Mitch replied.

"That negative feeling is their energy. Some people are just born negative, giving off that type of energy for the duration of their lifetime. Others possess a lighter energy, while still others are nothing but positive. It has nothing to do with gender; anyone can be positive or negative. The earth flows in the same energy. Each individual on this planet contributes to the flow of that energy. The lighter we become in our thoughts, words, and deeds, the more we reflect the positive. The more we fight, judge, or condemn, the more we allow the negative power to influence and chase away the light. We are linked to the divine through this flow of energy. Positive or more increased energy has been marked throughout the centuries by either monuments, like this one, or by buildings. Each one creates a voice to the divine. Clear so far?"

"I guess," Mitch blurted out, even though he was lying through his teeth.

She continued without skipping a beat. "The ancient teachers knew how to close off the rest of the world to connect with this energy. Meditation allowed their personal energy to connect with the monument, enabling them to store information. Kind of like a light bulb. You turn the switch, and the connection inside the bulb creates the illumination. These stones are storehouses of information if you have the same ability. They could be considered to be the first libraries of energy. Tools were used to carve the faces of these stones, giving us clues as to what information the stone housed. They used a variety of symbols to convey their message."

"Like hieroglyphics?" Mitch asked.

Gillian smiled at his recognition. "Precisely." She looked around at her friends. "Would anyone else like a turn?"

Pip and Genevieve shook their heads.

"You're doing great, Gill. Keep going," Pip remarked.

"Thanks!" Gillian replied excitedly. She picked up the leather-bound book, opening it to the first page. "Look at the stone and tell me the symbols that you see."

Mitch strained his eyes at the well-worn carvings. Even though the weather had not been kind, the symbols were still prominent. "There are a number of them," he commented. "I see a mirror, a horse with two riders, some sort of arch, an hourglass, a spiral, a moon, a bird, a skull, and a circle with a cross inside it."

"Good. Remembering the crest you saw at the museum yesterday, is there anything on this monument that was also on the crest?" she asked.

Mitch tried to remember. Truth be told, he wasn't paying as much attention as he probably should have. He took a stab in the dark. "The bird looks familiar."

"Woo hoo!" Pip yelled.

Gillian nodded her head to encourage his continued participation. "The bird is a dove. The crest has a dove on the right side, and there are multiple meanings, but two of the most obvious are tied to a clan, which is the Tribe of Dan. The dove is commonly tied to the phoenix. According to manuscripts, the phoenix was an ancient bird present at the time of creation, knowing secrets that even the gods were unaware of. It has the ability to regenerate itself after it turns to ash, being reborn from the smoldering residue. The Tribe of Dan used the dove as one of its symbols before their migration into the west."

"The phoenix?" Mitch questioned. "Is that the same bird in the Russian folk stories, The Firebird?"

"Different cultures adopt symbols and utilize them in their own stories to convey the same information. Do you see the moon, close to the top? Anything familiar about it?" Gillian asked, leading him to the answer by pointing to her cloak.

"Your pins," Mitch replied sheepishly, feeling silly about his response.

"Crescent moons, to be exact. The crescent-moon symbol is a visible sign of the Goddess. There are many symbols referring to the Goddess, just as there are many goddesses, such as Isis, Hathor, and Sophia. All divine and powerful in their own right, they maintain balance with the masculine side. I think that is what Pip was trying to convey. Although, she did rather it poorly."

Pip stuck out her tongue.

"Mature, Pip. May I continue?" Gillian teased with a smirk. "The crescent moon reveals to others in our community that our minds, as well as our energy, are enlightened. You see, Mitch, the Goddess holds three powers: creation, preservation, and destruction. The original followers determined that when the energy of the Goddess attaches itself to an object, then the object can wield all three of the powers. Since the moon possesses the same three powers as the Goddess, it became the prominent symbol."

"Like the stone in the museum!" Mitch exclaimed.

"You can charge any object with energy, like a battery, and it will wield it. Without energy, it's just a useless shell. It can be charged with positive, negative, preservation, destruction, anything you desire. The stone in the museum possesses healing powers as well as protection. Even your stone possesses power."

Mitch tightened his grip on the stone in his right hand, wondering what power it could hold. The power to control, the power to heal, the power to destroy. Anyone who harnessed the powers she described could be invincible.

Gillian noticed his mood change. "Don't get any bright ideas, Doctor Brody. In the wrong hands, power can be corrupted. We were told that you aren't of that mindset."

"I can't use it for my own benefit?" he asked.

"You certainly can, but when you use power for selfish reasons, you open a whole can of karmic worms that we don't have time to discuss." Mitch frowned at her response. "To put it bluntly. You play, you pay."

Mitch smiled, nodding at the slang she used. Gillian surprised him. At first glance, she appeared aloof, but during this encounter, he found her to be highly intelligent, sensitive, and compassionate. He felt lucky to have met her.

She caught him smiling at her. "You look like you could use a snack." Reaching into her pack, she handed him an apple and a granola bar. "Quick break for everyone. Take a gander at the scenery. It's quite remarkable."

Biting into the apple, sweet juice run down his throat; somehow his hunger had taken a backseat to the morning's events. He hadn't felt hungry until he tasted the juicy fruit. He meandered to the other side of the peak to survey the view. Gillian was right; it was breathtaking. The valley below was quilted in differing shades of green with white thatched cottages nestled among the farmlands. Fluffs of sheep grazed on hillsides, defying the laws of physics with their tiny hooves. The heather fields were alight with the day's last rays of sun and more vivid. Completely alone in his own little world, a hand on his shoulder surprised him.

"Pretty remarkable," Pip stated.

"'Remarkable' doesn't do it justice. I'm not sure there are words," Mitch whispered.

"You know, it's funny. We drove past that sheep farm on the way up here, and now it looks completely different," Pip admitted. "Isn't it interesting how when you look at something from a different perspective, you gain a whole new meaning?"

Mitch gawked at her in awe as she walked away. It seemed peculiar that someone as young as Pip sounded full of wisdom. For all the questions and mystery that surrounded him over the past few days, he did enjoy the company of the people he met. They had given him a great deal of information to absorb, information that fought against fundamentals he had been taught in school, but there was something unique about these people that made him desire to spend more time in their world.

Genevieve stepped forward, gaining Mitch's attention by waving her hands. "I have been asked to be less abrupt in my delivery. In my defense, it's only because people are hard headed and don't listen. They close their minds to anything different from what they have been told as truth. Most people are not asked to think, and in fact, are not encouraged to do so."

Clearing her throat, Gillian broke through her sister's rant. Genevieve stopped. "Tell me, Mitch, which symbol speaks to you?"

Mitch once again surveyed the carvings. His curiosity peaked after Gillian's explanations of the dove and the moon. One symbol did stand out from the rest simply because it didn't fit in. "The skull."

"Interesting choice. Why?" she asked.

"I associate skulls with death, Halloween, or pirates, and I am pretty sure that none of those are the reason it was placed there."

A hearty laugh escaped Genevieve's mouth. "Pirates? I'll have to remember that one." She took a deep breath and continued with a stern tone. "Actually, the skull is regarded as the vault of heaven. You see, there are spiritual communities who believe that the soul is encased within the head, which accounts for the mass amounts of beheadings as a form of punishment. If they chopped off your head, then you wouldn't be able to reincarnate to cause more trouble."

A thought popped into Mitch's mind. *What was it that Mother would say?* She would spout the verse often when he wasn't telling the truth, professing that his eyes gave away his true intentions. "The eyes are the windows to your soul," he whispered.

"There is a widespread belief that our dome-shaped skull is regarded as the soul's spiritual center, often referred to as the heaven of the human body. Many communities of thought have not only continued this belief, but are examples of skull worship. For example, the legendary Queen Guinevere belonged to the Cult of the Severed

Head. When her son suffered an untimely death, she kept his head in a bag. Shocking, I know, but she felt that by traveling with his head, she would be able to keep his soul from returning to a far more grue-some fate at another's hand. Some considered it madness, others a mother's sorrow, but she knew of the ancient wisdom and practiced it quite openly."

"The Templars and Masons use a skull for ceremonies, which judging by the ring on your finger, you already knew." Her statement caused Mitch's eyes to widen. "Skulls have been an important symbol of knowledge, rebirth, initiation, and spiritual perfection since the beginning of documented time."

Genevieve looked at Mitch sitting on the ground. He continued to look perplexed, making her feel inadequate as a teacher. Gillian was much better. "What about crystal skulls?" she asked.

Scratching his head, Mitch replied. "I saw some blurb about them on a conspiracy-theory show."

Genevieve rolled her eyes. "Ah, bloody hell! Conspiracy shows are all alike. Although I sometimes watch, 'cause the theories come close to truth, but end up in an alternate direction. Why did people carve crystal skulls? Why not carve crystal crosses or hearts or brains or kidneys?"

"I guess you would carve a heart because you can't survive without it. But then again, you can't survive without a brain, either." Mitch laughed. "And I can't see anyone being taken seriously who worshiped a crystal kidney."

All three women laughed. His humor, for them, was confirmation that he was opening up to new ways of thinking.

"The skull reveals wisdom and knowledge, and like the stones, they are vessels of energy. Since they are made of quartz, a material known for its energetic properties, the skulls house information and communicate with the user or each other. Energy flows as a vibration that you can feel. Some resonate on a base tone and are slower, some pulsate, and some are higher and faster. These tones give the energy its rhythm, almost a melody, which allows the information to come through from the angelic realm. Once trained, our brains know how to convert these tones into words and feelings. Do you think you have a better grasp on how this works?"

Mitch lied. "I guess so."

"Good, one more symbol before our time is through. The hourglass speaks of the passage of time, but also brings forth the potential to return to beginnings. It flows from top to bottom, and when turned, from bottom to top, is also in the flow from the divine to the earth. Knowledge is passed from the celestial to the terrestrial and back again, which is constant, without end. In a sense, it isn't us against them at all; it is all of us working for the good together." Genevieve inhaled, preparing to complete her lecture, when Pip interrupted.

"We stop here. Learn anything?" she asked sarcastically.

Feeling overwhelmed, yet peaceful, Mitch admitted. "I feel as if I could stay up here forever."

Pip laughed. "Well, we aren't done yet. Open your pack; we have a few parting gifts for your participation. First, the leather-bound book. We have taken the liberty of sketching the symbols from the monument for your reference. Use it as your journal for notes, other symbols, and other information you deem important." Placing the book gently into his outstretched hands, she blew out the candle and handed it to him. "Take this candle. Light it when you need inspiration, allowing the white light to cover you in protection. Lastly, we present you with an object of knowledge. This small bowl has always held the anointing oil of a monarch, ceremonial wine, the blood of the fallen, or healing waters consumed by the sick. One particular alabaster jar, owned by Mary Magdalene, performed all four of these tasks during her time and training as a high priestess."

Pip winked at him. "How about that for dramatic?"

Mitch laughed. "Not bad."

Gillian removed her cloak, placing it neatly into her pack. Mitch noticed her place the pin back onto her sweater.

"Gillian, may I ask why you wear the pin without your cloak?"

She smiled. "Like the ring on your finger, I am recognizable to those who are like me. And to those who aren't, they may ask a simple question, and I'm given the opportunity to enlighten."

Mitch looked down at his ring. "People never ask about my ring; they just stare at it."

Gillian shrugged her shoulders. "Pity." She noticed the light changing on the mountain. "We better get a move on before we run out of light. I didn't think to pack torches."

The four started down the dirt path exhausted but exhilarated. By the time they reached the car, night had begun to overtake them. Dimly lit from behind, the blazing colors of the heather were no longer visible with the setting sun.

Pip cranked the car's heater to high, revved the engine into reverse, and turned the stereo up. The three women sang along to the radio as Mitch dozed off, delirious from both the company and the climb. "Don't get too sleepy. I suspect there will be two gents with a bottle of scotch waiting for you at home," Pip casually mentioned.

Mitch kept his eyes closed, allowing sleep to take him. He couldn't think of anything better than what awaited him back at the hotel.

11

Graham stared in disbelief at the numbers blinking on the monitor. He didn't like to rely on numbers; they were often unreliable. As a physician, he had to rely on numbers and statistics, but the roller coaster of this case created a reliance on more than data in a chart. He needed to rely on gut instinct if he was going to pull this one off. He watched the girl sleep in her bed and scratched his head at the dismal reality her condition presented. Over the last few days he had flooded her system with drugs, meant to halt the organ failure. Nothing worked. This was the first case in his career where he would admit that he had no idea what to do. It was an uncomfortable position to be in for someone who thrived on professional arrogance. He liked to be the hero, receive the accolades, and in this instance he feared admitting defeat would allow people to relish his shortcomings far too much. His ego ruled his career with an iron fist, without permitting his attachment to the lives he held in his hands.

In nursing care, the early morning hours dictated routine assignments, such as checking IV lines, administering medications, and documenting vital signs. As Graham watched Daphne perform each task flawlessly, a sick feeling arose in the pit of his stomach. A clinician at heart, he didn't have a high opinion of home care. It tended to employ sloppy nurses who were incapable of handling a hospital environment, leaving a tremendous margin for error. He preferred the sterility of the hospital, where events were controlled, meds were readily available, and people were trusted to perform admirably. Daphne had never given him cause for mistrust, but lately, there was some indefinable something that was wrong. For two people who had virtually grown up together, she was surprisingly distant.

"Daph?"

She responded quietly. "Yes, sir."

Graham placed his fingers beneath his chin. "I'm taking the bull by the horns and admitting her this afternoon."

"Her mother won't like it," Daphne commented without looking at him.

Graham shook his head. "I don't give a damn what she likes or dislikes. Her child's life can be managed better in the hospital than here at home."

"Have you cleared this with Dr. Brody?"

"He put *me* in charge!" Graham barked. "Get her ready for transport while I make the arrangements with the hospital."

Daphne stood up, making sure she kept her back to him. "And her mother?" She whispered, curious as to how he would convince Lillian to admit her daughter to the hospital against her will.

"I have a talent for convincing people of what's in their best interest," Graham stated casually.

An unfamiliar ring of a cell phone broke his focus. Crossing the threshold, he faced Daphne to see if she would answer it.

Reaching into her pocket, she quickly pressed the silence button. "This is a personal. Would it be too much to ask for a little privacy?" Graham respected her request, but made a mental note to speak to her about personal calls while on duty, especially with a critical patient. Daphne glanced at her young charge, making sure she remained asleep, while the phone in her pocket vibrated angrily. "You have impeccable timing," she snarled into the phone.

"My, my. You are *not* a morning person."

"No sarcasm, just orders," Daphne requested.

A pause followed. "What is the latest on the girl?"

"She goes in and out of consciousness more frequently, but two major problems have popped up."

"Which are?"

"The substance makes the visions more vivid and increases the number of episodes in a day. But it's becoming more difficult to regulate her during them due to the widespread organ failure. There have been a couple instances where I almost lost her," Daphne admitted callously.

"Keep administering the vials without altering the dosage. It needs to be consistent in her system for the effect to remain gradual. What is the other problem?"

"Wellington is admitting her back to the hospital and I won't be able to continue with the plan. Too many prying eyes."

"It is all falling into place, as I have predicted. Play along as if you are leaving your post and marvel at my brilliance."

Daphne's short fuse flared. "How much longer am I keeping the charade going? They aren't stupid men, especially when reunited. You can't keep Brody in Europe indefinitely."

"Tomorrow Brody will come in contact with someone who will ensure that our devoted doctor is taken care of. Stay on course, and don't forget to smile. No one appreciates Nurse Ratchet."

The phone clicked off before Daphne heard the footsteps. She jammed the cell phone into her pocket, returning to chart Tamara's daily statistics. The doors flew open as Graham strode back in the room. She hoped he hadn't been eavesdropping outside the door. She was getting the distinct impression that although they shared a history, he no longer trusted her. She might have to revert to their youthful past and flirt a bit to distract him. The thought left a horrible taste in her mouth, but a little sacrifice might be necessary for her goal to be achieved. She'd come too far for anything to stand in the way.

Graham barged into the room. "Spoke to Lillian. Damn, she's stubborn. I hate people who refuse to see reason. This is her child, for Christ's sake!"

"Did you call the hospital?" she asked, scratching her pen across paper.

"The ambulance will be here in an hour. The nurse's station has my orders," Graham remarked.

"I will prepare the equipment for pickup by the supply company and go home, since my position here is terminated." Stroking his arm seductively, she added, "It's been wonderful to see you again, Graham, even under these circumstances."

Graham recognized her fake smile from their youth. He used to fall for it hook, line, and sinker as an adolescent. But since his experience with women had increased over the years, so too had his ability to recognize the games they played. "Since Brody personally assigned you to her case, you're stuck. You'll be one of her primaries in the unit, until Brody orders otherwise. You can accompany her in the ambulance."

Daphne remained silent while she double-checked the IV line. She stepped away to oversee preparations for her charge's breakfast, when alarms on the monitors rang angrily. She rushed back to the equipment and yelled for Graham.

"What the hell is going on? Her stats are all over the place!"

"She's having another one!" Daphne shouted.

"Another what?" Graham grumbled.

"Episode," Daphne defined. "She has a few a day now, and yesterday I almost lost her during the longest one."

Graham shouted uncontrollably. "Almost lost her? This is what you guys meant by 'episode'? Grab the oxygen bag. We need to stabilize her! Hang on for me, Tamara. Just hang on."

Even though she was just on the brink of waking, the lightness in Tamara's head had become more frequent with each passing day. She usually welcomed the dreams, but the experience was no longer pleasant. Feeling her body float farther and farther away from the chaos, she heard Daphne and the new doctor screaming at each other as they poked and prodded her body. She could smell, hear, and feel each experience as if it were truly happening. Yet she was never able to speak to the people in her dreams. She was the silent participant with each of her two feet in two completely separate and distinct worlds, neither one bringing comfort or joy these days. She only experienced pain and frustration. A misty haze introduced the latest dream.

The room was filled with guests, all enjoying the festive atmosphere. People socialized with cups in hand filled to the brim with wine. Laughter and anticipation filled the room as more guests arrived through a door at the far end. Both men and women were dressed in attire suitable for their celebration, their heavy robes dyed in white, brown, red, and blue. While flickering candles set an environment of intimacy, women quickly shuffled around the room, serving the men.

A hush fell over the crowd as a young man clothed entirely in white entered the room. His shoulder-length brown hair blew in the breeze, and he smiled casually at the guests. Men immediately rushed to his side, speaking excitedly as they escorted him to the long table in the center of the room. The young man sat down and graciously thanked his hosts. Each man competed for the chance to be near him. One of the elders took the seat to his right, a true position of power and trust. Three women obeyed the command to serve, placing wine, bread, fruit, and meat on the table. The remaining men took their places at the table, enjoying the feast laid before them.

Their lively meal included conversation on a variety of topics, such as local politics, marriage contracts, and crop estimates. Three women cleared the table, placing a fresh cloth on top, securing it with white candles. The men fell silent as a fourth woman entered. Also dressed in all white, a blue cloth sash hung from her left shoulder, and a golden moon secured the robe at her neck. Unlike the other women, her head remained uncovered, her long brown hair curling at the ends. Her beauty was unmatched, and a quizzical smile danced at her mouth. The young man adjusted his chair and gazed in her direction.

The golden center of her eyes danced with the flickering light of the candle. Removing a delicate alabaster bowl and a blue stone from beneath her robes, she held them gently. One of the men handed her a small vial of liquid, which she emptied onto the stone in the middle of the bowl. Kneeling down before the man in white, she placed each one of his feet separately into the bowl. She poured the liquid over each foot three times and quietly dried each foot. Upon completion of the anointing ritual, she handed him a white cloth embroidered with a crescent moon. The young man took the offering and placed it in his lap.

The brown-haired beauty reached across the table, extinguishing the white candle with a small breath of air. Cupping his open palm in hers, she dripped the liquid wax onto his palm as she outlined the shape of a star on his hand. Her voice was barely that of a whisper as she spoke to him of his destiny. His purpose was to be one of healing and rebirth, though also lonely and challenging. She admitted her fear that the pain associated with such a task could prove too immense to handle alone. She offered her assistance, should the need arise for him to reach out to someone who understood the ridicule that he would endure on the pathway to greatness. Her sympathy over the suffering that lay ahead was sincere, while her understanding of it was not. A tear graced her porcelain cheek while the words "tragic end" escaped her lips.

The young man simply smiled and laid his hands upon hers, bringing her comfort through his eyes. He chose to use his presence to enlighten and bring balance, knowing that there would be tremendous strife over his message, and decided not to yield. A lesser man would have fled, knowing the circumstances.

She was educated in the arts of the priestesses, but knew deep in her heart that she would never be able to accept a task of such supreme sacrifice.

Though he was willing to accept this sacrifice, she knew there had to be an alternative. She told him that she would use her network of associations to ensure that his "intended" demise would be altered to include survival. With the completion of her duty, she rose to leave.

The young man watched her intently as she walked toward the entrance. She exited into the darkness with the grace befitting a queen. As the door closed behind her, the young man continued to watch the exit with the hope of her return. All around, men conveyed their congratulations of his anointing.

Confusion set in. Eyes that were not his own surveyed the faces of the men standing to his left and his right. His body felt weak, his mind was fuzzy, and it no longer belonged to him. Pushing people aside, he stumbled toward the long banquet table to quench his thirst from the heat in the room. The floor spun as he sipped from a cup of wine, unable to stop this newfound motion.

Throwing food off of a metal tray, he held it close to the candlelight. The reflection no longer showed a king, but instead illuminated the terror in a young girl's eyes who had merely come to visit.

Tamara watched the scene fade away, feeling the tug of her return to the real world. She recognized familiar symbols from other dreams. Her mother's voice pleaded with her to wake up. Machines beeped wildly, with Graham screeching orders at Daphne. Light seeped through eyelids, flooding her eyeballs into a semiconscious state.

"Tamara? It's Mommy. Can you hear me?" Her voice was desperate. "Wake up, sweetie. I'm here."

With a sense of confusion, Tamara forced her eyes to open. Lillian hovered above her, smiling nervously. "Hi, baby." Her voice shook with raw emotion. Tamara could not respond, lacking the strength to speak. Her mother turned to Graham as he reset the monitors. She could see the fear in his face. "Are you sure she's stable enough to be moved?" Lillian shouted.

"She's being moved. If you want to go with her, get your stuff," Graham answered curtly.

Lillian smiled and kissed her daughter's forehead. "I'll be right back. It will be OK, sweetie." Tamara thought her mother looked defeated. Lately, she noticed the withdrawal and increased emotions. She worried about her mother more than her own survival. Tamara turned her head toward Graham. Her voice whispered a single word. "Earl."

Leaning into the girl, Graham spoke calmly, hoping she did not see the masked fear in his eyes. "Tamara, can you repeat that?"

She managed the strength to whisper once more. "Earl."

Confusion swept over Graham's mind, forcing him to ask Daphne. She looked up with a lack of patience. "Earl is her uncle. She tends to ask for him after each episode."

Graham watched the numbers on the monitors move into a range with which he was more comfortable. Before this moment, she was an intrusion into his life that he resented Mitch for bringing to him. She was merely a case, a number, a folder with information attached to it. But now, her fragile existence changed his mind instantly. It allowed him to feel compassion for someone other than himself. Offering an unspoken vow of devotion to her survival against all the odds, he would see this assignment through to success. Not for him, or his ego, but for *her.* "Do you need anything, Tamara?"

Tamara vaguely heard the ambulance arrive, knowing her time at home was gone. She was not afraid. She needed to utter one syllable. Defeated by her body and brain, she fell back into her pillow, exasperated. Slightly above a whisper, a quiet prayer aided her voice to discover its might. "I need Earl."

12

S tirring from the dream-induced fantasy of a girl in a flowing white dress, Mitch wiped sleep from his eyes. A gentle knocking on the door forced him to leave the oversized duvet and march across the room. Throwing the door open, his dream girl stood before him, beaming. Rather than be charming, he snarled instead. "Any idea what time it is?"

"Just rumbling out of bed, I see," Pip teased.

"Why is it I always seem to encounter you before coffee?"

Barging into his room, she handed him a cup of coffee before flopping down onto the bed. "Someone is cranky."

Mitch closed the door. "Unlike yesterday, I'd like to at least eat something before you start with me today."

She flirted with a wink and a smile. "Don't get your knickers in a twist. I'm merely your chauffeur to the next vacation spot."

"I'll get dressed and meet you downstairs," he suggested.

She bounced off the bed. "Drink your beaker of caffeine and meet me in ten minutes, no more, no less." Pursing her lips as she slowly closed the door behind her, she added, "Ten minutes exactly, Mitch, or I leave without you."

Sipping his coffee, Mitch felt the warmth seep into his brain. He knew she bluffed a bit about the time. Where would she go without him?

"Do I get a gold star if I'm early?"

"Pity that when he finally lightens up, he has to leave." Pip threw her head back, laughing.

Mitch watched her bound down the stairs. He packed lightly, unsure how long he would be gone. Initially, he was under the impression that it would only be for a few days, but at this rate he wasn't sure when he would get home. Putting on a clean pair of jeans and a black sweater, he threw the rest of his belongings into his bag. In the shared bathroom down the hall, he splashed cold water on his face, brushed his teeth, and stared at his reflection. He appeared rested and calm, almost peaceful, which unnerved him. He needed to recapture the mindset of saving Tamara without getting caught up in what was swirling around him. Choosing to end the charade early, he welcomed the urge to get the hell out of dodge.

He overheard Duncan and Pip arguing from below. He admired the ease of their relationship, wishing he would have had that with his father. It was just one of the many things he regretted since his father's death.

"I can't take that one. I have to go the back way. Cuts off loads of time."

"Pip, I'm perfectly aware of your need for speed, but your safety is paramount. That road is a death trap. If something happens, no one would be around for miles. Be smart," Duncan insisted.

Pip smirked. "I like that road. It has adventure written all over it."

"As well as accidental death. But who am I? Just some old man who raised you, protected you, fed you, and clothed you."

"Good guilt, Dunc! Back road it is. And for the record, you said 'old,' not me," Pip teased.

The two laughed as Mitch approached the reception desk. "Ah, there he is. And right on time. Seems we have worn off on you, old boy."

Pip glanced at her watch. "Thirteen seconds to deadline. I would say that gold star is all yours, Mitch."

Duncan laughed at his daughter's wit, reaching over to pinch her cheek. "Chip off the old block."

Ripping the bag out of Mitch's hands, Pip walked away. "Say good-bye to Mummy. I'll be back after I'm done."

Duncan grabbed Mitch's hand. "It has been a pleasure seeing you again. You've grown into quite a fine young man." Laughing deeply, he added, "If you ever tire of the colonies, you have an open invitation to visit the civilized world." Mitch fought the urge to embrace him. Odd how he had come to respect him over the past few days.

Without warning, Duncan shoved a cell phone into his hand. "Should you need advice, a fresh perspective, a little guidance, don't hesitate to call. This phone is secure. One of us will always be at the other end."

"By one of us you mean…?" Mitch asked.

"Stewart and I. Oh, every now and then Pip may have it. She likes to feel included, you know. Just turn it on and press the speed dial."

Mitch glanced at the device. It was the newest smartphone on the market, which was a little intimidating. Gadgets smarter than people made him nervous.

Duncan playfully slapped him on the back as they walked across the foyer. Outside, the familiar Range Rover had Pip in the driver's seat. She waved to her father as they sped onto the highway, this time headed south. Mitch couldn't help but sing along to the radio. For a few minutes he didn't care about the final destination. This was a good time. The pause between tracks broke the haze from his mind. "Uh, Pip? Where exactly are we going?"

"To the train station."

"Train station? OK, then what?"

"You ride the train until it stops; get off and go to the location on the piece of paper I gave you."

Mitch looked confused. "You didn't give me a piece of paper."

She grabbed a small piece of blue paper and handed it to Mitch. "Isn't this in England?" he asked.

Passing a slower vehicle and narrowly missing an oncoming truck, Pip responded without skipping a beat. "Of course."

"Why am I going back to England? Seems like a lot of juggling back and forth."

"Look, Mitch, I don't make the rules. I don't even know all the details of this madcap adventure. Dunc gave me the location and told me to take you to the train station, and that's what I'm doing." Turning onto a dirt road, she added, "Any more questions?"

Mitch nodded his head. "Just two."

"Which are?" she prodded.

"Explain to me why you were so heated yesterday about the witch thing. What's the big deal?"

Without warning she stalled the car in the middle of the road. "I am heated from the lies that, for centuries, have suppressed women in an effort to control the masses. In ancient times, women possessed authority. They were priestesses who held priceless knowledge sought after by powerful men. They ruled their own kingdoms as well, if not better, than the men. Then, out of the blue, this whole religion thing is created, and poof, women are subordinate to everyone. And those who question authority are being called witches. Makes me sick."

Mitch commented, "Wow, talk about women's lib."

His joke stifled Pip's foul mood. "A little passion never hurt anyone, but centuries of lies have. What's your second question?"

"If you start driving again, I'll ask you. This road makes me nervous; it's so deserted as to be almost spooky."

Pip laughed, stepping hard onto the accelerator. "For the record, too many people know about this road for it to be spooky." They laughed together down the bumpy country road. "Well?" she asked.

"Well what?" Mitch asked.

"Your second question?"

"Oh, yeah. Do you know any more background on the Dan Family? I'm intrigued."

"I know quite a bit about the Tuatha de Danaan. What do you want to know?"

"All the gory details."

Pip cranked the volume down on the radio, allowing the music to become the background theme to their journey. "The Tuatha de Danaan is an ancient race, with the earliest record of their existence dating back to Ireland in eight hundred BC. They were a supernatural tribe of the goddess Danai of Argos, or in layman's terms, the goddess Danu. They were considered to be the world's most noble race, alongside the early dynastic pharaohs of Egypt."

Mitch interrupted while she took a breath. "Define 'supernatural' for me. 'Cause when you use that word, images of ghosts and Ouija boards come to mind."

"I define 'supernatural' in terms of the gift of perception," Pip explained.

Mitch purposefully teased her to see how far he could push her without inciting anger. "Like gypsies at a fair?"

"Not that campy. Perception is the ability to commune with other forces and gather information pertaining to an event or an individual."

Mitch pretended to copy her words into an invisible notebook. "Man, that sounds serious. Should I be taking notes?"

Pip shook her head. "Only if you feel the need, you cheeky bastard. Shall I continue?"

Waving his hand, Mitch responded, "By all means."

Pip carried on. "These people eventually assimilated into Hebrew culture, becoming known as the Tribe of Dan. They held the symbols of the snake and the Lion's whelp, which are ancient symbols of a dynastic line of kings. Their crest also included a cauldron, harp, spear, and stone."

Mitch interrupted. "You guys gave me a stone and a cauldron over the last few days! Are those connected to this family? And the snake from the crest? It all fits into this family?"

"I doubt that Dunc would give you the actual cauldron or stone. Those are probably in a museum somewhere, or more likely on the black market, but you did receive the same items associated with the tribe. Those objects belong to the descendants who became high kings for the Irish, Picts, and Scots. This led to some pretty mighty dynasties, not to mention founding the nation of Scotland."

Mitch's brain smoked with information while Pip veered back onto the main highway. She watched his struggle to believe what she had told him. "You are being given information. What you do with it is your own choice. I am not here to convince you what is or isn't truth. Everyone has free will."

"You don't make this easy, do you?" he asked.

"In what way?"

"My mother used to give me the same guilt trips. Worked like a champ every time."

"If you feel guilty, it's your own choice. I am merely a messenger of information. You can walk away thinking I am full of crap or one of the most brilliant people you have ever encountered. Either way, it has no effect on me. You have to be clear with yourself." Pip left the music low as the two sat in silence for the remainder of the drive. Once they reached the town center of Pitlochry, Mitch saw the train station on the last block. Pip pulled up to the front of the historical building. "End of the line, Mitch. Blessed be."

Mitch looked at his newfound friend, extended his hand, and smiled. Pip seemed disappointed at his gesture. He wondered how someone could hold so much passion in her life without the ability to play mind games. He had never known people who didn't have an agenda to benefit themselves. People like Pip, the twins, Duncan, and Stewart seemed to be few and far between.

He waved as Pip pulled away from the curb. She rolled down the window and yelled, "Don't forget to call Graham, you cheeky bastard!"

Surprised, he yelled back, "How do you know about Graham?"

Returning the volume back up to a level that promoted hearing loss, she smirked. "Didn't anyone tell you? I know everything!"

Mitch watched her car zoom past others in its path. Entering the terminal to escape a cold blast of wind, he took out his cell phone to check the time. He thought it would be better to wait until he was on the train to call Graham. Besides, if an emergency had popped up with Tamara, Graham would have called. Deciding to buy a snack to tide him over, he couldn't resist a Lion Bar. One bite of the delectable concoction left him sure that it was just short of heaven on earth. Moments after finishing his coffee, the train boarding was announced. Quickly finding a seat, he dialed Graham.

A female voice answered. "Hello?"

"I must have misdialed."

"No, don't hang up! You must be Dr. Brody! Dr. Wellington is finishing orders for your patient and asked me to answer his phone."

"Are you assisting him at the house?" Mitch asked.

"What house? He admitted her to the hospital four hours ago and just completed the latest labs."

"Hospital?" Mitch bellowed. "What the hell? She's supposed to be at home! What lab is he running?"

"Hold the phone, Colonel, don't misplace your rage on a nurse doing her job! You put me in charge, and that's how I am acting," Graham interjected.

Mitch relaxed slightly. "Graham, what's going on?"

"Tamara took a turn. Her so-called episodes are more frequent, her vitals are dipping too low during them to keep her stable in a home environment, and according to my records, all her major systems continue to shut down. None of the meds that I ordered are helping. They may be buying her more time, but they aren't reversing any damage. I put a call into Maier for his advice, and readmitted her to have or gain any hope of survival."

"I had no idea she was speeding toward the finish line this fast. I'm sorry I put you in this position, Graham."

Graham heard the change in Mitch's demeanor. "You know I love a challenge. In this instance, however, I wish you had told me about those episodes in greater detail."

"How many is she having?"

"According to Lillian, she was having maybe one or two a day before you left. Now we have documentation indicating upward of five in a twenty-four-hour period. How long has she had these?" Graham asked.

Mitch wondered how to explain. "Since she was a little girl. We called them 'episodes,' but they are more like visions of historical events. At times she is a majority player, where she experiences the scene as the actual people, and then other times she watches in the background as if she were stuck in a movie. She's been studied by dozens of doctors, even top academics. Some organizations labeled her as crazy, others wanted her committed, and some considered her dangerous. One guy even said she was a pathological liar, because what she was describing went against recorded fact. They all concurred that she was fabricating the visions to get attention."

"Is she?" Graham probed.

"I've been in her life since the day she was born, and I've watched her grow. I may not understand why they are happening or exactly what they are, but I am confident that Tamara isn't one to lie for attention," Mitch admitted.

"Hopefully Maier has answers. His secretary was adamant that he's occupied with another project, but he'd get back to me this week. I went ahead because I didn't know when I'd hear from you again."

"Wish I had thought of him! Did Lillian flip out when you moved Tamara back to the hospital?" Mitch teased.

"A little, but I laid down the law. To be honest, we are getting a lot of closed doors without any open windows."

"Meaning?"

"We aren't any closer to finding the culprit in this illness since you left, things are monumentally worse for her condition, and our time is screeching to a halt. Each hour becomes more crucial to finding the key to her survival, yet no one seems to care or find the time to help," Graham admitted.

Mitch heard the defeat. "This is extremely frustrating. I keep hoping the answer is right around the corner, and yet there are dead ends everywhere. And instead of being concerned about a dying girl, they all seemed more concerned with me."

Graham huffed. "It's hard to be you."

"That is not what I am saying! I feel your frustration! I am in the thick of it as well!"

"Well, you haven't witnessed the horror of her episodes, or you would be scared straight too. Put your foot down with these people. You still in the Highlands?"

"No, I'm headed back to London. Feels like I'm backtracking." Mitch removed Pip's piece of paper from his pocket, planning to inform Graham of his latest plans, when he was interrupted by someone approaching his seat. He lifted his ticket into the air toward the individual standing next to him. "Hang on a sec, Graham; they want to collect my ticket."

"Are you Dr. Mitch Brody?"

Mitch stared into a seemingly familiar face, which was not instantly recognizable. "I am."

"*The* infamous Dr. Brody who streaked naked across the quad of our medical school during commencement week?"

The light bulb went on, and a shiver ran down his spine. "Julian Kingman. That drunken dare, until this exact moment, was something I'd managed to block out."

Julian tossed his head back in laughter. "Drunk, my ass! You and Graham were always claiming alcohol as the excuse."

"Mitch, you still there?" Graham shouted through the phone.

Mitch suddenly remembered the phone in his hand. "Hey, Graham, you'll never guess who just popped up out of nowhere. Your old pal, Kingman!"

"Kingman? I hated that glory-seeking SOB! That guy shadowed us for four years!" Graham yelled.

Mitch laughed nervously, hoping Julian hadn't overheard Graham's comment. "When can I call you back?"

"Make it around four hours. I should have all the tests back by then. Kick Kingman's ass for me," Graham snapped, and then hung up.

Julian remained in the aisle glaring at Mitch. "Still tag-teaming your medical inadequacies?"

Recalling his own experiences with Julian in school, Mitch answered the lethal question. "Good friends are the best medicine."

Ignoring Mitch's sentiment, Julian asked, "Mind if I sit down?"

Mitch dodged the question, hoping Julian would take the hint to sit elsewhere. "What are you doing in Scotland?"

Stowing his briefcase above their seats, Julian claimed the spot by the window. "I was attending the World Health Organization proceedings for protocols regarding pandemic status and outbreak."

"Still working with infectious diseases?" Mitch asked.

"Of course. I spend the majority of my time in Europe, which I prefer to the United States, but I keep an apartment in New York for emergencies as well as those pesky visa requirements."

"Sounds like you're pretty successful. Am I to presume you're headed home to the States?"

"Not quite yet. Have some unresolved business in London before a business meeting in Switzerland." Julian smirked, thinking of the legs on the blond beauty he referred to as a meeting. "What are you doing here? I thought you believed that the East Coast was the only place to live."

Mitch laughed as he recalled that remark. He was young, naïve, and had never traveled outside the United States. Julian, it seemed, had an iron-clad memory. "Spent a few days with an old friend in the Highlands, and he recommended seeing a monument in England before I go home."

"I love history. Which one?" Julian pressed.

Slipping the piece of paper back into his pocket, Mitch decided that his history with this man outweighed any potential threat. "Glastonbury Abbey."

Julian retained his smirk. "One of my favorite locations in Europe!" He paused, looking out the window. "I do have some time to kill and I am quite adept at history. How about we see it together?"

Mitch winced. The less time with "Kiss-up Kingman," the better. The man made his skin crawl, but he couldn't manage a rude excuse since he implied an offer for company. Pip did say that he should learn to look at things in a new way, which convinced him to begin with Julian. "It'd be nice to have an acquaintance tag along."

"Great! Let me pull out my Blackberry, and we can download some info on the Abbey grounds before we get there. This should be a fun adventure," Julian exclaimed excitedly.

Mitch smiled uncomfortably at Julian. He weighed whether or not to squash the man's excitement with his desire for a nap as he watched Julian peer at his handheld device. He seemed harmless enough, and Mitch's tendencies to isolate himself needed a sweeping change. Julian's medical background, as well as his current course of work, could prove helpful in the future. He hadn't considered the possibility of an infectious disease in Tamara's case, but Julian's unexpected appearance had to be a sign. A meeting of the minds couldn't hurt. If Graham could set aside his ego to call for reinforcements, then so could he. "OK, Julian. Give me all you got."

13

The only positive aspect to the seemingly endless ride to London was that it was over. Julian hadn't stopped talking since the train left the station. His need to fill silence with endless trivia was annoying. Mitch feared it would take an act of violence to shut him up. Thoughts of simply pummeling him with a fork directly into his eye socket popped into his head even as they exited the train and hailed a cab.

"Off to the Abbey?" Julian asked, taking a break from his lecture on historical locations. He was positively chipper.

Mitch rolled his eyes at Julian's enthusiasm. "I have a standing hotel reservation, and tomorrow I have a scheduled appointment to attend."

"I thought we were going to see tourist sites."

Mitch had to pause or strike the man. "My appointment is at the Abbey. I assumed you could get souvenir booklets from the gift shop and fill me in on all the necessary information once my business is complete," Mitch snapped.

"Where are we staying tonight?" Julian asked.

"Again," Mitch huffed, "*my* standing reservation is at the Ritz. I don't know where you will be staying."

"I *love* that place! Wouldn't it be great if we got adjoining rooms?" Julian blurted out. "We should have dinner in the restaurant so we can catch up!"

The idea of a sharing anything more with Julian made Mitch's stomach churn. He regretted having asked him to tag along. Another classic flaw for Mitch, always giving people the benefit of the doubt when he knew deep down there was a snowball's chance in hell that they had changed. The naked truth was that Mitch invited him because he was lonely for a recognizable face. He would have invited his dentist.

Not unlike his arrival a few days prior, the black cab approached the curb at the Ritz. Mitch's gaze caught John's familiar face at the valet station. "I'd be better off traveling with him," Mitch thought while Julian paid the fare. Mitch heard John's iconic greeting as he opened the door.

"Welcome back, sir! Pleasure having you stay with us once more."

Mitch firmly shook John's hand. "Good to see you too! Missed you the day I left. They finally gave you a day off, huh?"

"Day off?" John inquired.

"I assumed you had the day off when you weren't at your post that day." Mitch chuckled. "I always assumed you lived upstairs, since you rarely take time off."

John glanced nervously at Julian. "Live upstairs, sir? That's funny. I don't mind the extra hours. They make for a fine paycheck," John joked.

Mitch winked. "An admirable work ethic is nothing to be ashamed of. You've impressed me through the years with your dedication."

"Thank you, sir. Have a good stay!"

Julian's eyes shot daggers at John as the two men entered the hotel. "Why are you nice to that guy?" Julian asked Mitch.

"Should I ignore him?"

"He's a common worker, Mitch. *You* are above them. Try acting like it," Julian sniped.

His brazen comment caused Mitch to halt midstride. The comment was made by an arrogant, privileged hothead who enjoyed making people feel inferior. It was out of character from his memories of Julian at medical school, where he was dying to fit into Mitch and

Graham's social circle. He aspired to be part of the popular group without success; now Julian's professional success had turned him into a snob. Mitch saw his error from the train. People can change, but whoever Julian was now, Mitch still didn't care for him.

Again, the reception desk was occupied by Bridget's unforgettable presence. The last thing he wanted, after the roller coaster drama of the last few days, were her innuendos and propositions. He fantasized of how Pip would respond to someone like Bridget. Her dulcet tones broke through the dream of verbal carnage that Pip was capable of inflicting.

"Dr. Brody! I kept your room ready, as requested, but I can always add something special." She winked, turning Mitch's stomach into knots.

"Not necessary, Bridget. I'm a little tired tonight."

Leaning over the counter to present him with the room key, she whispered, "Maybe you should get straight to bed."

Mitch ripped the key from her hands. "I'm headed there now."

Watching him scurry away, Bridget felt remorse at not following through with her plan to be at his door half clothed. Unsure of his return, she traded all her days off with other employees in order to be here when he came back. Thank God it was tonight. She fantasized about the two of them as husband and wife, seeing herself as a woman of luxury with his budding career. The dutiful wife in the beautiful house with two perfect children portrayed as the enviable lifestyle on countless magazine covers. She had a habit of being attracted to the power and confidence of each successful man she met, making herself readily available to each of them. Every time she found a man who had the ability to afford her a certain lifestyle, they followed the same pattern of using her for a one-night stand then disappearing in the morning. Her childhood had not included any lessons in confidence for her to be successful on her own. So she deferred to being the arm decoration for a powerful man. The lesson was solidified with each new boyfriend her mother brought home. Bridget learned that love only came when she became an object. Her latest conquest was proving to be an exception, announcing that he wanted a future together. He wasn't Dr. Brody, but he *was* a doctor. He could fulfill all her dreams. At least, she hoped he would.

"I didn't know you were coming!" she gasped. "Why didn't you phone me? I would have made myself more presentable for work today!"

Julian looked her up and down with tightly pursed lips. It didn't matter what she did to make herself look better, she was an extremely attractive woman in any presentation.

"The trip was a surprise after my conference ended. Do you know if John was successful with the intended target?"

Bridget looked uncomfortable as she surveyed the entrance for other patrons. "Did you ask him when you arrived?"

"I couldn't ask him with Brody around, you idiot. Did you forget your brain today, or is your hair too tight in that bun on your head?" Julian spat.

Placing a hand on top of her head, Bridget blushed. It had taken her a while to get the hair perfect without any strays, and she thought the curls framing her face looked pretty. "If you don't like it, I won't do it again."

Julian softened his tone. He could count on her insecurity, which intensified his ability to manipulate her. "Sorry, dearest. It's been a long trip. Do you think you could give me a room close to Brody, my little Grecian goddess?"

Bridget managed a small smile as her fingers flew across the keyboard. "I cleared the rooms across the hall this morning. Which one do you want?"

"Doesn't matter. You pick and meet me there when your shift is over. I'd like to mess up that tight hairstyle," Julian suggested.

Bridget leaned over the counter to kiss him, but he pushed her back behind the desk. "Have I done something wrong?"

"Decorum, remember? I don't care for people watching."

Handing him the room key, Bridget brushed his fingers. "Enjoy your stay, Dr. Kingman."

Julian posed one final question. "Are the accommodations free of pests?"

With a renewed confidence, Bridget looked at him. "No bugs in *your* room, sir. I can't vouch for the others."

A small amount of pride filled Julian's chest. Bridget was turning out to be more useful than he expected. He knew she desired a prestigious lifestyle, which he could give her. But as a wife she could jeopardize his carefree existence. He learned through associations with others in lofty positions how to utilize the people around him for personal benefit. He liked her, but just for the time being. Riding up the elevator to the third floor, the vibration from his cell phone surprised him. Obviously, the veil of secrecy was lifted for the evening. "Using your listed number to call me is quite a risk."

"Don't speak to me as if we are on the same level. Update your location and events thus far."

Julian didn't want to risk his position. "I'm in London at the Ritz on my way up to a room across from Brody's."

"Did your girl accomplish all you promised?" An image of Bridget flashed in his mind. He really did think she was pretty. "Without issue or intrusion." Silence filled the receiver, as Julian dared not speak first. He knew his employer's patience was not something to toy with. "And tomorrow?" he asked.

"Travel to Glastonbury. I'm unsure who the contact is in Scotland, but I remain hopeful that it is the Professor."

"The Professor has left the States?" Julian asked excitedly.

The voice avoided Julian's question. "Follow Brody through his tour. Go back to acting like the naïve medical student I met years ago, and you should be fine. Try not to be a pompous ass. Don't underestimate Brody's powers of perception, Kingman. After all, he is brighter than you."

The elevator doors opened as the phone went silent. Shoving it back into his pocket, Julian rolled his shoulders to straighten his back. His employer knew which buttons to push on a regular basis. When the pair met, Julian was a young, innocent people pleaser. With one firm handshake, Julian knew the man possessed the ability to make or break his career. He made it a priority to stay in contact with the man, as well as do anything to gain his favor. Once he saw the fruits of his labor, any task paled to the bounty of rewards he was offered. His employer fulfilled his promises by delivering the power and prestige Julian required. Swiping the key card on the door, a familiar giggle escaped the dimly lit room. Facing the king-sized bed, he barely made out Bridget's figure lying seductively across it. Closing the door behind him, he thought the spoils of war were worth the fight.

Julian's customary verbal lashing was surprisingly absent during their ride to the Abbey. He sat with arms folded, staring out the window. Mitch tried to engage in small talk, but it seemed Julian wasn't in the mood. This piqued Mitch's curiosity, as he tried to keep his concentration on the day at hand. He felt inside his coat pocket for the cell phone Duncan had given him. It had become an emergency lifeline.

"You're awful quiet today, Jules," Mitch probed.

Julian decided to go along with Brody's banter. It was the easiest way. "Had a hell of a time falling asleep last night," he muttered.

"Did you hear the couple on our floor? Man, were they loud! Someone sure had fun," Mitch joked.

The thought of Bridget's pleasure reentered Julian's mind. She tended to scream when reaching climax, adding to the intrigue of their rough games.

"You'd think that in a place like the Ritz, the clientele would be a bit classier. Must have been an expensive prostitute."

Mitch laughed. He thought the exact same thing.

As they approached the grandeur of the Abbey, Mitch tried to get rid of Julian for the day. He wasn't sure if he would need to continue the rest of the trip in secrecy, but since Duncan hadn't mentioned otherwise, caution seemed to be appropriate. "Hey, Jules, do you think you could take your own tour during my appointment? We'll be discussing issues of a personal nature," Mitch said.

"I was looking forward to a tour together," Julian replied.

Not wanting to draw any more attention to his situation, Mitch surrendered. "How about if we ask when we get there and see what happens?"

"Here we are!" Julian announced.

Glastonbury Abbey reflected the march of ages upon its ancient site, with the more recent cathedral at the front. A gift shop graced the middle of the property, with a tea shop for the weary traveler to warm up from the elements. In the rear stood Lady Chapel, holding the distinguished title of being the oldest building on the property. It stood in a ruinous state. The architecture that remained held but the memory of a period of gentility for the current generations.

Upon their entrance to Lady Chapel, a petite woman with silver hair greeted the two men. She was impeccably dressed in an expensive wool suit, matching scarf, and heels that clicked on the stone floor. Sunlight broke through the arched window casings, dancing around her feet as if she were standing in the middle of a spotlight. Her blue eyes surveyed the young men with the softness of a grandmother combined with countless years of wisdom and experience. "Which one of you is Mitchell Brody, and why is there an escort to his appointment?"

Mitch stepped away from Julian. "I'm Mitch Brody. This is a colleague of mine, Dr. Julian Kingman. He's tagging along for the day. I hope that's OK."

Her eyes questioned Julian's involvement, as he stood in front of her with a smirk plastered on his face. He memorized her facial features as a reference, in case he would need to describe her to his employer. "My instructions were not for two doctors. But, if he is with you, there must be good reason."

Motioning for the men to follow her, she stepped to the location of where an altar once stood. "The hallowed ground on which you presently stand is dedicated to the memory of Joseph of Arimathea.

Records indicate that his remains are buried within the grounds as a memorial. The man was pivotal in safeguarding one of the most precious relics from biblical times. He carried it to this property following the crucifixion of Jesus and is immortalized in a stained glass window, portrayed in this photograph. He holds the artifact in his left hand, a position of divine reverence for its meaning and importance."

Following her finger as she pointed to the open book page in her hands, the two men viewed the brilliant window. The portrayal of an older man dressed in a dazzling blue robe was masterfully captured with a golden cup gracing his left hand, while a staff occupied his right. Mitch stared at the window, searching for any hidden symbols or clues, as instructed by Pip. He kept his ideas regarding the imagery to himself until he would be able to record them in his journal back at the hotel.

The woman snapped the book shut. "Joseph was a wealthy entrepreneur with a minimum of twelve different business dealings, as well as a considerable metal trade from the Middle East, into what we now recognize as the European continent. Since he played an intimate role in the crucifixion of Jesus, there are several different accounts of his true identity, ranging from a simple businessman to the father of Jesus's mother, Mary. If in fact he was a family member, it would explain his behavior before, during, and after the crucifixion."

Mitch took advantage of her brief pause to interrupt. "Excuse me; your knowledge on this subject seems extensive. May I ask your background?"

Spinning on her heels, her irritation was apparent. "Your interest in me is complimentary, but not merited. It is merely my job to relay information pertinent to your education. However, since it appears that you are the type who won't stop asking until you are satisfied, I will give you a brief synopsis. I am professor emeritus at a rather large university in America, am able speak as well as write seven ancient languages, have written several books on ancient history, and have become the first female commander of a prestigious secret organization. Does any of that quell your curiosity?"

Julian smirked at her frankness, wondering if she was the Professor. He hoped she was, given that she had just fallen into his lap with little effort on his part to capture her.

She spun back around, facing the altar area once more. "Joseph of Arimathea held vast amounts of land surrounding the area in which Jesus preached. If he was an uncle to Jesus, then his behavior should raise no questions. If not, then his involvement raises questions pertaining to his participation with notable organizations of the time. Without going into a full-blown lecture, the simple facts are these: He owned the plot of land upon which Jesus was crucified, owned the tomb in which he was laid to rest, met with Pilate to negotiate the terms of possessing the body after the execution, and then traveled to this area between 30 and 32 AD with what is said to be a precious relic belonging to Jesus."

Since history never interested him, Julian eased himself onto a visitor's bench. He decided to pay little attention to her lecture, feeling it wasn't something he needed to participate in. He opted to catch up on his e-mail with his Blackberry while he had the opportunity for a private moment.

"The relic is the cup in the window?" Mitch asked.

"The cup is part of it. Documentation exists that Joseph brought two cups to the abbey. One contained the blood of Jesus, which was caught after his side was lanced with a spear, and the other contained the sweat from his brow. On the other side of much-heated academic debates, some historians claim that the cup was a chalice that held wine from the Last Supper."

"*The* Holy Grail? *The* Cup of Christ?" Mitch sputtered.

Smiling at his recognition, she applauded his mental prowess. "You know your history, Dr. Brody?"

"I know my legends," he admitted reluctantly.

"You believe it to be legend without a basis of truth?" she countered.

"I think there are dozens of tales of the Holy Grail, ranging from popular movies to bedtime stories with knights fighting dragons, but I don't think anyone has come across concrete evidence for the so-called Grail Quest."

Placing a hand on his shoulder, she looked deep into his eyes. "If you are aware of the quest, then you know much more than you let on."

Aware of the bait she dangled, Mitch answered vaguely. "Maybe I do, or maybe I'm not the naïve doctor you believe me to be."

"I don't doubt your intelligence in the least. I don't consider anyone on a quest to be vapid," she confirmed.

Surprise filled his face as Mitch removed her hand from his shoulder. "On a quest? What makes you say that?"

"Isn't that what you are doing here? I know a person's life is at stake, but you are still on a quest, or rather have been placed on one without your knowledge." Chuckling to herself, she added, "I love when they do that. It's so much more amusing this way."

Mitch's head throbbed. He hadn't signed up for any type of amusement. He had promised an old friend that he would try everything in his power he could think of to save her child. The truth was he wouldn't do this for anyone else but Lillian. Deep inside, he didn't care what label they stuck on this trip, as long as it was successful.

"We have a walk to take," she announced. "There's something I would like to show you, with your friend's approval." Julian waved his hand, keeping his eyes fixed on the small screen in his hands. He knew that no matter where they were headed, if she was the elusive Professor, he had her trapped.

Passing through the altar area of the chapel, the pair slid through a carved wooden door at the rear of the sanctuary. Once inside a darkened chamber, the woman lit a candelabra. The illumination sent inhabitants scurrying along web-laced walls toward the ceiling. Before continuing any further, she touched Mitch's shoulder once more. "There isn't anything that I mentioned in the chapel that your friend may not have already heard. From here on out, the information I give you is meant for your ears only."

"Where are we going?" Mitch whispered, his voice echoing off the walls.

"To show you what few people have the opportunity to witness."

"Am I allowed to ask questions this time?" he blurted out, feeling comfortable enough to mock her previous comment.

With a wide smile, she patted his shoulder. "That's how we learn."

Navigating their way down a narrow flight of stone stairs, the temperature dramatically plummeted. Mitch zipped his coat closed for protection against the emerging dampness. Approaching the bottom, the sound of water rushing below them filled his ears.

"Careful going through this part, and mind your feet. The sides are narrow, the water is cold, and the current is strong. I don't want to lose you to the river!" she shouted above the thunderous water.

"Where are we?" Mitch shouted back as he watched water rush past his feet.

The swift water flowed from an unknown source. The tunnel was too dark for their candlelight to penetrate. Walking on a narrow strip of earth to the right of the river, the woman led Mitch to a small bench cut into the stone wall. Placing the candelabra on a ledge above his head, she asked for him to join her on the bench.

"We rest in an ancient catacomb located below the chapel. It holds two springs of water that merge into a singular source. The springs have an unknown origin, but their importance is significant. This area of Glastonbury was known as the Island of Glass, due to the number of glass-like appearances created from the multitudes of lakes surrounding it. One of these springs is named the White Spring, because of its milky appearance, while the other, the Red Spring, has a rust appearance and is associated with the regenerative properties of snake's blood. This place of glass was a center of initiation and education for the Druids. My mention of the colors red and white correspond with a number of symbolic elements, including the balance of male and female, the rock quarried from the hills of Atlantis, and the phoenix. Ancient documents remind us that the Phoenix, whose very name translates into the word 'crimson,' comes alive when combined with a white stone. The power of the two rivers combining results in divine balance."

"Like the healing stone in the Atholl museum?" Mitch asked.

"The universe consists of balance. Without balance between the opposites, chaos ensues. A certain amount of chaos is needed to maintain balance, but too much results in darkness, such as wars, famine, and of course plague. Balance must be restored in order to preserve universal law."

Watching the water rush past, Mitch felt a new energy pulse through his body. He imagined people standing in long lines with buckets scooping up water from the springs, believing in the healing properties. "The point of all of this is balance?" he questioned. "The crest, the symbols on the stone, the object they gave me are all about balance?"

"Restoring balance is Tamara's destiny."

Feeling protective over his young patient, Mitch yelled, "She's dying! Is that considered a restoration of balance? Her death would make it all better? That's ludicrous!"

The woman remained calm in the face of Mitch's tirade. "Her visions will aid in the restoration of balance and of what has been lost."

"You're telling me I can't fail because if she dies then all hell breaks loose?" Mitch shot back.

Her hand reached beneath the bench and retrieved an article in a silky blue cloth. Unwrapping the tightly bound fabric, she revealed a gilded cup. The former luster had diminished over time, but the beauty of the craftsmanship remained. Placing the cup into his shaking hands, she clasped them around the base. "This cup is your third object, similar to the one Joseph brought to this area." Staring deeply into his eyes, she asked his permission to continue with the lesson. Feeling the cold metal in his hand, Mitch's curiosity renewed, and he silently nodded.

"As I previously mentioned, this area was a Druid center, but it held its own separate symbols with the veneration coming from the earth. The town was constructed on a mound consisting of seven concentrically carved circles. Each level was surrounded by a river with the two springs occupying the bottom. This structure created a labyrinth pattern, or a cone shape, which was an important energy principle of the time. Because of the energy between the earth and water, the Druids considered this place a holy entrance to the otherworld. The location was chosen not only for its energetic properties, but also for the water's glass reflections. Looking into the stillness of the river, they saw the roots of trees reflected back to them as evidence of the entrance. They believed this place could transport you to the realm of God."

Facing the water, she continued. "The number seven has spiritual significance in relating to the seven chakras of the body, the seven patriarchs, and the seven archangels, or rather messengers, who descended from the heavens to spread their message. It is noted in various manuscripts around the world that those who have knowledge of the number seven are initiates into the mysteries."

Mitch took a stab in the dark at assembling the puzzle pieces laid out before him. "Back up a little. You mentioned something about the color red and snake blood. There was a snake on the crest at the museum. Are they related?"

"The snake and the crest are intertwined," she replied.

"In what way?" he pressed.

She managed a smirk. "With your intellectual capacity, you might be able to figure it out. Use the book you were given to write it down and piece it together." Reaching for the cup Mitch held in his hands, she moved her hands above his, palms down as she lightly touched him. "What is a cup used for?"

"It holds things, you drink from it, and it's pretty," he blurted out without thinking.

His response made her chuckle quietly. "Let's continue on the thought process of it holding things. Would you define it as a vessel?"

"Sure. A vessel, a container, whatever."

"Is a vessel *only* an object?" Confused by her barrage of questions, Mitch found it hard to follow. "Let me pose this another way. Can a *person* be a vessel, or is the title left solely to an object?" She pressed, unable to release her questions from the ether.

"If you go back to the whole energy thing, I guess we are all vessels of some sort," Mitch replied.

Smiling broadly, she placed her hands in prayer form. A small chant escaped her tight lips. "Joseph of Arimathea came here with a vessel following the crucifixion of Jesus, but not just what he holds in the window. I have had the distinct privilege of viewing documents stating that he was accompanied by a young boy, whom he left here to be educated by the Druids. That child was the vessel meant to be filled with knowledge by priests educated in the same spiritual manners, as he would have had in Joseph's homeland. Why do you think Joseph would risk bringing him here and not keep him in the Middle East?"

"The instability of the area after the crucifixion with the occupation of the Romans?" Mitch blurted out, surprised at the intelligent answer that came from his lips.

"I'm impressed. I'll be sure to tell Pip how well you performed today."

The mention of her name brought a smile back to his face. He missed her laugh and was ashamed to admit a crush was developing.

"Different faiths were rounded up, and all individuals related to Jesus's ministry were persecuted. The political games following the crucifixion increased, with each faction vying for the control of the masses with their own interpretations of Jesus's messages. Some disciples capitalized on his absence by establishing organizations in his name without any correction from the Master." Retrieving the cup, she delicately rewrapped it into its satiny shroud. "We best return upstairs, or we will pique your friend's interest. Remember your silence about what you carry. If any explanation is necessary about the cup, you are to inform anyone who asks that it is an antique reproduction you came across while vacationing in Europe."

Mitch was anxious to know its true origin. "Is it?"

She taunted him while reaching for the candelabra in the alcove. "Ask yourself if you believe we would entrust you with the genuine article."

Julian completed the last e-mail from his office when Mitch surfaced, looking bewildered. The burlap sack he carried caught Julian's eye. He was unaware that Mitch would be retrieving any items along this journey, a tiny detail someone had neglected to tell him, which pissed him off. Standing up from the bench, he stretched his arms above his head, watching the two exchange a quick embrace. Julian approached them cautiously, directing his questions to the woman. "Where did you guys run off to?"

"Dr. Brody mentioned an urge to see the monk's cells from the original monastery. It proved to be quite interesting," she replied coldly.

A growl emerged from Julian's stomach, signaling his need for a meal, and to cut their conversation short. Mitch remarked, "I think that's our cue to leave." He extended his hand in gratitude, shaking hers with a comfortable grip, and thanked her once more for her time. Mitch headed first down the aisle as Julian lingered. Mitch had exited the chapel before the woman was able to halt his departure. Snapping her arm back down, Julian interjected. "If you value your life, you'll give it to me instead. "

Tossing a small piece of paper into her mouth, she gulped it down before Julian's hands met her throat. "I'll pass along your reluctance to my employer. Once he hears of your uncooperative nature, I am sure he will see fit to dispose of you in a swift manner. Don't think that I don't realize who you are." He glared at her with his eyes narrowing. "I could kill you right here and be the hero for eliminating the Professor, but I would hate to take that privilege away from a man who has searched for you for fifteen years. It will do his revenge-riddled soul more good than it will mine." His grip tightened. "Do you have any last words, Professor?" he said, sneering.

"*Inquirentes autem Dominum non minuentur omni bono,*" she whispered, matching his glare of hatred.

"And that means what, teacher lady?" Julian asked sarcastically, using his fist to break her nose.

She fell to the ground. "They that seek the Lord shall not lack any good thing."

14

The young boy walked beside his uncle, tightly gripping his hand. His feet dragged across the sloppy earth, reflecting the nerves churning in his stomach. The short stride of his legs forced the boy to take more steps than his uncle, who seemed to gallop. Sensing the boy's trepidation, his uncle stopped their advance. "Nervous?"

"We're a long way from home," he whispered.

"Your new teachers are knowledgeable, and it will seem more like home faster than you think." His uncle squeezed the boy's hand. "Each new experience can be intimidating at first."

Yanking his hand out of his uncle's grasp, the boy abruptly halted. "Can I go home if I don't like it?" he pleaded.

Recognizing the look of terror in his nephew's eyes, the older man bent down. "Going home is no longer an option. Your mother's directions were clear that our home is in this place. Your focus is the education you will receive. I will handle anything else of concern."

Pleading bordered on begging. "Can't my brother be here?"

His uncle stroked the back of his nephew's hands, knowing he had to try and explain. "Everyone has his or her own part in this world. At this moment, yours is to absorb all you can from these new teachers. Your brother's role is different. One day your paths will combine, but that time is not immediate." Glancing at the light dancing through the tree limbs, the man was concerned that their slow pace was fighting against them. "We must hasten our steps."

The tiny path through the woods made walking side by side difficult, but after the arduous trip they'd encountered to reach this destination, the boy felt safer being as close as possible to his uncle.

The arid desert they departed from a month ago was in stark contrast to the lush greenery that enveloped them now. Mature trees reached the highest points of the sky, with moss dripping from their trunks. At their base, small clusters of mushrooms and ferns bathed in the damp shadows. Morning mists rolled through the foliage, giving the forest an unnatural glow. Animal noises echoed through the brush. Without an entourage, the two travelers weren't terribly concerned with the issue of their safety, and they took comfort in being far away from any Roman threat.

When the foliage finally thinned, the young boy caught a glimpse of a thatched cottage with smoke rising from its chimney. A dog barking in the distance broke through the wood's silence, signaling life beyond the trees.

Quite suddenly, they stepped into a clearing filled with a community of cottages. People occupied with morning work paid little attention to the two new arrivals. Women held children's hands, while baskets of goods graced their hips, on the way to the village center. The aroma of cooking meat and bread filled the air, making the stomachs of the two travelers growl with hunger. Arriving at the center, his uncle purchased two apples from a vendor's wagon.

Biting into the crisp outer skin, the boy allowed the juice to drip down his chin. Using the sleeve of his new woolen cloak to wipe it away, his uncle shook his head in disapproval. Nearby, a small girl giggled at the boy's sopping chin as her mother pulled her along the narrow pathway. He envied the girl being able to hold her mother's hand. It was a sharp reminder that he was alone.

Finishing the apple more carefully, the boy watched his uncle seek directions from a vendor selling freshly baked bread. Motioning for him to follow, they made their way beyond the village to a large hill at the outskirts of the community. Before him was a curious hill with seven levels. At the top, a large stone building stood like a beacon of light. The boy stood still in amazement. So engulfed in the scenery, he was unable to finish his bread before hearing his uncle announce their arrival. "Quickly finish your meal before the elders approach. Your behavior is a reflection on the entire family."

Shoving the last piece into his already full mouth, a man clothed in a dark-brown robe approached from their right. With the hood of his cloak hiding his face, his voice took on a mysterious and ominous demeanor. "Welcome. Your travels were good?"

His uncle refrained from shaking the man's hand out of respect for his position. "I expected some delays, but gratefully we encountered none."

"You are to be taken to the high priest upon arrival."

The hooded man pointed to a pathway carved into the hillside, showing them the way to the top. Climbing higher and higher, the boy could see across the tops of the cottages to the trees from which they had emerged. They didn't seem so big now. The rising mist from the ground below engulfed the village, making it invisible. It was covering the hill, overtaking the path they had just taken, and began to overtake the varying levels. The stone building that was visible from the village below was actually a main building with six smaller ones scattered throughout the immediate area. A small reflecting pool sat in front of the main building. Reaching the top, both of the men, young and old, stopped to catch their breath.

Their guide excused himself, disappearing behind the massive wooden doors of the main building. The smell of incense escaped into the morning air as the doors shut behind him. Within moments of his departure, the doors reopened, presenting a small group of men dressed in identical brown robes. An older man, in white, stood out in the center. Unlike the others, whose faces were concealed, his was exposed. The length of his white beard came to his chest, while the fingers on his right hand encircled a carved staff. The small band approached the travelers, with the man in white to be the last. Glancing down at the boy, he extended his left hand in a sign of peace.

"You are most welcome to our place of learning," he announced, a melodic tone in his voice.

The uncle bowed his head in reverence. "We are honored he has been accepted. We were afraid that after recent events, his education was insufficient. We are grateful that your community is willing to perform the task."

Smiling at the boy, the man asked a basic question. "And his name?"

His uncle looked startled, causing him to stammer, "J-J-Joseph."

The man stepped closer to the boy, laying his left hand upon his head. "Joseph is a strong name for one so fresh with youth. You have the beginning of great strength. It surrounds you." Daring not to move, Joseph cast his eyes upward toward the man. "Can you feel it dwell within your body?"

"No," he whispered, afraid to speak any louder.

"You will," he promised.

Turning back toward the boy's uncle, the man directed the rest of his questions to him. "He is of Arimathea?"

"In an extended way."

"Does he have extensive knowledge?"

"His mother instructed him, but only briefly before our departure."

"She is of the white?"

"She visited this isle in her youth."

"My priests will accompany Joseph to his quarters. Tomorrow we begin his preparation. You brought the chalice?" Reaching into the leather sack that rode upon his back, the uncle produced an item wrapped in blue silk. He handed it to the man in white. "Come inside. We will discuss the consequences of its arrival."

His uncle dutifully followed the man toward the double doors as the priests motioned for the boy to accompany them into one of the smaller buildings. Unsure of his new environment or the people who inhabited it, Joseph made one last attempt to maintain contact with his uncle. Before he could disappear behind the massive doors, Joseph shouted at him.

"Uncle! I'm afraid!" he cried out.

His uncle emerged from the doors, smiling at his young nephew. "Learn all you can while you are here, and keep your mind open. I will return to you in two weeks' time, and you shall be without fear. Go with them to prepare." Holding his right hand up with his palm facing his nephew, the boy glimpsed the faint outline of a five-pointed star beneath his skin. "I believe in you," he added.

Those last four words gave Joseph the courage to follow the priests. His uncle had never said that to him before, and he discovered that he could in fact feel the strength that the man in white spoke of. The massive doors began to close; a final thought entered his mind, compelling him to share it. "Uncle! Wait, one more thought!" he shouted.

"Go ahead, Joseph!" his uncle shouted back.

"Dr. Brody! Dr. Brody is in trouble!"

Tamara's mind raced before having a chance to focus. How did that young boy know the name of her doctor? Were the drugs beginning to affect every miniscule aspect of her life? Eyelids fluttered open to a welcome relief. Earl sat next to her hospital bed, as if they were back at home, reading through their journal. Trying to lift herself off the pillow, Tamara lacked the strength. Admitting defeat this time, she slowly turned her head to the right.

"Earl?" she whispered.

Shocked at the frailty of her voice, Earl rushed to take her hand. "Hi, Princess. Pleasant dreams?"

"Get the book," she whispered.

Earl quickly retrieved the leather-bound journal that held all of her visions since preschool. Together they created an accurate account of each one, with margin notes of hidden meanings. Earl opened to a blank page, preparing to transcribe her latest adventure. "Was there something unique about this one?"

"They shouted a name," she stated, out of breath from the outrageous confession. "It was like they knew who we are."

Earl scribbled a few notes onto the page. "A name of someone you know?" he asked.

"Yes!" she exclaimed.

Earl sat down on the edge of her bed. "Tamara, your visions have been about past events, not future ones. How can someone from the past tell you about someone you know now? That would be an interesting change in your abilities."

Tamara chose her words carefully. She wanted to shout at him, force him to do something, but he was one of the only people in her life who didn't think of her as mentally unstable. She didn't want to give him a reason to change his mind. "At the end, the little boy shouted a name and a warning. We have to do something!"

In a feeble attempt to calm her nerves, Earl lifted her hand into his own. "Tell me what he said, and we'll take it from there." A wave of nausea swept over Earl's face as Tamara repeated the last words she heard before waking. Her words drove him from of his chair and into the hallway. The force of the door slammed Daphne against the wall. She cursed Earl under her breath while picking up the towels that she had dropped onto the floor. She opened her mouth to verbally assault him when he shouted for Lillian.

Still scooping up the towels to refold them, Daphne answered him with seething anger. "She went for coffee."

Earl looked at Daphne crouching on the floor. His questions regarding her motivation to care for Tamara were growing daily. "Tamara just woke up."

She quelled her anger and changed her voice to a more patient tone. "Does she need something?"

"She had an upsetting episode, and I need to speak with her mother," he replied.

Daphne wasn't buying the excuse. Footsteps down the hall halted her opportunity to grill Earl for more information.

Lillian appeared. "Earl, is something wrong?" She dashed down the hall, assuming that his call meant a problem with Tamara. The bags under her eyes reflected the barrage of enduring stress. The clothes that once hugged her well-toned physique now hung loosely. Instead of taking the time to care for herself, her hair was arranged into a tight bun, accentuating her fatigue.

Her rapid transformation distressed Earl. He found it difficult not to worry about Lillian along with Tamara. Lillian assumed the role of the family matriarch after her mother's death a few years ago, holding the position with the same strength and dignity. His greatest fear was that her daughter's illness would claim both of them. "She's fine, Lillian." With a side-glance toward Daphne, he added, "Can we speak privately?"

Planning to eavesdrop anyway, Daphne exited the hallway by entering Tamara's room. She left the door slightly ajar to give the impression that the two were alone.

Lillian approached the subject gently. "Did she have another rough one?"

Earl attempted to calm her shaking hands by holding them. "This vision spoke to her, Lillian. This changes her abilities."

"Let me be the judge of that. I know her abilities, Earl. I'm her mother. I know her better than anyone else," Lillian admitted.

Earl felt the sting of her words. "The vision was a young boy and his uncle. They were at an ancient place of learning in Scotland. At the end of the vision, the young boy told his uncle that Dr. Brody was in trouble."

Lillian's jaw dropped to the floor. "That doesn't make sense. The meds might have something to do with this. I'll ask Daphne if any doses have been changed lately." As she walked toward the door to her daughter's room, Earl grabbed her from behind.

"Lillian, if the vision said he's in trouble, then he's in trouble! He must be warned!"

"Mitch is perfectly safe. The two of them aren't even linked, so she couldn't possibly know his status. It's a ridiculous notion to propose."

"What if it isn't!" he pressed. "It *is* possible, Lillian. It's happened before."

Covering her eyes, she hung her head. "Why is this happening to my daughter?" she asked. "Is this my punishment?"

Earl held her as tears turned to sobs. He could feel the bones of her ribcage protruding from beneath her blouse, knowing that words were not enough. "Have faith, Lillian. No one else has the strength to endure this battle like you do. Don't forget that."

Still with her head buried in his chest, she exhaled deeply and asked, "What should we do?"

"When was the last time you spoke to Mitch?" Earl asked.

"A few days ago."

"Let's call to make sure he's all right," Earl suggested. "If he is, then we can question Tamara's vision. If he isn't, then we have things to discuss."

Daphne watched Lillian wipe tears away and leave Earl's embrace. She enjoyed watching Lillian cry. It made her feel powerful, which was intoxicating. She slipped out from behind the door. "Is everything all right Lillian?" she asked in her sweetest voice.

Lillian fell into her trap. "Daphne, have you spoken to Dr. Brody lately?"

Maintaining her innocent demeanor, Daphne answered. "Define 'lately.'"

Earl interjected. "She means within the last twenty-four hours, nitwit!"

Clasping her hands in front of her, Daphne pursed her lips. "I'll contact the office to see when he last called in for messages."

"Thank you, Daphne. That would be extremely helpful," Lillian remarked, shooting a look of aggravation at Earl.

Daphne sauntered down the hallway, scrolling through the list of contact names in her cell phone. She was aware of the time difference, but given the current situation, she was sure her contact wouldn't mind. At least she hoped so.

"I presume you have important information at such a late hour?"

"I do," Daphne whispered.

The demand was succinct. "Be quick."

"The patient had another episode tonight. This time, the dream mentioned Brody. Now everyone is in an uproar, thinking that the dream is real. What's his status?"

"Have I ever confided in you regarding any details? I don't recall having done so, and I'm certainly not going to start now."

"What do you suggest I tell Lillian?" she asked.

"You have a tremendous gift for lying. One of your more endearing qualities, I think."

"And Brody?"

"I'll have to reschedule his demise."

An unexpected wave of fear shot through Daphne. It had never been her intention to have Brody killed. She just wanted him to know what it felt like to not always be the bright, shining star at the center of attention. This wasn't what she imagined when she initially approached the man who would become her employer.

"Will I be informed when it happens?" she boldly asked.

A sinister laugh shot through the air. "I can have you informed when the deed is accomplished."

Turning her phone off, she prepared a statement. It would take juggling on her part with the involvement of several different people to pull it off. The girl just changed the field of play in a dangerous game. Smoothing the wrinkles out of her scrubs, she placed a sincere smile upon her face, convincing herself that she could follow through with one humdinger of a story.

15

As he exited Glastonbury and progressed to the car park, Julian was oddly quiet. Mitch felt relief with the last lesson, satisfied that he was not floundering alone. Instead of feeling like a pawn with an unknown agenda, he was part of something bigger. Surrounded by subterranean, swirling water, the vitality of the past events remained current. His conversations regarding the presence of energy and its flow were brought to life when viewing the water. The day brought clarity from the tangible facts of the lessons that he had been given. He felt the energy surge deep beneath the earth, and his anticipation to feel it again was paramount.

Even with Julian, their travel back to the hotel was blissfully silent. Neither man needed to ask questions about their time apart in the abbey. Each one was content to carry on as if personal business was carried out without any details needing to be given. The drop of blood on Julian's cuff left a question in Mitch's mind. But the issue was easily explained as a scrape from one of the stone walls he had brushed against. Upon arrival, the two men exchanged a polite dismissal and an empty promise to touch base before venturing alone to their rooms.

Mitch rummaged through clothes in his suitcase before finding items buried toward the bottom. Placing the three objects on the bed in order of receipt from left to right, he catalogued what he had received: the blue stone collected from Duncan, the bowl from Pip and the twins, and finally the chalice, still encased within its blue silk wrapping. The stone appeared as if it should be paired with something equally as brilliant, such as a gemstone, but instead sat with two random objects that would have looked more at home on a dining table. Duncan mentioned that each teacher would bestow an object of importance, but the objects' use would come later. Gently placing them back into his suitcase, the phone interrupted his moment of silence.

"Good morning, Dr. Brody!" Bridget chirped.

"You're cheerful this morning." He sighed, disappointed to hear her voice. He couldn't escape her no matter what time of day or night.

"I'm always cheerful knowing I get to speak to you. There is a message for you, and the caller seemed insistent that it be relayed immediately."

"Is anything wrong?" he asked, curious as to what, besides Tamara, could be so urgent.

"No, they mentioned you had a business appointment today and forgot to give you the address."

Thinking back to his exit from the abbey, he recalled that the woman failed to give him any information regarding the next location. She must have been thrown off by Julian's presence and the safest way to relay information was a phone call. It amazed him how these people all knew where he would be when he never told them. He laughed at his naïvety.

"Let me in on the joke," Bridget said.

"Just thinking to myself. What's the address?"

"I've never been there, but I have heard it is quite pretty. Loads of history, too. The lady said for you to be at Southwark Cathedral at one o'clock."

"Did she mention who the meeting would be with?" Mitch asked.

"She only mentioned the time and place. Don't you know who your appointment is with, Dr. Brody?" she asked sarcastically.

"Was there anything else?" he snapped.

"She said to remember that you are a soloist and not a duet. Does that make sense to you?"

Mitch laughed out loud. "It makes perfect sense."

"Too bad you have to be alone. I get off at noon," she suggested.

"Trust me, Bridget; you wouldn't want to witness the dullness of my meetings."

"You'd be amazed at what I'm willing to endure for the right man," she admitted before disconnecting the call.

As with previous conversations they'd had over the years, there was a point where Mitch felt uncomfortable with her level of flirtation. At times her comments bordered on obscene, making a professional relationship awkward. This trip confirmed for him that she was a woman who used her sexuality to get what she wanted, and since he wasn't that type of man, her directness was an issue. He decided that a change in venue was in order for the duration of his stay in-country. He transferred the three objects to his briefcase and packed the rest of his belongings into his suitcase. Following a brief phone call to the manager, he was assured his suitcase would be messengered to alternate accommodations.

While Mitch chose his words carefully with the manager, Julian wore a hole into the carpet, pacing across the hall. "Come on, damn it! I haven't got all day!" he grumbled. He had been made to wait in the past, which didn't bother him, but after the conversation a few days ago, he felt like a disposable grunt rather than a partner in the operation. Walking toward the bathroom, he decided that if the phone didn't ring in the next thirty seconds, he would cease his participation and move on to better things. The phone's vibration caused him to shut the shower off. "I don't wait around!" he warned.

"Remember to whom you are speaking. You may not wait for others, but you *will* wait for me."

"I thought after my message last night that you would have the decency to return my call with haste. Instead I slept with my damn phone. Does that sound equitable?" Julian demanded.

"My opera tickets were more important than your little drama. Regardless of what you believe in that narrow-minded brain of yours, I have everything under control."

Julian slammed his fist against the cold tile of the bathroom wall. His throbbing knuckles took his mind off the annoying fact that this time he wasn't in control—a truth he managed to avoid in other enterprising situations. "What do you intend to do about it?"

"The deadline to remove the obstacle is ahead of schedule. Today is the day to prove your loyalty."

Julian faced his reflection, peering at the materializing stress in dark circles, gray hairs, and a pale tint to his skin. He was never informed of the physical and psychological ramifications he would endure for this job. He didn't appreciate presenting himself in any manner that was less than perfect.

"Can you?"

Julian narrowed his eyes into a menacing expression. "Of course."

"I need to know what the old bitch told Dr. Brody yesterday."

Julian froze. He wasn't aware that his presence was needed on the tour that Brody took through the abbey. He assumed his duty was simply to accompany Brody to the location, not tag along on any worthless tour. "I told you last night that she destroyed the paper with the next location."

"What education did she give him about the abbey?"

"I didn't follow them once we were in the chapel. I didn't think it was important," he reluctantly admitted.

A deep sigh echoed through the connection. "You were instructed to gather all information regarding Dr. Brody's appointment at Glastonbury. Don't you think that would include any information he was given by the person or people he met there?"

"I guess so," Julian stated, bored that this was being blown out of proportion.

"Staying within the realm of guessing, do you guess that it would be important to know what he is being told so that we may use it as an advantage in the manner of our treatment of the little girl?"

Without thinking, Julian asked, "Yes?"

"Grab a pen and paper, writing down what I tell you verbatim. This time you will not be guessing."

Julian did as he was told, knowing that if he continued to dislike the direction his employer was taking, and he would bail out without warning. After all, he didn't need this to reach his ultimate goal of prestige. There were others who were willing to help get him there.

16

itch patted his brown briefcase. Just thinking about the objects inside made him nervous. He knew that the point of the trip was to remove him from the comfort zone and think in a different way. Nostalgia crept in for the effervescence of Pip and the twins. Retrieving the cell phone Duncan gave him, he pressed speed dial and waited for answer. The phone rang to a generic voice mail. He decided to leave a message. "Hey, Duncan, it's Mitch! I'm on my way to Southwark Cathedral, and I was feeling a bit lonely, so I thought I'd call. Glastonbury was fabulous! I think I am finally getting the whole energy notion your assistants have been drilling into my head. I have some questions for you. I'll call back when I'm finished with this lesson."

He shoved the phone back into his pocket as the cab slowed down. Feeling generous, he handed the cabbie a large tip. His mood was lighter than it had been in months. The anticipation of what he could encounter next raced from the tips of his toes to the top of his head as he made his way toward the cathedral's entrance.

The bell tower pointed toward the heavens, summoning the faithful to worship. Black-and-white stone gave a first impression of decay, but upon closer observance, the dark façade chronicled chapters in history. The main building and bell tower had been built at different periods, but their craftsmanship was unmistakable. Flowers graced pathways as people dashed about on their way to a nearby train station. Melodic chiming from the bells beckoned Mitch to enter the building.

Instead of a historical monument to tour, this was a working parish. Hymnals and prayer books dotted the backs of pews, showing wear along the bindings. Fresh flowers decorated the altar, giving its stern nature a welcoming feel. The stained glass windows displayed their brilliance on the stone floor as sunlight pierced through each color. Mitch dropped a five-pound note into the collection box, reading the latest news regarding community projects and humanitarian efforts. Both school children and adults worked to collect supplies for underprivileged children while canned food was collected for the hungry, both locally and abroad. The thought of their actions brought a tiny drop of regret to Mitch, as he felt he should do more community outreach rather than ignore the needs of those less fortunate.

Lit by a combination of modern electricity and glowing candles, the cathedral gleamed with amber light. No other visitors were present as Mitch toured the interior. Bright greens and blues of a memorial to William Shakespeare popped out at him. Footsteps approached from behind.

"Hi, handsome!"

"What are *you* doing here?" he asked as calmly as he could without shouting out of his frustration.

Bridget seductively batted her eyelashes. "I told you I was off at noon. You didn't mention whether or not I should join you, so I took a chance. Besides, I needed to see you one last time."

Deciding to play dumb, he asked, "What makes you think I'm leaving?"

Taking a step closer to him, she whispered, "I was the one who transferred your bags to your new hotel after being written up for inappropriate behavior."

Mitch rubbed the back of his neck. "Sorry, Bridget. I didn't realize he would take it that far."

"How about if I call you Mitch, since you already feel I've crossed a line?" she suggested. "Besides, it's not my responsibility to ensure that a patron doesn't misinterpret my behavior for anything less than professionalism. I can assure you I'm very professional." She ran her tongue over her lips. "You didn't give me a chance to show you how professional I can be."

Obviously, she was an individual who couldn't take a hint, so he would have to be blunt. "I have business that requires my undivided attention. You need to go home, grab a different guy along the way, and play games with him."

Bridget tossed her hair behind her shoulders. "I give you a little harmless flirtation to make you think you could ever be with someone of my caliber and you fall for it hook, line, and sinker—because deep down you're not only lonely, you're pathetic."

Mitch failed to curb his anger as he began to rush past her. "Bridget, just go. I have someone to meet!"

"Yeah, me!"

The comment stopped him dead in his tracks. He spun around in disbelief, expecting another battle of one-liners. *"You?"*

"After they called, I changed my work schedule to accommodate the time, and here I am, ready for your lesson. The question is, are you OK with me giving it?"

He never recognized anything that would lead him to believe that she was involved with Duncan's group, but honestly, he had never looked. He hung his head to avoid eye contact. "I'm sorry, Bridget. I had no idea."

Walking slowly toward him, she stopped inches from his face. Her tapping foot echoed across the stone walls. "You're learning that things aren't always as they seem." Mitch found it even more difficult to look her in the eye. She led him toward the altar. "Over the past few days, you have seen amazing pieces of history. Each one relates to the other. This cathedral is another piece of the puzzle. I was chosen because of my love for this church. I grew up in this congregation and still attend services every weekend because the energy is so electric." Her honesty showed a nicer side of Bridget.

"We are standing in the oldest church in London. There has been one on this site since 606 AD, with findings suggesting this was also a worship site for Romans and Pagans. Being next to London Bridge, it provided the only entrance to the city of London across the river for centuries. It's also located at the oldest crossing point of the tidal Thames." She snickered. "You could say that it is the heart of a cross-roads of time and spirituality. The congregation here understands the unique history of this place, so the members continue to promote the well-being of humanity through their good works. Did you notice the projects on the board at the front?" The pride for her church community was evident. Mitch couldn't help but be swept away with her passion.

"This church has also had its fair share of celebrities. William Shakespeare attended services here while he was a registered Mason, and to your left stands his monument. Tons of tourists come here and offer their donations just to photograph the memorial."

Loosening the tight grip on his briefcase, he placed it on the floor to remove the journal. He opened to a blank page and asked, "Does Shakespeare have a correlation with the hidden symbols?"

She peeked into the open bag. "Uh, huh."

Glancing at carvings on the walls for any recognizable symbols, Mitch asked, "Which symbols are important?"

Bridget kicked the briefcase away from his reach. "I'm just sup-posed to give you the history. Someone else will teach you about symbols."

Mitch turned to face the altar. "When do they get here?"

"Now!" a voice bellowed from the entrance. Julian Kingman stood within the doorframe.

"Julian?" Mitch asked in disbelief.

"In the flesh," he confirmed, strutting like a peacock toward the altar.

"You said you were here for a World Health Organization conference."

Julian stood before Mitch with a broad smile. "Obviously that wasn't the only conference."

Looking toward Bridget, Mitch said, "I'm confused."

Stepping onto the altar platform, Julian approached slowly. "Didn't Bridget tell you that I was coming?"

Mitch shook his head, trying to comprehend the roles these two people played in the organization. "She didn't mention who was coming. I didn't realize you knew each other personally."

Julian patted the top of Bridget's head. "Silly Bridget, always forgetting the small details. But then again, an air of mystery surrounding what we're doing is needed. Don't you think, Brody?"

"I didn't know you were associated with the group."

"Associations are delicate things, Brody. A person shouldn't televise their closest relationships to every Tom, Dick, and Harry. It wouldn't be appropriate," Julian sneered.

Mitch glanced at Julian's hands for the ring he was accustomed to seeing, since it was the one commonality that bound them together. Both the collar of his jacket, as well as his hands, were bare. Not one symbol graced his physique. Bridget passed the briefcase off to Julian as he took a seat on the altar steps. Patting the stone steps to his right, he said, "Sit down, we've got loads to talk about." Mitch reluctantly sat down. Bearing in mind that there were others who knew more than he did, he relaxed his suspicions.

Drumming his fingers against the leather, Julian asked a direct question. "What's in here that's so important, Brody?"

"The artifacts that the other teachers gave me."

"Wouldn't it be smarter to keep them in a safer place than this flimsy bag? Do you think the objects are safe out in public like this?"

"Safer than sitting in a hotel room, begging to be stolen."

Julian nodded. "You assume they are safer in your presence? Explain to me how I presently possess them. I'm no expert, but it seems your plan has already failed."

Mitch hung his head at the mistake. "I need to pay more attention," he admitted.

"No hard feelings, Brody. Just don't want this precious cargo to fall into the wrong hands. What are your plans?"

"Duncan instructed me to collect an artifact from each teacher, and he said that when the time was right, I would be told what to do with them."

Julian drummed a quiet rhythm upon the leather. "Duncan?"

"Didn't he send you?" Mitch asked.

"There are a lot of different people in control these days."

"I'm not familiar with the differing levels of authority. How about you show me the symbols we're here to discuss?" Mitch suggested.

Julian grimaced. "One final question. Do you plan on taking the items to the Professor?"

His question flustered Mitch. The only professor he could recall was the teacher at Glastonbury who gave that title as her chosen profession, but Julian had also met her that day. If he needed something from her, surely he would have asked, instead of waiting to question Mitch in a different location. The shrill tones of a cell phone pierced the silent sanctuary. Mitch held up his index finger to accept the intrusion. Bridget replaced him on the step.

"Hello?" he mumbled.

"It's Duncan. What's going on, son?"

"Julian and I were about to get down to business."

"I thought you mentioned sightseeing." Duncan said.

"You sent Julian Kingman to meet me at Southwark Cathedral for the lesson. Would have been nice to get a heads-up about that one, but that is a separate discussion," Mitch teased.

"Listen carefully, Mitch. I didn't, and neither did anyone I know, send you to Southwark."

Blood raced to his head with an intense throb. "Julian wasn't sent by your organization?"

Julian's fist raged against Mitch's cheek, the phone flew from his hand, landing Mitch behind a pew close to the entrance. "It's rude to take a personal call during a business meeting. Didn't anyone ever teach you that?"

Mitch had foolishly ignored his instincts with Bridget, and Duncan just confirmed his paranoia of danger. He spied his briefcase sitting on Bridget's left, next to the altar. He needed to think fast if he was going to retrieve it. "Calm down, Julian. No one ever died over accepting a call at an inappropriate time."

"That you know of," Julian grumbled.

"Maybe we can compromise," Mitch bribed.

Julian shoved him hard toward the altar. Stumbling across the steps, Mitch's body settled at Bridget's feet. "I see you're acquainted with Dr. Kingman." Her smile melted into a smirk. "He didn't have many kind words to say about your earlier years together. Seems you weren't very kind to him. Bet you're regretting that now." Bridget snatched the bag away from his grasp. "No, no, Dr. Brody, you need to listen to my brilliant boyfriend before receiving a prize."

Julian sauntered toward him while Mitch racked his brain for an escape plan. Uncertainty plagued him as he tried to figure out if they wanted the relics, the information, or both. If negotiations were successful, Mitch hoped he would leave this encounter with only a few bruises. Exchanging a quick kiss with Bridget, Julian bent down to Mitch's level. "Here's how it's going to work, Brody. I'll ask questions, and you'll answer. I'm not a beat-around-the-bush kind of guy, so we'll get straight to the point. If I like your answer, then I'll leave you alone."

"And if you don't like the answer?" Mitch dared.

"I have ways of getting the answers I want," he replied, cracking his knuckles in a show of force. "You'll tell me what my employer needs to know."

Julian's confirmation of a second party intrigued Mitch. His best tactic might be to play both sides against each other. Remembering the lack of self-confidence Julian possessed as a young man, he hoped he hadn't changed too much in that area since graduation. Mitch taunted him to see just how far Julian was willing to go. "There's an employer? Sounds about right. You never were a leader."

A swift kick to the stomach left Mitch gasping for breath. "May that be a reminder of who's in charge. I call the shots. Where's the Professor?"

"I don't know any professor," Mitch whispered as a sharp blow across his jaw forced his mouth open.

"Wrong answer, Brody. Is he with the girl or with you?"

Moving his bottom jaw back and forth, Mitch tried to remember if he had been introduced to anyone with that title. He repeated, "I don't know any professor." Another heavy kick found his abdomen.

Julian laughed. "Don't be a hero, Brody. Tell me where he is so I can pay him a little visit. I promise it won't be as painful as this one's turning out to be."

Watching Mitch painfully writhe on the ground created a bubbling of compassion inside Bridget. Brute force made her question the integrity of the man with whom she was intimate. She assumed she would be an accessory to a simple petty theft or at the least harmless fun. But not this. "Jules, lay off for a bit. He's bleeding."

"Shut up, slut," Julian snarled.

His response stunned her. "Jules, just take the case and go. Wasn't that the plan?"

Julian's eyes were fierce with hatred. "The plan has changed. *Shut up!*"

Mitch tenderly raised himself to a sitting position, wiping blood away from his jaw. He watched the exchange between Julian and Bridget, recognizing an opportunity for escape. Since his first attempt at playing the employer card failed, he thought Bridget might possess the possibility for assistance, if she could maintain her courage. "Listen to the lady, Julian. Obviously *you* have the advantage. You win. You're the *big* man."

Throwing his head back with laughter, Julian's temperament shifted again. While finding humor, the split personality relished the pain of the human condition as long as he was the one to inflict it. "I've always been the big man, Brody. Pity that no one, until recently, recognized my talents and abilities. I think my performance today is good." Kneeling down on the steps, he bent over to grab Mitch by the back of the head, forcing their eyes to meet. "Where is the Professor?"

"I swear to God, I don't know a professor." Fist met bone with an echoing crack. Mitch was sure the blow delivered a break to his jawbone.

"Stop it, Jules!" Bridget cried, rushing to Mitch's aide. She used a Kleenex from her pocket to wipe the blood from his chin.

"Get away from him, Bridget," Julian warned.

In a moment of defiance, Bridget countered, "No. I didn't sign up for this. You told me that we would play a little mind game, steal his case, and then go on holiday. I don't care what kind of grudge you have from school. He's not even fighting back!"

"I told you to *get away* from him!" Julian bellowed.

Bridget continued to tend to Mitch. She was never afraid of men who yelled. In her experience, yelling was a sign of desperation. "What are you going to do, Jules, beat me up too?" she challenged. As she faced Brody once again to assess his wounds, she said, "I don't believe you are man enough to hurt me."

Julian silently removed a gun from his pocket, pointing it toward the two people on the floor. "I don't need to hurt you, darling. In fact, I don't need you at all."

Ignorant of any threat, Bridget took a deep breath before turning to face Julian. She weighed her options. Would she be able to live with him or even herself after witnessing Brody's murder? "Julian, this has gone way too far. Put the gun down, and let's go. You don't want to do this."

Moving the gun's barrel from Mitch to Bridget, Julian changed his target. "You're wrong, Bridget; I *do* want to do this. I've wanted to do this for a long time. I get the perfect opportunity to seek retribution for the treatment I endured when we were in school."

Bridget stepped toward the altar, planning to use it as a protective shield. "All of this *is* about some stupid grudge! You're an idiot, Jules. Look at you now! You have it all! Whoever is telling you to do this isn't worth it. Make up some lie, and we'll go away. No one ever has to know you were involved."

"Oh, this isn't about a grudge. I'm carrying out orders. The revenge thing is just a bonus," Julian grumbled.

Reaching the altar, Bridget blindly felt the top for anything she could use as a weapon. "Jules, come on. If you love me, like I know you do, you'll stop all this nonsense and go. I won't tell a soul."

In the heat of their argument, Bridget and Julian moved farther away from Mitch. He silently crawled toward his briefcase. Grasping the top handle, he silently slid down the steps, using the pews as a possible shield from bullet fire. He felt only a slight obligation toward Bridget's safety, assuming Julian wouldn't pull the trigger if he were willing to continue speaking with her. Slipping behind the third pew from the front, he pushed himself beneath the rows and headed for the entrance.

Julian planted his feet shoulder-width apart with his gun directed at Bridget. He assumed he would have more emotion, but to his surprise, he was empty. The only emotion was pure excitement. The power was intoxicating. "I *did* love you, Bridget, and very well, I might add. But, I never *felt* love for you."

Tears flooded Bridget's eyes. She couldn't believe what she was hearing. She had been so blind. Covering her face with her hands, she sobbed as Julian noticed Mitch's sudden disappearance. Wheeling around in all directions, Julian screamed, *"Where is he?"*

Bridget choked out the words, "You need me. I know you need me."

Julian turned. A single shot rang out as her body crumpled lifeless to the floor.

"Wrong, darling. I don't *need* anybody."

Julian's vantage point at the altar kept all the exits within his sights. Even though he couldn't see Brody, he knew escape would be impossible without being heard. Since the doors remained locked, he knew Brody had to be near. He walked down the center aisle, moving the gun back and forth. "Mitchy, come out and talk, buddy. Now that we're alone, we can finish this without being nasty. I didn't mean to hurt you. I did it to impress the lady, and now that I've done away with her annoying presence, the two of us can be civil, can't we?" Julian scanned the pews on either side of the aisle as Mitch's ankles cleared the last pew at the entrance, where his discarded cell phone lay.

Peeking around each pew, Mitch saw that Julian's approach was much too quick for an exit. His best chance was the side door. The danger was a second secret scamper past Julian to the center of the cathedral.

Julian continued his progress toward the main entrance. "Mitchy, come out and talk. We're old friends, and that's what friends do. I value true friendships, and I would never hurt you as a personal choice. Come on, Mitchy…Let's be friends!" Julian proposed.

Mitch crawled on hands and knees along the right side back toward the altar, quietly pushing his briefcase in front of him. But Julian's footsteps pursued him on the stone floor. Mitch scanned the walls for a new hiding area. Hearing Julian's echo behind him, Mitch darted under the pews to his left and worked his way toward the center aisle.

"I'm not going to beg for you to appear. How about I make a quick phone call for someone to pay a visit to Graham. He could end up like Bridget here, which I would actually enjoy."

Mentioning Graham was a low blow. He longed to choke the breath out of Julian Kingman, but it was futile to think that way without a weapon. He had to get the hell out of there.

Rolling the gun around in his palm, Julian continued the game. "Graham isn't as tough as you are. He's a big talker, but I bet he would be far more fun to kill. Oops, cat's out of the bag. I *do* have to kill you. After all the crap I swallowed from that pompous ass back at school, Graham would be a pleasure to get to bump!" Mitch reached the altar and saw Bridget's body lying at its base. "Come on, Mitchy, this is all just business, but Graham will be a pleasure. I'll make sure my eulogy is extra special at a combined memorial. You did always want to die together, right?" Julian stopped in front of the Shakespeare monument. Trying the door to the left of the statue, he felt the secure lock, knowing there had not been an exit. He walked toward the stone-faced poet, preparing to fire his weapon. "Now we do it the hard way," he warned.

Slamming his briefcase into the left side of Julian's skull, Mitch bellowed, "When has it ever been easy with you?"

The blow knocked Julian off his feet, sending the gun flying from his hands. Mitch pursued it as Julian grabbed his foot, bringing him crashing to the floor. Mitch swung his body around, reaching the distance to grab the gun, while Julian's arms pulled Mitch's legs back toward him. Using his fingers to reach even farther, Mitch pulled his body toward the gun. Julian progressed up his legs to his hips, as Mitch used his left leg to break Julian's jaw. Stunned by the force of action, Julian's body flew backward, giving Mitch an advantage to grab the weapon. Mitch aimed at Julian's chest with the intention to fire only in defense. Julian lunged forward, capturing Mitch's waist. Hands flew from both men in an effort to secure the weapon. Mitch's knee met Julian's chin. The bone cracked from impact. Finding strength to stand, the two men faced each other as they wrestled back and forth for the gun.

"Give it up, Mitchy. You can't beat me."

"I already have, years ago. You've been trying to keep up ever since."

The mention of Mitch's superiority fueled Julian's rage. He screamed, using every bit of strength to yank the gun from Mitch's hands. Mitch returned Julian's effort with his own additional strength, using his shoulders as leverage. The fight reached a fevered pitch, with Julian surging forward, pointing the gun toward Mitch's vital organs.

"You're done, Brody," he said, sneering. A second shot echoed through the cathedral amid screams of horror. Mitch looked past Julian to a group of school children standing at the entrance with their teacher.

Fearing capture for a crime, Julian released his grip on the gun and fled out the side door.

E. R. BLAKE

Panting from their struggle, Mitch reached down to grab his briefcase, feeling a bolt of pain pierce his midsection as a wide smear of blood crept across his stomach. Hoping to evade any questions as an accessory to Bridget's murder, Mitch slipped out the same side door, while the teacher ushered her students out of the cathedral.

Mitch quickly found the cell phone Duncan had given him. Standing against the outside wall of the cathedral, he pressed speed dial. The release of blood confirmed that his time to reach help was limited.

"Please tell me you're OK!" Duncan shouted.

"I'm wounded. Tell me what to do."

"Where?"

"Gunshot to the abdomen. Not sure how severe, but since I'm feeling dizzy, I would say he got me pretty good."

"Can you walk?"

"Barely," Mitch sputtered.

"I'll talk fast. I contacted a couple to run interference for you during this bogus meeting. Go to London Bridge station next to the cathedral, and they'll meet you."

"Where at the station?"

"Outside the terminal."

A crackling sound signaled that the phone would soon be useless. "Duncan, I can barely hear you." Before the signal was lost, the words "yellow car" were the only ones he heard accurately.

Sirens broke through the cellular connection, as emergency crews arrived at the cathedral. Mitch clutched the briefcase tightly across his stomach, applying pressure to the wound, and headed toward the station. This recent turn of events made him question his ability to complete his task. The wound had made that decision for him, causing him to hope that he would meet up with the couple before he blacked out from an extreme loss of blood. He obviously wasn't a good judge of character, given the circumstance with Bridget and Julian. His ability to trust people was severely compromised.

With the terminal in sight, he squeezed his eyes shut a few times, clearing blurry images in front of him. Scanning the cars in front

156

of the terminal, he saw two yellow cars at the curb. An older couple claimed a modern coup at the highest point of the terminal. The second, a Mini Cooper, was closest to the entrance with a younger couple leaning against it. Taking a second to decide, he chose the older couple. They looked more like the type of people Duncan would send. Seeing Mitch from across the street, the older woman smiled, waved, and motioned to her husband. The man turned toward Mitch and slipped a gun from the lining of his coat. As bile rose in Mitch's throat, adrenaline reclaimed its place in his body, surging Mitch forward in a slow run.

Dodging through passengers headed for various trains, Mitch attempted to get lost within the crowd. With his pursuer almost upon him, he headed for a departing train. Unable to continue the pursuit, he slowed down, allowing the crowds to overtake him. Pressing the briefcase tighter against his body, he ducked behind an elderly woman in a wheelchair as the man rushed past. Feeling a pinch in his left arm, Mitch fell to the ground. The people above continued their path toward the trains as the world darkened. With consciousness abandoning him, a strong pair of arms lifted his body up off the floor. A man's muffled voice uttered the words, "Let's get him in the car before anyone spots us. We're due the *big* reward for this one."

17

The house was dark. Newspapers piled up on the front porch signaled desertion. All the shrubs and plants drooped with neglect, showing crispy brown edges on leaves. It was the perfect backdrop for a peek at the way the other half lived. Walking around the perimeter of the home provided no alternative entrance without being seen from the street. The only course of action would be a rear entry through the back garden.

Not one lock surrendered to force, even in the back of the house. Forcible entry was not an option. The operation had to go smoothly. A mental pause provided the necessary clarity to solve the puzzle. Bending down at the back door, the mat was the obvious place for a key. Not there. The top of the door jam, nothing. A wind chime hanging from the eaves swayed with a small breeze. Made of miscellaneous metal household items, it created a deeper tone than the common small cylinders. The middle object stood out from the rest. An old key with weathered patina carried a card with the handwritten words, "The Key to Life." Jackpot. Yanking it free from its bonds, the metal slipped effortlessly into the lock.

Careful not to arouse suspicion, in case a meeting was taking place in the basement, the intruder slowly creaked open the door. The overcast sky filtered limited light through the windows, providing just enough to navigate the room to a beacon in the dining room.

It seemed almost humorous that such a priceless artifact would be left without security in an ordinary house. Hidden relics in plain view provided a certain amount of anonymity, if the people who knew about it were trustworthy. In this instance, the more people who knew, the more opportunity there was for betrayal. It wasn't something that anyone wanted to happen, but it was something that needed to happen.

Viewing the Exile Carpet in the display case was different this time. Opportunities presented themselves to gaze upon its symbols and secrets through the years. But today, the importance of securing the treasure would finally serve a higher purpose than sitting in a case, waiting for its destiny to arrive.

The cold steel of a pocket knife slipped through the wires connecting a key pad to the case, and the absence of a red light indicated that the alarm was successfully dismantled. As the glass door was peeled away from the wall, the musty odor of the carpet wafted forward and filled the air. The knife severed the cords, and the carpet slid into gloved hands and was rolled quickly into a poster tube. The display case was left open to serve as a warning for trusting the wrong people.

Foolishly, trust remained with this family, regardless of the betrayals they endured.

Slithering through the back door one last time, an individual who was free from the bonds of family dared to smile. This was someone who demanded respect and loyalty without obligation to repay the debt.

The next time the Exile Carpet saw daylight, it would pledge its allegiance to a new family and a new power base.

18

The small car darted in and out of traffic at high speed, causing the other drivers to swerve, swear, and gesture. "You might as well post a sign telling the world that we're felons on the run by the way you're driving, Quinn. *Slow down!*"

"We have a deadline, Eleanor! We agreed to deliver Brody at a certain time, and I'm a man who keeps his promises."

"Since when?" she said, sneering.

"In case you haven't noticed, this is a *big* assignment. He doesn't hand these out to everyone. We're on our way up, baby! Plus, by the looks of our charge, he might not be so fresh when we arrive. Quinn glanced at the covered body in the backseat. "Are you sure you gave him enough?"

"How am I supposed to know? At least the bleeding has slowed." Eleanor glanced over her shoulder at the pile of blankets. She made sure that Quinn placed him faceup so she could monitor changes during the car ride. "I don't know what else to do. I tried to patch the wound as best I could, and the drugs help a little, but he needs serious attention. I didn't know he would be in such a state."

"Same to you, buddy!" Quinn shouted as another pointed gesture flew toward him.

Smacking him on the arm to reflect her disapproval, Eleanor showed genuine concern for their guest. "He's been out a long time. Are you sure you gave me the right stuff?"

Barely missing a delivery truck, Quinn swerved into a different lane of traffic. "I don't know, Eleanor! Stop asking stupid questions. They know what they're doing, even if you don't."

"And you do?" she shot back at him. "You're the all-knowing, all-powerful Quinn?"

"You said it, not me. Besides, you're the one who begged to come along. I thought I was flying solo."

Eleanor folded her arms across her chest. "Well, excuse me for wanting to get out of the house for once. You're the one who said we're a team, and now that the opportunity presents itself, you have to be the one who shouts orders at me. Some husband you are."

Unsure how to respond to her latest ranting, Quinn instead focused on the muffled ringing of a cell phone coming from the backseat.

Eleanor was worried. "We may be in a bit of a pickle. That thing has been going off for an hour. Someone's trying to reach him, and if he doesn't answer soon, they're liable to get suspicious."

Quinn ignored her, handing her a cell phone. "Let them know about his phone. Ask them what to do if it keeps ringing."

Eleanor dialed the number listed on the back while Quinn used the rearview mirror to check on Brody. She was right; he had been out a long time. He fell into their arms immediately, and Quinn suspected the damage was worse than he initially thought. He didn't know anything about medicine, but on all the cop shows he watched on TV, if a victim was shot in the stomach, they usually didn't last longer than the commercial break. Since their trip was longer than that, he began to worry.

"He said to keep doing what we're doing and *not* draw attention to ourselves. He'll sort out the phones when we get there. Don't get pulled over, you maniac." Placing the phone on the dashboard, she pulled a bottle of water from between her feet. "Think I should give him more water?"

Quinn checked the rearview a second time, looking for policemen on the highway. "Yeah, keep him hydrated. He has to be able to answer questions when we arrive."

The bottle trembled in Eleanor's hands as she put it to Mitch's lips. She didn't like guns, and the situation made her fears come alive. Mitch's wound was a subtle reminder of the type of danger they were in every day by agreeing to get involved. Seeing it all firsthand raised serious doubts in her head of whether or not she could stomach the task she would be asked to perform. With each passing mile, her quiet house seemed like an oasis.

Following the shot in his arm at the train station, Mitch was aware of the drug entering his system as he began to lose consciousness. When they stuffed him into the minuscule backseat of a car, he kept his eyes closed, which would prove to be a disadvantage in identifying them to authorities. He remained focused on their voices to distinguish them from any others that may appear. Over the last few hours in the tiny backseat, he floated in and out of consciousness from his wound as well as the drug. His lack of movement slowed down the blood stream, allowing him to retain more blood rather than losing it quickly on the run. Mitch surmised that they had administered some sort of sleeping drug out of fear that their captive could bleed out.

The continuous ringing of his phone could only be Graham. During his brief periods out of the sleeping void, thousands of drastic images flooded his brain regarding Tamara. What if she had died? What if she was dying at this very moment? He didn't dare answer the phone under present circumstances, so he laid there listening to their repetitive argument. The setting sun cast a pinkish glow to the car's interior, providing enough light for Mitch to inspect his battle scars. He could not physically inspect the wound without drawing attention, so he gingerly moved his fingers to where the bullet had entered his body. A sizable hole in his abdomen from the gunshot hid beneath a makeshift bandage. Whoever laid the homemade bandage on his wound did a fairly decent job. His jaw was swollen, yet moved freely, indicating that it had not been broken. He wasn't so sure about his ribs, but it was hard to distinguish which pain belonged to what in that area. The water was a welcome relief to the dryness in his mouth.

As Eleanor shifted in her seat in front of him, Mitch abruptly shut his eyes, dropping his arm back to his side.

"Quinn? Do you think it's time to give him another shot?" she asked.

Glancing down at the dashboard clock, Quinn shook his head. "Ten more minutes. Good Lord, Elle, do you want to overdose him?"

Wringing her hands in her lap, she fidgeted in her seat. "Look, Quinn, I'm doing my best. The fact that he was shot makes me nervous. What if it were you or me?"

"You're daft! You have to expect a little danger. That's what makes it exciting!"

With the setting sun as a backdrop behind his head, Quinn seemed angelic. Eleanor didn't like to think of what could happen, so she didn't think about it at all. With every ring of the phone, fear crept into her mind. There had been days during her daily chores at home when she wouldn't answer their phone out of fear that Quinn lay dead somewhere. With all of the increased activity over the last six months, she had been right to question it all. "Are we stopping for a bite?" she asked nervously.

"No time for a formal sit-down. We need petrol, but we're OK until Dunkeld. You can grab a bite from anything that's open if you like."

"Time for the shot now?" she asked again.

Recognizing her timid nature, Quinn softened his delivery. "Yes, Elle, you can give it to him now."

Mitch felt a familiar wetness grace his lips, combined with a stick and burn sensation to his right thigh. The difference with this shot was that he remained alert. His body's reaction to the first one had been automatic drowsiness. They were trying to help him remain alive, at the very least. But the reasoning behind that made him anxious. He listened as driver and passenger lost themselves in a discussion about her mother's upcoming visit. Daylight had almost disappeared, and Mitch strained his eyes to view his captors. He guessed they were midlife by the gray battling the brown color for dominance in their hair. From the inane information they traded, he learned that the woman named Eleanor was a homemaker, while Quinn's occupation was questionable. When he grabbed hold of Mitch at the train station, he was stronger than he appeared, leading Mitch to believe that his chosen profession must involve heavy lifting. There were only two things that he was confident in assuming: these two people had never left their small town until today, and this was the first time they had done something like this. He hoped they would play it safe.

"Get your purse out, love. Just a few more kilometers."

"Are they reimbursing us for our expenses? I don't think our budget can afford this trip if they don't. You don't make a millionaire's wages, Quinn," Eleanor barked as she produced a silver coin purse from her bag.

"If you don't knock it off, woman, I'm going to lose it. Getting reimbursed is your worry? There are a few more worries here at the moment. After you get your snacks, make sure you double-check the bandage before we're off again. We're making excellent time, but if we stop again, we'll be late, and he'll be angry. And I don't want to deal with angry."

Pursing her lips in defiance, Eleanor glanced sideways at her husband. "Let him be angry. We have the cargo, and he can wait. He's not God, you know."

Mitch felt the roar of the engine slow as they veered off the highway. Quinn was anxious to impress his superior. From the manner in which he spoke about this assignment, his success could result in a sizable advance. Being unfamiliar with the small towns and villages of the British Isles, Mitch wasn't able to pinpoint where they were stopping. For all he knew, they had crossed the Chunnel into France. This uncertainty provided no comfort.

"There!" exclaimed Eleanor. "That one's open, and they have a small café. I'll pop in for a sandwich while you fill up the car."

With the car halting beneath a bright canopy of lights, escape from the backseat would prove challenging. Mitch knew that any hope for a speedy getaway depended on Eleanor and Quinn being absent from the vehicle as well as the immediate area. Eyes still closed, he reached beneath the seat, assuming that when they grabbed him they remembered his briefcase. Feeling the familiar worn leather under his fingertips spelled success, while every muscle screamed at the small movements he forced them to make after hours cramped into the same position. Mitch knew that if he could slip past the gas station, into the dark of night, his luck would change.

Quinn opened the driver side door, as Eleanor requested a favor. "Come with me? I don't want to walk into a strange place alone at night."

"No one will suspect anything, just get your snacks." Quinn's patience level was dangerously low as his focus remained on their passenger in the back seat. He wanted to dump his cargo and receive his accolades.

"Please, Quinn!" she begged. "Escort a lady into a café, for Christ's sake. After all these years, you could remember how to be a gentleman."

"Leave Christ out of this, you raging lunatic." In one sweeping motion, Quinn slammed the door shut and walked toward the café with his wife.

Leaping into action, Mitch grabbed his briefcase, popped the rear hatch open, and rolled onto the pavement. Standing for the first time in hours was painful. He rolled his shoulders forward, hugging his briefcase close to his body for support. Quickly estimating an evacuation route, he scanned the pump area for a direction. Luckily, a number of vehicles cold hide his departure as he painfully crept behind them, making his way toward the road. The dim lights of a village a few city blocks away from the station became his new goal.

Each step became increasingly painful as he realized that the last hours spent "resting" in the back of the smallest possible space weren't beneficial. Slipping behind a bright-blue cargo van, he watched Quinn and Eleanor walk back toward their yellow vehicle, another argument in full swing. Adrenaline propelled Mitch onto the road leading to the village. Limping into the darkness, he attempted to gain a sizable lead in order to find adequate shelter. Lighted shop windows illuminated enough of the village for Mitch to navigate. As he looked toward the center of town, a gruff voice cried out in the darkness behind him.

"Oi! Get the car, Eleanor, and I'll run after him. Drive past and block him in." Quinn bellowed.

Hiding inside an alleyway, Mitch watched the yellow car zoom past him. Eleanor was not paying much attention to all the possible nooks and crannies that afforded disguise. He might not be that fortunate with Quinn. If he caught Mitch, one blow could render him useless for the remainder of his life. Mitch's only advantage was the small distance he created between them.

Scrambling back onto the village streets, Mitch scanned the area for a better vantage point. Not far from his current location, a bell tower silently stood guard. "A church is always open to people seeking refuge," he muttered to himself as Quinn's heavy footsteps grew louder. Eleanor drove past the center a second time while Mitch ducked behind a large fountain.

Lifting his feet seemed an insurmountable task, as their weight increased with each effort. His vision was beginning to blur. "A few more feet," he gasped, forcing his body to perform. The sounds of footsteps and squealing tires became distant as Mitch fought to keep himself from succumbing to the increased damage he inflicted upon an already deteriorating body.

Reaching the church before the shadows overtook him, he seized the handle of the main doors. Locked. Limping around to the first set of doors on the side of the building, he yanked the handles hard. Locked. Shouts by Eleanor and Quinn were prevalent as he reached a second set of doors on the right side of the church. Locked. "Damn it, doesn't anyone trust anybody anymore!" he screamed. Advancing upon him quicker than he could walk, Quinn and Eleanor caught up with his retreat as a full-bodied bush provided adequate cover.

"This is bad, I tell you, just bad," Eleanor sobbed.

Quinn drifted toward his wife. "Calm down. While you were driving in circles, I alerted him to our situation. He wasn't pleased, but he also wasn't surprised. He said to try to find the doctor while he sent backup." Unable to compose herself, Eleanor wilted into his arms. "Stop crying, Elle. It will all work out."

Utilizing Quinn's shirt as her personal handkerchief, Eleanor asked, "Was he very cross?"

Lifting her chin to gaze into her eyes, Quinn joked, "Nah, I told him it was your fault."

Humor proved to be the best remedy for the tense situation, and the couple headed into the darkness, searching for their lost possession. Mitch shifted his plan back toward the main entrance, hoping to locate an unlocked passage. His initial energy had greatly diminished, and his head felt like a stone on his shoulders. Looking down at his feet, the faint outline of fresh blood surrounded his shoes. He no longer felt pain, but rather the sensation of floating, as he reached for the handle on the main doors once more. Pressing down on the cold metal, he felt the lock give way as the door swung open. Stumbling up the stone steps, he fell onto a piece of carpet gracing the top step of the church. Rolling over onto his back, a great pressure exploded in his chest. Gasping for air, Mitch clung to the briefcase across his stomach.

Rushing through the open doorway, Quinn acknowledged someone else within the darkened church. "Sorry, we lost him, sure gave us a fright, but we did as we were told. We did bring him to you."

Before descending into the deep recesses of his mind, Mitch glimpsed the fuzzy outline of a young woman looming above him. "Right on time, Dr. Brody, with briefcase still in hand. Most impressive, indeed."

Finally admitting defeat, Mitch willed himself to die. If he had to go, this would be OK. With this new feeling of drowning adding to his instability, he no longer cared whom he was in the presence of, be they friend or foe. Looking at the woman, he used his final breath to whisper one word. "Sanctuary."

Graham had phoned Mitch three times in fifteen minutes without a response. Not sure if this was a feeble attempt to blow him off for more exciting pursuits or an actual emergency, Graham persisted anyway. After three hours without an answer, he admitted defeat.

"Wow, a female actually exists who won't return your phone calls? I wasn't made aware of hell freezing over today, but anything is possible. Look on the bright side, Wellington, if women have begun to ignore your advances, the fault might lie with the full moon."

The sound of her voice made the hairs on the back of his neck stand on end. She made him feel inferior, lost, and aggravated. Very few women were complicated enough to keep him interested for very long, and complication was the one thing he could count on from Channing Bradley. She consistently maintained an air of confidence while the world spun out of control. She was methodical and practical, and her superior technical skills at times bordered on bravado. She was the only female that brought him to his knees in an instant, forcing him to like her despite his competitive nature. The thought of sharing a future together made her dangerous. It broke all of Graham's barriers, allowing him to present the human side of his nature rather than the steady stream of professional courtesies he extended. After closely working with Channing over the past five years, she still possessed the ability to give him butterflies.

"For your perverse curiosity to be satisfied, it wasn't a female, it was Brody, and his phone must be off."

His comment made her snicker as she placed a stack of files on top of the nurse's station. "So it was your wife and not some random girlfriend. How unusual for the two of you. But then again, if I were Mitch, I wouldn't return your calls either."

"What do you want, Bradley? A world of exclusive pediatric conferences not in session today?" he snapped.

Graham used her last name as an informal address for two main reasons: She was one of the only female colleagues in their medical field that tolerated all the male arrogance, and it masked his feeble attempt to keep her as "one of the guys" while denying his true feelings for a married woman. Named after her grandmother's family, she carried a name on paper that could be viewed as either male or female. The ambiguity was intriguing to anyone reading her credentials. Channing Bradley was a force to be reckoned with in every aspect of her life.

She weighed her options of a reply. "Jealous that you weren't invited?"

"No, unlike others in this field, I perform at a consistent level, at which so-called famous doctors should be performing. Sadly, they fail to do so because their personal indiscretions take precedence over their profession." There was a hint of bitterness to his voice.

"You're mad that they invited me to speak rather than you. I have little doubt that one day you'll get your chance, Wellington. Someone somewhere will recognize your talent." She was never mean-spirited in their exchanges, but she did give him a fair share of teasing. She enjoyed putting him in his place every now and then to bring him back down to earth after all his lofty attempts in medicine. Graham Wellington was a dare devil who relished the tempting of fate by taking risks. This was the reason she questioned his position as department head. While she was envious of his title, deep inside she wouldn't mind taking a professional risk.

Graham stared at the computer screen with Tamara's vitals. She had been stable since her admission, her organ functions showing a slight improvement. While he was grateful for the positive turn, it made him uneasy thinking that at any moment the bottom would fall out, causing them to return to square one.

"Do you intend to continue torturing me with your intelligence, or is there a purpose to this visit?" He avoided looking at her.

"I'm looking for Brody. I need a consult on a case, and it's right up his alley," she admitted with a smile.

"He's indisposed at the moment," Graham snapped.

"The computer shows he has a patient in this wing."

"I'm in charge of her care while Brody is running errands somewhere in Scotland. They designated Brody as the physician on the chart due to his name being on record as her primary physician. I realize that the two of you share information regarding patients all the time with your weird little MENSA project. But since he's absent, I suppose I could take a look at your junk."

"The professional term is consultation, Wellington. Physicians use it as a tool for the betterment of patient care, which is something you're not familiar with, since you just referred to them as junk. It's not junk, it's a patient. Try some sensitivity for a change," she advised.

He took his eyes off the computer screen, staring at her for the first time. The sparkle in her brown eyes created an immediate loss of concentration, causing him to gaze at her forehead instead. "They wouldn't be here if they didn't have junk. That's our job, to get rid of the junk and send them back into the world to get more. It's not insensitive; it's emotional detachment from the business of medicine."

Feeling a sense of disgust at his perception, she answered, "It's a barbaric theory at best, but I have to admit, it has a shred of intelligence to it."

Raising his hands above his shoulders, he placed them behind his head, smiling as he leaned back in his chair. "Show me the goods, Bradley. I'll scratch your back, and you can scratch mine."

"You need a consult from me?" she asked excitedly.

"No, there's a spot on my shoulders I can't seem to reach. Would you mind?"

His comment merited throwing her pen at his head. "Jerk."

"Just doing my job," he replied, his pager vibrating on his belt. "Someone is in need of my barbaric methods of medicine. Leave the file, and I'll pick it up when I get back. You know I'm better at consults than Brody anyway." With a wink, he strolled down the hallway toward the elevators as a nurse approached the desk.

"Did Dr. Wellington leave?" she asked.

"Can you smell the overbearing odor of his cologne?" Channing asked.

"Not very well."

"Then he's gone," Channing confirmed. "Do you need him for something?"

"I had a few questions regarding the drug choices for Dr. Brody's patient."

Channing was intrigued. She would love to be involved in one of Brody's cases. Seizing the opportunity, she probed the nurse for more information. "Is that the one shrouded in secrecy? No one seems to know anything about her, including the staff."

The nurse looked around nervously. "We were all told not to speak about her case to anyone. There are even special nurses that Dr. Wellington handpicked to attend to her care. I think it's weird that a nurse specializing in home care is looking after her, but he makes the rules, not me."

The mention of a home-care nurse intrigued Channing. "Are there unauthorized personnel caring for a patient in this facility? That's not possible."

"She was on staff until a few years ago, when she was let go for questionable practices. Mysteriously, both Dr. Brody and Dr. Wellington got it overturned for her to be back as the charge nurse on this case. Dr. Brody chose her as the home nurse, and Dr. Wellington transferred her back here when the girl was admitted. It's all too confusing, if you ask me, so I just work my shift and don't ask questions."

Jotting down a quick note, Channing felt she could get away with two more questions before the nurse shut her down. "What questionable practices?"

"I wasn't privy to the details, but the gossip is that she had issues giving the wrong drugs, and lawsuits were pending. Seems she also had a mean streak. I heard from someone in the locker room that she liked to withhold pain meds until patients begged. Made her feel powerful."

"Would you mind pulling up the patient's record? Sounds like a fascinating case," Channing asked, feeling lucky.

Sensing that her job could be terminated if she interfered, the nurse logged off in the records program. "I can't do that, Dr. Bradley. Procedure dictates that you have to be asked by one of the assigned doctors on this case as a consult, and I don't have authorization to show you anything pertaining to this patient."

"Bravo, Laura! Five bonus points to your overall total!" Graham shouted, having snuck up behind the two women. "Stealing patients is a criminal offense."

"I'm not stealing anything, Wellington. I know you're stumped, or else you wouldn't be here. You like to get in, write orders, be the hero, and get out. Something must be above your head, or you wouldn't be here at such a late hour. Spill your guts, and let me help you." She stared into his eyes. "Is it too difficult to receive help from a woman?"

Considering her offer, Graham paused. "Tell you what, Bradley; it's blatantly obvious that you need something to occupy your time, so I'll throw you a bone. You can consult if it means that I can go home for a decent night's sleep. Besides, I wouldn't want you to get bored and take up knitting or some other mundane girly hobby."

He reached over the desk and typed his password into the computer system, retrieving Tamara's records. Deep down he knew that Brody wouldn't mind the added assistance if it meant success, but as a close personal friend, he knew it would create a mountain of insecurity within him. Regardless of egos or personal feelings, the final outcome had to be the health of the patient. He entered Dr. Bradley's code in the system, allowing her access as he threw the chart at her. "Get back to me with any questions. I'll alert the nursing staff that you are available for questions. Before you make any decisions regarding treatment, ask me first. There are a couple of unconventional issues that you should be aware of."

She cut him off. "Like the employment of a terminated staff member?"

Raising his eyebrows in her direction, Graham's curiosity was piqued. Her question confirmed a leak that needed to be sealed. "Where did you hear that?"

"A little birdie," she admitted. "You can't do that, Wellington. Last I checked, you weren't God."

Graham was quick to return the rebuff. "I know I'm not God, Bradley. I'm better looking!"

Though crass, his sense of humor broke the serious nature of their conversation long enough to allow her to refocus her attention to the patient. "Point made, Wellington. Continue your dissertation."

Crossing his arms in front of his chest, Graham rolled his shoulders back in an effort to appear more dignified. "I won't go into details now, since you seem to be getting plenty from the nursing staff. Pour over my notes, her records, add into the equation the chatter from the locker room and we'll have one hell of a breakfast meeting. Can't wait to hear what you come up with. As for me, I'm going home." He brushed past her, grazing her right elbow, which lay on top of the desk. The sensation of even the smallest part of her body gave him tingles. It was the primary reason he never shook hands with her. His attraction to her was dangerous for him to admit. "One final question: you on call tonight?"

Her focus moved from the medical chart. "No, I'm not."

"You are now! Thanks for the consult, Bradley. You're a peach! See you in the morning! By the way, I take my coffee with a small amount of creamer." He pointed his two index fingers at her in a gun shape as he backed down the hall. Before she could object to the sudden change in plans, his cell phone rang. "Oops, there's my date." He waved at her, shouting, "See ya later!

Channing watched him saunter down the hall until he slipped out of sight. She wanted to hate him, but knew that if her involvement in this case led to a victory, she could add another feather in her cap. Looking at the paper in front of her, she scanned the laboratory documents. There were results for toxins, liver disease, kidney disease, heart disease, cancer; the list was staggering for each system of the body. Yet each test failed to reveal any conclusive evidence for diagnosis, other than acute organ failure. Many diseases hold the potential for full-body surrender, like this young girl's. This challenge made medicine invigorating, and after reading a majority of the chart, she was itching to begin.

Quietly approaching Tamara's room, she stopped at the door to solidify the names of all involved personnel. Cracking open the door, a woman's harsh voice echoed toward the door.

"Come on, Princess, if you won't open your mouth, I'll force it open for you."

"No more, Daphne, please. I don't like that stuff. It makes me feel like I'm going to die," a small voice squeaked out.

A hearty laugh escaped. "You *are* dying, princess. I'm just trying to make it go faster. *Now open up!*"

Channing threw back the curtain by the door to see Daphne pressing a vile of clear fluid to Tamara's lips. "Just what do you think you're doing?" she demanded.

Unaware that a doctor would be looking in on her, Daphne panicked. She placed the vile in the pocket of her scrubs as she rose up off the bed. "Do you have authorization to see this patient?" she snarled.

Moving toward the bedside in one large step, Dr. Bradley looked Daphne straight in the eye. "I have more authority than you could ever imagine. What are you trying to do here?"

Daphne narrowed her eyes. "The medication that Dr. Brody and Dr. Wellington scripted. It's all there in the chart, if you're able to read."

Placing a gentle touch to Tamara's forehead, Channing felt beads of perspiration. Having a young daughter at home, her motherly instincts took control. She was no longer a consult; she needed to protect this child. "I'm sorry, Tamara; this is probably all a little bit scary. I'm Dr. Channing Bradley. Dr. Wellington asked me to assist in your case. Your nurse and I are going to speak for a minute outside, and then you and I can have a chat." Tamara smiled, grateful for her intrusion.

Turning her attention back to Daphne, Channing grabbed her elbow, leading her forcibly from the room. "A chat in the hall, if you please."

Once outside the door, Daphne yanked her elbow out of Channing's grasp. "No one touches me."

Channing sternly addressed her behavior. "Given the manner in which you were administering medication, I assume that you *are* the employee who was terminated for misconduct. We don't treat anyone in such a manner, and if I witness that behavior once more, you will be thrown out on your ass. Secondly, there isn't any script in the file that shows an oral medication. What you were attempting to force down her throat?" Channing paused. "Choose your words wisely."

Daphne stood her ground. She wasn't afraid of anyone, least of all some stuffy doctor who liked to speak as though she were superior to everyone around her. She remained confident that her position would not be altered, and she answered Channing's questions without fear of consequence. "I call that a victory. People often discuss my life in jealous tones. I believe you might need glasses, because the script is there in Brody's hand from the original orders." Daphne took a step closer. "As a bonus, no matter who assigns you to assist, I don't answer to you."

Taking a deep breath, Channing slammed the chart shut and returned to the nurse's station. "You're full of sass, aren't you? For your information, Dr. Wellington's order from last week to halt all previous meds overrides Dr. Brody's original scripts. If you need to return to nursing school to reeducate yourself on the basics, we won't hold your position. There will be a qualified nurse to replace you."

Daphne's mind whizzed through the chart engrained in her memory. She hadn't noticed that change, or she would have altered it. She had become complacent in the hospital setting, and with Channing watching her every move, she would need to play at a higher level. "I must have missed that. I must need a night off. I'll rest up and come back tomorrow with a brighter outlook."

"How about with a new attitude, or you won't be back at all?" Channing suggested.

"You like to talk big, but you can't do anything about me. I'm here to stay. I know people in high places," Daphne quipped.

Hearing the threat, Channing could think of but one rebuttal. "Trust me; the people I know are higher than you imagine."

Daphne took two steps closer to Channing, refusing to back down. "Honey, it doesn't get any higher than the people I associate with."

Marching down the hall, she felt Channing's stare as she slipped the rubber stopper back onto the vile in her pocket. One skipped dose won't kill her. "But the rest of them will." She smiled. Given the surprising addition to Tamara's medical staff, a late-night phone call to the proper authority was imperative. An occupied stairwell forced her to hide in the shadows.

"You've got me!" Graham cheerfully announced into his cell.

"Who have I got?"

He didn't immediately recognize the male voice or the accent, which caused Graham to respond with his own question. "Whom have I got?"

A thick East European accent responded. "I'm sorry, but I'm calling for Dr. Wellington. My secretary gave me this number, but it must be incorrect. Sorry to have bothered you."

Graham realized his mistake before the disconnection. "Dr. Maier? This is Dr. Wellington! I'm sorry; I was expecting your call, but not at this hour. I thought you were someone else."

A quiet chuckle came through the phone. "A caller of the female persuasion, I presume? If I recall correctly, the ladies did flock to your charisma."

Graham felt a blush in his cheeks, as a night during a trip to Vienna flooded his memory. "Why is it that people always remember me for my actions *out* of the medical arena and not for my talents *in* it?"

"Don't worry, Dr. Wellington. It most likely stems from the jealousy that you are so proficient at both," he teased. "Your message was marked urgent. How may I assist you?"

Graham sat down on the landing of the stairwell. "Are you still working in pathology?" he asked.

"I am wrapping up research on a newly discovered airborne pathogen for the World Health Organization. Seems the nasty bugger has reared its head in some small villages, and we are trying to determine if it is a highly evolved super bug, or lab created and released as an experiment," Maier stated.

"Lab created and released?" Graham asked. "What organization would claim victory for such an act?"

Maier snickered. "You would be amazed what people are capable of with the right motivation, Dr. Wellington. I assume you have an issue that requires my expertise?"

"Do you have time to take a look at a case? I'm stumped. I've run every lab imaginable and can't figure out the culprit. I have multisystem failure without a clear indicator of infection or disease."

A brief moment of silence occurred as Maier made his decision. "Is the patient stable?"

"For the time being. This thing likes to come and go. It's like fighting a ghost."

"Is the patient stable enough to travel?" Maier asked.

Jumping to his feet at the mere thought of transporting Tamara anywhere, Graham answered. "No way! It was touch and go getting her to the hospital from her house. I can't move her again until she has made strides toward recovery."

"That poses a problem, Dr. Wellington. For now, send me her chart, and I will see what I can come up with. I don't make promises, and it will take me a few days to assess the situation. I hope she isn't too critical that I can't use a careful eye to read through her information."

Graham slapped the concrete wall in a high five gesture. "That's terrific, Dr. Maier! I appreciate any advice you have, and I should mention that this isn't originally my case. Dr. Brody handed it off to me while he is out of town."

Dr. Maier cleared his throat. "Dr. Mitchell Brody? I adore him. You always did make a tremendous duo. I knew it from the moment we met at that conference years ago. You two wanted to conquer the world! Have you?"

Graham laughed. "Not yet, sir."

"No doubt you will. E-mail me the records and her background. I'll call you back in a few days," Maier stated, ending their conversation.

Graham shoved the phone back into his lab coat, skipping down the stairs two by two. He felt as if a gigantic weight had been lifted off his shoulders with the addition of Bradley and now Maier. If he and Brody couldn't crack this case, then those two would. He breathed a deep sigh of relief as he pushed open the door to the first floor, prepared to begin his first worry-free night in days.

Emerging from the shadows, Daphne overheard every tidbit of the conversation. Recognizing Graham's voice, she listened more carefully, in case he had finally been able to reach Brody. His questions regarding Tamara made her nervous. He was never one to ask for outside help, or to admit that he couldn't figure something out, yet he had done both. Watching his jovial bounce down the steps, she removed her own cell phone from her pocket and dialed.

"Yes, Precious One, what are you worried about now?"

The endearment threw her concentration. "Why are you being nice to me?"

"'Precious One' is what I call the cat before I kick her. The same goes for you. What do you want?"

"There's a new doctor on the case. Graham included her as a consult, and she stopped me from giving Tamara the vile tonight. She's a pain in the ass. Plus, the nurses are gossiping about my past indiscretions. I can't hide here very well."

A sigh filled the line. "Your tedium is annoying, Daphne, and I didn't bring you on because I valued that quality. Stop your bitching and do your job. I have always taken care of you in the past, and I do not plan on altering that now. That is, if you don't press too much."

Annoyed for showing weakness, Daphne asked, "What do I do now?"

"Play nice, and remember one important fact: Everyone is disposable, Daphne. Even you."

Daphne closed the phone tightly, holding it up to her mouth in astonishment. For the first time in her life, she felt afraid.

19

Trembling fingers ran the length of a metal chain hanging around her neck, with the tips tracing each intricate detail of the diamond-inlaid crescent moon. This timely heirloom had been passed down to each worthy female in her family for the last ten generations. Some desired it, but lacked the focus to achieve it, while other members were born with the ability to see past the diamonds into what the pendent represented. The lucky few wore it until their own daughters were awarded the honor. Tears rained upon the gold chain as she fought against the possibility that her daughter would never get the opportunity to wear this piece of history. She was coming into the age where she should be addressing her talents along with ancient wisdom, but this illness halted any hopes for her future. The thought of not being able to watch her daughter grow into a woman, fall in love, have a wedding, or give birth to her own child was too much to fathom. She wept for the tragedy that swirled around her only child.

A gentle voice whispered through her sobs. "Lillian? Tell me how I can help you."

Resting her body against the wall, she didn't feel that she could stand any longer. Hearing the serene voice echo in her head, she succumbed to the traumatic state, slumping into a pool onto the floor. She wanted her vibrant, loving daughter back.

"Oh my God, Lillian!" the voice shouted as two strong hands lifted her back into a vertical position. "Lillian, can you hear me?"

Dropping her hands from the necklace, she raised her head to see who had spoken. An unknown woman held her frail body in her arms, her brown eyes reflecting a tender kindness. Lillian instantly recognized the characteristics of compassion, empathy, and determination in the woman's eyes—three traits they shared in common.

Stepping out of the woman's grasp, Lillian replied, "Stress certainly exacts a price." She attempted to brush the wrinkles out of the clothes she had been wearing over the last few days, afraid to go home in case Tamara took an even graver turn. Tucking a few stray hairs behind her ears, she hid the necklace from view beneath her blouse. "Do I know you?" she asked.

"My name is Dr. Channing Bradley. Dr. Wellington asked me for a consult on your daughter's case. I came searching for you to get some answers to questions regarding your daughter."

Her bright smile and calm demeanor created an instantaneous trust. This first impression gave Lillian the feeling she had whenever Mitch was around: a feeling of safety, knowing that everything would work out. Like a badge of honor, Channing Bradley carried instant trustworthiness.

"Is Tamara OK?" Lillian asked frantically.

Channing calmed Lillian's quivering hand. "She's resting comfortably. I have a few questions regarding family history as well as her latest treatments with Dr. Brody. Can you spare a few minutes?"

Lillian nodded as Channing led her toward a bank of chairs. The hour was late, and the area deserted. Lillian felt comfortable enough to open up and be honest for the first time in months.

Opening the medical chart, Channing clicked her pen, preparing to take notes. "Let's tackle big issues first. Any history of heart disease, liver disease, cancer, stroke, or heart attack?"

Briefly contemplating her family's background, Lillian forced herself to think past her current situation. "My mother fought breast cancer, my father had a fatal heart attack when I was fifteen, and other than that I'm not sure. Why?"

"I would like to get a more accurate patient history to rule out any underlying causes that we might be missing in order to properly diagnose and treat your daughter."

"You think there is something Mitch and Graham overlooked?" Lillian asked with a new panic to her voice.

"I think we need to rule out every possibility in order for Tamara's health to return. I want to make sure that we are doing all we can for her. Please don't be alarmed, Lillian. This is something I do with all my patients, and since I didn't see these things mentioned in her chart, I thought I should ask," Channing stated.

Lillian ran fingers through her disheveled hair. "It doesn't surprise me that there isn't a family history in her records. Mitch has known Tamara since birth, and he has been an extended member of my family since childhood. He was there when my father died, and he was instrumental in getting my mother the right care for her breast cancer. I don't know what we would have done without him."

"Did your mother die from breast cancer?"

"She died as she intended, in her house, at the age she wanted, with all her good-byes said. It seemed strange to me, growing up, that my mother knew when she would die. It used to creep me out a little. In the end it was exactly how she had described it. Cancer had nothing to do with it," Lillian stated casually.

Quickly writing as much information as she could, Channing knew that an intriguing account of Lillian's beliefs required a deeper explanation. But it would consume too much precious time at the moment. A different conversation at a later date would be a better fit. "Do you know of any other serious illnesses in your family?"

Lillian shook her head, "I would have to look it up in my mother's book. She kept a record of that kind of thing with our genealogy. Said she wanted to know what she had to look forward to." She chuckled at her last remark. "Too bad she never saw this coming."

"Saw what coming?"

"Tamara's illness. She used to tell me that Tamara was destined for great things, that she would come into her own at a fairly young age, but never saw this demise. I wish she would have at least warned me about this."

Making a few more notes, Channing placed her pen on top of the chart. "You keep saying your mother 'saw' things. Can you define that?"

Wringing her hands, Lillian feared she had revealed too much. Still feeling somewhat safe in Channing's presence, though, she continued. "She was an intuitive. All the women in my family have been to an extent. They have the ability to converse with spirit as well as convey information pertaining to future events."

Channing couldn't help but notice the nervous manner in which Lillian used her hands. "Intuitive? I'm sorry if this sounds insensitive, but is that similar to a fortuneteller?"

"Good God, no!" Lillian exclaimed. "My family has a gift of knowledge that very few people come into contact with on a daily basis. It tends to make people uncomfortable to talk about in the open, but mark my words: they come running for advice regarding their lives when they know it's behind closed doors. Everyone wants to know what their future holds; they just don't want to do it where other people judge them."

"You know, I went to a fortuneteller once who was dressed up like a gypsy with a crystal ball at a state fair when I was twelve. She told me that I would change lives, and then she charged me a dollar. Madam Mystic, I think she called herself," Channing admitted. "Is it like that?"

"The people who travel like that tend to feed off the public's curiosity as they mock the true gift others possess. Gives the authentic ones a bad name." Lillian looked down at her feet, hoping that Tamara's name would not be mentioned in reference to this art. She preferred that this new doctor not treat Tamara any differently because of her personal beliefs regarding her abilities.

Leaning a bit closer, Channing asked, "Is that why Tamara has secrecy around her case, because she is gifted?"

Proceeding cautiously with her next statement, Lillian smiled. "My mother recognized Tamara's gifts early. She possesses a power I don't fully understand yet, and I'm her own mother."

Channing's mind swam with questions as a nurse interrupted their dialogue. "I'm sorry to interrupt you, Dr. Bradley. The lab results from this morning are ready. You told me to get them to you right away." She added nervously, "Plus, your husband is holding on line one."

Tucking the chart under one arm, Channing made her apologies to Lillian. "Would it be crass of me to ask if we could pick up where we left off later?"

Lillian agreed to a future meeting. Her attention shifted as she watched Earl quietly slip down the hall. Given the direction he was headed, he had to have come from Tamara's room, and he seemed in a hurry to get to his new location. She followed quickly as he darted past nurses on their way to other patients in the wing, past loved ones leaving the hallway after a late-night visit, ducking into a small waiting room at the end of the hall. The door was marked as a surgical waiting room.

Entering the vacant room, he extinguished lamps decorating three side tables. Leaving a single one lit, he sat down on an oversized chair and removed a leather-bound book from his coat pocket. Lillian watched him open the book, dialing a number on his cell phone. Turning his back to retrieve a dropped object, Lillian recognized an opportunity to creep into the room, hiding in one of the darkened corners. "Hey, Ted, its Earl. I've got some new information for you."

"Wait a sec, let me grab my notebook."

Earl looked round the room nervously for any sudden movement. "We've got to get this going!"

"OK, OK I'm ready. She must have given you some more?" Ted asked.

"Just you wait, Teddy boy! The episodes are becoming more frequent, and her visions are superb. They are taking on dimensions I never imagined. It's thrilling, to say the least. Let me put you on speakerphone so I can see my notes better." Lillian's blood boiled. "Can you hear me clearly?" Earl asked.

"Yes. The last time we spoke, you mentioned that the latest vision was of Glastonbury."

"You're correct. You have most of the vision with the exception of the last bit, which is, of course, the most critical. The young boy spoke to her, actually spoke to her, Ted!" Earl exclaimed.

"So, not only is she having visions of historical events, but now the events are speaking to her?" Ted asked, slightly confused.

"Exactly! And the people in the visions are giving her information regarding current people and events. In my experience, this has never happened before! There is a mind, body, spirit connection here that has yet to be documented. We are on the precipice of a new era in historical research," Earl announced.

Ted cut him off. "You can't define it as research, Earl. There isn't a historian or academic who would consider her accounts credible as tangible evidence to support the claims, no matter how much they differ. They'll say she's a girl who has dreams that are alternative conclusions to historical events and nothing more."

"Sounds to me like you've already been speaking to these so-called academics," Earl interjected.

"I'm not disloyal, Earl, just concerned. I kicked the idea around to a few people. This isn't just your reputation on the line anymore. I prefer not to be remembered as some quack who lost position at the University level due to this theory. There has to be viable data to silence the nay Sayers. You know that." Ted admitted.

"What about Edgar Cayce? He had psychic visions and interpretations and wasn't labeled anything other than credible."

Ted chuckled. "Cayce! They labeled him dangerous from the beginning and discredited him on multiple levels. Plus, he wasn't attempting to rewrite textbooks with a notebook full of dreams from a young girl."

Earl tapped his pen on the page, absorbing the advice from his old colleague. "She has one thing Cayce didn't. Her visions aren't in a controlled environment where they can be corrupted by outside influence. That's what they said about Cayce. Her visions are the product of a clear channel during sleep. She can't be influenced or manipulated while she's sleeping."

Clearing his throat, Ted answered, "They will respond that during a sleep cycle her brain could be manipulated to produce these visions, or that they are the manifestation of her subconscious brain releasing information that she was told. I think we could explain those points without scrutiny, but the more pressing matter is the communication from the visions directly. That could be a little trickier to explain as they attempt to discredit us all."

"Run it through your brain and give me all the differing perspectives," Earl demanded.

Ted ran his thoughts fluently. "Clearly there's a stronger spiritual connection developing that we overlooked. I didn't think it could happen, but it has a substance to it that could be groundbreaking. It's going to make one hell of a published article, not to mention the fact that history and religion could be altered forever."

"Not an article, old friend, think bigger. I see a book or two with all of this. My little Tamara is going to secure my retirement," Earl announced. "By the way, did you hear back from the publishing house?"

"No, but I did hear from an interesting fellow this week. Said his name was Rothschild and that he had read some of your preliminary theories regarding Tamara's case and was intrigued. He's been following another young lady with the same propensity, only at a lower level, for ten years. He said he wanted to speak to you personally, said he could shed some light on some questions you might have."

"That's remarkable, Ted! Should we send him our most recent notes on Tamara and ask his opinion?" Earl suggested.

"I have another call. E-mail me your current notes, and I'll see about getting them to this Rothschild fellow."

"I'm still at the hospital, but I'll e-mail them to you first thing in the morning. Did this guy say where he was from?" Earl could hear Ted's other phone line ringing in the background.

"Somewhere in Europe, I think. I don't remember the country. I've got to go. Talk to you tomorrow."

Earl breathed a deep sigh of relief at the chance that his theory with Tamara would be taken seriously. Standing up to leave the room, a resurgence of energy flowed through his body. The outline of a woman in the doorway halted his departure abruptly. Leaning toward the closest table, Earl switched on the lamp to reveal Lillian with a look he had not seen before.

"Lillian! Is Tamara OK?" he asked anxiously.

"Cut the crap, Earl! I sincerely hope that wasn't Ted Knickerbocker from Boston University on the phone. He'll be in a world of hurt with the history department when I get through with him," she warned.

Earl would have to tread carefully. A scorned woman could make a fire-breathing dragon afraid, and a mother protecting her offspring could defeat any creature great or small. "Lillian, we were having a friendly chat about Tamara. You know how unique she is, combined with the fact that she has valuable information to share with the world. Surely you wouldn't deny humankind the lessons she could teach!" he proposed.

Lillian resisted the urge to punch him between the eyes. "You know, Earl, I didn't say a word when you paraded all those so-called professionals around Tamara when she was younger, under the guise of research. I even held my tongue when they turned their findings into a witch-hunt of my daughter by labeling her a freak with developmental insufficiencies. But I will not allow you to financially benefit from her after all she has suffered. I don't care how close you have been to this family. This ends now."

Earl sat down with a loud thump. "Lillian, think about this clearly for a minute. With the publication of this information, I will deify Tamara. I can recant those professionals' opinions and theories. She will be a star!" Earl knew the comment was a long shot as soon as he uttered it.

"You believe she wants to be a star? She wants to be normal! She wants to be a kid who goes to school without others pointing and laughing. She wishes she could walk through a mall without people whispering behind her back. It's her time to come into her own power, not continue to have her differences publicized." Lillian ripped his coat open, tearing the journal from his pocket. "This journal represents her trust in you, and you want to capitalize from it! The thought makes me sick! But more importantly, *you* make me sick. How dare you do this to people who have loved and trusted you?"

Guilt suddenly overtook him. Tamara only trusted Earl as someone to convey her visions to. He couldn't deny their special relationship, yet he could not deny that she had the ability to alter preconceived ideas. "I have the right to say whether her story should be told. And I know you don't want to hear this, but if she doesn't make it, she can live on through our work."

Lillian threw the journal, narrowly missing his temple. "How dare you even suggest that she won't survive! She has to survive! *She will survive!*" Tears welled up in her eyes. "There isn't any other option. Mitch will fix it; he always does. *He'll fix it!*" she screamed.

Earl reached for her hand. "What if he can't, sweetie? We have to prepare for Tamara's life purpose to be fulfilled some other way." He tried to convince her as he squeezed her hand. "I can make that happen."

Lillian allowed him to touch her regardless of the anger. She couldn't deny that he had been the one by her side through it all. His loyalty was undeniable, and deep down she knew that he really did love Tamara. "I can't give that outcome any energy. I have to continue to love her and stay positive. That's what she needs."

Earl purposefully mentioned a sore point. "What does Tom say about all of this?"

She forcibly wiped the tears from her cheeks. "He's away on business, and I can't get hold of him. He left right before Mitch and said he'd be back next week."

"Where is he this time?" Earl probed.

"I don't know. He keeps it all pretty secret," Lillian confessed.

"Shame that with his daughter ill, he can't alter his business plans," Earl suggested.

Lillian recognized his attempt to bait her into switching her anger to Tom. "Tom's business is important. He doesn't know she's taken this turn. This is *my* problem, and *my* responsibility, not his."

"He's her parent too, Lillian. Don't assume all the burden if you don't need to. Tom has broad shoulders to lean on. Use them."

She pulled away from him, backing up a few feet. "Tamara has always been *my* responsibility, which has nothing to do with the number of parents she possesses."

Feeling immense sorrow, Earl looked at her broken form. "Lillian, you put that on yourself. Your mother would never have put that kind of pressure on herself or you."

His casual mention of her mother jogged her out of her tear-filled haze. "My mother knew this. She knew it all. She and I discussed it several times. I take this responsibility *very* seriously. I was chosen. This is *my* path, *our* path together."

"I didn't mean to insult you. I know how serious you are about Tamara and how deeply you love her. I believe that on some level, it's your love that keeps her here. A mother's love is a distinct bond that can't be explained. I merely implied that you can share the obligation with Tom as your partner," Earl said, trying to make amends for the bridges he may have just burned.

Lillian stared Earl in the eye and smoothed stray hairs back into place with her palm. Their conversation reminded her of a promise she had made before Tamara was born—a promise she made while praying on bruised knees for a child during infertility treatments. "I don't care what anyone thinks, Earl. Tamara is *my* daughter, *my* responsibility, *my* love. It is a holy obligation that is misunderstood by everyone and recognized by no one." Walking toward the door, she grasped the hard wood with her right hand. Before slamming it shut, she glanced back toward Earl. "Having a child means wearing your heart on the outside of your body at all times. It isn't something to be taken lightly. And I won't allow you to steal mine any longer."

Earl felt the room rattle from the force of the door slamming shut. For the first time since being introduced to this family thirty years ago, he felt the pang of loss at their potential absence. For the first time in thirty years, he hung his head and wept.

20

*L*it from above, her lifeless body cast a heavenly silhouette. Dim lights around the room hid the crocodile tears of sorrow as they streamed down the cheeks of her family. Two nurses flanked the bed, turning off the machines on either side. As the screens darkened, their crying turned to wailing despair. One nurse exited the room while the one who remained gently laid Tamara's hands across her stomach. Leaning toward her patient one last time, she whispered a small prayer and tiptoed out of the room. Lillian rushed to the bed, throwing herself on her deceased daughter's body. Kissing her head, hugging her tightly, and singing their nighttime lullaby, she wept for the tragic demise of the love of her life. No mother should have to bury her child, she sobbed into the atmosphere.

While parent and child shared a final embrace, a new light appeared above the bed, casting a brighter glow. The new illumination brought a re-newed sense of peace to the barren room. A feeling of love increased in such a dramatic way that tears flowed free without any replacements. Lillian laid her daughter back on the bed as she continued to sing their special song. With each lofty note, an invisible, silvery cord ascended from Tamara's body. Higher and higher it climbed, until it breached the ceiling, seeming to stretch far beyond it. With a small tug from above, Tamara sat up in her bed, alight with the ceiling's glow. She looked at her mother, rocking and singing, and at Earl, who sat in the corner crying. Reaching out to touch her mother, she was unable to feel the sensation of skin-to-skin contact. Hovering above her bed, she shared *her good-byes with her mother and Earl, preparing to ascend into the peaceful light above.*

The overwhelming peace urged her to fly out the window, shouting its presence to anyone who had the ability to listen. Smiling at the release of pain and turmoil from her body, she watched the hem of her white dress billow as if in a pool of water. Before reaching the ceiling, the cord halted without warning. Prompted from above, Tamara turned toward the doorway. Drifting slightly toward the door, she whispered to the man standing on the threshold. "I can't hold on much longer. They've come for me."

"*No!*" Mitch exclaimed, ignoring the pain from his abdomen.

"There, there, doctor man. Lay back down. We aren't through with you yet," a female voice whispered.

Startled by the dream, Mitch was unaware of his surroundings. Before his loss of conscious thought, he felt that he too was dying. With his mind still fuzzy, he was unable to distinguish reality from fantasy. He hadn't spoken to Graham in days, and the possibility that Tamara had passed could be a reality. Even though he had never given any real credibility to the powers above, Mitch offered up a silent prayer for Tamara.

"Bad dream, huh? Or maybe you're a screamer? Which is it, bad or screamer? Important information to have at our fingertips should more delicate matters such as these present themselves. Or you anger the wrong person during interrogation."

Blinking his eyes into focus, Mitch gazed into Gillian's brilliant blue eyes. It took him a moment to register who she was as he felt her fluttering hands on his stomach.

"Gillian?" he asked.

"I was afraid that after this whole drama, you might have a touch of amnesia. Glad to see you back among the land of the living."

"Where am I?" he asked, scanning the room they occupied.

"Pip's house. Duncan said to bring you here for safekeeping. Don't worry; you've had excellent medical attention," she casually remarked.

Mitch's mind raced with questions. "Wait a sec. How does Duncan have the resources for medical attention to come see me? And furthermore, who the hell were those people at the train station, and why was I in their car? How long have I been out? And—"

Gillian raised both hands, shielding her from the barrage of questions. "Whoa, cowboy, hold on a second. I'm done here, so I'll go get Pip. You're supposed to be resting. If you get yourself in a lather and rip open those sutures, I'll do you in myself." She stood up from the chair and walked across the room. Before closing it behind her, she made one final demand. "Do not get out of that bed. You're still pretty delicate."

Mitch smiled. It felt good to see her again. Her eyes had a way of making him nervous and joyful at the same time. Taking the opportunity to survey his surroundings, Mitch noticed that the room held an element of cheer. It was elegant, without being overstated, feminine without being over the top, and most importantly, comfortable. The walls were painted a medium blue, with curtains framing the large windows in a sunny yellow with shades of blue flowers. Underneath the window sat a wooden storage bench with cushions in coordinating blue-and-yellow plaid fabric, and throw pillows in blue, gold, red, and green dotting the top of the bench. On the floor, next to the bench, sat his briefcase. Mitch breathed a sigh of relief. The realization that he had risked his own life for the case's objects hit him like a ton of bricks. He had never risked his life for anything before, yet now he was willing to do so without question. It was a change he never saw coming.

The queen-sized bed was the height of comfort, with a goose-down feather bed atop the mattress. Footsteps signaled Pip's arrival as Mitch turned his head toward the door. A maple rocking chair next to the door caught his eye. He wondered if she had sat in the chair, rocking through the night, watching him sleep. The thought of being in her presence brought tingles of excitement shooting through his pain-riddled body.

Without warning, the door flew open. Instead of the usual ponytail, her golden hair hung beside her face, with loose curls at the end. A smile plastered on her face, Pip entered the room with her typical swagger, dressed in jeans and a navy T-shirt promoting the phrase, "Keep Calm and Carry on." Recognizing the immortal quote of Winston Churchill during World War II, he laughed at how fitting it was to both her personality and his own situation.

"Well, well, Sleeping Beauty is finally awake! Man, when you do drama, you *really* do drama. Dunc can't hold a candle to you. Bit jealous, I think." Pip sat down in the rocking chair.

"It's true; I like a bit of flair." He laughed, staring into her slate-blue-gray eyes.

Pip threw her head back in laughter. He enjoyed watching her laugh. Her entire face lit up in pure bliss. "Brody, you are a wild man! I hadn't the foggiest notion that you would go to such extremes to get your information, or salvage what he gave you." She pointed to the briefcase. "It's commendable."

"I like your shirt."

Pulling the cotton fabric away from her skin, she viewed the white words upside down. "Fitting, isn't it? Good old Churchill. He was a brave bugger, just like you. Maybe you're related," she suggested. "How are you feeling, by the way? I haven't seen Daddy in a state like that since I almost set the hotel on fire at the ripe old age of ten."

Mitch's discomfort came in the form of stiffness through each muscle. His body felt like a ten-thousand-ton brick had been placed on top, without any relief. Not wishing to seem weak, he played down his injuries. "There is a small amount of pain from the gunshot, and I'm a little sore all over, but nothing major. Could use something to eat."

"Doctor said no solids until he checks you tomorrow. I'll have the twins make you up some broth. Gillian's been feeding you for the last few days. She's tremendous!"

"Feeding me?" he asked, concerned by the thought of how they had been nourishing him.

"She treated you like a wounded animal, using a syringe filled with homemade broth to feed you like a baby bird. She's good at it. The doctor cleared it since we didn't have an IV set up and we didn't want to draw any unnecessary attention to ourselves by renting more equipment. We kept it at a minimum, with the ultrasound device being the last to go. But the doctor said when he comes tomorrow, he'll take it with him. He still wants to double-check your gunshot wound."

"You actually have a credentialed physician looking after me? It's not some country bumpkin who plays around with medicine as a hobby?" he teased.

"Country medicine, my ass! When the call initially came in, I assumed you had a superficial wound to your arm or leg. I never imagined that you were given a fatal blow to vital organs. We were lucky."

Mitch felt the layers of bandages across his midsection. "Lucky, indeed. Mind if I ask some questions?"

"Gil said you were eager to get started. Shoot." She placed her feet on the side of the bed, with the rocker poised in a comfortable reclining position.

"How about being shot by an old friend at a false location? How in the hell did that happen?" he asked, failing at hiding the anger in his voice.

"We're just as confused. No one on our side sent that guy to you; nor do we have any clue who he is. You'll have to fill in the blanks in that department. First, who was it that shot you?"

Mitch snorted at her cavalier attitude. "I went to medical school with him. He was the last person in the world that I would assume to threaten my life. His name's Julian Kingman and disappeared quicker than I could out of that church. I have absolutely no clue where he would be now."

"Was the church the first time you've seen him since med school?" she probed.

"No. He approached me on the train down to London after you dropped me off. He said he was here for a World Health Organization conference, and he was going to London for downtime. I thought he was OK, so I mentioned I was going sightseeing and suggested we should do it together. I didn't think too far beyond that," Mitch replied calmly.

"What happened after that?"

"We got to London, I had my room still open at the Ritz, we stayed there, and the next day we went to Glastonbury."

"He accompanied you to the Abbey?"

"He came with me to the Abbey, but never went beyond the chapel walls, if that's what you're worried about."

"Did he meet the teacher?"

"Yeah, but she never revealed her identity to either one of us. Hell, I don't know anything other than the credentials she rattled off."

"Did he see what was written on the paper she gave you?"

Shaking his head, Mitch replied, "She never gave me any paper. I got a message from her the next morning telling me where to meet the next teacher. I went to Southwark, not knowing who to expect when Bridget showed up first."

Who's Bridget?" she asked, deep wrinkles appearing on her forehead.

"She's one of the front-desk clerks from the Ritz. Whenever I stay there, she flirts with me, and when I first saw her, I assumed she was there to proposition me, but she mentioned that she was one of the teachers. She acted like she knew what she was talking about, so I didn't question her involvement."

"How does Julian play into this scenario?"

"Bridget told me that another teacher was arriving to instruct me on the hidden symbols in the cathedral, which is when Julian appeared. I was confused, but nothing on this excursion has been anything other than confusing, so I trusted him. It couldn't have been an accident that we bumped into each other on the train. I didn't suspect anything was wrong until Duncan called."

"Daddy called, flushed the bunny from the bushes, you got shot, and then what happened?"

The deep sigh Mitch breathed into his lungs caused him to wince with pain. "I spoke to Duncan a second time, and he told me to meet a couple with a yellow car at the train station. That's when they chased me."

"I'm kind of fuzzy on that bit. Why did you run away from Quinn and Elle if Daddy told you to meet them?" Pip asked.

Mitch's recollection of the events raised his blood pressure as if he were reliving the series of dramatic sequences. "There were two couples. My phone didn't have a clear connection to hear the description, and all I heard was something about a yellow car. I wasn't clear on who was there for me until an older guy pulled a gun out of his pocket."

"Wait a minute! Two couples with yellow cars? Can you describe them?" Pip asked, producing a small notebook and pen from of her jeans pocket.

Mitch recalled every minute detail of the couples up to the chase through the village of Dunkeld for Pip, and she furiously wrote it down. When he finished his description, she placed the notebook on the bed and pursed her lips. The look of shock mixed with panic was evident across her face.

"Stroke of luck that Quinn got to you before that other bloke. I can see why you ran away. You should make amends to Quinn and Elle. They were frantic about the whole episode, and they were marvelous."

Mitch thought back to their random arguments while in the vehicle. They both seemed like novices, and he asked Pip why they were chosen to meet him.

"They're old family friends. Quinn is a Coper and always wanted an important assignment from Daddy. There wasn't anything more urgent than retrieving you, so he gave him the chance. They were on a mini holiday in London and were overjoyed to prove they were ready for tasks. They're good people, Mitch."

"Given the circumstances, they didn't seem like it, but their fights were entertaining."

Pip laughed. "Yeah, they disagree about everything! Make up better than they argue, which is how they have seven kids at home. That motherly instinct saved your life, though. Elle gave you antibiotics all the way up here and stopped most of your bleeding. She kept you alive." She watched him try to sit up. "What did we tell you about trusting people?" she reminded him.

"You told me not to. I don't know *who* to trust anymore!" he exclaimed, on the verge of shouting.

"If your feelings told you something was wrong, why didn't you listen?" she asked honestly.

Mitch didn't do feelings. After the loss of his relationship with Brooke, he kept every feeling bottled up inside until the point of boiling over, when he would resort to extreme exercise to handle the stress. It wasn't exactly healthy, but it worked. "I don't know." It seemed like the safest answer.

"Truth is, you are far too trusting for your own good," she stated, directing her eyes to his bandages. "The problem here is that you're afraid to tell anyone to bugger off for fear that they might think less of you, allowing guilt to rush in. You take every Tom, Dick, and Sally for their word, even if it puts you in danger. Am I close?" she asked.

Mitch turned his head away. "Yeah, that's about right," he admitted.

"I thought so." She brushed her fingers against his chin, moving his head back toward her. "Any more juicy details you have for me concerning the church theatrics?"

Thinking about his exchange with Julian made him irate. "Come to think of it, he did say something weird. He asked me about the Professor. Is Duncan a professor?" Mitch innocently asked.

Pip's rosy complexion turned ashen white, with her eyes growing larger by the second. "What did you tell him?"

"I don't know any professor." Watching her reaction turn to horror, he asked, "Is there someone I haven't met who uses that title?"

Pip jumped from the chair. "I need to call Daddy. I'll send Gils in with the broth. You'll need your strength for the days ahead."

Her sudden desire for departure seemed out of character. "Is something wrong, Pip?" he asked.

Keeping her back toward him at the door, she bowed her head and whispered, "The game has changed," as she slammed it shut behind her. Safely outside his room, Pip placed her forehead against the wall, taking slow, deep breaths. Gillian walked down the narrow hallway toward her to attend to Mitch's recovery.

"Two steps ahead of you as usual, Pipster! Thought he might like some broth under his own strength, instead of out of some dumb syringe." Seeing Pip's position against the wall, Gillian asked, "What is it?"

Keeping her eyes locked on the flowered carpet beneath her feet, Pip relayed her conversation with Mitch. Upon hearing the name of the Professor, Gillian dropped the bowl of broth onto the floor.

"He asked specifically about the Professor?" she asked, panicking.

"Yes," Pip confirmed.

"*No one* but the inner circle knows about him. What does this mean?" she asked, raising her voice.

Pip picked up the empty bowl and placed it tenderly into the hands of her friend. "It means two things. One, I have to call Daddy, and two, we have a traitor in our midst." She stepped away. "You need more broth."

Gillian watched her friend slump down the hallway. This was a new side to Pip. Through all the scolding she endured during their adolescent adventures, she had never looked defeated. Her body reflected the stress of the situation while adding to the equation the possibility of failure. Without making any more demands of their bond, she silently walked toward the kitchen to acquire more broth for their patient.

Duncan sped along the highway with Stewart rambling away in the passenger seat. Since receiving Pip's frantic phone call, he had made a few of his own. It made sense that Pip's suggestion at an inside job was accurate. He racked his brain for anyone suspicious, but could think of no one who might fit the description. He couldn't allow Mitch to be the bait for a second attack, but in the end, the girl was the key. Unable to ignore Stewart's incessant questions any further, Duncan cut him off. "For the love of all that is holy, would you *shut it!*" he bellowed.

"Change your tone, you old poop. I'm stating facts out loud so that we might figure this out together. It's not my fault that you placed us in this predicament," Stewart remarked.

"I don't appreciate the accusation that this responsibility lays solely on my shoulders. I didn't get us into anything. Something has gotten into us. I'm trying to salvage all we have worked diligently to protect before it is lost." Duncan sighed. "Your endless chatter isn't helping."

Stewart glanced out his window. "I'm merely trying to help," he muttered under his breath.

"Try harder," Duncan suggested as they passed the same fountain Mitch had used for a hiding place several nights before. Pulling into the drive in front of Pip's cottage, Duncan addressed his friend with orders of behavior. "And for God's sake, don't let the cat out of the bag before we explain things properly. He doesn't need to know all the ins and outs of the organization and why he is here before the proper time. It will spook him back to the States. Follow my lead." Turning off the engine as Pip approached the car, he added, "You know how important this is, Stewart."

Stewart didn't like being ordered about, especially when he and Duncan were co-commanders. Duncan knew his temperament and reputation for being a hothead who spoke too much when cornered, but he didn't need to speak to him as if he were a child. Duncan may be right, but Stewart didn't have to like it.

Pip embraced her father tightly. "What do we do now, Daddy?" she whispered.

Duncan patted her back as he released his hold. "We follow the sage advice printed on your shirt. Keep Calm and Carry on. There isn't any other option."

Stewart stepped up to the pair. "Chin up, Pip. I called the others, and they are aware of the situation. The wheels of progress are in motion. Where is our young doctor?"

Pip motioned toward the house with her head. "In his room. The doctor arrived ten minutes ago to examine him. He said his recovery is remarkable. Must be those herbs that Gillian's been adding to the broth. I swear, in another life, she must have been one magnificent apothecary."

As the trio approached the white-washed Dutch door, Stewart was the first to make a suggestion on approaching their guest. "He must be told about the girl."

Duncan opened the door and led them inside. "I agree. He must know a bit. Especially with her new developments."

Stewart grabbed his arm. "And his father?" he asked.

"Maybe," Duncan told him and kept walking.

Pip left the two men to join Gillian in the kitchen. Genevieve was due any minute for their weekly poker game. The two men walked down the hall in silence, each one mentally preparing for a difficult conversation. Though each one hated to admit it, they were each scared to death at the reaction of their new young friend. They heard the final bits of dialogue between Mitch and the doctor as they approached the door to his room.

"I'm OK?" Mitch asked.

"Right as rain in a few more days. I would still like for you to rest as much as possible. No long walks or hikes anywhere, and if you feel pain or weakness, sit down. Doesn't do anyone a bit of good if you try and play the hero. Just recover."

Mitch's inquisitive medical nature took hold. "Did the bullet hit any vital organs that I should be concerned about?"

The doctor placed the wand back into its position on the hand-held ultrasound device. "You're lucky; the bullet is lodged between the intestines in a small crevice. Haven't ever seen that before in my life! Since there was no exit wound, it will have to be surgically removed sooner rather than later. Wouldn't want it to create a sepsis situation, but for right now, you're OK. Your loss of blood was substantial, but nothing that wasn't easily remedied here. We gave you a few pints when you arrived, and you've come through it nicely. When you are ready in the next couple of weeks, and everything has died down, call me and I'll remove the bullet." He handed Mitch his business card.

"You're a surgeon?" Mitch inquired, surprised at the man's credentials.

"I *am* many things, Dr. Brody. A surgeon is merely my career." He smiled as he prepared to leave. "Not bad for country medicine," he commented, slipping out the door past Stewart and Duncan in the hall. He acknowledged them with a nod of his head as they swept past him to see Mitch.

Mitch couldn't help but laugh at the doctor's joke. Pip had obviously told him the sarcastic comment he had made. He didn't have a clue what the standards of medical care were in this region; he had assumed the worst. Another reason he liked Pip—she didn't let him get away with anything. It reminded him of Brooke. Too much reminded him of Brooke on this trip.

Stewart was nothing but smiles when he saw Mitch sitting up in bed. "My boy, you look better than the women described. Why, you aren't pasty at all!"

Duncan pushed him out of the way with an elbow to his ribcage. "Don't crowd him, Stewart! I'm sure he was a bit pasty in the beginning, but his color is much improved. You must thank Gillian for all her tending to you. She really has done a marvelous job!" He sat down in the rocking chair previously occupied by his daughter as Stewart pulled a second chair up to Mitch's bedside.

"Gillian took care of me? I assumed it would be Pip," Mitch said with disappointment in his voice. He had hoped it was Pip who nursed him through the ordeal.

Stewart answered first. "Oh, she was here off and on. This is her home, you know. Safest place we could think of after she found the device on you at Dunkeld Cathedral. Gillian took care of your daily needs since she has experience in these matters."

Mitch looked confused. "What device?"

Looking nervously toward Duncan, Stewart continued, "The locator device. Didn't they tell you that they found one?"

Crossing his arms, Mitch answered, "Funny, they hadn't mentioned it yet. Why don't you two explain?"

Duncan rolled his eyes. "We will, dear boy, but first, let's discuss the Southwark incident. Did your friend Julian tell you who he was working for?"

"He mentioned an employer, but didn't give a name. He seemed distressed that he even had one. Then again, Julian never did care for people to be above him in anything." Mitch smoothed out the sheets and added, "For the record, he's not my friend."

Stewart laughed nervously. "No worries, old chum. We have our best people looking into the matter. We'll find out who's behind this in no time."

Annoyance was clear on Duncan's face as he removed the small notebook from his pocket that Pip had used earlier. "Before I ask Stewart to leave, so that we may converse privately, there is some information that only he can give you regarding Tamara."

Upon hearing her name, the hairs on the back of Mitch's neck stood on end. "Tamara? I had a disturbing dream about her. Do you know if she's OK?" he asked, anxious for any answer, good or bad.

Stewart addressed Mitch's question. "I spoke with our contact there this morning. She has stabilized a bit, but her visions have taken a new turn. She recently had one concerning you being in danger, which we were notified about right after your voice mail to Duncan. You hadn't yet been attacked, but the coincidence is astonishing." Stewart paused before he asked, "May I inquire as to the content of your dream?"

"Her soul parting from her body in a heavenly glow. It was beautiful, but frightening." Mitch recaptured the vivid light in his mind as he spoke. "Wait, you said she had a vision about me?"

"You know about her visions?" Stewart asked.

"Of course I do. I was the first person her father confided in when they began. She was five, I think, but they didn't really manifest on any regular basis until she was about seven or eight. Until that age, they just said she had historical dreams."

"And did her so-called dreams ever involve people current in her life at the time?" Stewart asked, probing for any information he had not yet been privy to.

Mitch shook his head. "No, just pictures of people in old-fashioned costumes. Her parents told me that it was like she was watching a movie."

"She had a vision pertaining to current people just before your attack. This confirms a theory we have had for a while," Duncan interjected.

"Which is what?" Mitch asked.

Stewart once again took control. "Tamara is unlike any girl we have ever come across. You now know The Three and their powers are off the charts when they are together, but apart, their abilities diminish. Always meant to be together, I suppose. Anyway, Tamara's gift is extraordinary. Her vision including you indicates that her soul has the ability to spiritually reach into current energy, entwining it with energy of the past. It is difficult enough to connect to someone on a soul level in this energy field, let alone other time periods. In addition to this rare ability, it seems that through all that you have recently been taught, your energy level has reached a point where Tamara's soul can speak to yours. It is a breakthrough that has arrived earlier than anticipated."

Mitch suddenly felt tiny in the presence of these two men. He wasn't sure if they were being entirely honest with him and their intentions toward Tamara. In her defense, he bombarded them with questions.

Duncan stretched out a hand to calm Mitch's frazzled nerves. "Hold on, son, we don't mean her harm. We were informed of the gift she possessed on the day of her birth."

"And how do you know all of this?" he shot out at them.

Stewart responded first. "We have members all over the world who keep the secrets of our organization, along with its people, safe. One member, who is an intricate part of this arena, gives us firsthand information about Tamara. Please believe me when I say that we have never wished her harm; nor do we now. We are trying to maintain her safety until the time comes for her to fulfill her destiny."

A single thought shot into Mitch's brain. "The Professor!"

Stewart nodded. "You are correct; that individual does give us insight into Tamara's condition. But at no time has the information ever compromised her safety or that of her family."

"Who is the Professor?" Mitch prodded.

"It would be wrong of me to divulge the identity at this time. There are factions who wish to do great harm," Stewart told him. "When the time is right, it will be revealed to you."

Mitch pressed further. "Does Tamara know?"

"Only that this person is part of her life. Nothing more," Duncan answered.

"Why would anyone want to hurt this little girl?" Mitch asked, fearful of the answer.

"Tamara's gift is powerful, and power makes people hungry. They want the ability to control others, to feel bigger, to be better than the lot they were given, and when they become powerful, it performs as it intended. It corrupts them, turns them into someone unrecognizable to anyone who knew them before. There are few individuals on this earth who can handle the effervescence of power. I believe to steal what she has and use it for one's personal agenda would be the intent." Stewart looked drained. "Remember, those who can't possess or control seek to destroy what cannot be theirs. The pure act of destruction gives them the power they seek."

Duncan patted his old friend on the back. "Stewart, I think Pip had some tea in her cupboard that she could stand to share with you. Why don't you try some? And I'll be there shortly."

Stewart retreated to the kitchen with fatigue-filled eyes. Though he looked utterly exhausted, there was a peace about his presence that indicated the lifting of a giant weight off his shoulders. Mitch was unsure how long Stewart had kept the information about Tamara a secret, but confiding in him just this little bit made Stewart feel tired, and at the same time, lighter than air. The messages were finally out in the open.

Smiling at Mitch, Duncan made a simple statement. "The journey needs to be stepped up a bit now, lad, with this new threat." He grabbed Mitch's right hand. Mitch felt the pounding of his blood through his veins within the tight grasp. "Can you do this, son?"

He didn't know. He didn't know about any of this. People knew about Tamara all over their area, due to the countless number of specialists who had come to try to diagnose her, but he never dreamed that people overseas knew about her. He promised Lillian that he would do whatever it took to ensure Tamara's future. Did he have the courage to see this through? Could he be a knight in shining armor, aiding in the fulfillment of a legacy that the world desperately needed?

Duncan attempted to convince him to move forward. "We've faced invisible foes before and defeated them all. There are always people popping up to take their best shot at us. Our concern is that they know more than anyone ever has. They have a definite plan, and for the first time, we aren't sure where it's coming from. I'm confident that by the end of today, we'll have a clearer picture. When you turn on the lights, the darkness recedes to shadow. At least, that's what your father used to say."

Mitch didn't like the casual mention of his father. Some memories weren't too pleasant. When people asked about his family, he remarked only about his mother and sister in a manner that made people uncomfortable to probe any further. Only Graham knew the backstory, and he didn't tell anyone. "My father?"

Duncan's eyes turned soft. He knew there had been a rub there, so he approached it delicately. He wanted the boy to know who his father truly was. "As I told you before, your father was a great man. He defeated many foes in his tenure with us; he was one of the best leaders we have ever had. I learned a lot from him, and I was heartbroken after hearing of the accident. We were told that there was an attack coming, with your father being the primary target. He informed me that when it was his time to leave this world, he would greet it with a grateful heart for having been a father to you and your sister. He was willing to do whatever it took to keep the secrets of the organization safe." Duncan paused. "You won't have trouble finding courage, son. It's in your blood."

Mitch looked down at his hands, which were exact replicas of his father's. His father once told him that they had been passed down through generations of doctors, and it was up to him to keep their hands busy in the field of medicine. Mitch loathed that remark. "My father knew about Tamara?"

"He knew it all."

"Will I?" Mitch asked.

Grasping his hand tighter, Duncan replied, "After all your lessons." Mitch looked deep into the eyes of a man who was becoming his mentor. Duncan returned his gaze. "Can you?"

Without hesitation, Mitch placed his left hand on top of Duncan's. "I can."

"Good!" Duncan exclaimed, wrenching his hands out of their grip. "You'll stay here until you are back on your feet, and then we will get this wagon rolling. Lots to do before Tamara's arrival." He stood up out of the rocker, placing the notebook back into his pocket.

"Tamara can't come here; she isn't stable enough to travel!" Mitch exclaimed.

Smiling in his typical manner, Duncan responded to the outburst. "Oh, she will be. She has to be, or all of this will have been for nothing. That little girl has tricks up her sleeve that none of us has ever seen. I, for one, can't wait to see them!" He waved toward Mitch as he exited the room. "Get some rest this evening. I'll send the female persuasion in with some dinner for you. Good work, my boy!"

Before he slipped from view, Mitch shouted at him. "What about security? You said there was a locator device on me. If that's true, then they know where I am!"

Duncan popped his head into the doorway. "The locator device was taken back toward London with Quinn and Elle. No one has any clue where you are but us. Plus, who needs burly security types when you have Pip? Sleep tight!"

Mitch slipped further down into his warm duvet. The mere thought of Pip sleeping just a few feet away from him sent shivers down his spine. He couldn't help the feelings that began to occupy his mind. He drifted off to sleep as fantasies of walking through a field of wildflowers with Pip and two small children flowed into his brain. For the first time since his failed relationship with Brooke, he envisioned a future with someone special, and he surrendered to his fatigue with a smile across his face.

21

"You're telling me that U2 defeats the Rolling Stones in a comparison of the greatest bands of all time?" Mitch choked through laughter.

"That is the main point of my argument," Pip responded sarcastically, annoyed with his laughter at her expense. Her loyalty for the band ran deep, complete with schoolgirl fantasies about marrying the drummer.

Mitch continued to laugh at her sensitivity. A brilliant conversationalist, Pip could discuss any topic from pop culture and music to philosophical theories and history, even world politics. It had been a long time since a woman stimulated his mind, which was refreshing and challenging. He loved the way in which she stood up for things she was passionate about, even if that included a famous rock band. "I'm agreeing with you! I just find it odd that you feel so strongly about a rock band. You don't strike me as the type who feels passionate for things like that," Mitch noted carefully.

Looking at Pip's hands tightly gripping the steering wheel, Mitch knew he was dangerously close to making her angry. He wasn't sure why she was so sensitive and jumpy this morning, but he knew better than to make a bigger deal out of something so minor. "You strike me as bit cranky today. What's up?" he asked.

Whizzing down the A9 away from Killiecrankie, Pip drove with her usual reckless abandon. She tended to drive faster and more offensively when she was upset, and the news that there was a traitor among their group upset her terribly. The group had been founded upon a mutual trust with all members, and to think that someone had pledged the same oath with betrayal lacing their lips made her physically ill. Loyalty and respect were two characteristics she held in high esteem, and the disintegration of those traits on the generations of society through the years made her melancholy. The core of humanity was changing into a beast that she no longer recognized as anything she desired to be associated with. This group had been a safe haven from the greed of the world, along with a return to old ways that in her opinion should never have been forgotten. A threat from the outside was obvious and expected, but inside was incomprehensible. Above all else, it made her fear for her father. He created vulnerability through his trusting nature, and she prayed that it wouldn't claim him as the next victim. "It's one of those days." Keeping her eyes on the road, she added, "We have a bit to cover today, and I don't want to waste time."

If Mitch had learned anything about this fascinating creature over the last few days, it was that Pip was quiet when something was wrong. "Why don't you just tell me what's happening and get it over with? Might make you feel better."

Pip maintained her grip on the steering wheel, weighing her options. She was instructed not to tell him too much, in case he came across the wrong people once more. Duncan had increased security around her house during Mitch's stay, with nightly visits from organization members and local law enforcement. She had become accustomed to seeing people lurking in her bushes, while Gillian served coffee to sleepy-eyed men in the morning. Duncan forcefully ordered that Mitch was not to be left alone from this point on, including escorts to each new teacher for the remaining lessons. Tamara's arrival was the only point he was vague on. How he was able to pinpoint her exact travel dates when he didn't even know her health status perplexed Pip. When she posed this exact question to her father yesterday, he simply smiled and told her that she didn't need to be privy to all the information in his mind at all times. It was his standard maneuver in dodging a question. She found it extremely annoying.

Mitch watched her wrestle with her thoughts. "Who's the one who keeps telling me to open up and trust people, to listen to my inner voice? What's your inner voice saying now?"

Damn it, he's right, she thought. Her foot backed off the accelerator as her fingers loosened around the steering wheel. A small smile swept across her mouth. She looked at him out of the corner of her eye. "All right, smart guy. Clever tactic, using my own words against me. What do you think is going on?"

"I think there's a lot of concern about the Professor."

"Obvious assumption, Brody. Don't quit your medical career for a shot at investigation," she teased.

"Finally, sarcasm! I was beginning to think that you had been possessed by pod people who badly imitated the real Pip!" Mitch exclaimed. He watched her smile grow wider as she shook her head at his blatant mocking of her state of mind. "If it isn't the Professor or the threat to my life as well as the organization itself, it must be the pressure of trying to keep the operation going while pinning your hopes on the travel of a sick girl across a large ocean to ensure the completion of a prophecy. Maybe it's global warming?"

Pip could no longer contain her laughter. Mitch had an uncanny ability of bringing her back to reality whenever she felt trapped within the uncertainties of her mind. "It's been global warming this entire time! Feels good to have it out in the open."

The duo chuckled together as the vibrant countryside streaked by outside their windows. Without speaking, both gave each other a quiet strength that they had been lacking. The shared feeling that it was better to fight together than as a lone crusader against a hoard of enemies intensified. Safety in numbers felt best. Mitch found himself entranced at the scenic beauty that passed at breakneck speed. He was falling in love with not only the people he encountered, but with the entire nation of Scotland. During his recovery from the gunshot wound, he discovered a renewed sense of vitality, as if viewing the world through youthful eyes. And it was magical. He even considered telling Pip about his increasing feelings for her. Vulnerability no longer scared him, but he needed to find the right words before approaching her with any sort of a romantic proposition.

Pip hummed along to the U2 CD as Mitch broke the silence. "Where are we going today? Not a train station, I hope."

Her smile radiated confidence. "No more trains, I promise. Today, you're all mine, and we're not going that far from home. Just another mile or two."

"Another mile till what?"

"The scene of your dramatic collapse. I thought we could relive how you managed to drag yourself to the cathedral with a gunshot to your abdomen. I have a gun stowed in the back for such an occasion; we can make the reenactment more realistic."

Touching the sensitive area of his stomach, Mitch found her joke a little too close for comfort. He hadn't ever experienced that type of fear or pain, and he preferred not to relive that night. It was enough that the memory intruded each night in his dreams. "Let's leave the gun out of it and focus on my bravery."

Pip heard the tremble in his voice, sympathetic to his trepidation. "How about a little historic discussion during this last bit?"

Mitch laid his head back onto the headrest, focusing his gaze on Pip.

Reaching into the center console, she removed a small white brochure. The cover portrayed an artist's rendering of Dunkeld Cathedral with the word "welcome" printed in five different languages. As he scanned through the black print outlining the cathedral's history, he focused his attention to the story Pip had begun to weave about their destination.

"Dunkeld Cathedral rests on the north shore of the River Tay, uniting with the river Braan, nestled within the lush greenery of the Perthshire Hills. As early as 570 AD, Celtic missionaries built a monastery there, which was rebuilt in the year 848 AD by the king of the Scots, Kenneth MacAlpin. It suffered both desecration and destruction twice, following the Reformation in 1560, and the Jacobite victory at Killiecrankie in 1689 during the Battle of Dunkeld. It currently showcases various historic artifacts, including a hand-carved oak screen, a ninth-century Pictish stone, a ninth-century cross slab, and a Bible printed in 1611 as a rejected prototype."

Pip continued her explanation, describing in precise detail the mixture of architectural styles of Gothic and Norman influences as well as the coat of arms of the Atholl family. Mitch felt the hum of the engine lull him into a stupor, when a comment from Pip jolted him back into focus.

"Wait, did you say dove motif?" he asked excitedly, finally recognizing one small piece of the vast puzzle.

"Yes, the cathedral is dedicated to Saint Columba, whose name means 'Dove.'"

Scratching his head, Mitch recalled the dove carved upon the wooden crest outside the Donnachaidh museum. "Columba? Have we talked about him before or just the dove?"

"I don't recall mentioning him, but the dove has been mentioned. We'll get into more details regarding our friend Columba once we arrive at the cathedral. He's someone you'll need to remember if you want to understand how all this fits together in the end."

"He's the main guy?" Mitch asked.

Pip slowed the car down as they approached Dunkeld's center. The cathedral became visible in the distance, close to the fountain where Mitch sought refuge. "Sometimes it isn't *who* the person is, but *what* the person represents. Learn to look beyond the obvious, and you'll find what you're looking for."

"That's awfully profound for this early in the morning, Pip."

"I have my moments."

The morning light cast a mystical glow upon the cathedral. During his previous visit, Mitch's pain superseded any appreciation for the grounds, building, or surrounding village. With this fresh perspective, he absorbed the majesty before him. The recently mowed grounds dripped with drops from the morning fog. Flower beds displayed meticulous care, while weathered wooden benches dotted the landscape, waiting for weary visitors. Unlike the two other cathedrals he recently visited, a feeling of serenity surrounded him at Dunkeld. A part of his soul resonated to this unique patch of ground that his feet now inhabited. He was sure the connection occurred the night he lay struggling for life on its steps. Unaware of who he was or what he had been sent to do; it offered him the only gift it could, the gift of shelter. While Pip saw the events as coincidental, Mitch chose to view them as miraculous.

Smirking at her friend's newly acquired sense of the divine, Pip took his hand to lead him gently toward the entrance. Mitch's chest tightened with panic as he stepped through the double doors. A phantom pain shot across his abdomen, recalling his struggle to open the doors that night. As his hand winced beneath hers, Pip turned to face him. "Everything all right?" Mitch's fear was apparent. She placed his trembling hand upon her heart. "Feel that? I'm real, the fear is not. I've been fearful all morning, but you pulled me from mine, and now I'm returning the favor."

Mitch's hand continued its tiny tremors, although no longer from fear. The intimate placement of his hand against her body was almost too much for him to bear. Staring into her deep-blue eyes, he lost himself in the moment, knowing that at any second his natural instinct to kiss her would take hold. Avoiding the possible rejection that accompanied such a maneuver, he wrenched his hand away from her, rubbing it along his pants leg in the vain attempt to wipe away his feelings. "Thanks, but I'm fine."

Pip cocked her head to one side, pursing her lips in disbelief at his statement. "OK then, we've got loads to cover today." Handing him the journal she gave him almost a week ago, she stated, "You should write some of this down for future reference."

Pip sat down on the carpet that covered a small step behind her. Motioning for Mitch to join her, she began with a question. "What is the first thing you notice about Dunkeld, now that you see it in the daylight?" Taking a seat next to her, he looked around for anything that stood out. Since she had mentioned it in the car, the answer was the dove motif adorning the cathedral. Mitch pointed to the east window, where a dove had been handcrafted in stained glass amid the Christian virtues of fortitude, charity, prudence, justice, faith, hope, temperance, and patience. "Similar to the carvings on the stone that we showed you, the dove also has multiple meanings throughout the annals of history. This dove, however, is not hidden in its decoration, but is out in the open as the symbol of Saint Columba. He is also known as Columcille."

Handing a pen to Mitch, she indicated that he should take notes.

"Documents indicate that Saint Columba preached here for six months during one of his sojourns into the highlands from his home monastery at Iona. After his death, Kenneth MacAplin, the king of Scotland, had his relics brought here to Dunkeld and buried under this very step, to stop invading Norsemen from desecrating the remains. A carpet was commissioned to cover the step with the dove symbol woven into it, because Saint Columba was referred to as the 'Dove of the Church.'"

Mitch scribbled into his notebook, pausing at her mention at the saint's title. "Dove of the Church? Was he especially peaceful or something?"

"What do you remember from the day at the museum with Daddy?" she asked.

"We talked about the symbols on the family crest outside, the Tuatha de Danaan tribe, and the crystal ball in the case," Mitch commented.

Pip corrected his terminology. "Ball of crystal, *not* crystal ball. Saying it in that manner sounds like some cheap theatrical trick. Bear that in mind as we go along."

Mitch immediately apologized. "How does it tie in with that?"

Pip sat back against the step. "Let's see how much of Columba's life I remember from school." Her ability to weave history into a fascinating tale was one of the many remarkable gifts Pip possessed.

She began her tale with his birth, which was heralded by a prophecy to his mother, who was a member of the royal family of Tara in Ireland. "They christened him Crimthean, meaning 'Fox.' It wasn't until years later, when he began the Iona monastery, that his name was changed to Columba. The departure from his family was shrouded in controversy, death, and shame. One account stated that he had been exiled to Iona from his native land due to the illegal copying of a book of Psalms from Saint Finnian, resulting in the death of three thousand men at the bloody Battle of Culdrevny.

"The intention of his exile was to reclaim the number of souls he had slain in battle as penance. Columba demonstrated miraculous aptitudes with an ability to copy approximately three hundred books, with an eyewitness account mentioning light shining from his fingers while he wrote. This description showed an individual who was capable of all types of spiritual manifestations, even carrying his own staff, similar to a high priest's. He possessed an ability to converse with animals, in particular a white horse that wandered near to him during one of his many walks around Iona. In an effort to ward off danger as well as punish enemies, he periodically utilized visionary and prophetic incantations, which frequently resulted in the performance of miracles."

The tale of such an extraordinary individual caused daydreams of Columba's time period to flood Mitch's brain. He reveled in his own imaginings, when Pip shook his shoulder, disintegrating his boyish fantasies. "You still with me?" she quietly asked. Blinking quickly, Mitch nodded. "Good, 'cause the really brilliant stuff is coming."

"That wasn't the really good stuff?"

"Not at all! That was the tedious stuff, which teachers drill you on at university. The really interesting stuff is what lies in the shadows that we speculate about and dig deeper into. That's what gets me going, uncovering some secret clue that everyone else overlooked," Pip exclaimed.

Mitch folded his arms across his chest. "Tell me the good stuff."

"He foretold of his own death as an ascension into the sky by a brilliant light flooding his room. Also, he was known to lay his head on a stone pillow, similar to the tale of Jacob's stone pillow in the Bible. But my favorite account by far tells of his ability to prophesize the succession of a king by using the *Glassy Book of the Ordination of Kings*. Fancy name for a round ball of crystal, don't you think?"

A light bulb went off inside Mitch's brain. "Hold on a minute, a ball of crystal, the dove, a stone pillow, the royal family. Is he related to the family at the museum?"

"Dig deeper. Look beyond the obvious symbols to alternate meanings. Try breaking it down piece by piece. Start with the stone."

Thumbing through his notes, Mitch tried to recall what the three women had told him on the top of Ben Vrackie. "The stone holds and conducts energy." Putting the pieces together he exclaimed, "There was a stone found before the Battle of Bannockburn when the Templars arrived, which was the same stone I saw in the museum!"

Pip smiled with pride at a man who expanded his mind beyond expectations that even she held. "It is Columba's stone. What about the dove?"

"The dove was on the crest at the museum. Other than that, I haven't a clue how it could tie in, other than a possible family relation."

Smoothing out the carpet beneath the two of them, Pip traced the outline of a white bird held in flight. "The dove is an ancient symbol, which Christianity labeled as the physical manifestation of the Holy Spirit descending upon the earth. Other ancient cultures use it as the sign of the goddess Sophia, the mother of wisdom, the female counterpart to God the father. Doves were sacred to the pagan goddess of love. After Noah's survival from the flood, a dove carrying an olive branch arrived at his ark, signaling that God received his prayers. In old fables, souls who were fortunate enough to be blessed before death became doves." She paused, her eyes narrowing. "In Egypt, the dove is more widely depicted in carvings across from a serpent, showing an enlightened individual the balance of the sacred feminine, the dove, to the sacred masculine, the serpent. As for a family connection, that seems pretty obvious."

Furiously copying her words verbatim into his notebook, Mitch asked, "How?"

"The Clan Donnachaidh claims heritage from Columba through the Tuatha de Danaan, but I think that is the public persona. The crest you saw at the museum is one of two. That is the ancient crest of the House of Struan. There is another crest that doesn't show any of the symbols publically, which is the crest more widely used by the clan. The ancient motto was also changed somewhere down the line, making it all the more fascinating. *Scientas est postentia,* translated from Latin, it means 'Knowledge is Power.'"

"Is it?" Mitch questioned with a childlike innocence.

"The greatest leaders in history had knowledge on their side before trudging into battle. You can overthrow any power base with the right information at your disposal. It's not wise to enter into a situation blindly, without knowing what you're up against."

Mitch scowled at her last comment, assuming it was directed toward him. Realizing the unintentional slip, Pip laughed out loud.

"With you as an exception, of course, my dear Brody!"

Smiling back at her, Mitch admitted, "I don't have a clue as to what I'm doing here, but I hope I'm gaining some insight."

"You certainly are."

Their eyes met for a brief moment before Mitch returned to his notes. There was one piece of the puzzle that they had yet to discuss. "What about the stone pillow?"

Pip stretched her arms above her head. "Well, let's see, there are two big coincidences. The first being that the kings of Scotland were crowned at the Palace of Scone seated on a throne, which sat upon the Stone of Scone, or the Stone of Destiny. This has been associated with the stone book of kings that Columba held, even though the Stone of Destiny wasn't made of crystal. The second is that the crystal stone holds and gives energy, so if the owners laid their heads upon it, it would act like a superconductor, relaying information to the owners from the higher power they were intending to communicate with."

Mitch's head reeled from all the information.

Images swirled in his brain of an old man with a staff wielding a magical stone, while three thousand men died at the mere glimpse of it. Knights on horseback whispered secrets as they rode into battle. A dove circled above him, bathed in radiant light from above, touching the earth like a feather, turning into a beautiful raven-haired woman dressed in white robes. The woman reached out her delicate fingers to touch him as his shoulder felt a sting.

"Mitch?" Pip shouted. "Mitch, are you all right?"

Moving his head from side to side, all he recognized was cold stone beneath him. "Pip?" He asked in a groggy voice, "What happened?"

"You went all pasty and collapsed," she answered, helping him to sit up. "We better get you something to eat. We've been sitting here awhile."

Grabbing him around the waist, she lifted him to his feet, and they made their way toward the Chapter House's tea room. Once inside the shop, Pip gingerly placed him on a chair. As she walked away to place their order, Mitch watched her hips sway within her jeans. He found her tough when needed, intelligent, nauseatingly rational, and surprisingly tender. Thinking he might have scratched the surface of this fascinating creature, he caught himself staring idly toward her with his mouth gaping open, a small puddle of drool forming in the left corner. Setting two mugs of coffee down on the table, she knocked his elbow out from underneath his hand. Mitch's head jerked downward. So much for gentle, he thought. Sitting down in the opposite chair with a thump, she scowled as she reached for sugar packets in the middle of the table.

"Anyone home?"

"Daydreaming," he replied.

Blowing steam away from the hot liquid inside her cup, she raised it to her lips. "Daydreaming about what?"

Creating a lie rapidly, Mitch responded, "Just ancient battles."

"You normally look all googly-eyed when you daydream about battles and death, or were you thinking naughty thoughts about the counter girl, of which you are too petrified to confide the truth to me?"

Mitch raised the mug to his lips as a distraction from the blatant questions. Desperately wanting to shout from the rooftops that he had fallen head over heels for this woman, he didn't dare. He wished he could throw the table off to the side, grab her in his arms, and kiss her passionately to show her that she was the most invigorating individual he had ever met. She reminded him of Brooke, but with a zest for life that she had lacked, making Pip the perfect combination of it all.

Instead, he lied, "You caught me."

Turning the corners of her mouth down into a frown, she showed her disapproval for his choice in the female persuasion. "Typical choice, Brody. Big boobs with a tiny waist to match her brain, no doubt. Men are all the same. You don't want a challenge, you want Barbie."

If you only knew, he thought, continuing to avoid the issue by enthusiastically consuming his beverage. Several silent minutes passed before he found the courage to speak to her again.

"Why the coffee break?" he asked.

"You looked a bit peaky around the edges, and since we hadn't eaten since breakfast, I felt a meal of some sort was in order. You're still on the mend," she stated.

The counter girl interrupted by serving two plates to their table. She smiled flirtatiously at the young doctor, ignoring Pip altogether as she tipped the second plate dangerously close to spilling its contents onto the floor. Before the food took flight, Pip lunged forward, "Thanks just the same, but I think I'll take it from here," she remarked sternly to the girl, who flashed her best smile toward Pip before sauntering back behind the counter. Mitch dove into his sandwich, driven by a sudden onslaught of starvation.

Feeling the reenergizing effects of a Ploughman's sandwich in his body, Mitch revisited their conversation about the stone of Columba. "When you gave me the stone on Ben Vrackie, were you giving me the ceremonial stone of Columba?"

Wiping her mouth with a napkin, Pip replied, "Sort of. Your stone represents *all* magic and ability through an organic substance that retains energy. Remember, the stone is only one part of the team; the user is just as important. You have to be able to connect to the energy and wield it for a higher purpose, excluding selfishness."

"You mean to tell me that throughout history, people never used a powerful object with selfish intentions? I find that impossible to believe," Mitch suggested.

Pip narrowed her eyes in concentration, "Oh, everyone has an agenda, even a saint. I think Columba was part of something bigger, and the stone that foretold the next king in his hands could certainly have been politically driven. He could have felt pressure from family members to select someone they needed for a particular base of power, or he used his own abilities to shape the areas he visited with an enlightened sense of teaching that had been solidified from Egypt, Atlantis, and the Middle East." Pip looked down at her plate. "I believe it all ties together in one way or another."

"How so?" Mitch asked.

"People in organizations have tried to remind humanity of what we lost. It's difficult to convince people to think outside the box, but to switch gears and believe something that wasn't written in the Greatest Book of all Time can be folly." Pip sighed deeply, staring at her half-eaten sandwich.

The weight of responsibility on Pip's shoulders was suddenly crystal clear. With one comment, he had witnessed the price her passion exacted.

Along with the wisdom she gained from her education, she had been instilled with a sense of duty to pass along her enlightenment, which wasn't simple. He could tell that, along the way, she had experienced her fair share of defeat at each person's declaration of disbelief.

"How do you know it's true?" he probed.

Blinking back tears, she answered, "How do you know it isn't? How can people believe in a God they can't see or hear, and yet blindly speak with such conviction that the answers to their problems lie with him? How can people read an inaccurate accounting of history, which has been thrust upon them by the very people who wished to control them, and negate other records of illumination?"

Mitch whispered, "I don't know."

Wiping tears from her eyes, she added, "That's what this is all about! Restoring the balance to the light, to the way things were when everything was in perfect harmony. When love was the common thread weaving us together, when a person in need was offered a hand from a stranger, and others were comforted during sorrow. The balance has been tilted for too long, and with your help, Tamara can make it right."

Startled by the casual mention of her name, Mitch's eyes reflected astonishment. "Did you say Tamara can make it right?"

Realizing that she had leapt across the boundary Duncan established, Pip quickly cleaned the table in front of her. "There is more you need to learn before that topic can be delved into with any kind of comprehension." Seeing his look of disappointment, she added, "The next couple of days are crucial. Your next teacher is a gem; she'll answer all your questions."

"*All* my questions?" he asked, raising an eyebrow.

Standing up from her chair, Pip laughed. "Well, maybe not *all*, but a fair amount. You have three more objects to acquire before you can even hope to know it all. You're only halfway there," she joked.

Mitch laughed with her as they made their way back into the late-afternoon sunshine. Blinking at the cathedral's tower bathed in warm sunlight, he felt content with his presence in the world. He took an oath to help his fellow man as a doctor, and yet through the corporate greed of insurance companies, it was easy to fall prey to the financial gain of the profession without concern for the human being before him. A handful of doctors that he knew, including himself, had tried to stay true to the oath. There were moments when they threw caution to the wind, slipping invoices of service into the trash for individuals needing assistance. Those colleagues consistently reinforced his faith in a greater good for the cause of humanity.

Without warning, Pip slipped her arm behind the crook of his elbow. Mitch felt the warmth of her breath upon the base of his neck, sending him into a rarified form of intoxication. *This is the moment,* he though. This was the moment he should profess his growing feelings for her—in this picturesque setting. It was the most romantic moment he could think of. As he opened his mouth to speak, Pip cut him off. "So, Brody, have a girl or two back home?"

Mitch stammered, "N-n-no. I don't have time for dating."

"Pity that." Pip asked, "Do you fancy girls?"

Quickly defending himself, he asked, "Is there a lingering question?"

"Stewart did say that Graham was your chap," Pip interjected.

Mitch recalled the conversation back at the inn, when Stewart assumed his relationship with Graham was more than platonic. "I haven't found the right one, I suppose."

She gripped his arm tighter as they meandered toward the car. "Speaking from personal experience, when you meet that one person, you'll know, because it hits you like a ton of bricks. I met mine, here in this very garden, and in this cathedral is where we'll be married."

She was correct about one thing; her statement hit him like a ton of bricks. Unable to catch his breath, the fantasy bubble of a life with Pip popped from existence. "You're engaged?"

Shoving him playfully in the ribs, Pip asked, "Is that so hard to believe?"

"No, I thought guys would line up around the corner for a chance to take you out, but a fiancé is something different. Congratulations!"

"Will you come?" she asked sweetly.

The pair stopped midstride, facing each other, Mitch trying to look at her as if she were his own sister, and Pip trying not to compare him to her fiancé. "I would be honored."

She placed a soft kiss upon his cheek. "I'm the one who is honored."

Mitch closed his eyes, relishing the tender moment.

Pip grabbed his hand, dragging him back to the car as the sun descended into the horizon. "You say you don't have time for girls, but I know one particular girl who will stop you in your tracks."

Mitch cleared his throat, pursing his lips at the assumption that she had the faintest notion of the type of girl to pique his interest.

He had to admit that the conversation was a welcome relief from the heavier topics they discussed. Entering the familiar car, they pulled out of the car park. "And who would that be?"

Cranking the volume back up to deafening, U2 blared through the speakers. Pip slammed her foot down on the accelerator. "You'll see."

22

*B*are feet delicately skimmed moss-strewn stones toward the castle tower. Flowing robes caught the morning breeze with an air of mystery, femininity, and whimsy. Blustery wind whipped through auburn hair, forcing her to lift the hood of her sapphire cloak around her face, covering it completely. Her outstretched arms cradled a long bundle wrapped in black velvet. Flanking her left and right side, two young women, dressed in forest-green cloaks, walked cautiously through the wind, each holding flickering white candles. The trio approached the fortified structure with great care, trying to be as quiet as possible. Battle was to commence in a few short hours, and the king had not been properly prepared for his forthcoming task.

Two guards at the front gate moved aside to allow their safe passage into the castle. A gate opened to an interior courtyard, where the women joined a white-haired man in jewel-toned robes, a long oak staff clutched in his left hand. Watching the women approach, he addressed their status by bowing deeply while raising his right hand over his heart. The two younger women bowed in return, while the older simply nodded her head.

"Priestess, we are humbled by your presence and express our most reverent gratitude for the gift you bestow upon our royal successor."

The priestess withdrew the hood from her head, her blue eyes blazing in the surrounding firelight. "It has been seen that he is the chosen regent."

He answered confidently. "I have seen it with my own eyes, and I discussed the matter with his mother, for her approval."

"And how has she responded?" she inquired.

"With swift and determined approval, Priestess. She comprehends the task for her young son. She hesitated but for a moment, and is aware of his life's path."

Glancing to the young women standing on either side, they drifted silently toward a doorway on the other side of the courtyard. "They go to prepare the young man. You and I will confirm his appointment as well as survey the forces assembling below." The man stretched his right hand toward a bench carved into the stone wall.

She sat first, placing the bundle on the cold stone. The man sat to her left side, leaning his staff against the wall. Due to the early hour, the courtyard was empty. The woman placed her left hand, palm up, toward the man, displaying a five-pointed star emblazoned on her hand. Placing a small, transparent ball into her palm, she wrapped her fingers around it and closed her eyes. A low hum surrounded the bench area as the two sat listening to the ball's eccentric melody. With her meditation complete, she returned the ball to its owner, whispering a small blessing as she did so.

"Are you satisfied with the confirmation, Priestess?" he asked, placing the ball inside his robes.

"You have foreseen correctly. The young man is to rule, but for how long is uncertain. There is shadow surrounding his reign. Factions are in place before he ascends that conspire against his light. They are aware of his associations and seek to destroy the ancient teachings that threaten their control."

"A dilemma without end."

"Without our assistance, his reign will not last the day. It is the reason we arrived swiftly at his mother's insistence."

"She contacted you before I was given the opportunity?" he asked.

"She has been a member since her youth. She was brought to us by her own mother, who knew the importance of receiving our education. She remains one of the brightest we have. I have queried her on matters she has brought forth, without question. She has a remarkable connection to the stars. They tell her many things that come to pass. Accompanying her rare talents comes a mother's heartache from witnessing the possible demise of her only offspring. There is not always comfort in possessing such talents."

"Surely with our combined efforts, the young man will take the day," he stated.

The woman bowed her head as she folded her hands into her lap. "Indeed, the combined power of the high priest and priestess can succeed, but the real task comes in the heart of this young man. He will not only be tempted to withdraw, but also to perform atrocities against his fellow man, and be faced with the decision to surrender his forces or retreat for victory another day. There are factions both within as well as around this young man. I do not see an easy path."

"He has more strength than I have seen in a royal sire—even more than his father, who possessed great conviction to his purpose. I have confidence that this young man will be able to rise to all expectations."

"I pray you are correct, sir, and I pray that what I have seen will not come to pass," she whispered.

The man's eyes turned tender as she spoke about his young king. He had personally raised the young man from infancy, sheltered by the wisdom of the Druids, and allowed his personal feelings for the boy to overshadow his better judgment. He had become a second father to him, when his true father was found savagely beaten and left to die. A week after the funeral pyre burned, the high priest consulted the sphere in order to receive the name of the next to rule. He was shocked to discover that the young man had been chosen. Due to his age and inexperience, he assumed that an older cousin would be granted rule until the day when the young man grew into a fit ruler.

The family was deeply concerned at the announcement, yet graciously accepted the prophecy. Hostilities between the kingdom and southern invaders came swiftly following the young man's ascension to the throne. Their threat of invasion was an issue the prior sovereign managed to keep at bay, but his passing presented an opportunity for invasion success. They knew the young king was inexperienced in battle, and his victory would be impossible to achieve. They had begun their assault two days prior, marching without challenge through the kingdom, until they arrived at a neighboring field, ready to overtake the castle at any moment. While the sun began its ascent into the sky, enemy forces were seen outside the castle walls. Guards alerted the high priest. His immediate response was a request for aid from the high priestess. Her presence at the castle had been swift.

"Are your forces assembled, Priestess?"

"They are preparing for conflict. Our advantage is the element of surprise. Very few are aware of a woman's presence in battle, let alone at the point of increased vulnerability. As is our tradition, we will achieve confidence through the Goddess as well as the Divine Creator. They will provide the protection we require. The balance of sacred masculine and feminine must be upheld."

"How many have you?" He hoped her response would reflect a greater number than the one he imagined in his head.

"We number a few hundred. I have instructed the younger priestesses to remain in instruction, focused on their studies. They are not to be included in this conflict."

The high priest breathed a sigh of relief. A few hundred would be tremendous assistance to their already weakened force. A recent illness had decimated their full force, decreasing the numbers for battle. They would need all the help they could muster for any type of victory. It was not only a tradition to have women on the front lines of battle, but also an honor, considering the addition of their Goddess energy. The ancient teachings were a priority to all who lived in the kingdom, as parents took great pride in sending a son or daughter to be educated by the high priest and priestess of the realm.

The priestess turned her gaze toward the window. *"The light has changed; the young man's time is close. It is time to complete the preparation."* She rose from the bench at once, grasping the bundle across open palms. *"Please escort me to his chamber. It is time to greet our future king."*

The high priest ushered her through an open doorway, leading to two staircases, one spiraling upward and the other down. They climbed toward the bedchambers and meeting halls on the second floor. Reaching the second floor landing, they turned to their attention to a small door at the end of the hall. The high priest and priestess whispered a small blessing upon the room. Upon completion, one of the young priestesses allowed them entry, nodding in reverence to her superiors.

"The future king has been anointed with oils and waits in anticipation of your arrival."

"If we are welcome, then we shall bestow our gift upon him."

The priestess crossed the threshold, surveying the room to confirm that the necessary accessories had been laid out. A white cloth emblazoned with the five-pointed star of the Goddess as well as the adjoining symbol of the crescent moon adorned the stone floor. Additional candles cast a radiant light within the darkened chamber, and the wooden shutters were closed, enabling their ceremony to be undetected by prying eyes. The future king sat in a high-backed chair at the opposite side of the room, his newly forged armor glimmering in the candlelight. His mother stood to his right, smiling as she watched the priestess approach the center of the painted cloth. The high priest stood to the priestess's left side, motioning for the future king to join them within the star's center. A quick glance to his mother gave him the reassurance he needed to cross the room.

He came face-to-face with the high priestess for the first time, and eleven women clothed in white robes surrounded the trio, encircling them with clasped hands. They whispered a blessing in song, each voice blending in perfect harmony. Her robes shimmered with an incandescent light of black and dark blue. Raising her face toward the ceiling, she closed her eyes, extending her palms forward toward the center of the star. The stars on her hands glowed from an unknown source. The fabric of her robes flowed in an undetected breeze. A crescent moon necklace with a brilliant sapphire shown at her neck. The future king looked around at each face, nervous about the day's coming events. Sensing his fear, the priestess addressed him.

"You have been chosen to lead this land with a combined reverence for the wisdom you were taught as well as the purity in your heart to perform each task with knowledge beyond your years. There is confidence in your ability to succeed far beyond assumptions at your youth. Your name was seen within the sphere, which informs us of your call to sovereignty. Your part is the most difficult. But do not think that your mother's is any less challenging. It is far more difficult to watch your child struggle than to go through the struggle yourself. Look to her for guidance as you are questioned about your inexperience from those who will seek to steal authority. Walk with a clear head and a selfless heart. Look to those who give you true knowledge, not to those with hasty solutions. For it is they who could be your undoing."

The future king nodded, fearful to look directly into the priestess's eyes. His mother instructed him not to be nervous, but he couldn't help but feel anxious at the energy he felt flowing from her. He felt as if he was in the middle of a *whirlpool. The singing of the priestesses created a vibration that made him drowsy. His lack of sleep was taking a toll, and the adrenaline that coursed through his veins hours ago had dissolved.*

The high priest unwrapped the bundle from the priestess. Beneath the heavy cloth lay a glittering sword with a sapphire-jeweled handle. The brilliant facets of the gem cast a deep-blue light upon the walls. He instructed the man to approach and lay his hands on top of the blade. Fingertips brushed the metal, and he flinched at the warmth it radiated. The priestess addressed him a second time.

"Your feet grace the inner sanctum of our temple. It is unwise for you to travel to the halls of our sacred space at this time, for the enemy has many eyes. Eyes who seek to destroy the purity that we represent. For that reason, we have re-created the heart of our temple here upon the floor, in the hope that it will energize you with the power we hold close to our hearts. It is in this place that the Goddess protects and guides us all, most of all, you." The stars on her palms flashed at her mention of the Goddess, glowing more intensely. "Before you is a weapon as well as a symbol of the duality of the universe. For you cannot have strength without courage, victory without defeat, sorrow without joy. The object is one of seven needed to obtain one's own true enlightenment within the forces of the universe and the master teachers who dwell within it. You are given this object on this day in the hopes that it will aid in your quest for truth. Be warned: during your quest, this object is only as powerful as the master who yields it. Use it, as a tool for unnecessary destruction and justice will come to you at your own hand. It recognizes only the white and not the dark. Approach with caution, for if you stray from the light, it will leave you to your own demise."

He grasped the hilt with his right hand, feeling an electric shock surge through his arms. As he jumped back from the volt, the priestess smiled. "You have challenges before you, but also victories. Listen to your heart, for it will never lead you astray; retain the loyalties of your youth without the blinders of innocence. In the days to come, may you remember that we are not only with you, but are now a part of you."

She placed a golden pin in the palm of his left hand. The future king looked down at her final gift, recognizing it as the one his mother wore each day. His mother wept in acknowledgment of the gift. He glimpsed at the priest-ess with eyes that transformed from an adolescent's to those of a wise sovereign. He clasped the pin within his fingers, feeling the shape of the crescent moon against his skin. Courage began to flood every pore of his body. The king felt the day's victory belonged to him, and he knew his reign would be prosperous.

23

Bright sunshine broke through Pip's bedroom window. She and the twins made Mitch feel like a family member during evening poker games at the kitchen table while they laughed through various topics. Some evenings, their foursome expanded to include Duncan and Stewart, fresh from an argument, looking for a distraction from their heated debates. Members would poke their heads in to say hello, hold a quick meeting with Pip, and dart back out again. He questioned Gillian regarding all the activity surrounding the house. Her only retort was that Pip preferred chaos to solitude. Since Pip was an only child, Gillian explained, she made lifetime friends who acted as substitute siblings. As they discussed the isolation of an only child, Mitch confided about his own childhood with a sister. They had been close as young children, but drifted apart after his father's sudden death. Mitch became preoccupied in being the man of the house, leaving a pitiful amount of time to be an adolescent, while his sister withdrew into the shadows of questionable friends, secretive behavior, and petty theft. He viewed the death of his father as severely impacting his life, but until this moment with Gillian, he never noticed how it impacted his sister. If he had paid more attention to her needs, maybe her high school years would have been better.

Having been a guest in Pip's house for one week, he considered throwing away his medical career to become a permanent fixture in her life. He contemplated speaking to Duncan about a quiet position at the inn as he courted Pip and created a picturesque life in a fairytale world. After their day in Dunkeld, reality struck like a mallet on his head when Pip casually announced the existence of a fiancé. Throwing the duvet over his head, he rolled toward the window, wishing he could erase any romantic feelings he had developed for her. He hoped to complete his appointed task with a shred of dignity left intact, but the chemistry between he and Pip could prove too difficult to ignore any further.

"Do you plan on getting something accomplished?" Genevieve asked, standing in the doorway of his room. Mitch stayed under the duvet, ignoring her obvious attempt to rouse him.

"Is sulking one part of your personality that we should consider charming?" she asked, baiting him to engage in an argument. Mitch continued to ignore her.

Walking toward the bed, Genevieve added, "Look, I hope you don't sleep au naturel, 'cause I'm about to throw those covers off you and wouldn't appreciate the shock." Mitch grabbed the corners of the duvet tightly, trying to avoid the ambush. He shifted his body weight toward the other end to compensate for the new intrusion. He braced himself for the theft, which never came. Instead, Genevieve spoke to him in a surprisingly tender voice.

"I'm going to be honest with you. I know how you feel about Pip. I've seen the way you look at her, following her with those come-hither seductive eyes. You aren't the first to become infatuated with her; it's natural to be drawn to Pip because she's amazing. But so are you, and you deserve to be happy. You deserve someone who follows *you* the way you do her, and you'll find the right one. This, if Pip has her way, will be much sooner than you think."

"Does she know?" he asked from his hiding spot beneath the duvet.

"Of course not," Genevieve answered. "Pip goes about her life thinking that men are oblivious to the fact that she's even a woman. She thinks they all consider her one of the guys, when in reality they are just as scared as you are to tell her how they feel. Their passive natures combined with her mental intimidations have kept her from many a boyfriend. There were many tear-filled nights during our youth when Gillian and I tried to reconstruct her self-esteem from a shattered crush. Finally one guy came forward, shared his feelings, and won her heart. The two of them are tremendous compliments to each other, and I think their marriage will be a good one."

Mitch removed the shield from his face. "She's happy then?"

"The happiest I've ever seen." Genevieve's hand brushed hair out of his face, exposing the mist in his eyes. "You still have a place in her heart, and in some ways it's stronger than if you were her spouse. You have the place that is reserved for true friends and secured by unending loyalty. The corner you have carved out in her heart can never be compromised by anything as petty as some of the issues married couples endure."

While her words comforted Mitch, the selfish part of him didn't want to hold a place in her heart, but secure a place in her arms. Looking into Genevieve's eyes, he felt her own tremendous strength surging toward him, assisting him out of his slump. He began to pull the duvet away from his body, as Genevieve's eyebrows raised, questioning whether or not he was clothed. She expressed disappointment when he raised himself from the bed, wearing a pair of sweatpants and an old T-shirt.

"It's always a long shot, but one worth taking," she said, winking in his direction. "Get dressed. Gillian's making fresh scones with her famous blueberry preserves, and she'll be crushed if you don't join us. You've got another busy day ahead of you, so you'll need all the energy you can muster." Heading toward the doorway, she paused while Mitch began to make the bed. "By the way, your secret's safe with me."

This new side she had exposed established a newfound respect for a woman he previously judged as a reflection of her sister. Twins possess a unique ability to trick people into believing they are a singular entity, when in reality they are separate individuals. The realization that Gillian could have a tender side through the thickness of her skin was a sweet surprise. Genevieve was the nurturer, while Gillian remained detached and aloof, but their conversation showed an intricate attention to detail that Genevieve used to approach every day of her life. He dressed quickly, wanting to get to the kitchen as soon as possible, uncertain how much longer he would be a guest in Pip's house. Approaching the kitchen, he recognized two voices instead of the usual three. Pip's voice of enthusiasm was mysteriously absent.

"I already told you, he was wearing pants, you giant perv!" Genevieve yelled at her sister.

"I asked you again because I didn't hear you the first time over the mixer. Bloody Hell, Gen, you make me out to be some sort of infatuated freak!" Gillian exclaimed.

"Well, aren't you? You're constantly picking up after him, doing his laundry, baking for him, and you make that insipid laugh at all his jokes. If you don't fancy him, then you sure fooled me," she responded, tapping her fork against the wooden table.

Gillian turned off the mixer, pointing one of the beaters dripping with cream directly at her sister's head, daring Genevieve to give her an excuse to throw it. "It's called being hospitable, Gen. And as for the pants comment, I asked to make sure that you didn't barge into his room like a stalker." She flicked a small piece of cream off the end of the beater, which landed in Genevieve's hair.

"Stalker, huh?" Genevieve stood up from her chair, armed with a bowl of blueberry preserves. The two girls squealed with anticipation of an impending food war, when Mitch's silhouette forced them to relinquish their weapons prematurely. Gillian spoke first, as Genevieve seized the opportunity to repay the cream that landed in her hair.

"Good morning, Mitch! Slept well, I hope," she quipped, wiping blueberry preserves from her left eyebrow. "Scones are almost ready. Sit down, and have some coffee. Gen, get Mitch some coffee."

Genevieve sat back down, lifting her coffee mug toward her mouth. "He knows where the coffee is; he can get it himself."

Gillian shot her sister a look of contempt. "He's still healing, Gen! Just get the bloody coffee already!"

Mitch raised both hands in the air as a sign of surrender. "Ladies, I'm perfectly capable of getting my own coffee. But if its bloody coffee, I'm not sure my stomach could endure that."

Gillian threw her head back in a giggle. "Mitch, you are too funny!"

"There!" Genevieve shouted. "That's the fake laugh I was telling you about!"

Gillian shot her sister a look of disgust as Mitch placed his hand on her shoulder. "It's not fake, Gill, it's just girly. It was a dumb joke made in the vain attempt to get you to laugh, and it worked! Aren't I lucky?" Genevieve rolled her eyes. After pouring himself a hearty dose of freshly brewed coffee, he sat next to Genevieve at the table. "Where's Pip this morning?"

Gillian placed a plate of fresh scones, eggs, and ham in front of Mitch, beaming widely at her latest culinary achievement. "She's having breakfast with Harry, of course. It's Wednesday. Their weekly ritual includes an early morning hike followed by breakfast. I expect her any minute to retrieve you."

Genevieve pushed her plate of food away. "And with any luck, Harry will be with her, and you'll get a chance to meet him too. Won't that be fun?" she stated, openly mocking Mitch's crush. He smirked in recognition of her snide comment, while Gillian sat across from the two of them oblivious to the secret they shared. The three sat in silence over the next few minutes, consuming their breakfast and sipping coffee. Mitch was the first to break the stillness that surrounded them.

"Any idea of the agenda today?"

Genevieve grabbed a piece of paper, suddenly interested in making notes. "We're not supposed to mention anything."

Gillian glanced at her sister with frustration on her face. "We can say a little, Gen. We can tell you two things about your teacher: what we call her, and where she's from."

"She's not from the UK?" he asked.

Genevieve, who had been unwilling to relay any information, answered first. "She's a yank like you; only she's been living here for quite a while. Owns her own shop in Pitlochry called the Toad's Pocket. What would you say she sells, Gill?"

"Trinkets and handmade items. Very charming shop—we love going there for high tea, which she has every afternoon. Thank goodness she doesn't sell all the touristy garbage you'd normally see. I think she's simply magical, myself, which is why she's known to her closest acquaintances as Fionn Briosag."

"The White Witch," Genevieve muttered. "They call her the White Witch."

The hairs on the back of Mitch's neck stood on end. "You're taking me to a witch?"

Gillian waved away his fear by shaking her head. "Not a real witch like you see at the cinema. She's known by that name for her tremendous insight as well as her ability to make good things happen. Too much stigma has been put on that word since the Middle Ages, with the witch-hunts here and in your country. What it comes down to is that people have always been afraid of the true power of women, and because of that fear, they labeled it as dangerous, heretical, and placed the name 'witch' upon it."

Genevieve put the pen down. "There are some called 'witch' who prefer to dabble in things that they don't understand and can't control. It's those people who are dangerous, creating the stereotypes we see today. But back in the days of the ancients, everyday people utilized their local people of magic to assist them in all aspects of their life. Today we call them freaks and cast them out of society."

Gillian placed her hand on Mitch's. "Don't look at her as the stereotype. Look at her as your teacher, regardless of background, reputation, or outward appearance. Sometimes people are completely different beneath the surface than what you originally think."

Genevieve returned to her writing. "Yeah, Mitch, some are complete nut jobs!"

Gillian ripped Genevieve's place setting from the table with disgust. She took Mitch's empty plate away from his outstretched hands as he laughed, turning to start the dishes that had piled up in the sink. Turning the hot water on at the faucet, she looked out the window as a ball of dust congregated at the front gate. "Must be Pip!" she announced, returning to her usual chipper demeanor. She watched Pip open the garden gate and stride toward the house with mud covering the lower portion of her sweatpants. "Oh, and she's alone, no Harry today. How unfortunate, I wanted to speak with him."

Genevieve smirked, unable to voice out loud the comment floating in her head. She found human nature fascinating in its avoidance of honest communication for the sport of playing games. There were moments when she stirred the pot to witness an individual's dance of evasion, making her an intricate member of the game-playing society, though she would never openly admit it.

Pip burst through the door of the kitchen, tracking mud from her hiking boots onto the freshly mopped floor. Rushing to the refrigerator, she guzzled a bottle of water against the rush of cold from the open door.

"Pip!" Gillian shrieked, "At least remove your boots! I just washed that floor this morning!"

Tossing the bottle toward the trash can, she missed it by a few feet, angering Gillian even more. "Calm down, Granny, its fine. Just wait till it dries and then sweep it up. No need to get your knickers in a twist." She looked at Mitch still sipping his coffee. "You ready to go, sunshine?" she asked.

He smiled at her bravado. "Ready as I'll ever be. Let's go meet the witch."

"You two are about as discreet as a bull in a china shop." She directed her attention toward Genevieve. "What else did you tell him?"

"Nothing terribly important, just her nickname," she replied, clearly annoyed.

"Right then, let's get on the road. We have a bit of a drive today, but it is well worth it. You'll get to see some stunning countryside with the flowers all in bloom. I love this time of year!" Pip exclaimed, grabbing two more water bottles from the fridge.

Mitch departed the kitchen to grab a jacket, amid girlish giggles and remarks about the nature of Pip's morning with her betrothed. Regaling them with tales of their intimate moments, Mitch laughed at the frankness of their dialogue. Grabbing a jacket from the closet, his eyes fell upon the briefcase sitting beneath the clothes Gillian had hung up. He decided not to take it, convincing himself that this was the safest place for it to spend the day. Second-guessing the decision, he retrieved the stone and shoved it into his pocket. It had become an extension of him, and he felt safer with it on his person than sitting at the bottom of a dark closet.

As in recent days, the pair tore out of the driveway on their way to some semisecret location, with Mitch using his time in the car to catch up on sleep. Today felt different. A tension flowed between them, stemming from his fear that she was aware of his personal feelings. She didn't pressure him into conversation, casually stating their travel plans to Stirling and increasing the stereo volume. It felt as though he had just closed his eyes when Pip announced their arrival.

Nudging him awake with her elbow, she whispered, "Come on, Sleeping Beauty, you don't want to miss this view. It takes my breath away every time."

Stark-white houses crested with thatched roofs dotted the countryside in tidy little clumps. Horses meandered through meadows, chomping wildflowers that popped up to bask in the warm sunshine. An enormous tree-filled hill supported a castle at its peak, while a spiral tower lay beyond. Lit from the sun in the east, the tower seemed to touch the bottom of the clouds as they rolled past in the gentle highland breeze. "Which hill are we climbing today?" Mitch asked, finally daring himself to speak.

"The castle is to your right is Stirling, and the grand tower you see in the distance is the Wallace Monument. That's where we're headed."

"The castle I recognize," Mitch told her. "I came here as a kid with my dad. We never toured the monument, but I'm guessing it was erected for William Wallace, the hero of the Scottish War of Independence."

Grinning from ear to ear, Pip replied enthusiastically. "You surprise me with your knowledge of Scottish history, Mitch! People have heard the tale of William Wallace, but that's due to Hollywood magic, not credible lessons."

Mitch couldn't stop himself from teasing her. "You mean he didn't look like Mel Gibson with long hair? I thought he was dashing."

Shaking her head, Pip applied her foot to the gas pedal, propelling them forward at an even faster pace. "We're a little late, due to my morning with Harry. By the way, in case you weren't aware, I don't normally escort people to meet teachers. I was given orders."

"By Duncan, I presume?" Mitch asked.

"Until we have concrete evidence of who was behind the attack at Southwark, Daddy didn't want any chances with your safety. From here on out, you will be escorted to and from each lesson."

"By you?" he inquired, fearful that she would say yes.

"I have you for the next few days, but beyond that I can't tell for sure. Daddy should know something by then," Pip stated.

"It's been a week!" Mitch remarked, shocked at the intensity of his voice. "Surely he has to know something. This is ludicrous!"

The car screeched to a halt in the middle of the road. Pip's anger at his callous remark raged free. "Look, Brody, we're doing our best to figure this out. While you have lain around my house recovering from your ordeal, good people have stayed up many long nights trying to locate the person who has infiltrated our organization. We're not dealing with an amateur here; they know what they are doing. And more importantly, they know how we operate, which makes this a delicate procedure. We must act as if we know nothing while attempting to flush the bunny from the woods. Don't act as if my father hasn't done anything." Her last words came in the form of a deafening shout. "He does *everything*!"

Waving a white flag of surrender, Mitch apologized profusely. "I'm sorry, Pip; I know your father is doing all he can, and I appreciate you helping me."

Putting the car back in drive, Pip acknowledged his apology. "We're all a little on edge these days. No offense taken."

They sat in silence for the last few miles. Pip was right about one thing today; the countryside was breathtaking. Suddenly the concrete jungle of city life no longer held its shiny luster. He would have chucked it all to own one of the pristine farmhouses they passed on the road. The car wound its way up the hill toward the monument, with buses full of tourists bursting from the windows, their cameras ready to capture the splendor of the scene. The architectural design of the tower was marvelous. Insight into the complexity of the man they honored in stone was evident in the location of the monument. Just as Wallace would have wanted, the tower overlooked the majesty of the fields below, as if he were inside peeking out. The massive stonework reached toward the sky as an extension of the land itself. Graceful spires sat atop arches culminating in a magnificent peak where an observation deck held dozens of people shooting video or waving to others meandering below.

Pip parked the car among the masses visiting for the day, joining them on the walk to the monument. Mitch glanced to his left and right as they walked, hoping to capture his first look at the so-called witch. Watching his nervous movements, Pip pulled him away from the hordes of tourists. "You look like you're having a bloody fit. Calm down, will you?"

Releasing his arm from a firm grasp, Mitch ignored her suggestion and continued to scan the crowd. "I'm on the lookout for the witch. We're meeting her here, right?"

"We're meeting at the top. Stop looking like a paranoid freak!"

Stepping back into the crush of visitors, Mitch blended into the crowd. Grabbing a booklet at the entrance about the tower, he entered the stone building with genuine interest. Inside the exhibition hall, a glass capsule stretched from floor to ceiling, encasing a massive sword, said to be owned by Wallace. Visitors gasped as they viewed the scope of the weapon, winding their way to the staircase leading to the observation deck. Pip motioned for him to join her at the staircase as everyone marched in an orderly fashion along the stone steps. Some held small wands to their ears spouting facts in various languages.

Pip smirked. "Two hundred and forty-two steps straight up to the top. Think you can handle it?"

"Lead on," Mitch instructed.

Halfway up the staircase, Mitch's calves began to burn. There were a few instances during their climb when he stopped and clutched his aching side, as Pip continued and others passed him by. Breaking through the doorway of the observation deck, the sunlight hit his eyes with blazing intensity. He felt someone grab his elbow as he lurched to the side. Turning to the right to dodge their grip, Pip's voice broke through the brightness. "This way."

Leading him to the far corner of the tower, they looked out upon the valley below. Differing shades of green formed a patchwork quilt, as farmers tended to fluffy flocks of sheep. The bustling town of Stirling showed a steady stream of traffic from the main highway, while clouds floated past, creating oddly shaped shadows dancing across the ground. Remembering a game he played as a child with his sister where they created shapes out of cloudbursts, Mitch turned his head toward the cool, crisp breeze.

A voice from behind stirred Mitch from his daydream. "Pip, I didn't think you'd be the one to bring him. What a lovely surprise!"

Pip rushed to the woman's side, embracing her warmly. "How's our girl?"

"Busy as ever. She sends her regards. Said she would e-mail you later."

Pip backed away toward Mitch. "Here's your witch, Brody."

She certainly didn't look like any stereotypical witch Mitch had ever seen. Her frosted blond hair touched the bottom of her ears, where frogs of carved ivory dangled from each lobe. The frames of her glasses shone with an iridescent blue, and gentle dove-gray eyes peeked out beneath them. She was sophisticated with a smidge of whimsy as her black pants continued into her black top adorned with crepe-colored roses at the neckline. A bright-yellow jacket kept out the chill, while a golden crescent embellished in the center with two sapphires graced her lapel. She carried a long black velvet bag, tied at the top with a red satin ribbon, in her left hand.

The woman watched Mitch in silence. Then taking his hand in a firm handshake, she commented, "The pleasure is all mine, Dr. Brody. I've heard quite a bit about you."

Mitch shook her hand as his own trembled between her fingers. "Are you really a witch?"

The woman laughed. "My reputation with this group precedes me. The girls like a little shock value with new people, and Duncan has quite the flair for the dramatic arts."

Pip sighed deeply. "He knows all about the drama, I'm afraid."

"Ah, yes, the unfortunate incident last week. I spoke to your father this morning, and he's already whittled down the list of possibilities. Amazing guy, your dad. Think of me more as a priestess than a witch, Dr. Brody. Although between you and me, riding a broom would be fantastic fun!"

Mitch couldn't help but laugh. "What would you like me to call you?"

Raising her index finger to her lips, she whispered, "You may call me Boggs."

The women embraced a final time as Pip announced her departure. "Call me when you can no longer tolerate the buggar!" she cried, raising her hand above her head. When Pip had vanished, Boggs focused squarely on Mitch, looking him over from head to toe. He watched the tourists milling around him to divert his attention from her intense gaze, which was beginning to make him extremely uncomfortable.

"Why is there pain, Mitch?" she asked, looking beyond him at the greenery below.

The question caught him off guard. "It's the body's way of signaling a problem." He wrinkled his brow. "No one has ever asked me that before."

She shook her head. "No, you misunderstand me. I'm asking about *you*. Why is there pain in your life?"

Mitch didn't follow her train of thought. "I suppose it's because I'm a doctor, and pain is part of the job description."

Boggs spun him around to face her. "Let me tell you something upfront about me. I don't mince words. I will tell you how I see things in complete honesty. I don't believe in playing games or dancing around an issue in order to get an answer. You might have to work a little harder to come up with a truthful response, but I can assure you that at the end of this, you will thank me for my frankness. You still have a considerable amount of work to do before you reach the conclusion of this so-called quest. And speaking from experience, if you don't prepare properly, the final outcome can be altered considerably." Removing her glasses, she raised her chin upward to see him more clearly. "So, I'm going to ask you again. Why is there pain in *your* life?"

Taking a deep breath, Mitch flashed through his life thus far, coming to a basic conclusion. "Maybe it's the old saying that God doesn't give us any more than we can handle. He must trust me an awful lot."

Placing her glasses back onto her nose, she pointed her index finger into his chest. "That's a copout, Brody, and a load of crap! God brings us challenges, and *we* determine what we can and cannot handle. Human beings are classic examples of pure avoidance, where we avoid every situation that comes our way until it brings us nothing but pain. We don't like to confront; we like to ignore in the hopes that the situation will disappear. But it doesn't work that way, does it? Have you had a situation that you ignored because it was too big a problem for you to deal with?"

Mitch avoided her gaze. "Who hasn't?"

She continued. "Could it have been the time when you buried your head into what you were being told to do rather than getting to know the man behind the title of 'Father'? Or the time when you hid behind the responsibility of taking care of your mother and your sister after his death? Or when you chose not to fight for the woman you loved, without considering that she wanted you to chase her to prove your feelings?"

Mitch cut her off. "Wait a sec; you're attacking me with information that someone has fed you, without knowing any other facts. Those are obviously pain-filled situations, and anyone would have reacted the way I did."

Crossing her arms in front of her chest, Boggs smirked. "I know more than you think. I know information about people that they haven't told anyone before." Pointing to the moon pin on her lapel, she added, "I have been blessed with gifts from the universe as well as have an extensive education in ancient teachings. To put it mildly, I know things."

Skeptical at her arrogant statement, Mitch asked her to prove her ability. Boggs closed her eyes and raised her head toward the heavens. "Why did you erase Graham's signature and replace it with your own on that woman's chart?"

No one, not even Graham, knew he had taken the responsibility for the dosage mistake. "I was protecting a friend," he blurted out. "We were new residents, and during a tense moment, he froze and didn't calculate the dosage correctly. It could have happened to anyone."

"She almost died," Boggs whispered.

"I know," he replied, staring at the stone beneath his feet. "But she didn't, and when I found out that there could be a malpractice suit brought on by the family, I falsified the document so Graham wouldn't have his license revoked."

"You chose to take the heat and face the possibility of your career ending?"

"Yeah, but unlike Graham, I had a B plan. I didn't have a father breathing down my neck to live up to the family name, and I didn't have the added pressure of a long line of ivy-league family members who became tops in their fields. I just had my mom, and she was proud of me no matter what I did," Mitch confessed.

"Was it loyalty or pain that made you do it?" she asked, shooting the arrow of truth deeper into his chest.

"A little of both. Deep down I wanted to leave the program, and in my mind a mistake like that was better than quitting."

"You chose the pain of distrust from your colleagues rather than follow your passion?" Boggs questioned.

Bowing his head, Mitch's small voice replied, "Yes."

Boggs slapped him on the back. "Finally, we're getting somewhere! You can't take this kind of leap of faith without knowing the man you are inside! It's not about how people see you, but how *you* see you." Smiling sincerely, she led him to a bench at the opposite end of the observation deck, abruptly changing the subject as they sat down. "Don't you just love to people watch? I find them fascinating, from their fashion choices to the way they talk to the people around them. You can tell a lot about people from the way in which they treat others." She chuckled at an elderly couple arguing over where to have lunch, while a young boy held within his mother's arms gazed into her eyes and tenderly kissed her cheek.

"How did you know about my residency? I didn't tell anyone about that; Graham is even fuzzy on the details."

Keeping her gaze on the little boy and his mother, Boggs answered bluntly, "In scientific circles, I am labeled as an intuitive psychic. I tap into the energy of an individual and communicate with my spirit guides to receive information concerning a soul's energy. Yours is quite spectacular, with a lot of push and pull going on, and you struggle with the tiniest things." She turned her head toward him. "Let's table that dialogue for another time and get to the real reason we're here."

She untied the scarlet ribbon at the top of the bag she carried, sliding out the artifact contained within. In the glittering sunlight, the golden hilt of a sword peeked from beneath the black velvet, followed by its silver blade sheathed in protective metal. Laying the sword across her lap, she folded the bag neatly, tucking it underneath the blade. The antique had been engraved at some point in its existence, but since the engravings had faded, a closer examination was necessary to pinpoint what lay hidden within the metal. Someone had taken excellent care of this sword, loving it enough to delicately polish the metal without desecrating the engravings.

"Instead of asking you a bunch of questions pertaining to what you do or don't know about swords, I'm just going to get right to it. Everyone has different teaching methods, and mine is to teach, ask questions, and then teach some more. OK with you?" Mitch sat silently, nodding his head for her to continue. "The sword is a symbol not only of warfare, but as I hope you may have already guessed, spirituality. The sword has the ability to create kings, strike down or disfigure humans, establish power for a leader, punish an enemy, rally the troops before battle, and reverse it all with an incredible ability to heal. Its healing capabilities lie in the realm of healing the land following the coronation of a ruler that is more enlightened than the previous. Throughout periods of history, leaders have come to power who were required at that moment due to their ability to see past their own needs for the betterment of the people they governed. There is an ancient symbol, adopted by the medical community, that distinguishes healers from other members of society. Would you be able to draw it for me?" Boggs asked, withdrawing a small notebook and pen from her purse. The symbol immediately come to his mind, so she sat quietly and waited for him to remember what was embroidered on his lab coat.

"Are you talking about the two snakes entwined around a cross?" he asked, unsure of his answer.

"That symbol of healing was adopted from an ancient community before the time of Christ called the Therapeutate. They were revered healers who dealt with the mind-body connection, believing that the mind could conquer physical ailments of the body and vice versa. They were what we would now refer to as naturopaths, in that they dealt with holistic medicines of herbs to heal the sick. They were present during the life of Christ, and rumors have circulated that he may have spent some time in their community before creating his own." She smiled warmly. "I'd say you were born to be a healer, Mitch."

Mitch returned her smile, not knowing what she meant by the compliment. "How does the sword come into that symbol? I always thought it was a cross, not a sword."

"Couldn't it be one in the same?" she asked. "Look at the sword on my lap. Doesn't it resemble a cross in the manner in which it is built? You have the hilt, the cross section, and then the blade. Within the healer's symbol, the snakes represent yet another aspect of enlightenment, which is the Gnostic illumination of an individual through their snake system, known as chakras. Every person has a channel through his physical body where illumination travels, which is the spinal column, culminating at the crown chakra, also known as the head. Since the time of the Therapeutate, this practice has been known as the Kundalini. When a person reaches this heightened state of awareness, their ability to converse with the powers above is wide open."

Boggs paused. She knew it was a lot for anyone to take in, least of all a man who had been tricked into coming on this mission. She was impressed by his willingness to accept what he had been taught so far, but his ease of acceptance would be challenged as information became more difficult. They were asking him to abandon his prejudices and jump feet first into an abyss without a safety net. In her experience, people were reluctant to loosen their grip on the preaching they received throughout their lives and try to comprehend something different. It didn't make them wrong or her right, it just made her melancholy that narrow-minded thinking could still prevail while solidifying organized religion as still one of the mightiest forces on the earth.

He sat there watching the people walk by, trying to concentrate on what she was saying, when in reality all he saw was the pen in his hand the day he changed the signatures.

She nudged his shoulder. "You still with me, kiddo?" Mitch smiled. "Forget what I said earlier; put it out of your mind."

He took a deep breath, stretched his arms into the air, and cracked his neck from side to side. When he was done, he pointed his finger at her, signaling that he was ready for more.

"First the snake. Serpents represented the energizing life force of the Supreme Spirit as well as being the worshiped form of the goddess of knowledge, known as Sophia. The snake reflects enlightenment in its highest form, the sacred male to balance the sacred feminine, and during its progression through history, it morphed into the dragon. The dragon symbol was the epitome of the Holy Spirit as it moved upon the waters of time, and members of the dragon court might wear an insignia of a dragon curved into a circle, with a red cross of the Rosi Crucis. We connect the dragon to some very influential families, such as Uther Pendragon, the legendary father to King Arthur. If the snake represents the path toward truth, then the sword that it is entwined around is the ability to cut through to the core, where truth lies."

His focus gradually reappearing, Mitch continued to silently sit beside her. She recognized his internal struggle, but continued anyway. "Name for me one of the more famous swords in history. I already gave you a clue, so it should be easy."

"Excalibur!" he whispered.

"No need to whisper, this isn't anything secret, and if people hear our business, maybe it will enlighten them a bit." She leaned closer to him. "I'm not into espionage. The more you know in this life, the better equipped you are to deal with what you walk through. And you're correct. The legend of Excalibur was a gift to the newly crowned King Arthur to prove that he was worthy to receive the throne, with differing accounts of how he actually received it. Some say he pulled it from a stone, while others explain that the Lady of the Lake, who was the head priestess of Avalon, gave him the gift. Whatever tale you espouse as truth, the core issue remains that the sword was given to Arthur with the intention that he wield its power to create a utopian society, hence Camelot. Even Saint Michael carries a blue flaming sword as the great defender. It is he who, according to the Catholic Church, destroys the dragon as the warrior angel of God."

Mitch scratched his head. "Didn't you just say that the snake and the dragon were one in the same?" Boggs nodded. "So if he destroys the dragon, couldn't that be symbolic of the destruction of knowledge? Why would a messenger of God be instructed to do that?"

Boggs smacked him on the back in approval. "Mitch, you're brilliant! He wouldn't, which makes it pretty apparent that it is a symbol of the heads of the church wanting to destroy true knowledge under the fear that people would start thinking for themselves. A church without followers is no church at all, which brings us to our location today. Why do you think we are at the Wallace Monument?"

"Because of the huge sword downstairs?"

"Ask any Scotsman about famous swords, and the first one they will speak about is Wallace. As you can tell from the size of the display case, it is rather large, and no ordinary man could wield such a weapon, but Wallace was hardly a country bumpkin. He was a learned man, an intelligent man, and as portrayed on film, a brave man. He knew what true loyalty was to his family, his friends, and his nation. He gathered people around him because he wasn't afraid to show what he stood for with the potential to die for his passionate beliefs. He helped create a revolution empowered by tens of thousands of countrymen, all willing to accompany him into the unknown. One of those men was Robert the Bruce. You can see how in both Arthur and Wallace, the sword gave the men the ability to slice through to the truth, becoming exemplary leaders to those who needed both guidance and hope."

Boggs extended both hands to Mitch, who grasped them reluctantly. She felt a slight tremble emanating from him. "Recognize the greatness within yourself. Each person has the capacity to achieve what lies deep in our hearts, but most are afraid to leap. Fear plays an intimate role in the demise of achievement. Fear is doubt, fear is darkness, and fear is unproductive. Regain control of your contribution in this life, and fear will take a backseat." Mitch felt compelled to embrace her, which he did rather awkwardly. She patted his back as if she were his own mother, returning a sense of comfort to his already shaken demeanor. He pulled away as tears trickled down his cheeks, wiping them away with the back of his sleeve. Boggs very sweetly handed him a tissue. "Don't be such a guy. Your tears are merely a re-lease. Welcome them and move on in a positive manner. You've done good work here."

Crumpling the tissue into a little ball, he shoved the evidence of vulnerability into his pocket. As he did, a little girl confronted him from his right side. "It's OK, sir, I cry when I get scared too." Her smile reached from ear to ear as she walked away with her mother.

"Isn't it amazing that children automatically know truth, speak their minds, and the adults in their lives teach them to suppress it and lie, since it isn't considered correct or polite to speak the truth? It's pure fascination to me," Boggs commented.

Mitch watched the little girl walk toward the other side of the observation deck, glance over the side, and quickly turn around with her eyes closed. Her speaking to him made him realize that he did want a family, did want a future, and wanted to be the person who sang the fears out of his child's head. He suddenly ached with long-ing for having small hands clasp around his neck in a loving embrace.

Boggs placed the sword back into the black velvet bag, tying the ribbon in a delicate bow at the top. Mitch held out his hands to receive the sword, assuming it was one of the objects he needed to retrieve.

"What are you doing?" she asked him.

"Aren't you giving that to me?"

Standing up from the bench, Boggs replied, "Not yet. We have one more stop to make. Any other teacher would indeed give it to you now, but I think we can get some more work done at a second location that isn't far from here."

The two descended back down the stairs, through the exhibition hall, and out into the car park without speaking, each one lost in thought. Mitch noticed that her walk became a little swifter as she joined the crush of people on the gravel. She stopped abruptly at a black Mini Cooper, looking from side to side past all the cars around them. "Is this your car?" Mitch asked, walking to the passenger side.

"No, it's not, follow my lead," she whispered, and then announced loudly for others to hear, "Damn it, I left my purse inside. Hope no one has taken off with it; we need to go and report it to the guards before anything happens."

A man three aisles away watched them saunter toward the monument. His stride kept up, so much so that Mitch realized they were being followed. Upon reentering the exhibition hall, Boggs approached a guard in a navy-blue rain slicker with the Wallace crest. They exchanged a few words as he discreetly slipped something into her hand. She beamed, while the man from the parking lot closed in on them. Extending his hand to grab Mitch's back collar, the guard moved forward with a silky rope in his hand. Shoving Mitch out of harm's way, he apologized for the inconvenience of the closure of the hall for cleaning purposes. The man, upset by the change of plans, shouted obscenities at the guard. Boggs steered Mitch out a back door reserved for employees, leading to a separate parking lot on the side of the building. They stopped at silver Mazda, parked a few feet from the door. Revealing a set of keys in her hand, she unlocked the door, told Mitch to get in the car, and started the engine.

"I love the Templars," she announced. "Always there in a pinch."

"That guard was a Templar?" Mitch questioned, still rattled by the presence of a man following them.

"Duncan promised protection. You'll find that from here on out, they will be around you, even if you never notice them. They have a grand tradition for protecting what is precious in this world. And right now, that includes you."

Mitch breathed a sigh of relief. "Where are we going?"

"Stirling Castle."

"To do what?" he asked.

"To walk in the footsteps of greatness."

24

"How about a little music?" Boggs suggested, loading a CD of Air Supply into the car's stereo system. The distinct love ballads flooded the speakers as the pair wound their way from the Wallace Monument. Clearly a fan of the American pop group, Boggs seemed transfixed by the melodies, at times even closing her eyes to the road, lost in the rapture of music. It reminded him of his mom, who enjoyed embarrassing him as she drove him and his friends to and from school, belting out the same songs with her tone-deaf singing. Looking back, it seemed that his mom was a relatively normal parent, but when he was a kid, he thought she was out of touch. Having Pip as a chauffeur had spoiled him a bit. He had grown accustomed to getting somewhere at breakneck speed, but the opposite seemed true of Boggs. She was content to motor about at an easier pace.

"How's your mom doing these days?" she inquired.

"She's busy with her charity work at the children's hospital and keeps to her garden club. Stays home more than I think she should, but she has a great set of friends who look after her when I can't." Perplexed by her question, he asked, "Do you know my mom?"

"We go back a few decades to university days, before she met your dad. We lost touch about the time your sister was born. I sent her a few notes here and there after your dad passed to let her know that her support base still existed, even with him gone. She's stronger than you think." Boggs chuckled. "In fact, she buried my sorry behind a time or two at meetings. She's truly gifted."

"The only time she left the house was for the market or her women's clubs meetings. Did you two attend the same club while you lived in the states?" Mitch asked.

"Oh, no, she attended a few organization meetings with your dad right after he was named master. Her abilities, especially when it comes to you, are very acute."

"Are you referring to psychic things again?"

"Your mom has the ability to tap into your energy with a precision I have rarely seen. She was never concerned about you until after your father passed, but your sister maintained a constant thread of fear in her mind," Boggs replied as her driving landed them behind an even slower moving truck.

"What was there to worry about with my sister? She never rebelled, did as she was told, and acted like the perfect child, while I was the one who went through the rebellion phase after the accident. I thought that since I had just been made an adult, I could act like one in a variety of ways." Mitch admitted openly.

"Like drinking?" Boggs asked.

Mitch folded his hands onto his lap. "Yeah, I tried to hide it, but my mom caught me a couple of times and gave me some lecture about enjoying my childhood while I had the opportunity. I listened to her, but thought that I no longer had a childhood, because it was stolen from me the night my dad died."

"That wasn't her fault, Mitch; neither was it your father's intention. Accidents happen whether we like them to or not."

"I assumed the responsibility on behalf of my father. I stepped up." Mitch bowed his head and whispered, "I always step up."

Boggs discovered an opportunity to pass the slow-moving truck ahead of them in a sudden burst of speed. She waved at the driver as they passed, answering Mitch's statement at the same time. "That's the point right there. *You* assumed the responsibility to take care of them. No one appointed it; *you* took it. This is a pattern you seem to follow. You put the unnecessary burden onto yourself while swimming in the muck it creates. The perplexing thing about you is that, unlike your sister, you don't complain."

Mitch's cheeks flushed red with rage. "Leave her out of this!" he seethed. "She never complained."

Rolling her eyes, Boggs looked annoyed. "Are you kidding me? She was nothing but a complainer! She kept journals to the effect. Did you know that?" Mitch shook his head in denial. "Your mom found them in her room when she was seventeen. She was developing into a type of person your mother was afraid would become lost. She expressed a desire to have wealth, power, prestige, and worst of all, control over others. According to her writings, your sister's greed was insatiable. She had a couple of instances of shoplifting with her friends, and your mother was called on several occasions by the principal for bullying a weaker individual at school."

Mitch scoffed at her remarks. "That's not possible. My mother would have told me. I was the man of the house."

"But you weren't her parent, you were her brother. It wasn't your position to discipline. Because of her self-destructive path, your Mom contacted us to enroll her in a special school to help her find her way. Do you remember her final year of high school?" Boggs asked.

"I was in med school at the time, but I do remember my mom saying that she had been accepted into a gifted program," Mitch replied.

Beginning their ascent up another hill, Boggs waved her hand in Mitch's direction, as if swatting at a fly. "Merely semantics. That gifted program was a girl's school that educated young women in the spiritual arts alongside academic programs. Your mother was familiar with that school because she attended it as a young girl. The pin she wears is the symbol of her graduation, which is identical to my own, except the two stones represent my granddaughters. Your mother bragged that your sister learned a great deal at school, with the most important lesson being that she possessed no extraordinary talents of her own, making her lash out even harder at those who did. She judged them as freaks, and she sought out others who would stop at nothing to destroy them. It has been your mother's greatest heartbreak."

Mitch could only think of one question. "Why?"

"A bond between a mother and a daughter is unbreakable. A woman feels compelled to instill in her daughter all of her own wisdom through the mistakes she has made. Your mom believed that she failed your sister, and that guilt created the recluse she has turned into over the last ten years. The two women in your life never had any speck of a relationship after she was sent away to school. Now, I'm afraid your sister has made a pact with someone who cares very little about her, but who can give her all the material goods she so desperately desires."

Thinking about his sister's hardships, he felt the same guilt his mother carried. "I should have paid more attention to her needs. That's what big brothers are for."

The laugh escaping Boggs's lips surprised Mitch. "You don't change, do you? Even when you're told that you put pain and pressure on yourself, you repeat the process! Let's try something. I'm going to ask you some simple questions, and you answer them with short, honest responses." Mitch sat in silent agreement. "Are you her parent or her brother?"

"Brother?"

"Are you responsible for her path as well as your own?"

"No?"

"Is it absolutely necessary for you to assume the suffering of those around you at all times, no matter what the consequence for you?"

"No?"

"Is there a reason you're answering each question with uncertainty?"

"Yes?"

"And that would be because?"

Mitch answered from his heart. "I'm trying to figure out what you want to hear and not be honest with myself."

Boggs smacked her hands against the steering wheel in celebration of his breakthrough. "Bravo! Now we're getting somewhere! It's quite difficult to look at ourselves in a different light, especially when that light is discolored by the poor choices we make." Mitch frowned. "Don't make that face, Mitchell. You're not weak; you have a good heart, which you can't give away to all Toms, Dicks, and Harrys who ask you to carry their burdens subconsciously. Those are their burdens, *not* yours. All people have to lie in the beds that they make. Some are messy, while others are neat as a pin, and at the end of the day, karma is a bitch."

The bold lettering on a sign straight ahead of them returned a flood of memories into Mitch's brain as he choked back tears pooling in his eyes. "What does karma have to do with it?" he asked, rubbing his eyes until he no longer felt dampness.

"Our actions set about a chain of events that may lead to different results in this life or the next. It's like being in school. If you don't learn the lessons and can't pass the grade, then they hold you back. It's the same on a spiritual level. If you don't learn the lesson, you are doomed to repeat it sooner or later. Things in your life have led you to this point, this task, and this karmic debt. *You* are the one who has to assist Tamara through this. *You* were chosen long before we ever got involved. Your name, like hers, was written on the stone to complete this journey together. You must embrace the past, live through the present, and create the future." Boggs pulled the car into an empty parking spot and turned off the engine.

Leaving the keys in the ignition, she turned to face him. "Take a moment to examine your life, and you'll see that there aren't any subtle coincidences where your path is concerned. On the contrary, there have been glaring signs pointing you toward a destiny. Why on earth would you be lifelong friends with Tamara's parents, and why did they make you her godfather, if not for the reason that you were meant to be? Can you think of anyone else who could possibly bring the passion to it that you do?" Taking a deep breath, she added, "Graham was meant to be her doctor for this leg of her adventure;

your involvement with her care was merely the catalyst to propel you forward."

Mitch sat still, slowly breathing in and out, trying to process all the questions she threw at him. The mental strain was comparable to the family therapy sessions he had to endure after his father's death. He handled that situation in much the same manner, answering questions with questions, telling the therapist what he thought he wanted to hear. His flaw this time was having someone who saw past all that. "I don't know," was the answer he could give, because truthfully he didn't.

Dropping the volume of her voice to a hush, she asked, "Is that the best you can do?"

"For right now, yes it is. I don't know if you are aware that this is all new to me. One day I was sitting in the hospital trying to figure out a dying girl's chance at survival, and the next thing I know, I am thrust into a world where people are shooting at me and I'm given information that I am expected to believe without question." He looked straight ahead.

Boggs's voice rose a little higher. "We don't have time to coddle you! Time is something we're in short supply of these days. Your father knew the risks and took them without question. He knew truth would speak to his soul, and so he asked very few questions. Are you unable to do the same?"

"I am not my father!" Mitch seethed.

The vibration from his outburst shook the parked car, as the two of them stared into each other's eyes. Mitch didn't feel like he had any fight left to continue with whatever she had planned, and he secretly hoped that she would take him back to Pip's house. He felt the urge to be alone on a long walk, where his destination was no longer important. Security be damned; he needed to be on his own.

After a few moments, Boggs broke the ice. "You are correct on all levels, Mitch. However, nothing worthwhile is easy." She laid her hand on his, which trembled through anger. Her hands were surprisingly soft and gentle. "Please think about Lillian. She has known your path with her daughter from the beginning. Now she has to sit by, helpless to aid in the survival of her only child, while she keeps unwavering faith that Tamara will not perish. Would you be able to have such faith?" She looked at him as a single tear streamed down her cheek. "I'm not sure if even I would have the strength to endure what she has without wanting to rip someone's head off."

Lillian's face flashed before him the day he left the hospital room. He had signed orders for Tamara to go home, while in his own mind he lacked the confidence that she would survive. He hoped for a miracle when he was embraced by his old friend, he smiled at her daughter, and he walked out of the room. "She is remarkable. She's always been remarkable, but you're right, no mother should have to endure this type of pain."

Her grip tightened. "If not for yourself, do it for them. Continue this journey with Tamara and Lillian in your heart. They are the ones to be saved." Mitch took a moment to nod. "Besides, we'll have plenty of time to work on you when this is all over. My hourly rates aren't that bad," she joked, playfully patting his hands.

Mitch laughed at her attempt to be funny, feeling much more comfortable than he had all day. "Tell me where we are and why we're here."

"Oh, no, this one's on you. You tell me where we are."

The masonry's creamy exterior had yellowed since his last visit, but the strength of the massive structure was undeniable. One glance at the fortified outer walls returned him to a young boy sitting in a car with his father. "Stirling Castle."

"You remember your trip?" she asked quite candidly.

"Just as big and foreboding as this one is turning out to be." Mitch laughed at how it did seem a little smaller now that he had grown up. "I don't remember much about the history, though. Duncan and Stewart did mention that they found the stone from the museum here the morning before a battle. Other than that, I'm stumped."

Boggs clapped with enthusiasm. "Good thing I'm always prepared." She reached under her seat, pulling out a well-worn book with brightly colored tabs extending from the pages. She pulled at a blue tab, opening to a page regarding Stirling Castle. "I used to embarrass my daughter with this book. We toured Scotland for a few summers, and I used this tourists' blue book to outline which historical places to visit. She told me to burn it the last summer we were here, but I just couldn't. I can't resist a good travel book or historical marker."

Mitch could only imagine the type of daughter Boggs created. Given the manner in which she spoke about their summer excursions, it sounded as if she was similar to a boyhood Mitch. He would tag along during family vacations, daydreaming of more stimulating locales. While Boggs droned on about the castle's residents of James IV, James V, and Mary Queen of Scots, Mitch felt the same drifting of his attention as if he were sitting in the backseat of his parent's car. Mary was the castle's most famous prisoner before being hauled off to the Tower of London, under the Queen's orders, for execution by beheading for the treasonous act of being a threat to her throne. Before departing for her impending doom, Mary summoned the presence of a family who had guarded her since birth. For their service as well as their silence, she bestowed a gift upon them. An artifact revealing secret symbols of a spiritual education both she and Tamara have received. Mitch's interest piqued at Tamara's name, but he wasn't fully present in the lecture until she mentioned the Battle of Bannockburn. For some odd reason, he held a fascination about the battle. "Sorry, can you repeat the battle part again?" he asked.

"Holding this castle was a key element leading to the Battle of Bannockburn." She closed the book with a thump and threw it onto the dashboard of the car. "Let's tour the grounds."

Mitch stepped out into the brisk air, wishing he had worn a thicker jacket. He was impressed by the care the building received during numerous renovations. The painstaking attention to detail was everywhere, in the way scaffolds where placed against the aging mortar to the direction of pathways for tourists during their visits. Boggs walked ahead of him, pointing out features of the castle, quoting from memory the statements she read in her tourists' blue book.

"What does this location have to do with what I need to know, besides Robert the Bruce obtaining the stone here?" Mitch asked as they walked.

Without skipping a beat, Boggs answered him swiftly. "Every place of significance on the earth's surface holds the energy and memory of the event that occurred there. This castle has been significant during many events in Scottish history. Once we turn this corner, we will focus on three important facts for our discussion today." They followed the path around to the great hall on the other side of the building. Cloistered within overgrown ivy, a small dark door hid within the camouflaging vines. Five narrow steps led into a long garden area on a lower level. Three weathered wooden benches dotted the green grass, surrounded by flowering vines climbing their way to the top of the wall. Boggs led him to a remote section of the garden, where visitors were not permitted. Turning to face him, she squinted from the blinding glare of the sun.

"Before the Battle of Bannockburn commenced, Bruce knew he was outnumbered, knew he could not be victorious, so he asked for help. When a person who acts on behalf of others without personal gain asks for aid, he or she is awarded assistance without question. Bruce received his assistance in the form of the Clach na Brataich, or Crystal Charm Stone and military reinforcements as mounted Templars on horseback." Mitch felt the inside of his pocket for his own stone, thinking that he could feel it pulse.

"Bruce not only received aid from the Templars, but from Druid priests who summoned old magic to protect the Scottish soldiers. The traditional practice of Druid priests was to create a magical line in front of the army, protecting them from harm, which I believe led to victory. Magic in its purest form isn't all bad." The wind blew harder at her mention of magic, whipping the flowers so forcefully that they almost bent in half.

"There is a memory of a prophecy held here from long ago. An ancient text tells of a princess who shall be born of parents possessing the abilities to see beyond the realm of this world into another. This princess shall create a shift in the energy of the world, thus bringing about the desperate change of humanity. The task appointed to her by the heavenly realm is to restore the wasteland that humanity has created, restoring the necessary balance for humankind to continue. Without this balance, we are cursed to repeat every historical cycle, every plague, every war, and every sorrow. We must get back to the mindset of loving each other, learning from each other, and supporting one another, or we will be erased." Boggs folded her arms in front of her chest and waited for either a question or response from Mitch, whichever came first. "The part of my historical lesson regarding Tamara and Mary is a vital part of this information." She rolled her eyes. "Men always hear the conflict of battle and perk up, but refer to a high-profile female, and it becomes yawn central."

Mitch apologized. "There is a connection between the princess who went to the tower, Tamara, and the princess of prophecy?"

"Boggs tapped her toe impatiently. "Do you know what hangs in Tamara's family home?"

"There is a glass case with some old weaving inside," Mitch stated, surprised that he remembered the house's details.

"That old weaving is called the Exile Carpet. It hangs as a symbol of its guardians' status as high priestesses in education and enlightenment." Boggs waited for a reaction from Mitch, who stood with a blank stare in his eyes. "It is passed down through generations of guardians to ensure that its message of hope endures. Mary was a guardian when she handed it over, with specific instructions, to those who were sworn to protect it. The princess in the prophecy carries the responsibility of protecting the Exile Carpet, which is needed in the final ceremony, for the high priestess to restore humanity's wasteland."

Surveying his environment, Mitch couldn't help but wonder why the wind whipped furiously around them and yet nowhere else. Could it be possible that magic existed in this world, staring people in the face, and yet the blindness that they created toward it blocked their view of its majesty? Sure, he was a little more accepting of the notion than he was a week ago, but if anyone possessed magical abilities, it was surely the women he had met on this trip. All of them in some way, shape, or form had shown him magic, and he had no choice but to look over the edge into the deep end of the pool and jump.

"That's a pretty hefty job for anyone, let alone a little girl," he answered.

Boggs smiled. "It's been a big job for a number of master teachers throughout the centuries. We have a tendency to believe for a bit and then march back into our old ways of finger-pointing while blindly following false leaders."

Mitch took a deep breath into his lungs, feeling a small ache from his wound. "Tamara is going to need all the help she can get." At the mention of her name, the wind ceased as suddenly as it begun. Birds chirped from their nests, clouds effortlessly glided past them, while flowers raised their heads back toward beams of the sun. Boggs was right. Magic *was* all around.

Taking two steps toward Mitch, Boggs posed a loaded question. "Who said we were talking about Tamara?"

He faced her in a defiant stance. Mitch knew she was testing him. "Why else would I be here if it wasn't Tamara? She has all the characteristics you mentioned; she's had them since she was a little girl. Now her life hangs in the balance, and I, as her doctor and her godfather, have to find the key to restore her health as well as her spiritual balance. "

"That's a pretty hefty job for anyone, let alone a doctor." Boggs remarked, quoting his words.

"I guess it is."

"Keeping all of this in perspective, let's soldier on and see what we find." Boggs suggested, leading him along the castle wall. A large statue of Robert the Bruce stood across the lawn, with the Wallace Monument silhouetted in the distance. The two figures stood in stark contrast, yet complimented each other as beacons of strength protecting the countryside. Approaching the statue, a glimmer of metal shone into Mitch's eyes. He squinted, trying to make out the object that sat in front of the base of the statue's pedestal. Boggs stopped midstride, allowing him to continue alone. He didn't need to glance back at her, knowing that the shiny object was meant for him. A miniature hum escaped his pocket, as the stone began to rise in temperature. The warmth emanating from his pocket intensified with each step. He reached his left hand forward to grasp the hilt of a sword, which stood straight up in the ground. The metal came alive under his touch, sending a spark of electricity into his body. Drawing the weapon from its resting place in the earth, he laid it across his palms, as Boggs had done at the monument. Upon closer inspection, he noticed that the markings were identical, even in the same locations. He didn't see Boggs carry the sword onto the castle grounds, so with his brow furled, he turned to interrogate his teacher.

"How do you think it got here?" she asked, not allowing him to ask speak first.

He summed up his response with a single word. "Magic?"

Placing her index finger onto the tip of her nose, she answered, "Precisely."

"This is another object that I need for some mystery thing that no one will tell me about, right?" Mitch asked, feeling the metal vibrate in perfect harmony with his stone.

"This is merely the fourth object. You must receive two more to complete the circle and begin the process of healing. Wheels have been set into motion regarding Tamara's well-being and the completion of her own task. All the objects that you have been given and are yet to receive will be utilized for the completion of her destiny. It is vital that this congregation of objects must be collected under the purest of circumstances, which is why we felt it necessary to educate you before giving any of them to you."

"What creates purity?" he asked, still wrinkling his brow.

Removing her glasses allowed her the opportunity to look directly into his eyes without obstruction. "Love," she said. "Love is pure. The love in your hearts that beat together at the right moment, combined with the hope that remains for humanity's success, allows channels to open and information to be received. It's as simple as that." Placing her hand onto his chest, she felt the rhythm of his heart beating faster and faster from adrenaline permeating his system. "Unconditional love is one of the most powerful forces on earth. Love can eliminate fear, doubt, and darkness; all you have to do is summon it." She withdrew her hand and embraced him, feeling the sword press into her torso.

Mitch pulled away from the embrace first, placing the sword in the sheath that Boggs held out to him. He wrapped it in the black velvet bag she removed from her purse and retied the red ribbon at the top.

"Let's get moving," she told him. "Pip will be getting worried. I'm sure that the Templar back at Wallace told her about the man following us, and I wasn't truly honest about what we were doing today."

"How so?"

Boggs quickened their pace past tourists, who were lined throughout the lawn area. "I didn't tell her we were coming here. We were supposed to stay at the monument, but I had a feeling that I could get you to open up more because of the trip you made with your father, and I was right. Don't you hate it when that continually happens?"

Consumed with sharing personal stories of vacations gone wrong, neither one noticed the man behind the wheel of a black sedan. As the two approached their vehicle, he grabbed a cell phone from its plush resting place amid the upholstery. His orders had been to follow them at Wallace Monument, to make contact while there, and to place another locator device onto the doctor before they left. Dialing the phone number listed in the contact list, the click told him he had a connection.

"I had them, sir, but the woman noticed me before I could place the device on him. She used some idiot guard at the monument to get in between us. I suggest that I keep on this case a little longer. I'm confident they will return to the girl's house for the night, and I can slip it on him then."

A muffled whisper through the receiver commented on the man's inability to perform as promised and then relayed the next set of instructions.

"I think we need to lay a little low, since they expect something to happen. I'll call you when it's completed." The man pushed the power button, disconnecting the call, and threw the phone into the backseat. Watching the silver Mazda pull out of the parking lot, he slowly began his pursuit, maintaining a safe distance between the two vehicles. He needed no further instructions.

25

A tiny boat danced upon white-capped waves with five passengers huddled together for warmth. Tightening their cloaks to protect them from the freezing spray, the youngest passenger, a girl of eight, stared up at millions of stars glittering like rare gems in the night sky. An older man next to her pointed out each constellation as they twinkled above. He hardly missed an opportunity to teach her something new, especially when her eyes were full of wonder. The little girl absorbed every piece of information with contagious enthusiasm that made her a pleasure to educate. She leaned into the man for added warmth, and he embraced her gently as they gazed at the heavens together.

The two women dressed in matching sapphire cloaks sitting toward the stern focused on the nearing shoreline and small spots of light that guided their vessel through the surf. The powerful arms of the young man who steered with the current slowed his paces, allowing the water to propel them forward to land. Through the darkness, four torch-bearing females in white stood ready to greet the new arrivals. As sand met the wooden hull, the torchbearers walked forward to assist with the last few feet of their voyage. Pulling the boat further onto the shore, they aided the two women first, followed by the young girl and the man who continued to hold her hand. Her green cloak wrapped around her small frame, the girl's emerald eyes sparkled with the light cast by the torches. The torchbearers parted to reveal a fifth woman standing behind them. Also dressed in white, her cloak shone brightly from an iridescent pattern embroidered into the fabric. Her long brown hair waved from the breeze off the ocean. She stepped toward the women in blue, extending her hands, palms up, in a sign of welcome and peace. The younger woman mirrored her hostess, bowing her head in recognition of the greeting. The women embraced, yet tears of sadness fell from their cheeks.

The lady in white whispered, "The ordeal is complete?"

The lady in blue choked back her emotions to keep from sobbing. "Yes, Priestess."

The priestess peered into the eyes of her friend. "The plan was executed without complications?"

"There were unforeseen circumstances, but we are safe and the future is secure." The woman in blue removed the hood of her cloak to reveal a crescent pendant hanging from her neck. "Sarah is safe, which is our first concern. I assume my uncle has already arrived?"

"Yes, Mary, he arrived three days ago, regaling us with the tales of your escape. I am humbled by the level of bravery you have shown. What you completed is no small task," the priestess remarked.

Mary bowed her head in gratitude for the compliment. She didn't feel very brave. She felt like a frightened rabbit, fearful that the slightest tremor would bring about her death at the hand of a fierce predator. Each time she gazed into the eyes of her daughter, Sarah, she felt a renewed strength to continue. Their escape had been swift following Jesus's punishment. Threats not only came from the Romans and the temple priests, but also from Simon Peter, who seized the opportunity to denounce his following of Jesus's teachings in order to establish his own version of a spiritual path. The male disciples went into hiding, while the female disciples remembered their roots in the Temples of Isis and returned to their roles as priestesses. If it hadn't been for the wealth and influence of her Uncle Joseph, Mary was unsure if their flight into Egypt would have been as smooth.

Mary motioned for her daughter to accompany her next to the priestess. Stepping forward, Sarah continued to look back at the man, who encouraged her to move forward. Taking her mother's hand, she glanced up at the woman standing before her and began to tremble. Sensing her fear, the priestess spoke softly.

"*Sweet Sarah, there is no need for fear. We are protected by powers beyond your current understanding, but you will recognize the service of the Magi.*" Four muscular men stepped from the shadows into the light. Dressed in traditional Egyptian uniforms, each carried a broad sword at his hip. She recognized each of them from the temples where they had sought refuge. "*Scrolls were sent requesting their aid when we learned the date of your arrival. They will accompany you as long as you are here.*"

Sarah breathed a sigh of relief at the presence of the four men. While in the Egyptian temples, she hadn't felt fear from any outside influence as long as the Magi were present. A peace surrounded her because of their protection. She felt as if she were encapsulated within a magic bubble that could not be penetrated. She smiled, acknowledging their service. Returning her smile, the tallest man addressed the group. "*We have lingered too long and should retire for the evening.*"

The priestess agreed. "*The night has eyes that are difficult to see, I am afraid. Let us follow the path leading to secure premises for the evening. Tomorrow we will obtain a permanent location for you all.*"

"*Thank you,*" Mary replied as she held her daughter's hand and asked for the other two passengers to follow. The torchbearers mixed with the Magi, the four passengers at the center of a circle, creating a shield of protection from anyone wishing harm, while the priestess led the group toward their accommodations. As their feet felt the transition from sand to a compacted dirt trail, Sarah felt comfortable enough to speak to her mother.

"*Is this the end of our journey?*"

Mary squeezed her hand affectionately while she kept her focus straight ahead. "*There may be brief adventures for educational purposes, but the difficult times should be behind us.*"

"*Should be behind us?*" Sarah repeated.

"*Yes, little one. Without adversity, the challenge would not be as sweet when it is defeated. We learn from the rocky road as we gather strength from that knowledge.*"

"*But the torture of our loved ones is over?*" Sarah asked softly.

"*For now,*" Mary whispered. "*We will all have to contend with a small amount of torture of being away from the places we love while we make a new*

269

life. But as for the physical pain that has been endured, it is over. I am sorry you had to witness it at such a young age. That was not our intention."

Sarah stared at the back of the priestess's white cloak, straining her eyes to make out the symbol embroidered in shiny thread. A serpent coiling to the sky sat on the left, while a winged disc sat in the middle, a dove gracing the right. Identical symbols adorned the entrance to the temples at Heliopolis, and while the priestesses there wore different clothing, the symbols remained consistent in the training they received. Sarah hoped that one day, like her own mother, she too would wear the priestess symbols.

The landscape was foreign to Sarah, who was used to feeling the desert sand beneath her feet and the hot wind blow at her cheeks as the sun baked mud into hard clay. This land had a moist chill in the air that would be hard to get used to. Even in colder times, the desert didn't have the dampness that this place held. A small community of buildings came into view, lit by torches strategically placed around the site. No one but the small band of people walking the trail was visible due to the late hour of their arrival. Tonight, the added pressure of making a positive first impression was eradicated, as a soft bed was all the weary travelers desired.

The priestess stopped at a large building, as she bid the travelers goodnight, informing them that she would see them when the sun rose in the morning. The torchbearers retreated as well, while the four Magi led them to a small building a few feet away. With the Magi secured outside, as they had been in Egypt, Mary led her party inside.

At the center of the circular building, a fire roared to the top of the ceiling, where a small hole allowed the smoke to clear. Four beds encircled the blazing warmth with fur blankets for additional comfort gracing their simplicity. The only man of the group sat on the bed closest to the door, with the second woman next to him, while Mary and Sarah took beds across from the door. Sarah felt much safer sleeping through the night knowing that anyone who wished them harm would have to go through four Magi as well as her uncle before accomplishing evil.

Since they fled their homeland, her nightmares had gotten worse, and sleep did not come easy once night fell. In her more recent dreams, she saw herself upon a large cross, crying out for help, while those around her ignored her *pleas. Each dream brought her a newfound terror that proved difficult to shake during the daytime, causing her to retreat farther and farther away from human companionship. Sarah laid her head upon the softness of the pillow, wrapping the fur around her chilled body, and allowed fatigue to overwhelm her. The trip, the lack of sleep, and the anticipation of what could come around any corner suddenly took its toll, allowing her to succumb to her body's need to rest.*

It would be the first time in months that she would sleep through the entire night without dreaming.

Smoke from the extinguished fire woke her before the sun had its chance to peek through the ceiling. Stretching her body in different directions, Sarah raised up from the comfort of her bed, feeling refreshed and energized. Today was the first day of her new life, new identity, and new home, and she intended to make the most of the time she had here. She expected to see the others still sleeping in their beds as she looked around the room. She faced the disappointment that she was the only one left. Her immediate thought was that something had happened in the night, and she was left alone. Fear had a convenient way of settling into the deep recesses of her mind and having its way with her emotions. Venturing out of the building, she encountered two of her Magi faithfully guarding the doorway. They smiled as she greeted the small rays of sun beginning to bounce their beams through the tree limbs. The taller one acknowledged her presence respectfully.

"Good morning, Princess."

"Good morning," she replied, with a tiny smile. "Are you aware of where my mother has gone?"

He pointed to the large building they passed in the night. "She and your uncles are meeting with the priestess. Your aunt is tending to the kitchen to ensure you get nourishment that is familiar to you in this strange place." Winking at her, he added, "She has shared some of your meal with us. You will be satisfied."

Her smile extended from ear to ear. He was her favorite of all the guardians, the one who took walks with her and let her just be a girl, away from the pressure of her family, away from the uncertainty of her future, and away from the gossip mongers of the villages. He never asked questions. He simply escorted her wherever she dared to travel, prepared for any threat, and let her be a child. She trusted him like no other and was happy that he was chosen to accompany her here.

"I'm glad she gave you breakfast. I'll tell her you finally find her cooking acceptable." Walking away from him, she heard him laugh as he explained the joke to the other guard. She liked to tease him, he explained, which made her more like a daughter than an object to guard.

Imposing wooden doors shielded the entrance. Round copper doorknobs jutted out from the wood, causing her to use both hands to open just one door. The smell of incense permeated the air as her eyes adjusted to the candlelight within the interior. Her two uncles were arguing, and the one who sat beside her on the boat from Egypt spoke first.

"Joseph, I understand your point, but we do not dare another excursion so soon."

"Lazarus!" Joseph yelled. "You are a fool! They only know a small amount here, if anything, and what they do know has traveled farther than you to reach them. Information becomes distorted. Do not be lulled into thinking that you are completely safe."

Sarah walked into the open room and saw her Uncle Lazarus standing across from her Uncle Joseph, looking as if he would strike him. She had never seen him so angry.

"Joseph, safety will be a concern for a lengthy period of time. Mary and Sarah in particular. The young one is greatly traumatized. You don't hear the night-mares that she has in her sleep, as I have. It concerns me," Lazarus admitted.

Joseph approached Lazarus, placing his hand on his shoulder in a gesture of kindness. "We have been through a great deal, but we have survived to see another beautiful day. The plans we made prior to Jesus's arrest were impec-cable. The Roman Pilate was accommodating once the money was delivered and saw to it that all was performed as requested. We're all safe."

Lazarus looked into the eyes of his friend and family member. "Are we?"

"For now, we are."

"And Jesus?" a voice from behind them asked, breaching their perceived soli-tude. "Is he safe too?" The two men whipped around to see Sarah standing across the room.

Lazarus was the first to reach her, embracing her tenderly. "Jesus is safe, little one," he whispered. "The priests are healing both his body and his soul. He will return when he is ready." Grabbing her shoulders, he looked deeply into her eyes. "Until then, you have nothing to fear. We are all with you."

Joseph strode toward her with outstretched arms, ready for his own embrace. "I haven't seen you in months, little one. You have grown a bit since your departure from Egypt."

His embrace was not as tight as Lazarus's, and he quickly withdrew from her. He seemed to act increasingly nervous around her the older she got. When she questioned her mother about it, she told her that it was because he was used to a little girl, and her becoming a young woman made him feel old. Sarah never thought of her family members as older; their hair just turned different colors.

"Good to see you, Uncle," Sarah remarked. "Is my mother here?"

Lazarus was the first to respond. "She is with the priestess, in morning prayers, as well as securing the plans for your education. It seems we are to stay at this location longer than previously assumed, but it is necessary. Your Aunt Martha has been preparing a meal for you. Why don't you eat until you are called?"

"Yes, Uncle," Sarah replied. He showed her where delicious smells lingered in the air, and she slowly walked toward them, intent on trying to overhear more of what her uncles were debating.

Disappointed by their silence, she walked through a doorway leading into the large kitchen area; Sarah was surprised to see her mother and aunt laughing by the fire. She hadn't seen her mother happy in many months. The strain and pressure had been apparent on her face for almost a year, and a smile rarely graced it.

"My dear Sarah, come sit with us and eat something. I have much to tell you."

Martha grabbed a third stool and placed it between the two women. She softly pulled Sarah's hair back from the front of her face to fall behind her shoulders. Her fingers twirled the curly ends, making them more pronounced. Before turning to attend to Sarah's breakfast, she placed a kiss on the top of her head.

"Why are the uncles arguing?" she asked.

Mary sighed, placing a bowl of steaming tea on the ground. "Each one wants the same thing, but in different ways. Oftentimes, men arrive at the same conclusion, but from alternate directions."

"How long are we staying?" Sarah asked, taking a bowl from her aunt's hands and balancing it on her lap.

"Since you began some of your training in Egypt within the Temple of Isis, the priestess would like to question your knowledge to determine how to proceed while we are here. I am confident you will surpass all her expectations, since you have already proven to be a gifted healer."

"And what will you do while I am learning, Mother?" Sarah inquired.

Before answering her question, Mary reached into her blue robes, grabbing a small bag and a book. She placed the objects on her lap as Sarah's eyes widened in recognition. "I intend to pass on my experience and knowledge to those who have the ability to read the written word, so that generations of humanity will come to know that we have lived and discover their own strength."

"Like the men who followed Jesus?" Sarah asked.

In their homeland, the Jewish priests forbade women to participate in any type of education. Sarah heard from her Aunt Martha that some of the women who followed Jesus's path had gone against the priests in secret and maintained their own accounts of spirituality.

"They spoke of rules to follow, and I speak from the soul." Mary picked up the small bag and handed it to her daughter. "This is now yours. Use it wisely, and the grace that I have been given shall also flow into you."

Sarah accepted the small bag, feeling the weighted contents in her hand.

When she was younger, she would feel the objects from the bag's exterior, trying to guess what it contained. One time, she thought she had felt one of the objects jump when touched, which had frightened her, and she had not gone near it since. This time, as she held it, the entire bag seemed to come alive with a tiny vibration running from her hand into the rest of her body. While Sarah contemplated the gift, Mary opened the small book and removed a dried lotus flower from between the pages. Placing it gently into her daughter's hands, she smiled at the young woman who was appearing before her eyes, as the little girl began to evaporate. "It was the last lotus of the season. I took it, for you, as a remembrance of the temples. Use it to recall warm days filled with wonder as you begin your journey of self-discovery. I have tremendous pride in you, Sarah. You will do great things."

Hearing her mother's pride was too overwhelming to bear. She threw the bag and lotus flower onto the ground and embraced her mother. They held each other tightly as Sarah sobbed for all the things she should not have seen but had to endure. Mary stroked her hair, as she had with Jesus before they removed his body.

"You are my miracle," Mary whispered.

Tamara's eyes flew open as the girl embracing her mother retreated to the dark recesses of her mind. She had seen these four travelers before, but couldn't place them. Rubbing her eyes to eliminate the sleep from their corners, the glass case at Gammie's house popped into her head. The four faces embroidered into the remnant of the carpet were the same from her vision, leading her to think that maybe this vision had been a dream manifested from the carpet. Tamara began to doubt her ability as her mother entered the hospital room carrying a small potted plant: a lotus blossom.

"Hi, sweetie," her mother chirped. "Have a good nap?"

Her mother's voice seemed more and more strained these days, leading Tamara to believe that she knew more than she let on. She internalized everything and spoon-fed Tamara information that she deemed imperative.

"You look worried. Anything you want to talk about?" she asked, placing the plant on the windowsill.

Tamara had asked about the carpet hanging in the dining room on numerous occasions. It was a priceless artifact that should not be touched by a child's hands was the only explanation offered. It seemed ridiculous at the time, but now, lying in her hospital bed, she wished she could stare at the carpet a little closer. She must have been staring blindly at the wall for her mother to ask her again if she was all right.

"Yeah, Mom, I'm fine. Just a weird dream."

Lillian brushed Tamara's hair out of her eyes. "Do you want to talk about it?"

Tamara allowed her mother to console her. "I'd rather wait for Earl."

Lillian forced a smile. "Sweetie, Earl is busy with his own personal agenda and won't be here for a few days. I'm sure we can tackle this one, and then the next time you see him, you can tell him everything. How does that sound?"

Tamara knew something had happened. "No offense, Mom, but I didn't think you would understand what I'm talking about. Maybe you could just call Earl and ask him when he *can* be here."

Lillian enfolded Tamara's hands within her own. "I asked Earl to take some time off from the hospital. He has some larger issues on his plate and needed a reprieve. He'll be back when his business is wrapped up." She looked down at her daughter's hands, still amazed by how closely they resembled her own. "Why don't you give me a test to see how much your old mother knows? I think you'll be surprised."

Arguing with anyone took a physical toll on Tamara. Her blood pressure rose, sending monitors into hyperactive alarm mode, resulting in stern lectures from her nurses. Daring the risk of her mother thinking she was completely crazy, she closed her eyes and described the vision. Her mother kept their hands linked throughout the entire story, squeezing her hand only twice.

When Tamara finished her explanation, she opened her eyes and stared into her mother's smiling face. "Why the smile?" she asked nervously.

"Because, my dear daughter, you have finally come into your own. I think it is safe to say that your training began long ago, without my knowledge, within the visions." She looked up at the ceiling and laughed. "You were right, Mom; I should have listened to you."

Scrunching her face in confusion, Tamara asked her mother what she was doing. "I'm talking to your Gammie, sweetie. She had the uncanny and somewhat annoying habit of constantly being right regarding an outcome or situation. And whenever we spoke about you, she was right on the money every time. I just never listened until now." She patted Tamara's hands the same way her Gammie used to. "You'll find as you get older that the things your parents tell you will not only come true, but will make perfect sense as an adult."

Tamara hadn't seen this carefree side of her mother before, which she liked more than the proper lady she usually portrayed. "So what do you think about the vision?" she asked.

Lillian made herself more comfortable on the bed as she thought of the best method of explanation. "Can you recall what is hanging in Gammie's dining room?"

"The carpet thing in the glass case," Tamara replied.

"It is the Exile Carpet, and it has been handed down through generations in our family as an heirloom, even though the people portrayed have nothing to do with our family."

Confused by her mother's vague terms, Tamara asked, "Then why do we have it?"

"Because it is a reminder to us all that hope remains for truth to survive, even under dire circumstances. Our family carries the responsibility of its safekeeping," Lillian stated.

"Hope for what?"

"That one day humanity will awaken from their hypnotic, deadened slumber and think for themselves; that history has the chance to be rewritten with the accuracy of lost stories; that humanity will return to its roots of kindness, servitude, and grace. It is a symbol that even when things are darkest, there is always light. Our family has retained the obligation for the Exile Carpet's protection since its inception in France. Each generation of female guardians understands the magic it holds, until the day when the high priestess will regain her throne in the temple to repair what has been broken."

Tamara's head began to throb. "Don't talk in riddles, Mom."

"You can't rush from A to Z without knowing all of the letters in between! To appreciate the carpet or your vision, you need background information about the people you saw, who happen to be the same ones portrayed in the carpet. The young girl named Sarah has been identified by popular theorists as a princess born of noble lineage. Some theories identify her as the daughter of Mary Magdalene, while others identify her as a common slave girl that accompanied Mary Magdalene, her sister Martha, and her brother Lazarus out of the Middle East following the crucifixion. The artist who completed the carpet is unknown, but whoever it was, the person knew that the Magdalene made it safely out of the Holy Land."

"Where did she go? They didn't mention their location in the vision," Tamara said.

"Ancient accounts state that she landed in the south of France, which is why that area had such a tremendous veneration for her, and how the Cathar religion was established. There are manuscripts that say she lived in a cave and her remains lay somewhere in France, yet to be discovered."

Tamara began to feel lightheaded from everything her mother knew so easily. "Who were the Cathars?"

"They were a religious organization dedicated to the teachings of Mary Magdalene. The Catholic Church performed unspeakable horrors on them during the Inquisition, practically erasing them from existence." She leaned in closer and whispered, "Between you and me, I don't think they were wiped out. I think they just went public. You can hide better out in the open."

The Cathar religion intrigued Tamara, but she pushed it to the back of her mind, trying to remain focused on her vision. "How do you know it was Mary Magdalene?"

Taking a deep breath, her mother explained the different names for "Mari" within ancient cultures. "The name could be spelled in a variety of ways, from Marian and Mary to Marianne, Myrrha, and even Myrrhine. It was a common title for a woman educated within the Temples of Isis as a shamanic healer. During a period of great enlightenment, the temples afforded women the opportunity to claim their heritage as healers from all over the world. Due to the changing environment from a multideity belief into a single-deity system, the traditions of healing and priestess work was outlawed within certain communities, labeling women who had been taught to commune with the Universal Mother Goddess as heretical witches. Men rapidly became leaders while suppressing women's roles to complete their agenda of control. Within the Gnostic Gospels, Mary the Magdalene was often referred to as "Mary Lucifera," or the "Light Bearer," which was the highest honor they could bestow. It meant that she was a woman of extraordinary talent, who commanded the attention of many people. Her background as a trained Egyptian priestess led to hostilities toward her during her companion years with Jesus. A few of the male disciples were openly hostile toward her, intimidated by her natural abilities. People judge and condemn things they don't understand." She paused. "Just like they have with you."

"I don't get it." Tamara said. "All I've ever heard was that Jesus had male disciples, but the vision said there were women." She brushed a stray hair from her eyes.

"Female energy must balance out male or you get a preference that leans toward one side. You can't have black without white. Both must work together to obtain true harmony."

Tamara pressed her mother further. "Why don't books say that there were women?"

"Because that would alter the foundation of the church that Simon Peter built." Looking toward the doorway, Lillian checked to make sure they were still alone. "I think the organization was built around an idea that Simon Peter had, not Jesus. I have read various gospels, some written by women, and I didn't find a single quote by Jesus stating that his intention was to create a religious following."

When Tamara looked at her mother through a daughter's eyes, she saw a parental figure that said no to things like swimming without sunblock, running with a sharp object, cookies before bedtime or for breakfast, and television before homework. This new woman was fascinating, and showed an intellectual side. She would never admit to it out loud, but this discussion was better than anything she had with Earl. Desirous to learn more, she asked, "What do you think happened to Sarah after she hugged her mother?"

"She left her mother and traveled into Scotland, to the Isle of Avalon, to be trained by the priestesses, as her mother had been.

Mary stayed in France, but Sarah returned once her training was completed. You see the two of them portrayed as the "Black Madonna" in churches throughout Europe. In fact, Mary carries a stone in her right hand, which symbolizes her ability to heal."

Tamara sat straight up in bed. "Is that what was in the bag she handed to Sarah? A healing stone? One like Gammie's?"

Lillian nodded at her daughter's enthusiasm. "You come from a long line of healers on my mother's side. I was educated in the same beliefs, beginning at your age. You have the natural ability combined with visions of historical events, which makes your gifts rare."

Her casual statement about her gifts made Tamara feel self-conscious. "Is that why people studied me, because I was rare? Like some animal in a zoo?"

"Is that what you felt like?" her Mother asked, and Tamara simply nodded. "People studied you because you had a talent they didn't understand. I'm afraid that human nature took over for rational thought when they labeled you as anything other than extraordinary. I told you that people condemn things they don't or can't comprehend. Those doctors certainly weren't any different. Your father and I did it as a way of hiding you out in the open." Reaching under her daughter's chin, Lillian lifted her head up to gaze into her eyes. "Even parents make mistakes, sweetie."

Tamara saw the love her mother held deep within her eyes, and she knew the past was not intentional. Her parents, no matter how she had felt at the time, would never jeopardize their daughter. Sometimes she faked sleep to hear her mother whisper prayers at her bedside. They consistently requested that Tamara's burden be lifted and given to her mother. "What next?" she asked.

"Now, we wait to see what tomorrow brings and prepare for your own adventure, just like Sarah." Lillian raised her hands to the back of her neck, fumbling beneath the top her turtleneck sweater. Pulling off the crescent necklace, she handed it to her daughter, motioning for her to scoot up in the bed, so she could place it around her neck. "Now is your time. Now we make sure your destiny is completed."

Securing the chain around Tamara's neck, Lillian leaned back to see the pendant hanging gracefully from her neck. Seeing the moon hanging against her skin, Lillian could still see the little girl twirling in her nightgown with a petticoat hanging off of her head as she played bride.

"Gammie's necklace?" Tamara asked.

"It's your time to wear it. You are one hell of a special kid, and this is one hell of a necklace. But in order for you to be able to wear this symbol, with all that it represents, you will need one more thing." Reaching into her purse, Lillian retrieved a brown suede bag. Grabbing her daughter's left hand, she turned it palm up and placed the bag into her hand. Tamara felt the weight of the bag, and just like Sarah, the contents of the bag jumped. The small jolt surprised her.

"Is this the same one you and Gammie had? The one you never let me play with?" Tamara questioned.

"No," her mother replied. "This was carved especially for you by someone commissioned by your Gammie the day you were born; she knew that one day you would enter into the education that all the women of our family have completed. This one has been kept for you until you were ready."

Tamara carefully untied the top of the bag, revealing nothing but darkness. Holding the bag in the air, she let its contents spill onto her hand. The palm-sized green ball settled into her hand naturally. Throughout her life, she heard women in Gammie's house talk about healing stones and medicine bags, but she had never been this close to one before. Finding herself in uncharted waters, she had no clue what to do with it now that she possessed it.

"Just hold it, listen to it, and the rest will come later. Every stone reacts differently to each person it belongs to." Laughing, she added, "Boy, what I wouldn't give to have seen Mitch when he received his stone. I bet he flipped out!"

E. R. BLAKE

"Dr. Brody got one too?" Tamara asked, amazed that he was one as well.

"Yes, because just like you, he is completing a path of destiny. He has had to learn some lessons that aren't easy to accept, but are mandatory for his care of you." Lillian recognized the look of worry on her daughter's face. "He knows what he's doing, and so do we. The people he's with would never let anyone harm him. Especially now that the two of you are spiritually tied."

Tamara's eyes flew back toward her mother from the healing stone in her hand. "We're what?"

Lillian closed her eyes, knowing she had said too much. There was no other alternative than to explain the real purpose of Mitch's trip, unaware that their time was monitored by a shadow in the doorway.

Dr. Channing Bradley intended to enter the room to discuss the latest treatment options for Tamara now that she had stabilized a bit, but the conversation rendered her motionless. She was stuck between curiosity for the information Lillian offered her daughter and the instinct to leave the two women alone. She hated to admit that this family intrigued her. The concepts Lillian professed went against everything she had ever been taught in vacation Bible school as well as by her own family; yet she was hesitant to discount the validity of each fact. So she hid in the darkened doorway, her focus concentrated on the tales of Dr. Brody in Europe, when she too fell prey to a surprise from behind.

"Heard enough?" a soft voice whispered into her right ear.

The shock of the intruder caused her to spin around, the force nearly knocking Graham to the floor. Lillian and Tamara snapped their heads toward the door, while the two doctors apologized and backed out of the doorway together. As soon as the door latched shut, Channing approached Graham defensively.

"What the hell do you think you're doing? You don't sneak up on people in a hospital!"

Graham laughed at her tone. "Of course you do! Especially if that person is listening in on a private conversation that isn't any of her business. Did you hear anything juicy that would be worth mentioning in the nurse's gossip ring?"

Smoothing her lab coat, Channing despised his manner in getting under her collar so quickly. He had the annoying habit of popping up unannounced at the most inopportune moments in her life, which was usually when she was displaying her sympathetic human side, rather than the rational doctor she portrayed to her colleagues and staff each day. Dr. Brody would normally ignore her behavior, chalking it up to a different side without mention, but Graham liked any torment he could inflict upon her.

"I was there in a professional capacity to give Lillian the results from Tamara's labs this afternoon and to discuss a couple of treatment options."

Graham stared at her in disbelief. "And did you accomplish that in a professional capacity?"

Channing rolled her shoulders back, attempting to look taller. "I didn't get the chance. You snuck up on me. I'll have to go back later."

"That's one big steaming pile!" he exclaimed, flopping down into an empty chair. "Why can't you be yourself with me? It's not that difficult, Bradley. I've already formed an opinion, and it can't get any worse."

With limited options, Channing loosened the control on her image. She didn't like to get too close to fellow colleagues. Professional jealousy ran rampant in her field, culminating in an ugly episode where a colleague tried to steal one of her ideas, passing it off as his own, citing personal information that made her look like an unqualified fool. Graham didn't seem like the type to stoop to that level of thievery, so she pulled up another chair and sat down beside him. "All right, I was listening," she admitted.

Graham framed his wide-open mouth with both his hands in a look of shock. "You don't say!"

"Cut the crap, Wellington! Let's just get to the point, OK? Did you hear any of their conversation?" she asked inquisitively.

Graham slumped into a more relaxed position, placing his hands behind his head. "I've heard it all before. There's nothing new that I haven't already been privy to."

Now it was Channing's turn to look shocked. "You mean you understand everything she's talking about? The so-called 'gifts' of the family, the religious stuff, and now the stone? You've known about all of that?"

"That and more," he answered. "You seem to forget that Brody has known this family since childhood, and I've known them since medical school because of our friendship. Add into the equation that both Brody and I have been treating her for the past year in dual capacity, and the information network gets a little slimmer. Besides, Lillian doesn't have to lecture us on any of this stuff. It's brotherhood 101."

Channing shook her head in confusion. "It's *what* 101?

Graham sighed in fake exasperation. "Brotherhood. Mitch and I are brothers." He held out his right hand, revealing a silver ring wrapped around his finger.

Channing stared at the ring, unable to recall if she had ever noticed it before. She didn't possess the habit of staring at people's hands to check for jewelry. The symbols on the ring stood out against a white backdrop. A red eight-pointed star sat atop a gold crescent moon. Graham watched her study the ring with tremendous scrutiny. Before she had a chance to speak, Graham interjected, "Mitch has the same one. We bought them together."

He was the last person in the world who would belong to any organization with an interesting history combined with moral integrity. She saw him as purely self-involved to be interested in anything as trivial as assisting others in a charitable manner. The only question she could muster was, "How?"

Shrugging his shoulders, Graham explained that he was the seventh generation in his family to be initiated. At first he was hesitant, but when Mitch confided his interest, Graham wouldn't let him do it alone. "Actually, I think it was one of the better moves I've ever made.

I've learned more than I ever thought I could have, and the other brothers are like family."

"Mitch knows all this stuff too?" Channing asked, returning to the original point of their conversation.

"Sure. But I doubt he remembers it all. I bet you one million dollars he's floundering like a fish out of water in Europe right now." Graham leaned closer to Channing, whispering, "He gets flustered easily, you know."

"Do you *believe* it?" she asked, scrunching her nose.

"Why not? You're a doctor. Aren't we supposed to open our minds to the possibility of other options, other treatments? To be able to push the limits of what we think we know or can accomplish? Isn't that what medicine is all about? We're supposed to question the results and get to the root of the situation. This isn't any different," he stated.

Her silence prodded him further. "Come on, Bradley, you know I'm right. When have I ever steered you wrong?" Unable to answer, he filled in the blanks for her "That would be never." Graham stood up from his chair, kicking it back toward the wall. Extending his right hand to her, he said, "Let's get some coffee, and I'll answer all the questions you can come up with."

Channing looked at his hand, afraid to touch him. She questioned that his feelings for her were strictly professional and wasn't sure if this was another one of his ploys to make her feel uncomfortable.

"Come on," he coaxed. "It's just coffee."

Mimicking an invisible *X* above his heart, he promised no funny business. She took his hand, as assistance in standing up from her chair, but dropped it quickly once she got onto her feet.

"Maybe we could go over some of the options I was going to tell Lillian," she said, nervous to be alone with him without the topic of medicine.

Graham sighed as they began to walk. "There's that good old professional capacity rearing its ugly head again."

Channing stopped walking. "What?" she snapped.

He stopped two feet ahead, turning to look at her. "You can't accept that good guys exist, can you?" he asked her honestly.

Uncomfortable with the question, her knee-jerk reaction took on a personal nature. "Of course I do. I married the last one."

Watching her pass, Graham followed her quickened pace down the hallway. "Sorry to correct your misgivings, Bradley, but some of us are right under your nose."

26

Mitch sat in the backseat of Pip's car, speeding down the A827 along Loch Tay, with Boggs riding shotgun in the front seat. He was surprised that the twins weren't involved in this particular lesson. Genevieve, in her sarcastic tone, made a reference to "Pip's ulterior motive," which confused Mitch about the day's activities. After the remark, Gillian shot a devilish look toward her sister and patted Mitch on the back, reminding him to keep an open mind. Before Mitch could question her further, Pip pushed him into the car, where Boggs occupied the front seat.

The two women engaged in small talk, discussing various topics such as fashion, the store Boggs owned, gossip about people from the village, and finally a cousin who piqued Mitch's interest. Boggs was unclear as to how they were related, but the way she spoke about her, he presumed they all shared a branch on the family tree.

"I haven't heard from her in ages!" Pip exclaimed. "I send e-mail after e-mail without reply. What's she been up to?"

"Ah, this and that," Boggs answered. "You know her, Pip. Once she gets her teeth into a project, she forgets there is a world outside the library." She chuckled. "Tremendous work ethic, poor people skills. I'm afraid she likes the solitude, which I fear I had a hand in with her lack of siblings."

Pip patted her hand. "Parents tend to worry that they damaged their children, when in fact we all turn out fine. She rears her head on occasion, and we've managed to stay close after all these years. Nothing to go on about." Looking at Mitch in the rearview mirror, she asked rather pointedly, "Is she seeing anyone romantically?"

Knowing the direction Pip was headed, Boggs smirked. "Isn't a mother the last to know?"

Pip laughed, addressing her next question to Mitch. "Hey, Brody! You interested in meeting a hot dish during this trip, or are you business without pleasure?"

Mitch didn't feel the urge to engage in a battle of wits. He doubted that a blind date, at this point, would pique his curiosity enough to take his mind off of losing yet another phenomenal woman. All of his feelings for Pip reminded him of the pain he endured after losing Brooke, and the last thing he needed was a one-night stand with some cousin to satisfy her matchmaking skills. "I think I'll pass," he replied. "No offense, but I've got too much swirling in my brain to attempt to be charming."

"Aw, come on," she teased. "She's fantastic, and brilliant, and funny, and loyal to the gills. Plus, she has a killer personality. You'd love her!"

"Again, not interested."

Pip kept the topic of Mitch's imaginary love life flowing. "I think it would be perfect! Help me out here, Boggs!"

Boggs shook her head, denying Pip an ally. "This isn't my business. I'm here to help teach about standing stone circles and be an extra guard for the transfer. I don't get mixed up in this kind of thing."

"Not even for your own daughter?" Pip pressed.

"Not even for her," she replied.

"Wait a minute." Mitch interjected. "The person you want to set me up with is Boggs's daughter?" Pip nodded. "Is this the cousin you were just talking about?" Again Pip nodded. "So that makes Boggs your aunt?" he asked, confused at the family's lineage.

Boggs answered the question before Pip opened her mouth. "Haven't you had a person in your life that was close to your family who you referred to as an uncle or an aunt or even a cousin, without a blood relation?"

"No," Mitch answered quickly. "That's weird."

"You're weird!" Pip shot back defensively.

"Come on, children," Boggs stated. "Sometimes friends fill the void that family members can't create. It's all semantics. We consider ourselves family, and that's all that matters."

"I don't care what you call her, I'm not into anything romantic, and I would appreciate if you didn't arrange a meeting with her," Mitch sternly stated to the women.

Pip snorted. "You don't have a choice in the matter, Brody. She's the teacher we're taking you to today!"

Mitch turned his head toward the window again; trying to ignore the obvious setup. "Terrific," he mumbled, trying to focus on the hills surrounding the Loch.

Sensing the newly created tension coming from the backseat, Boggs unfastened her seatbelt and spun around. "Why don't we focus our attention on the job?" Mitch refused to look at her. "OK?" she asked.

Still looking away, Mitch quietly answered, "Yes."

"Pip?" she asked, looking in her direction.

Pip remained indignant. "I guess so."

Boggs spun back around toward the front of the car. "How about we give our star pupil a small amount of background?" Pip mumbled an answer as Boggs turned the music off. Staring straight ahead, Boggs directed her first question to Mitch. "What do you know about standing stone monuments, Dr. Brody?"

Mitch could think of only one. "Stonehenge?"

"Yes," Boggs confirmed.

"I saw a documentary a few years ago in the on-call room. Scientists were trying to re-create what it might have looked like, with wood and tarps."

"Do you remember anything else from the program?" she asked.

Images from the television screen shuffled out of his memory banks. "Theories about its purpose as a trading post, a spiritual center, a giant meeting hall, or a sophisticated calendar based upon the astronomical patterns of that time. I was paged and didn't get a chance to see the conclusion."

"Wow, Brody, I'm impressed," Pip mentioned.

"Remembering details is part of my job." Switching his concentration from the window to Pip's eyes in the rearview mirror, he managed a small smile. "Is that where we're going?" he asked. "Stonehenge?"

"Bloody hell, Brody! We're not taking you back to England! They shoot you there, remember?" Pip teased.

A tiny laugh escaped Mitch's lips as the defensive walls he raised during the dating conversation broke away. "Where are we going?"

Boggs slipped her glasses off, using a cleaning cloth to remove the smudges. "We're going to a stone circle site, which is conveniently close by. There is an archaeological dig going on, and you will be given your next lesson while Pip catches up with her cousin."

Pip looked sideways at Boggs. "Should I have a go?"

Boggs motioned for Pip to continue. "We'll take turns while we're in the car."

"Right then!" Pip said. "Standing stones are no different than your stone. Given the correct vibration level or melodic frequency, a trained individual can store information in the stones. It's like an ancient data processing center with records and storehouses. Some scientists have discovered that the standing stones around Great Britain have their own network with an ability to connect between regions. Mind-blowing huh?"

Mitch remained silent.

Boggs added to Pip's explanation. "One source has eluded the cleverest of researchers. Historians know of its existence due to very old documents, but they are unable to penetrate the opening." Mitch looked perplexed. "The Hall of Records in Egypt houses the most ancient documents, even from Atlantis."

Finding his voice, Mitch asked, "Is that the one inside the Sphinx?"

"Same one," Boggs answered. "One day three people will arrive at the door between the two paws and reveal the Hall of Records."

"How do you know that?" Mitch asked.

"Psychic." Boggs hummed in a melodic tone. "I saw it in a vision. The three people are related. I'm sorry to say that Tamara isn't included."

Mitch laughed. "This is about enough adventure for a lifetime." He watched the two women laugh at his joke. "Can the twins speak to stones?"

Pip's wide grin was apparent in the rearview mirror. "Only when together. Their gifts are strong when separated, but together, they are a force to be reckoned with. They're spectacular!"

Mitch directed his attention back to Boggs. "Can you play music to retrieve stored information?"

Boggs spun back around to face him. "You are sharp as a tack! Your teacher today has a theory regarding that very topic. Her dig site is also looking at the possibility that the Scottish war instrument of the bagpipes was created for the specific purpose of mimicking the necessary tonal vibrations to communicate with the stones. The underlying tone of the pipes could allow them to wake up."

"For argument's sake, let's say that I was able to open one of these stones. What would I find?" Mitch asked.

"You would find records of the high priest and priestess, events of importance that took place in the area, lessons to be learned on a spiritual level, and a record of master teachers who spent time here."

"Not the meaning of life?" he joked.

"The meaning of life is different to each person, Brody. Not unlike the concept of heaven. It's all subjective," Pip answered.

"Just like this trip," Mitch commented.

"Precisely," Boggs replied.

The last few miles of the car ride were silent. Pip focused on last-minute wedding details, while Boggs concentrated on a mental inventory of the shop. Mitch attempted to empty his mind of everything imaginable, which only succeeded in winding him up even tighter about the trip's outcome. As if the car knew Mitch could no longer survive the anticipation of what awaited him, they turned onto a dirt road past the village of Killin. Pip parked in an open field, with no visible monument in sight. Four other cars sat in the grass as empty testimonies that people were indeed out in this desolate area.

The two women exited the car first, pulling out warmer jackets and umbrellas. Pip announced that the site was within a grove of trees. The three marched in single file, with Boggs leading the way. Mitch desperately wanted to speak to Pip about why he had been tense with her over the last few days, but didn't want to inflict further damage to their friendship.

Reaching the sanctuary of trees, their shade provided cover from sprinkling rain. Boggs broke free from the well-traveled path, entering a lesser-known trail through the brush. Mitch strained his neck to catch a glimpse of the standing stones through a clearing when a low growl distracted him. A second and more distinct growl a few seconds later, closer to him, forced Mitch to slow his pace. Terrified to take another step, he searched for anything that would serve as a weapon. Finding nothing, he turned to face the predator. Out of the corner of his eye, silver-and-black fur over white forearms and paws appeared. Face-to-face with a creature whose teeth were fully bared, Mitch silently pleaded for peace.

The top of its head reached the curve of Mitch's hip. The girth of its chest would have held three of his palms. Ears flattened against its head, it resembled a giant wolf, with paws planted firmly on the ground. Beast and man stood three feet apart, yet Mitch felt the warmth of its breath. The animal took one step closer. Wincing in preparation for teeth to meet flesh, a rustle in the bushes broke the animal's concentration. "Kodiak? Where are you, girl?"

The animal released its defensive stance at the sound of an owner's voice. Its tail raised into a scorpion formation with the end resting on the small of its back. Two brown boots escaped the greenery, with a royal-blue leash dragging on the ground. A woman, dressed in denim jeans, a cream Arran sweater, and a navy-blue field jacket cleared the brush, clapping her hands. "There you are! You scared me to death!"

She linked the leash onto the matching collar around the animal's neck, which carried an embroidered crescent with three stars. Her brown hair hid the profile of her face while she bent down to kiss the animal's head. "Sorry if she scared you. Kodiak is my first line of defense. She's an excellent judge of character, which is why I keep her around. I've got hold of her now, so you can breathe again."

Mitch's breathing stood suspended. Her hazel eyes sparkled with intensity. He found it difficult to produce oxygen for his brain, feeling as if he were staring at an apparition. "Brooke!" he sputtered, bewildered by her presence.

She blinked her eyelids open and shut a few times, hoping to clear out the image of the man before her. Kodiak sensed the tension and returned to her defensive position. Looking up at her owner for permission, she decided to growl again. Brooke pulled at her collar, creating silence between the three of them.

"Is this a sick joke?" Mitch asked.

Brooke remained silent, not knowing what to say. She had been informed of a student to teach and was the obvious choice due to her incredible knowledge on the subject. It had taken years to get over their failed relationship and now, ironically after all her professional accomplishments, fate stepped in to press them back together. Her mind shut down with his presence in the woods. There were so many things she had wanted to tell him over the years, to pick up the phone and make amends. Hesitation won the mental battle each time the receiver sat in her hand. The first thought through the haze of her mind was an apology. Before she could make it, Pip burst through the brush.

"This is an odd method of introduction, certainly not ideal, but interesting at best." Making her way over to Kodiak, she scratched the dog tenderly behind the ears. "Still guarding our girl?" Kodiak's tail showed appreciation for the attention. "Quite a dog, eh, Mitch?"

Finally able to direct his gaze somewhere other than at the woman who had shredded his heart, Mitch looked at Pip petting the dog affectionately. "Looks more like a mean-ass wolf."

Pip tipped her head in disbelief at his brazened speech. "She may look menacing, but she's all love." The last part she stated in a tone normally reserved for small creatures or babies. At the change in her voice, Kodiak stepped in front of Brooke, jumping up to stand with her paws on Pip's shoulders, licking her face.

Mitch's anger at the current situation reached a boiling point, and he could no longer contain his pent-up emotions.

"Pip?" he asked in a stern manner. "Do you want to answer some basic questions right now?"

Helping the dog back onto the ground, she chirped, "Sure."

"For starters, what in the hell are we doing here?" he said, attempting to slow his rapid breathing.

"We're here for the standing stones. We explained it all in the car. Did your gunshot wound affect your brain?" she teased.

"How about explaining what *she* is doing here," he asked, using his index finger to point directly at a motionless Brooke.

Slapping her hand against her forehead, she apologized. "Sorry, where are my manners? Brooke, Mitch. Mitch, Brooke. She's the one that I was trying to fix you up on a blind date with because I thought you would be perfect for each other, but then you went all wonky about not seeing anyone."

He could do nothing but roll his eyes. "I am familiar with her name."

Pip linked arms with Brooke. Pip neglected to see how pale she had become. "She's the cousin I told you about, nitwit! Well," she said, laughing, "not blood cousins, but we've known each other since we were seven and got into loads of trouble. Just ask Duncan. You can't live through that kind of naughtiness and not be bonded for life." Nudging Brooke with her elbow, she asked, "Am I right?" Brooke continued to stare at Mitch. Their knowing glares lit a light bulb in her head. "Hold up! How do you know her name?"

He screamed, furious at the game she played. "Don't stand there and pretend that this lifetime friend of yours never told you that we dated. This is a giant setup that I don't appreciate and will not tolerate." Pushing past them, he headed back toward the car. "Game over!"

"Hold it right there, Brody!" Boggs yelled from behind. He did as instructed, but did not turn around. He wanted to be mad; it felt good to be mad, finally allowing the hurt an outlet. "You can go back to the car, allowing your emotions to get the better of you. Or you can stand here like a man, use your words, and communicate like a grown-up. You don't have to like what people tell you, but you do have to listen to what they have to say. Everyone is entitled to his or her own opinion." She added with a laugh, "And if you ask me, mine is generally the right one."

Her hand touched his right shoulder, rotating him toward the women. "Let's hear what you have to say, Mitch, and then calmly, everyone will take a turn until the issue is resolved. But remember one thing amid all of your anger, there is a life at stake." She winked at Mitch. "How about that for a guilt trip? Hard to say no." She stepped away, allowing Pip and Brooke to face him as well. Kodiak sat down on the trail, recognizing that a lengthy debate was about to happen. "Go ahead, Mitch, say your piece," Boggs advised.

He decided to start with Pip. Brooke would take more time. "All that talk in the car about some cousin, when the whole time you knew that Brooke and I had a turbulent past! Have you been setting me up to fail, knowing that this meeting would throw me off?" he stated, trying not to shout.

"Honestly, Mitch, I had no idea that you ever knew each other. I am an engaged fool who wants to see everyone paired up because of my personal happiness. I promise you, I had the best of intentions."

Cracking his knuckles, he added, "Did you think of a backup plan in case I failed your little experiment?"

"No!" she bellowed. "I swear on all the powers of the universe that I had no idea! She was meant to be your teacher based on her intensive research with the stones. Daddy never knew about a personal connection!"

"Liar," he spat at her.

"Cheeky bastard!"

"Deceptive shrew!"

"Sniveling ass!"

Mitch opened his mouth to retaliate when Boggs screamed above their tirade, "I'm responsible! I knew the connection and allowed it to move forward."

Her confession sent Mitch reeling. "How?"

Boggs filled her lungs with a deep sigh, letting the air pas through her nostrils loudly. "Mothers know things. Some things we know about even though our children would prefer them to remain confidential," she admitted quietly. "I knew about you from the moment the affair began. Mitch, Mitch, Mitch was all my sweet girl talked about! You consumed her every waking thought, and if I'm not mistaken, some dreaming ones as well," she confessed. "Your breakup devastated her. While you thought that she was cavalier in taking that position far away from you, she believed that you would follow. To make it all work out. To have the fantasy life every girl dreams of. That is what she wanted."

"Why drudge up all these painful memories?" he asked.

"Are you happy?" she questioned. "Have you truly been happy since you parted?" She pointed a finger straight at his heart. "You can lie to yourself all you want, but the happiness you seek lies in there. *You* are your worst enemy and always have been. Brooke isn't the enemy, neither am I, and neither is Pip. Why not just let go, embrace life, and live each day with as much enthusiasm as you can muster?"

The only response left him was, "I'm happy, damn it."

His answer lacked the passion she knew hid beneath the surface, the passion she saw at Stirling. Boggs contemplated her next words. Placing her hands behind her back, she approached with a gentler tone. "The universe sends people to our lives for a reason. Some are meant to teach lessons based upon what we need to know or are lacking in some capacity, whether through direct contact or as an example through behavior. Others are sent to awaken our senses and put us in tune with the weightlessness of love. And then there are those who are meant to pick us up, put us back on our feet, brush us off after a fall, and put us onto the path when we are misguided. Every person you come in contact with on this trip fills one of those roles. Maybe not the romantic one, but we remain hopeful."

Daring to take a few steps closer to him, she added. "Pip was correct; Brooke was chosen to teach you based upon her knowledge of the subject matter and nothing else. I was the one who knew the past you shared and failed to inform Duncan. If there is anyone you have a right to be angry with, it is me." Placing her hands under her chin, she batted her eyelashes. "You wouldn't begrudge a silly old woman a final chance at grandchildren, would you?" she chirped.

Finding a tiny smile seemed miraculous. He stared into her doe-like eyes. "I guess not," he mumbled.

Boggs clapped her hands. "It's settled, then. Pip, come with me, and we will leave these two alone to conduct business." She grabbed Pip by the elbow to lead her back up the trail, while shoving Brooke closer to Mitch with the other hand. Kodiak shuffled between them, almost causing Brooke to stumble. "This woman has a lesson to teach, and this man has one to learn. By the grace of all that is holy, they will find a way to see past their differences and focus on the job at hand, rather than their unwillingness to see the obvious."

Pip whispered to Boggs, "It would be a bloody miracle."

As the two women left the scene, Boggs whispered back, "From your lips to God's ears, my dear." Waving her hand, Boggs hoped her daughter would be able to get past her internal demons and complete the given task, no matter how impossible it seemed at the moment.

Mitch stood defensively, prepared for battle either with Brooke or Kodiak. Her beauty certainly hadn't diminished. He remembered her zest for life and ability to emerge victorious from any debate whether prepared or not. Maybe she had still cared about him when they parted, and maybe, just maybe, he had made the biggest mistake of his life by not chasing after her. He looked at the enormous dog, expecting more growling, but none came. It merely sat with a look that reflected his own confusion. Both of them waited for Brooke to acknowledge anything.

"Do you need to sit?" he asked gently. "You look kind of pale, Brooke."

Reaching up to her forehead, her hands smoothed the hairs on the top of her head. She stroked the top of Kodiak's head in a rhythmic beat.

Hoping to coax her into speech, he repeated his offer. "Brooke? Can I get you anything?"

Her gaze pierced Mitch's wall of defense. Her voice had a slight tremble. "What I *need* is answers to lingering questions before continuing this charade. You expect me to believe that load of..."

"There's no need to start swearing at me!" Mitch interjected. "We can have an adult conversation without sinking to that level."

"Because you're already there?" Brooke asked.

"That's not fair," Mitch snapped. "There were factors to consider before running off after you." Looking down at his shoes, he was unable to look at her. "Things were complicated."

Her shouting reached a fevered pitch. "*You* made it complicated! I *knew* you were going to propose that night, and I told you about the job offer to see if you would rise to the occasion or if you would hide your tail and run, which is exactly what you did. *That's* why we broke up, *you moron!*"

Mitch waved his hand in front of his face, trying to get her to slow down. "You *knew* I had a ring?"

Brooke cocked her head to one side with a look of disgust. "Graham," she announced. "He told me you purchased the ring and what you were planning. He thought he was helping me to make a decision regarding the job."

Swiping the bush next to him, Mitch intended to do more damage to it; instead he only made the leaves shake. "My best friend ruins everything! What are you going to tell me next, that he had some sort of weird crush on you too?"

Brooke met his fiery gaze. "I will not even dignify a comment to such a ludicrous accusation! It was you and he who had more of a weird love thing than he and I ever could." She kicked dirt with the toe of her shoe. "I went to Graham because he was the closest thing to you, knowing he would give me a straightforward answer about how to explain the job to you. I was torn between the possibility of losing you and losing what I had worked so hard for during my academic career." Quietly she added, "It would have been difficult for anyone."

Mitch watched the way her left sock dangled around her ankle while the right sock remained stiff against her leg. The realization that maybe she was the same person who left so many years ago created an ache that he had buried for too long. She was finally standing in front of him with the same emotions he too had swallowed. How could it be possible that after all the mistakes he made, he could be rewarded a second chance? "Why didn't you say something?" he mumbled. "Why didn't you give me a clue that you knew about the ring? That might have changed my perspective!"

Brooke laughed at his lack of insight. "Oh, yeah, I should have told you that I had secret information about the romantic plans you made and blow the whole thing out of the water, because what every man wants is to make the plans, sweat out the answer, and have his girlfriend ruin the surprise. That sure would have changed your perspective! You would have been pissed off, broken up with me, and gone off to fight Graham for telling me! How romantic."

Dismissing her tone, he retaliated. "It would have been better than what you did. I had no input! It was loads better to slip the ring back into my jacket, feeling as if you never cared. Good job, Brooke, another man crushed by your sensitivity!" He made the last comment intending for it to sting. It worked.

Tears welled up in her eyes, and instead of wiping them away, she let them roll down her checks. "I guess we can call it even, because that's the way I felt at the airport when I left."

Mitch suddenly felt exhausted. Each muscle ached from the strain of the years relived in moments. Feeling the need to lie down, he made a final attempt to put the past to rest. "Why would I beg you to stay?"

Brooke's eyes softened from the tears. "That's generally what men do. They fight for what they want, and for what they need."

Bewildered by her statement, a question popped into his near empty brain. "You would have stayed?"

She whispered, "Yes."

A flash entered Mitch's mind from his dialogue with Boggs at the Wallace Monument. She was absolutely correct! He chose the easy way out on a majority of life-altering judgments, when he should have planted his feet firmly and fought for what he wanted, even for what he believed! He was a man who learned to perform the seductive dance of avoidance, failing to recognize that the fight as well as the afterglow could be enjoyable. His life choices became crystal clear. "I'm sorry, Brooke," he confessed. "I apologize if I hurt you by making poor decisions."

Brooke's mouth hung open in disbelief. "Could you repeat that?"

He laughed at her distrust. "I'm sorry."

She tried to get the image of Graham pointing and laughing out of her head. She knew that if he were here, he would give them grief over their stupidity and force them to embrace. "I can't believe that you said those words to someone other than Graham!"

Smirking, he replied, "There's a lot I can't believe these days. I still can't believe I hopped on a plane and entered this roller coaster because Lillian told me to, even against my better judgment to stay with Tamara." He fondled the zipper on his jacket. "I'm certifiably insane."

"No, you're not, Mitch. You're finally finding your courage before the midlife crisis hits," she quipped.

Releasing a hearty laugh aroused Kodiak from her slumber. Mitch couldn't help but continue the outburst. "I thought this *was* the midlife crisis!"

"Oh, no," Brooke said. "You have at least two more days before the bottom drops out and it arrives full force."

Unable to contain himself, Mitch doubled over in a fit of laughter. Even Kodiak seemed unnerved by the immediate change in climate. She jumped up, prepared to pounce on anything that moved. Composing himself at last, Mitch faced two identical looks of confusion from Brooke and her dog. "Do you think you are able to put all of this away for the time being and teach me? I have a lot to learn."

Brooke glanced at Kodiak, whose tail slowly wagged an approval. "I think that can be arranged. Follow me."

He watched both Brooke and Kodiak meander down the path with the same rhythmic gate. He envied their tender connection. Kodiak was closer than anyone could be to her, and yet Mitch wasn't entirely sure the dog would accept being replaced by a human. It was obvious that if he harbored any romantic feelings for Brooke, he would have to convince Kodiak that he was worthy of the attention. It could prove trickier than meeting a girlfriend's father. The nice reality was that at least a father didn't pose the threat of tearing your face off with one bite.

Throughout their walk, Kodiak would glance at Mitch. He was sure her thought process was to keep an eye on him, but secretly hoped that if anyone jumped out of the bushes, the dog would rise to the occasion. He fantasized about a fight between an unarmed Julian and Kodiak at full strength. Smirking at the imagined outcome of Kodiak's success, he nearly collided with Brooke, unaware that they had stopped at a clearing in the trees.

"After two years of excavation, it still takes my breath away." Brooke announced, pointing to the megalithic structures one hundred feet away from where they stood. "Have you ever seen anything more beautiful?"

I can think of one, he thought, remembering the warm summer's day they spent swimming at the lake. He could still smell the fresh strawberries from the picnic she had packed as they lounged in the heat. That was the day he fell head over heels. The moment arrived when she emerged from the water, backlit from the sun with tiny beads of water glittering like diamonds on her tanned shoulders. That image was more beautiful than anything in the world.

"I asked you a question."

Mitch stammered out a quick response. He didn't feel the time would be right, after their argument, to drudge up any memories of their failed relationship. Instead of provoking further confrontation, he soaked up the grandeur and sophistication of the site.

Brooke unfastened Kodiak's leash, allowing the dog to roam. For a split second, the dog lingered, clearly trying to decide whether she should allow her master to remain in the presence of a stranger. She ran off toward a row of stark-white tents. The six tents stood on opposite sides of the stone circle, acting as home base for the graduate students who were hand selected to assist in the dig for experience as well as academic credit.

Mitch counted the number of stones in the area as thirteen. The seven-foot slabs lacked the decoration he saw on top of Ben Vrackie. Around the structure, deeper holes were dug in random patterns, where artifacts were unearthed. Small bits of pottery peeked from beneath the earth, waiting patiently for someone to reclaim it from its resting place. Red-flagged stakes marked various locations around the site, which made it seem like a crime scene.

He voiced his concern to Brooke as she chuckled at his inexperience, replacing the present scene with a medical one to make him feel more at ease. "This is my operating room, and the process in which I dissect my patient. The only difference between the two is that I take my time with very little funding at my disposal, while you fancy doctor types rush through procedures on your way to collecting buckets of money."

Mitch snickered. "The only *real* difference is that if I took this long on a patient, they'd be dead!"

"Good thing mine already are!" she quipped.

"Update me on the status of your patient," he stated, with his hands held behind his back, just as he would with an intern during morning rounds.

Brooke began, accepting her role as tour director. "The first thing people typically notice, aside from the size of each stone, is the number of them in the circle. Only a few remaining circles in the British Isles compose the mystical number of thirteen. Some circles may have the number, but the monument is no longer prevalent due to collapse of the stones. This circle is one of the best specimens we have encountered, along with the added bonus of artifacts from various locations both inside and outside the circle."

"What's significant about the number thirteen?" Mitch asked with genuine curiosity.

"Glad you asked!" Brooke exclaimed. "The number thirteen has a wide range of significances from astronomy and spirituality all the way down to a historical date that the general public consider unlucky. It has and will remain one of the most fortunate numbers in the universe."

The pair walked around the outer rim of the circle, while Brooke explained the theory of alchemy in great detail with its various properties for changing objects into precious metals. Her explanation included great scientific names such as Galileo, Copernicus, and Newton, who were extremely well versed in the practice of alchemy. "These men knew the secrets to the transmutation of metals into fine white powder that held both antigravitational and superconductive properties. They found that the records kept by the order of the Therapeutate were correct. It has the ability to fuse with our DNA, resulting in increased hormonal production, an enhanced immune system, and a balance of both sides of our brains." Brooke folded her arms against her chest as a sign of arrogance that she knew something about medicine Mitch did not.

"That's impossible." Mitch scoffed. "How in the world could some guy in the desert manufacture a powder that performs to such a capacity, let alone be able to track its progress through the body without sophisticated machinery?" He shook his head at her willingness to believe anything she read simply because it claimed to be historical evidence.

"Believe what you want, but just because something seems primitive doesn't mean it lacks sophistication. Some of our modern ideas have evolved from guys hanging out in the desert. I wouldn't be so quick to mock what you don't fully understand," she warned.

They continued their orbit around the circle until they reached the first white tent. Brooke completed her insight by explaining that within the alchemical process, the number thirteen denoted the exact number of stages leading to death as well as rebirth. She casually added that it was also the number of times the planet Venus revolves around the sun during the span of light years.

Folding back the entrance flap of the tent, Mitch grabbed her elbow. Brooke looked down at his fingers, feeling the same electric surge through her body as she had the first time he touched her, many years ago.

"And what about the historical date you mentioned?" he asked quickly, aware of a tingle through his arm as well.

"The date is the arrest and execution of the Templars by the king of France. It was on Friday, October 13, 1307, that Philippe signed the order condemning them to extermination. Thousands of Templars were hunted based upon the greed of a desperate Monarch who refused to pay back money they graciously loaned him. It is why Friday the Thirteenth is considered to be unlucky."

Mitch stared down at the ring that graced his finger. "I never knew that."

"Few do," Brooke answered quickly, slipping into the tent. Approaching a young man in front at a computer screen, she motioned for Mitch to peek at the astrological graph rotating clockwise in a perfect concentric motion. "We have been studying this site for two years and have discovered unbelievable coincidences." She pointed to smaller circles, stating they were the alignment of planets at the time the site was built. Distinguishing a red circle on the right side of the screen as it made its journey around the imaginary earth below, Brooke identified it as Saturn with a broad grin on her face.

"Which means what?" Mitch asked, unable to follow her pattern of thought.

Her excitement at the discovery was hard to miss. She yanked a second chart off the desk, showing Mitch a picture of Saturn illuminated in a darkened sky. "The brightness reflected off the planet is what made people refer to it as the Midnight Sun. They didn't have the widespread pollution we do, to cloud up the heavens, so their vision of astronomy was completely different. The Midnight Sun is used as an underground reference to the practice of alchemy. Plus, Saturn is the god of war, which brings us to another exciting discovery."

Stepping to the other side of the tent, Brooke stood next to a long, narrow table. She carefully peeled the tarp back to expose a weathered-looking spear, whose tip had been dulled from either the number of years sitting in decay or regular use. Brooke looked at him with a sparkle in her eye. "Well?"

"It's a spear," he stated, and his eyebrows rose as he questioned her pride over something that seemed trivial.

"It's not just a spear!" she screamed. "This spear coincides with the god of war and the Druids who made their home here. This spear is the only one we have found at the sight, and was clearly left as a sign of what was happening here." Growing frustrated at his lack of involvement, she tapped her foot. "Search your memory banks. Surely you have been told something on your trip that can correspond with what I'm showing you."

The only thing that popped into his mind was the day at Dunkeld with Pip, when they discussed a warrior monk named Columba. Taking a stab in the dark, he presented her with that answer.

"That's a tiny part of it. The spear is a sign of battle, as well as power. I'm going to assume that you have heard of the Spear of Longinus."

Mitch crumpled his face in concentration. "Is that the thing Hitler hunted during World War Two?"

"Anything else?"

He scratched his head, prying more information from his fingertips. "It's the same one that pierced Christ's side during the crucifixion?"

"Anything else?"

Mitch placed his hands in his pockets and muttered, "Nope."

Brooke delicately removed the spear from its resting place, holding it upright. "The Spear of Longinus, or Spear of Destiny, as it was often called, was taken to Constantinople after the crucifixion and interred within the walls of the Church of St. Sophia, which happened to be the greatest church in all of Christendom. Are you familiar with the goddess Sophia?" Mitch answered that she was the goddess of wisdom. "Before and during World War Two, Hitler dispatched large groups of researchers to all corners of the globe in search of priceless artifacts that would bring great power to the Reich. Some refer to this time as Hitler's Holy Grail quest, but some of us who studied the trip records agree that Hitler was aware of something larger. He studied the nature of alchemy and of a secret ceremony that required five sacred objects to bring about promised power. Fortunately for us all, he didn't succeed."

"The spear is one of those objects," Mitch reiterated to Brooke.

Stepping closer to him, she whispered a question. "Can you think of any others?" Mitch's jaw dropped at the thought of four objects in his briefcase. Brooke clapped her hand over his gaping mouth and backed him outside the tent, the spear still in her hand. "Let's return to the circle, shall we?"

He tore her hand away from his mouth as soon as they reached a safe distance from the tent. "Am I some guinea pig for an ancient ritual gone awry?"

Brooke motioned for him to calm down. Mitch wasn't ready to calm down. "Are you a weirdo cult that has an innocent girl in a compromising situation where she ends up as a sacrificial lamb?" Brooke continued to hush his outbursts. "I can't believe this, Brooke!" Mitch continued to shout. "How did you get wrapped up in all of this?"

Clapping her hand back over his mouth, she felt him struggle to free himself. "Would you please shut up? I don't need anyone alerted to my personal business! What we are doing with you and Tamara, by the way, has nothing to do with any cult or psycho conspiracy theories. We're trying to bring balance back to an earth in desperate need of it." Loosening her hand on his mouth, she asked, "Do I need to call Duncan?"

He muttered that he could be trusted as she released his mouth. "Walk into the center of the circle. It is precisely what I left our possible future for." Mitch flinched at her last remark, as if she had wounded him with an invisible weapon.

Reaching the center of the circle, Mitch felt intimidated by the massive power emanating from the collection of stones. Something encapsulated within the sacred heart of the site gave him chills that ran the length of his body. Brooke seemed right at home, and a bit more peaceful. Placing the spear carefully on the ground, directly in the center, she removed two coins from her pocket and walked each one to opposite sides of the circle, facing each other on the ground. She returned to the center, picking up the spear from its resting place with her right hand. Out of the corner of his eye, Mitch caught a small object dart across the ground toward the center, where it was joined by another. She motioned for Mitch to take a look. Taking a step forward, he picked up the two coins, perplexed by the fact that they were now stuck together.

"We discovered that stone circles were built to mark vortexes in the Earth's magnetic field, which is where positive and negative energy lines converge. Some physicists have dabbled in the theory that they could build portals to other dimensions, but I haven't found any proof to substantiate that yet." Folding her arms across her chest, she added, "The significance of Saturn's involvement is that when the planet reaches its peak in the night sky at the hour of midnight, the magnetic forces of the circle increase, resulting in a power surge. Few places on earth can brag about that detail, which means the sophisticated alignment of this space is truly remarkable."

Holding the coins piqued his interest in Brooke's work. He was amazed that anyone would be able to unearth information about a time so long ago without written documentation. In his world, theory didn't work; you needed cold, hard facts.

"Boggs mentioned something about a musical theory with the stones," Mitch said.

Brooke replied rather smugly, "Oh yeah, the bagpipe theory. I made a stab in the dark one night regarding the ability to store or retrieve information in the stones with music." She gently laid her left hand upon one of the stones. "I found carvings on this stone and thought, 'What if?' So I grabbed my handy MP3 player and poked around with some Highland bagpipe music. After a few minutes, the stone began to vibrate, mimicking the tone. I'm not done with my testing yet, so I would appreciate it if you wouldn't mention it to anyone else." She rubbed the faint outline of a serpent on the stone. "If I'm correct, the bagpipes weren't merely instruments of war, but were designed to capture the base note of tonal vibration and pair it with the upper octave notes, resulting in a frequency that enabled data to be set into stone. To a university committee, it's either completely brilliant or absolute folly." Looking across the circle at Mitch, she invited him to meet her on the other side. "Look at this snake. What do you think it means?"

"Boggs told me about the snake in the medical symbol and how it rose through the body, bringing enlightenment."

Brooke, still holding the spear, pointed out several zigzag patterns and spirals that accompanied the serpent. "The pairing of symbols often leads researchers into different translations. In this case, however, I did research through countless numbers of pairings and came up with my own translation. The serpent represents the self-energizing creative force of the Supreme Spirit. During its heyday, the circle was used for purposes relating to the balance of one's own soul energy along with creating the ability to commune with the Supreme Spirit." She further explained that when an individual's own serpent within is energized, the energy is said to rise through the charkas of the body, creating a union with the Supreme Universal Soul.

Mitch looked confused. "What?"

Laughing at his honesty, Brooke asked him a question off the present topic. "What did Saint Patrick, the patron saint of Ireland, do?"

"He drove the snakes out of Ireland."

Brooke enticed him further. "And what if I told you that the symbol for the Word of God, or rather Logos, was a serpent? The venerable emblem of the Holy Spirit itself, which moved along the waters of faith? How then would you look upon the act of Saint Patrick? Did he save Ireland, or did he rid it of its spiritual heritage?"

Her direct approach startled Mitch. He didn't recall her being brazen. Sure, she could debate anyone under the table, but she rarely took sides. It seemed now she had chosen sides, and she was protecting it with a commendable passion. "I would say that with all I know now, anything is possible."

"Coward." She smirked. "Here," she said, thrusting the spear into his hands. "This, as I alluded to before, is the last object you must obtain. Now the work begins."

Mitch scoffed. "Up until now this has been a vacation?"

"Still a smart ass," she replied. "Tomorrow, you and I are going to Oban, where my obligation for your safety concludes. I will hand you over to your final teacher, who will combine all the pieces of the puzzle."

"And tonight!" he teased, winking at her seductively.

She retrieved a small brown cloth from her pocket and wrapped the head of the spear, while at the same time punching Mitch's arm for the insinuation of an affair. "Tonight we stay at Pip's. I have a few things to discuss with my dear old friend, and you have items to fetch before we leave in the morning. Besides, I want to say hello to the twins. I haven't seen them in ages."

They exited the circle respectfully, heading back to the wooded path. Their initial tensions had evaporated into a newfound respect. Mitch fought the urge to hold her hand as it dangled close to his body. Before reaching the entrance of the woods, a shrill whistle escaped Brooke's lips, resulting in a large bounding animal. Kodiak regained her dutiful place beside her owner, accepting Mitch as the new accessory. "I don't go anywhere without Kodiak. She and I have been through too much for me to leave her behind like some common housedog. Mals are much too smart for that." She scratched behind her ears. "At least I think so."

They reached the area where the parked cars sat, in record speed, thanks in part to Kodiak's sprint through the brush. Brooke disabled the alarm on her navy-blue Volvo. The back hatch flew open, and Kodiak took her traveling place. Brooke stowed the spear carefully in the backseat as Mitch made himself comfortable in the passenger seat.

A pair of eyes Mitch knew well watched the newly formed trio from the thickness of the trees. The Ritz's valet sat alongside the burly man from Stirling. "You know the location of the house?" he snarled.

"It's the last place downloaded from the device," John answered sheepishly.

"Good," the man said, his eyes hidden by dark sunglasses. "We can take out more than just him. Kill two birds, so to speak."

The thought of witnessing murder made John nervous. He promised a certain amount of cooperation to Julian when first approached, but he didn't think that placing a locator device on Dr. Brody would result in Bridget's death and more. Julian was extremely angry after the cathedral incident. But John didn't begin to suspect he would be an accomplice to yet another heinous act. "Yes, sir!" he replied almost automatically.

"Don't be scared, little girl," the man snapped at John. "I'll be the cat catching the mouse, and you can be the bird that flies away when it's stuck in my paws."

John followed him to their waiting vehicle, nervous that maybe he had made a terrible mistake.

27

The solitude of a hospital cafeteria after hours was oppressive. During the daytime, it buzzed with activity from visitors of various walks of life, flashing smiles to those in need of extra support. At night, the scenery dramatically changed. Dimmed lights for late-night dining created a cavernous feel, void of any feeling.

In the farthest corner of the room, Earl sat in near darkness, playing with a wooden stir stick. Since his dialogue with Lillian in the waiting room, their face-to-face occurrences had been strained. It saddened him to think that their history could be erased over a simple misunderstanding. He understood her position as a mother, but what perplexed him was that she believed he was capable of placing Tamara in a position of harm. To him, the thought was grotesque. Why didn't life come with a rewind button?

His brief conversation with Rothschild renewed his hope, not only in the project, but also that if there were others as gifted as Tamara, she would have a support system throughout her life. With all of the information pouring out of Tamara these days, to find someone with identical abilities would be remarkable, but to have others possessing even greater gifts would be stupendous.

Earl never pretended that Tamara's revelations wouldn't benefit him. He owed this to her, to participate in a swift vindication after all she endured as a child. He couldn't bear the thought of another set of articles labeling her as a "freak of nature whose condition demanded institutionalization."

Placing the stick back into his tepid coffee, he pondered whether or not he should contact Rothschild this soon after their initial dialogue. He promised to get back in touch with Earl, but since time was of the essence with Tamara's delicate medical condition, he felt the sooner the better. Using his fingers to calculate the time difference, he removed his cell phone from his pocket, hoping his call would garner a warm reception. Feeling discouraged after four rings without an answer, Earl pulled the phone away from his ear as the man's voice greeted whoever was calling. "Is anyone there?"

"Yes, sorry, I thought no one would answer at this time of night," he admitted shyly.

"Then why did you bother calling me?" Rothschild snapped.

Earl felt intimidation pouring from this guy, as he tried to think of a witty remark. His inability to store clever remarks caught up with him the older he got. "It's Earl Hutchison; we spoke together a short bit ago about a girl and her visions. I'm not sure if you remember."

Dr. Rothschild sounded confused as to Earl's identity. "Is she in Europe?"

"No, sir, she's in the States. My colleague at Boston University contacted you before we spoke. You evaluated her once as a child with a team of specialists to determine her abilities. But since that time, she has grown exponentially in her gifts," Earl stated, prepared to hang up the phone with his tail planted firmly between his legs. "If you don't remember, then I am sorry to have wasted your time."

"Is the girl in hospital?" Rothschild asked, his accent heavy on the word hospital.

"Yes!" Earl exclaimed, "Yes, she is!"

"Vaguely," Rothschild replied arrogantly. "Let me grab my notes as a reference guide. Please hold."

Earl instantly felt foolish. His instincts were better than this. If Rothschild proved to be a European snob who preferred to flaunt his superior intellect, then he would rather not deal with him. The minute on hold felt like an hour, and he finally admitted that this was a monumental mistake. He began to disconnect the call when the man cleared his throat over the line.

"Ah, yes, the American. Her name is an odd version of Sarah. Is this correct?" he asked.

The manner in which Dr. Rothschild spoke left a bad taste in Earl's mouth. He was distant with a hint of condescension. "I would appreciate if you took this case seriously, Dr. Rothschild. We don't need to be partners if you don't feel we are up to your standard." The reception on Rothschild's end fell silent. "By the way, her name is Tamara. Please refer to her properly, or do not refer to her at all."

A robust laugh escaped Rothschild's mouth, catching Earl off guard. He expected the man to hang up on him, or call him every name in the book, not laugh. "Excuse me?" was all Earl could manage in his state of shock.

"No, excuse me!" Rothschild replied, still chuckling. "I tend to test people regarding their cases to see what their tolerance level is in how much proverbial crap they are willing to swallow on the pathway to academic celebrity. You would be amazed how many people will digest an enormous amount of dung just to get their fifteen minutes of fame. But you! I look forward to working with you, sir."

Still perplexed as to whether this guy was telling him the truth, Earl asked the obvious question, "You are on board?"

"I have not had a girl in her talent pool before. I would say her abilities are rare, but I find that if I open my mouth too soon, another girl pops up out of the blue to slap it shut. I am more cautious in my labels these days. Let me confirm that I believe we are in a brilliant position to make academic history. But I thought the same thing years ago when she was evaluated. I wanted to be in a superior position to swim upstream against the pseudointellectuals who cried for the popular vote of insanity."

It felt good to have someone in his own academic arena confirm his suspicions. "There aren't *any* others like her?"

"Tomorrow could be different, but for today, she is the only one," Rothschild repeated.

Earl furiously jotted down notes on a napkin. "Do you think she could be poised to raise serious questions in religion *and* history?"

Rothschild rustled through the pages outlining Tamara's visions. "What I find fascinating is her wide range of historical events. For instance, there are a few pages dealing with events from biblical times, which include Mary Magdalene, John the Baptist, Jesus Christ, and who I presume to be his brother James. Then switching gears into the genre of the Dark Ages in Europe with Druids and priestesses, and onto this latest vision in present time, which has me utterly intrigued. In my opinion, she is receiving information for a purpose. There has to be an underlying explanation why this is being brought into the limelight."

Earl agreed with the theory. "In my opinion, the biggest question we have is whether or not she is credible to the swarms of naysayers who are positioned to attack once we go public."

"Belief in her credibility will shine through with the right piece of evidence to support even one of her visions. Tell me, does she or her family possess any historical evidence from these visions?" Rothschild asked.

There wouldn't be tangible proof that Tamara was seeing was the truth, because they were visions, not archaeological sites. "What type of proof can she have? We're talking about events that happened thousands of years ago. How would she own a piece from that era?"

Rothschild's response instantly turned stern. "It is my experience, Mr. Hutchison, that subjects possess some small object that is either an original or a replica of an artifact that triggers these episodes deep within their psyche, resulting in the manifestation of visions. Does your subject possess any object that will explain her visions or could aid in their explanation?"

Imagining the Victorian house of Tamara's grandmother, he quickly visited each room in his mind for anything of historical significance. "She grew up in a house with a large collection of antiques from both Europe and the States, but I can't recall anything that could be linked to her biblical visions."

"Then you are wasting my time, sir." Rothschild spat through the phone.

"Please don't hang up, Dr. Rothschild! There is one thing that could be tied to all of this, but it isn't as old as we hope." Closing his eyes in order to describe the article better, he gave his best description of the glass-encased carpet hanging in the dining room.

"What you have described, sir, cannot possibly exist," was the whispered response.

"I assure you, it does. The carpet has been handed down through the generations, and it hangs in the house in a custom-made case," Earl confirmed.

Rothschild cleared his throat a second time. "That carpet has been lost for centuries, only referenced in manuscripts written by the Cathars and hidden before their destruction. It was rumored to have been sold on the black market for a ridiculous amount of money, and therefore untraceable. Are you telling me that the family you refer to are individuals who frequent the black market for ancient artifacts?"

In defense of his longtime friends, Earl's shout echoed through the empty cafeteria. "God, no! There isn't a snowball's chance in hell they bought it on the black market!"

"You put me in a compromising position, which leaves me no other recourse than to test the girl myself, in person," Rothschild replied.

Earl scratched his head with the pen in his hand. "I can arrange that with the doctors at the hospital. This would be the safest place, since they could monitor her while in vision state. When were you planning on arriving?"

"I am afraid you mistake me. You must bring her to me," Rothschild commanded.

Earl's jaw dropped open. "She's recovering from multiple organ failure!"

Rothschild sighed deeply to show his lack of patience with Earl's constant stream of negativity. "Didn't you tell me in an e-mail that she was improving?"

"Yes, but..." Earl answered.

"Then let her improve and move her to me. We have hospitals that are more than adequate should something happen to the girl," Rothschild interjected.

Earl dropped his pen, using both hands to cup his head. "Give me some time to see how she does, and then we'll see what arrangements can be made."

Rothschild's approval of his sudden change of heart was evident in the change of his tone. "I'll need you to bring the carpet to be deemed authentic." Earl gasped at his request. "If you don't produce the carpet with the girl, I will make sure that everyone in the academic world receives a copy of a scandalous article depicting you as an antiquity thief with black market connections."

Earl stammered, "But I..."

Rothschild disconnected their call. "Good day, sir."

Earl held the phone in his hands for a few minutes, stunned by the recent turn of events. How was he supposed to move Tamara to Europe with her mother's permission, let alone take the carpet with them? On one hand, he needed the vindication that Tamara would bring for his career after turbulent years of fighting for university tenure. But he couldn't risk her life or the relationship of a family for the sake of fame or fortune. Could he trust Rothschild with something as precious as Tamara? He stood up and approached the coffee machine to pour his third cup for the evening, acknowledging that the night just became unending.

Dr. Bradley briefly encountered Earl in Tamara's room, but it was all she needed to recognize him in the cafeteria. She peered from behind the ice-cream machine, which was her late-night indulgence when the day's stress proved too great. Fighting the impulse to offer even the tiniest bit of support, Channing quietly slipped past him, flashing her hospital badge at the cashier for payment.

Exiting the darkened cafeteria, she noticed that snack time impeded her desire to look in on Tamara before Daphne's shift concluded. Since their initial consultation, the locker-room gossip buzzed with stories of Miss Daphne's checkered past. Channing maintained a friendship with her nurses for several reasons: one, she flourished in the atmosphere of teamwork when trust existed without pompous titles, and two, by keeping her ear close to the gossip, she kept up with the pulse. During her fellowship years at the University of Louisville, professors taught that a doctor must trust the nursing staff, since they are the first line of defense and offense in patient care. Some of her colleagues took an arrogant stance toward their nurses and saw patients receive only basic prescriptive care. Channing didn't view anyone as less or more important than she was. People were people, and they were all deserving of her attention.

Taking the stairs two by two, she reached the third-floor wing in record time. *Not bad for someone holding an ice-cream cone,* she chuckled. During her residency, she frequently sprinted up the stairs while finishing her lunch. Lately, she hadn't relied on that talent, but she missed those days of not knowing what to expect. Tamara's case brought her back into the late-night trenches of the research library. Over the last couple of nights, Channing stayed to personally monitor Tamara, not only because of her distrust of Daphne, but because she was stumped over the current treatment plan. Tamara's vitals showed signs of stabilization, making it seem as though her body *was* capable of repair.

She rounded the corner to Tamara's room, attaching a small light to her lab coat. She often used it during evening hours when she didn't want to disturb patients. Hearing a laugh come from the door, she stepped behind two chairs. Channing caught a quick glimpse of Daphne exiting as she pulled a cell phone out of her pocket. Standing in the doorway for a moment, she checked for messages. The sound of her maniacal laughter made Channing's skin crawl. She needed to get to Tamara as soon as possible, hoping Daphne wouldn't linger.

Daphne looked around for any signs of activity on the floor. Seeing none, she slipped something from the nurse's station desk into her pocket and proceeded to walk down the hall. Channing revealed herself from behind the chairs as Daphne turned her back. She carefully opened the door to Tamara's room and stepped inside.

The lights were dimmed. Her periods of nighttime sleep had decreased since her return to the hospital, and she often complained about the brightness of her room regardless of the time. Graham and Channing took great pains to ensure that the evening nursing staff did as little as possible to disturb her. Channing flicked the small light on and approached the monitors. Seeing no obvious change, she felt confident that they had made a step in the right direction. Maybe their patient was healing. The only way to confirm the improvement was a double-check of her morning labs. If there weren't any glaring discrepancies, she could confidently report that the worst was over. Flipping through the drug-interaction log attached to the IV pole, her minilight slipped off and slid into the trash can, illuminating its contents. Kneeling down on the floor, she pressed the sides of the liner away from the center of the bin to reveal a plastic vile. Manipulating the light to investigate the vile further, a glimmering drop of fluid remained intact at the bottom. Careful not to spill whatever it contained, Channing lifted the vile out of the bin, holding it between her thumb and index finger for safekeeping. Rather than speculate, she prayed her favorite lab technician was still on duty.

The logical conclusion was that Daphne discarded it, but Channing knew better than to accuse without concrete evidence. Daphne was mentally devious—the type of person who would stop at nothing to obtain a goal. As she started down the stairs, Channing was pleading with her already fatigued legs to make the trek down four flights to the basement when Daphne's cackle reverberated off the metal handrails. Carefully peeking over the edge, the top of Daphne's head was visible one floor below. Channing sat down on the top step, pressing her body against the wall to hide.

"I gave her the last dose I had, so if you want to finish her off, you'll need to send more as soon as possible."

Channing dared to move closer to the railing, hoping to glimpse the phone number before Daphne hung up.

"A week is too long!" Daphne shouted. "She's already begun to stabilize because you told me to back off the dosage for a few days. I realize you take pleasure in her suffering, but it will force me to increase her dosage, which may kill her by mistake. Is that what you want?"

Channing wished she could hear the other side of the conversation. As if by some divine response to her silent prayer, Daphne switched the phone to speaker mode. Channing laid back against the wall, unsure if Daphne would venture up the stairs.

"By the way, where are you? There's so much background noise this time, sounds like a zoo or something," Daphne said.

A scratchy voice flooded the speaker. "I am watching my black beauties dance within their cozy confinement. If only humans possessed such ability. It would be most interesting to watch."

Animals, in general, filled Daphne with a fear that rendered her motionless. As a precaution, she opened each shipment from her employer with great caution in the off chance that he decided to send her one of his lethal beauties in conjunction with his normal parcel. The only part of an animal that she found intriguing was the tail of a rattlesnake that had been separated from its owner.

"Tell me again why I have to wait so long for another supply," she dared to inquire.

"As previously stated, a week is needed for the serum to be completely mature."

Daphne wrinkled her noise as if she smelt something rotten, but couldn't locate it. "Mature? Are you breeding those things?"

"Well, of course!" he replied smugly. "I need a fresh supply. I have wasted much of my inventory due to your incompetence. Even with your carelessness, events have taken a turn that have improved your viability. Instead of having to rid myself of your ineptness, I will employ your services, no matter how substandard, for a bit longer."

Daphne felt empowered. She took a risk by pressing further for additional information. "What's next on the agenda, omnipotent one?"

"Careful," he warned. "You wouldn't want to lose your head before its time.

She backed off, apologizing for her callous remark. He accepted her apology graciously and continued with his description of what the future held.

"But how?" she asked, when he had finished.

"Don't worry your pretty little head with details. Be amazed at the accuracy of what I imparted to you coming to fruition. I have received information that Tamara will be moved."

"And in the meantime?"

"Call in sick for the next couple of shifts. Let her stabilize. It will be that much sweeter when the final dosage is administered and her body can no longer handle the shock of the serum," he said, laughing. "Wish I could see it in person."

Daphne descended the stairs, hearing a shout float down from above.

"Bitch!" Channing yelled down, freezing Daphne's footsteps from proceeding any further. She looked up as Channing emerged from the shadows. "Actually, 'murderer' is better!"

Daphne closed her eyes into slits as Channing quickly made her way to the landing. "What did you dare call me?" she spat.

"I overheard your little friend on the phone. You can bet your sweet ass that the police will be informed." Raising the vile to eye level, she held it out for Daphne. "I found this in the trash can. Want to tell me what's in it, or would you rather wait for the trial, you miserable excuse for a human being!"

Daphne pursed her lips to keep from shouting obscenities back in Channing's face. "I haven't the foggiest notion what that is."

"You were the last one in her room tonight." Channing began to shout. "I watched you walk out, which at the very least makes you an accomplice to the maniac on the phone."

"You're following me now, Dr. Paranoid?" Daphne shot back. "That proves you're the wacko, not me. Shouldn't you be busy curing some sick kid rather than tailing me for doing my job? I could go to the medical board and scream harassment."

Channing shook her head, trying to erase the poison being thrown in her direction. "You can't do shit, and you know it! The board would never believe someone with your record. How about you just tell me what's in this vile, and I'll make sure the police handle you a little nicer than your average run-of-the mill criminal."

Daphne winced at the courage it must have taken for Channing to track her down. She hadn't had anyone follow her every move before, which proved to be an advantage in the past. Now she saw that she had been sloppy. "Careful, Doctor, I know people who will take care of you with just the snap of my fingers. If I were you, I would stay as far away from me as humanly possible," she warned, lowering her head in an ominous manner.

Ignoring her threat, Channing continued. "I heard your guy mention serum and some animals in a container."

Daphne simply smiled. "Sorry, if I told you, I'd have to kill you." Placing her hands on either side of her cheeks in mock surprise, she added, "Maybe I will anyway."

Channing took a step closer to Daphne. Checking her watch, she realized that this exchange was leading nowhere. She began her descent on the stairs, challenging Daphne for the last time. "I'd like to see you try."

Her manner infuriated Daphne. She watched her own hands extend to reach Channing's back. One small push is was it would take for her to lose her balance. As she fell, Daphne would take her leave back upstairs, exiling herself to the nurse's station as an alibi. It would be hours before anyone found Channing's broken body in the stairwell. Few people frequented the stairs after dark, opting instead for the empty elevators. A surge of strength welled up inside before she pushed.

Channing felt a small amount of pressure on her back and turned to see Daphne standing behind her with a look of contempt. Knowing what she was capable of, Channing braced herself for the moment of impact. She took a step downward as the door to the landing opened and one of her pediatric night nurses stepped onto it.

"Dr. Bradley?"

Daphne quickly withdrew her hands, shoving them into her pockets.

"Yes, Caroline?" Channing gasped.

"There's been a development with the patient in room 205."

"I'm right behind you," she replied. Daphne passed her on the stairs, whispering a snide comment as she went. Channing directed her attention to Caroline. "We don't have a patient in room 205."

Caroline smiled. "I heard your shouts from the hall and thought you might need a hand."

Channing threw her arms around Caroline in a deep hug. "I owe you one! Just name it!"

Caroline patted Channing's back stiffly, uncomfortable with the sudden show of affection. "Can I have Christmas off?"

Channing held onto her arms, keeping the nurse's body straight in front of her. "For the rest of your life!" she exclaimed. "I need to get this down to the lab immediately; can you alert them that I'm coming?"

Caroline nodded as she watched Channing sprint down the stairs with a renewed vigor. "You want me to ask for Rene?" She yelled.

Channing held her hand above her head, her thumb raised in the air as a sign of approval, holding the vile even tighter. Reaching the basement level at a sprint, she burst through the doors into another dimly lit hallway. If it weren't for the fact that this was where the larger lab was located, Channing would not feel the need to come down this far into the depths of the hospital. It reminded her of a bad horror show.

Throwing open the double doors to the lab, she was surprised to see techs still at work. The lab usually kept one or two techs overnight in case an emergency test needed to be run, or if results had backed up during the day, but this night, the techs numbered twice as many.

Crossing her fingers that the senior pathologist would still be working, she breathed a sigh of relief when she saw a desk lamp burning brightly on his desk.

Channing entered his office, expecting to see him sitting in his chair. Since it had been left unoccupied, she figured that waiting was the best decision for the moment. She made herself at home in one of the small chairs that faced his wooden desk. In the ten years she had known Dr. Rene Ansilar, she had never taken the time to look around his office. Looking at different frames hanging on the walls, she noticed that among all the credentials pertaining to his career, bright watercolors of his native Philippines jumped out from the cream paint. Shelves behind his desk housed a vast library on alternative healing methods. The power of minerals, crystals, and mind-over-body titles sat next to the hard-backed spines of healing techniques of ancient shamans, ending with a bronze statue of Buddha. The variety of material brought a different perspective to the man. She knew him to be thorough as well as diligent in his work, always going above and beyond the call of duty to assist a physician or find a miniscule piece of evidence that a technician overlooked.

"Dr. Bradley? What on earth are you doing here at this late hour?" Rene questioned as he entered his office, walking over to his desk. Placing a manila folder on top of a pile of others begging for his attention, he sat down in his high-backed leather chair and switched the desk lamp up to its highest setting.

"I'm sorry for barging in like this, Rene. I've been working on a case with Dr. Wellington, and I have something I would like you take a look at. I honestly didn't think you would still be here."

Rene smiled, revealing dark circles under his eyes. "I didn't think I would be, either, but your patient's results have me stymied. I wanted to run alternate tests on her last blood draw to see what we have been missing. Tamara's results perplex me on a myriad of levels."

Channing smiled at her old friend. "I have a nurse who is administering a secret drug that could be causing the widespread failure of her organs. Could that be a possibility?"

Using his elbows for leverage, Rene leaned forward onto his desk. "Please shut the door," he whispered. "No sense alerting anyone in the lab that there is the possibility of mischief afoot in the hospital."

Channing did as she was told, returning to hand the plastic vile to Rene. Shaking the contents gently, he placed his nose above it, allowing scent to permeate his nostrils. After several minutes of personal investigation, he removed all the pens from the holder on his desk, setting the vile carefully inside, making sure to keep it straight. Folding his hands across the desk blotter, he asked Channing how the vile came into her possession. She gave him a brief background of Daphne, her reputation, and their altercation.

He leaned back in his chair, placing his hands gently into his lap. "I see."

"Do you think this is the root of Tamara's illness?" she asked.

"Whatever is held within that vile could either be keeping her sick or adding to her demise," Rene stated rather matter-of-factly. "It's only logical."

"Can you test it for me without any formal results being given to the hospital? I'd rather keep this under wraps until we have concrete evidence," Channing boldly demanded.

"But the greater question is, do we have enough liquid in the vile to be tested?" Peeking over the edge of the vile, he added, "There may not be enough to test within a wide range of limits."

"What do you propose?"

Reaching for the file at the top of the pile, he opened it and laid it onto his desk. Retrieving a pair of black metal-rimmed glasses from his side desk drawer, Rene placed them on his nose and handed Channing a paper from the file. "This was a test I ran this evening with Tamara's blood platelets and a small tissue sample from her cheek. The results are disturbing."

"The results show a destruction of organs at a cellular level, meaning Tamara's organs are being decimated at their foundation. Without the means to completely regenerate new cells, her organs would completely fail. This explains the shutdown, but not the cause. What made you run this test without an order?"

Rene shrugged. "A hunch. All the ordered labs were inconclusive wastes of time. Each time we ran them, the same results came with no end in sight. Finally, after the last few days, her blood gases have been stabilizing, and her red count began a small but steady increase, which led me to wonder."

Channing thought out loud. "Poison."

Rene shook his head. "I don't think so. Poisons are traceable." Channing opened her mouth to contradict him as he held up a finger to silence her. "I realize that certain ones are not. However, in this case, with the vast amount of tests we have run on this poor girl, not only have we made her a human pin cushion, but we would have seen something pointing to either a manmade or natural toxin."

Utterly confused, Channing took a deep breath. "The man on the other end of the phone did mention an animal of some kind used to create a serum."

"Yes, but with the amount of matter to test here, it limits our ability to narrow the field in regards to animals." Taking his glasses off to rub his eyes, Rene stared at the ceiling. "Do you remember the trip we took to South America when we saw those children in the remote hilltop villages?"

"Vaguely."

"They had a similar pattern of cellular destruction. And in those cases we discovered the culprit was an amphibian that infiltrated their food source. That could be something."

A thought flashed in Channing's mind with Rene's memory of the Doctors without Borders trip they had participated in together. "You're a genius!" She exclaimed, while jumping out of her chair. "I need to look at my travel journal from Egypt five years ago. If my hunches are correct, you may have just cracked this sucker wide open!" Before exiting from his office, they collaborated on what tests to run under this new theory. "I'll bring notes to you later this afternoon. Think something could be ready by then?"

Rene shook his head. "Don't think so. It might take a few days, and I'll need another tissue sample from Tamara."

"You got it," she answered. "Anything else?"

With the office door now standing wide open, Rene whispered, "I'd keep an eye on that nurse, if I were you."

"I intend to do better than that," Channing answered.

28

*T*rembling hands removed a sterling-silver chest from a safe hidden within the wall. Placing it onto an intricately carved table in the center of a darkened room, the Apprentice secured the rest of the safe's contents from the outside world by locking the heavy door with a swift turn of his key. Pushing an oil painting of the French coast back into position over the door, he turned to face the chest.

For security purposes, the room was lit by golden candelabra, giving a metallic sheen to the chest sitting between the flickering candlewicks. The Apprentice felt the moisture from his palms. For a brief moment, he thought he saw the chest breathe. Erasing the thought from his mind, he tightly grasped the two handles on either side of the chest to lift it from the table. A knock on the door alerted him to the lateness of the hour, insisting that he report to the Master with the chest. No other instructions were given, and he was concerned whether this was simply another exercise in his initiation.

The Apprentice had never witnessed what the chest contained. When he was given the key to the safe, he didn't think to ask what reason there would be for it to remain hidden. Slowly climbing the stairs to the main hall, he stole a few moments to gaze upon the intricate symbols engraved within the precious metal. On the top, a skull rested in the center, while a ribbon with a Latin inscription curled beneath. Since he hadn't been educated in Latin, the phrase meant nothing to him, but he decided to research the words in the library.

With slow, steady steps he approached doors leading to the one room in the building where apprentices were forbidden to enter before their initiation was completed. The sanctuary. The sweat on his palms intensified as he raised his knuckles to knock on the heavy doors three times.

The voice of the Master boomed. "You may enter."

The Apprentice cautiously opened the heavy doors, using his hip to balance the chest. His first view of the sanctuary caused him to gasp for air. Since his family was of modest means, he had never seen crystal chandeliers before, let alone the size of the two that hung from the ceiling. Rich burgundy fabric draped the walls, graced with celestial bodies, while gilded candelabras the height of a grown man flanked a wooden altar in the center of the room. The white marble floor shone in the bright lights of the candles, creating the look of a glass-like surface, which reflected his stride. Thirty high-backed chairs adorned with burgundy velvet seats sat in two rows on either side against the walls. At the opposite end of the door, two thrones sat unoccupied behind a speaker's podium. Behind the massive altar, draped in blue velvet and finished at the ends with golden tassels, stood the Master. His hands were clasped together in prayer. He motioned for the Apprentice to come closer to the altar, despite the young man's apparent fear.

"Place it in the center, if you please," he stated, his voice resonating off the walls.

The Apprentice did as he was instructed, taking five steps away from the altar, bowing from the waist as he went. Keeping his head low, he waited for the Master to address him.

"Do you know why I summoned you?" the Master asked.

Silently, the Apprentice shook his head. He had not yet been given permission to speak in the sanctuary, let alone to the Master directly.

"You may stand straight and relaxed, young man, and do not fear to speak freely. You and I are the only ones to grace this space, and I feel we can dispose of the usual decorum for the time being," the Master stated in a softer tone than his first address. His years of experience in his position were evident by his gray hair and a gaunt look around his eyes. Sleep had become a luxury to him during the last few days, and he relished a time when he would be able to participate in the sweet release of slumber. He had been through this once

before, when he was younger, and knew that after the initial work was completed to secure the contents of the safe, instruct the new members of the guard, and put secondary plans into motion, his rest would come.

The Apprentice had only seen the Master on three occasions other than tonight, and on each occasion his two closest advisors accompanied him. The Apprentice tried not to notice the sound of his own heart beating loudly in his ears.

Once more the Master posed his question. "Do you know why I summoned you here this evening?"

Swallowing the lump in his throat, the Apprentice's voice squeaked, "No, sir."

Keeping his hands firmly clasped, the Master asked a third time. "Do you know why I summoned you here this evening?"

Reflecting a moment, the Apprentice boldly replied, "Because I have bravery in entering the sanctuary before my initiation has been completed."

A smile graced the Master's face as he fought the urge to laugh. "Excellent assumption, but I asked you to enter. Bravery cannot be shown in doing what you are told. Only courage can."

"Sir?" the Apprentice questioned.

"In times of great need, men abandon their directives in order to do what they believe to be right. In the instance of pure courage, the man who stands his ground and follows through with his required task is the brave one, regardless of what he feels should be done."

"Yes, sir," the Apprentice replied, absorbing the lesson.

The Master bowed and took three steps away from the altar. Keeping his eyes firmly on the silver chest, he gestured for the Apprentice to reapproach the altar. As the Apprentice took his final step to the altar, the Master asked, "Can you complete the task I am to bestow upon you without question or detour?"

With eyes widening at the possibility of what lay ahead, the Apprentice confidently answered, "Yes, sir."

Closing his eyes, the Master replied, "Good man."

Placing his hands behind his back, the Master asked the Apprentice to place his hands upon either side of the silver chest and read the inscription in the center. Ashamed of his lack of education, the Apprentice confessed his *ignorance of the Latin tongue. To his surprise, the Master didn't scold him, but instead spoke the phrase from memory.*

"And its meaning, sir?" the Apprentice asked.

Smiling once again, the Master answered, "Knowledge is power. It is the motto this organization has defended since inception. Remember the phrase for as long as you breathe, for in all its simplicity, it may unlock many doors for you in the future."

Over the next few minutes the Master coached his young pupil in the Latin phrase, repeating it slowly until the young man spoke it naturally. When he was convinced of the Apprentice's retention of the impromptu lesson, he instructed him to pick up the key on the altar and unlock the chest. Before raising the lid, the Master instructed the Apprentice to close his eyes, empty his mind of all thoughts, take three deep breaths, and slowly open his eyes when he was done. Opening his eyes, the Apprentice saw new things in the room he had not noticed before.

The walls of the room revealed four marble alcoves, two on either side, each reflecting the glowing light of the candles as they held their own treasures. To his left the first alcove held a glimmering sword, its jeweled hilt casting colored prisms onto the floor. The second alcove presented a silver chalice atop a gilded pedestal. On his right in the third alcove, a medium-sized cauldron filled the space, while the final alcove was filled with a tall spear, its tip sparkling from the minerals still intact. Upon a prompt by Master, the Apprentice opened the silver chest to reveal a white skull staring up at him with blank eye sockets. A chill ran down his spine as he gently lifted the skull from its confinement, allowing it to breathe fresh air. Placing it on the blue velvet fabric of the altar, the Apprentice slid it to the left edge of the altar as the Master handed him a small silver pedestal.

The pedestal consisted of four independent silver rods, handcrafted into curls at both the top and bottom, allowing it to hold the skull upright. In the center where the four pieces met, a blue sapphire, the size of his palm, floated on its own. Following instruction, the Apprentice lowered the skull onto the top of the pedestal as the Master lit two white pillar candles on top of the altar. The Master looked the Apprentice directly in his eyes as he explained the reasoning for the skull to be kept locked in a safe. As he spoke, the eyes of the

Apprentice became larger and larger until the space between his eyes and his forehead merged into a singular piece of flesh. The information spilling from the Master's lips would be considered blasphemous in certain circles, and the Apprentice knew that what he was being told would have been part of his initiation ritual, for there weren't many men in his position that would understand the information he now received.

When the Master completed his explanation, he retreated from the altar, once again clasping his hands in prayer in front of his mouth with closed eyes. The Apprentice gave him a moment of silence, and then asked a simple question. "What do you ask of me?"

"I demand two things: your undying loyalty to the organization you are about to enter, and your obedience, both to me as well as the ancient secrets that will be given to you. Are you capable of performing these tasks without prejudice or question of motive, should the need arise?"

The Apprentice stood a little taller. "I am."

"Are you able to walk your path, knowing full well that there will be others who attempt to change your beliefs as well as secure the secrets from you?"

"I am," he confirmed.

"Are you able to stand without fear alongside those who have also pledged their loyalty, even when the world around you labels you as heretic? Can you stand strong, not losing sight of what you have seen and heard, knowing deep within your heart that you have been shown the path of truth?"

Rolling his shoulders back, the Apprentice promised, "I am and will, sir."

The Master walked around the altar, placing his right hand upon the Apprentice's shoulder. Looking deep into his eyes, he bestowed the honor. "From this day forward, you shall be known to all who gather within these walls as The High Priest of Oannes. You are the keeper of the chest, and it is your duty to guard it, with your life if necessary, using your discretion in who shall be allowed to look upon its contents."

Reaching into the Apprentice's plain white nightshirt, he placed an aged scroll of parchment next to his skin. "Keep its story close to your heart, and do not forget that it is now your primary master. All others are secondary, even me. If there is a demon among us who wishes it harm, you will be told. The chest will be your guide in who shall be trusted. Finally, keep your promise and obey my every command from this day forward. There are times of great struggle ahead, and the loyalty you have shown this evening will need to be consistent."

"I understand, sir," the Apprentice replied, unsure of what demons the Master referred to.

The Master turned the Apprentice away from the altar to face the doors, leaving behind the chest, skull, and pedestal. Since he had just been given the task of safeguarding the chest and its contents, he felt uneasy about leaving it. As the Master began to push him toward the doors, the Apprentice pulled away. Still grasping the Apprentice by the shoulders, the Master sensed his apprehension and tightened his grip on the socket of his shoulder. With a few feet left before they reached the doors, the Apprentice slipped out of the Master's grasp, heading straight back to the altar. He stood courageously in front of the skull, his arms folded in front of him.

"I am sorry, sir, I cannot leave my charge," he stated sternly with a courage that surprised even him.

The Master spun around to face him. "I have chosen wisely. A lesser man would have left." He walked back toward the altar and instructed the young man on the proper placement of the skull on its pedestal within the chest. Securing the lock with the key that hung from the chest, the Master placed a second key in the Apprentice's hands, instructing him to keep it with the scroll next to his heart at all times.

"This way," he explained, "if a man wishes to do you harm and steal the prize for himself, he will alert you with his deceptive hand."

The Apprentice thanked the Master, grasped the chest with both hands, and began his walk toward the door. The Master remained at the altar, watching the young man and the chest depart. As the heavy door opened, the Apprentice turned one last time to face the Master. "May I ask a question, sir?"

Bowing his head in acknowledgment, the Master replied, "You may."

"Since this honor has been given to me tonight, will my final initiation commence soon?"

The Master blew out the candles on the altar in one breath. "You have been initiated at my own hand, brother. You require nothing else."

The young man beamed from the doorway, elated with his new position as both brother and high priest. It was the first time in his short life that he felt important. He closed the heavy door behind him, knowing that within a week, he would reenter those doors with his brothers, taking a seat in one of the chairs closest to the thrones at the back. The thought made his entire body tingle. His distraction of future events caused him to run into a stranger lurking beyond the sanctuary doors. Knocking the stranger to the ground from the weight of the chest, the young man hovered above the darkened form on the floor, straining his eyes to identify who he had become entangled with.

"Watch where you are going, sir." A female voice squeaked, unsure of whom she had run into, hoping it wasn't the Master.

"Pardon me, madam, but, you are not expected so close to the sanctuary. Is there a matter I can help you with this late in the evening?" he asked her, using a single hand to hold the chest while using the other to help her to her feet.

"No, sir. I have been summoned by the Master with specific instructions to bring him what I carry in my hands. I was told to show it to no one before placing it within the sanctuary."

Her bold proclamation of being allowed entrance to the sanctuary shocked the young man. He was told that women were not allowed past the doors, not even to clean! There were brothers assigned to such a task to ensure that the room remained undisturbed by those who had not been privy to its secrets. "I am sorry, but that is not possible, madam. Your presence is not permitted within the walls."

Her voice maintained its steady rhythm, unyielding to his stern warning. "It is I who am sorry, sir, for I have been called, and I will go, whether you permit it or not. You may stop me if you like with whatever means you have within your immediate grasp."

Sweeping past him, he felt her skirts brush against his pant legs, as her shadow walked toward the heavy doors. She knocked three times, as the Master's voice once again bellowed from within the room, permitting her entrance. As she opened one of the doors, the young man saw a piece of tightly rolled cloth held underneath her arm. Before entering into the forbidden space, she looked back at the young man standing in the hallway holding the silver chest. Her warm smile captured his heart. She paused briefly for him to ask her what it was she carried.

"A priceless artifact," she whispered. "An artifact that represents the truth of the past, as its very existence threatens the foundation of control for those who seek power."

Her answer confused the young man. His evening had been full of artifacts bearing the same title.

"What kind of artifact can do all that?" he whispered back to her as the doors closed.

"A carpet," she stated. "Merely a carpet."

29

The two strangers from the dig site hid within bushes surrounding Pip's cottage. Peering through the kitchen window, Mitch, Pip, and Brooke laughed at past memories. Brooke led the group through recollections of crazy adolescent pranks she and Pip created during summers together. Unaware of any threat beyond the glass, the trio continued their celebratory reunion with a second bottle of wine and increased frivolity. A phone vibrated in the outside vegetation.

"Gotcha," he addressed the man cowering behind a tree. "John, place the locator device on the car tonight before they have a chance to get away in the morning." He thrust a small black box into his hands. "Go get 'em, Tiger," he mocked, slapping John hard on the back.

"Do it yourself!" John snapped.

Cracking his knuckles, the man responded quietly. "He said for *you* to do it! If you like, I could tell him that you're frightened of a parked car." Reaching inside his coat to retrieve the phone, he added to his threat, "I'm sure he'll be pleased by that little tidbit of information."

Without another word of argument, John slithered across the gravel drive toward Brooke's Volvo. He shimmied underneath the belly of the vehicle, near the gas tank, released the adhesive backing of the box and firmly pressed it against the metal. Instead of a calm retreat back to the bushes, he sprinted across the drive, bent over in a feeble attempt to hide. A combination of nausea and stomach pain confirmed the return of his ulcer. Jobs like this often gave him stomach pain, but the number of antacids he consumed made him question whether the venture was worthwhile. He should have held out for more money.

John reclaimed his position next to the burly man, who was finishing another phone call. All John overheard was the confirmation of the device's placement. "Done there, Superman?" the man asked sarcastically.

John fought the instinct to punch the man square in the jaw. Since the size difference was acute, John knew the better course of valor would be to play along. Being a large, lumbering man could certainly carry the disadvantage of not being light on his feet, or so John hoped. "What's the latest?" he asked, genuinely curious.

"We take a little day-trip tomorrow with our new friends. We're to follow them, trap them, and give them the big sleep." The man laughed. "Just hope Julian doesn't beat us to it and take the fun away."

The mention of Julian's name sent chills down John's back. He involved John in the cat-and-mouse game he now played, under the guise that his momentous gambling debts would disappear. He failed to mention that the debts would be paid upon completion of further tasks, not just the initial plant of the smaller device back at the Ritz Hotel. He didn't like the way Julian conducted business. Better to pacify the brute sitting next to him as added protection, he thought.

"If we know where they're going tomorrow, why did I just put that thing on their car?" John asked naïvely.

Raising a pair of binoculars toward the window, the man spat out his answer. "We need to know the precise location, so that I don't have to sit my ass in any more of these bushes waiting for them to leave."

John wasn't aware of any plan to abandon their present location, so he pressed further, perfectly content with spending the night in bushes. "How is he sure of the next location? They could switch things up in a heartbeat."

"Come on, stupid, use your melon. He's on the inside! He knows every move before the doctor man knows. They keep him updated on each and every happening right down to the people he'll meet."

"How is that?" John asked.

Lowering the binoculars, the man looked John squarely in the eyes. "Look, I overheard a bit. You can learn a great amount of information by keeping your mouth closed and your ears open," he advised. "The guy has membership rings for twelve different organizations along with the credentials to back them up. Each ring opens the doors, and he waltzes right in."

The man returned his focus to the scene in the kitchen, ignoring John completely. John's jaw dropped at the realization that he was involved in something larger than he agreed to. This was supposed to be a simple job. One to clear his debts, gain more cash, and secure a work-free lifestyle for at least a year or two. His exit needed to be smooth, or else he would be next on the list of fun things to dispose of during an afternoon romp in the woods. Unexpectedly, the man stood up. When John questioned their departure from the bushes, the man demanded he get into the car without any further questions. John ignored the demand, pressing the man's buttons until he relinquished the evening's plans through sheer frustration.

"We have a room at a cozy country hotel in Killiecrankie, which isn't far from here." He surprised John with a hard slap to the back. "We're sleeping in the lion's den tonight, old boy!"

John followed the earlier advice, keeping his mouth shut and his ears open in the vain attempt of learning a bit of information to use as leverage. He would need it when they learned that he had installed the locator device, but failed to switch it on.

Fresh from their late-night comedy session, Brooke and Mitch faced the day with new respect for each other. The stories exchanged between the women showed a playful side to Brooke. He only knew her as a serious academic who took pride in both her achievements and intellectual prowess. Watching her laugh with pure abandon allowed Mitch to recapture the feelings he had the first moment he laid eyes on her. She continued to give him butterflies. He was hopeful his love for her could bubble toward the surface once more.

Fastening her seatbelt, Brooke looked in the backseat to check on Kodiak. Seeing that she was content in her place, she turned the key in the ignition and headed out of the drive. The silence in the car unnerved Mitch, as he was used to hearing a barrage of U2 music in Pip's car, or sappy ballads in Boggs's. The two stared out their windows for the first ten minutes, until Mitch could no longer stand the tomb-like atmosphere.

"Oban?" he asked uncomfortably.

"Coastal town of Oban. I have friends there."

Looking over his shoulder at Kodiak, he asked, "She goes with us?"

Brooke snickered. "Of course she does! No one ever gives me an issue when Kodiak is around, and she's used to going everywhere with me. If I left her somewhere, it would be catastrophic to her mental stability. She hasn't left my side since I picked her up as a pup."

Mitch didn't understand her attachment to the animal. "People let you bring her into public places?"

"Well, there *are* limits," she admitted. "But there is a place where she'll be comfortable for a few hours, and they love her."

Kodiak lifted her head, letting a quick howl escape her mouth as the car passed the turn-off for the dig site. "Not today, girl."

Mitch shook his head at the exchange. He didn't understand it, but he could respect it. He wanted to keep the conversation going before being bombarded with business in Oban. "Last night was fun."

A broad smile appeared on Brooke's face. "I haven't laughed like that in years! Pip and I had a wild time during those childhood summer visits. I forgot what an important part of my personal history she holds."

"I have to ask," Mitch said, enjoying her smile. "Did you guys really fry the electricity to the inn with a campfire?"

Brooke was unable to contain her laughter. "Oh, yeah! Pip had the wild idea of camping out under the stars, without any gear of course, and it didn't dawn on us to check for wires as we sat underneath the sign. When Pip lit that match and threw it on the pile, I thought we would catch the sign on fire for sure, but when the sparks came and the inn went dark, I feared for my life!"

"Why?" Mitch asked.

"The inn was full for dinner! I can still hear Duncan's voice bellowing our names. We spent the next three nights outside just to make sure he had calmed down!" she chuckled.

"And was he?"

"Was he what?" she asked, through laughter created tears.

"Was he calm?"

"Oh, yeah, he calmly told us that we were on strict kitchen duty for the duration of my visit. I had the worst dishpan hands when I got home!"

Mitch fell silent as his own memories of the trip with his father continued to haunt him. "Those must have been incredible summers!"

"Looking back, they were the best times of my life. Funny how when you grow up, the things your parents made you do when you were younger, that you hated, suddenly become the best experiences. It's frightening to think my mother was correct when she announced that I would thank her someday."

"I came here once with my dad at my mom's insistence and hated it; now I'd give anything to go back and share it with him again. I think I would appreciate it more from this perspective."

Brooke looked at him tenderly. "I didn't know you came here with your father."

Mitch returned her gaze. "Seems there is quite a bit we never shared."

"You didn't enjoy that trip to Scotland, but how about this one?" she asked, clearly baiting him.

Mitch huffed. "Secrets, strange people, and old objects to carry. Getting shot by an individual that I have known since medical school. Being chased while bleeding to death and almost being mauled by a giant dog. I'd say it's been a positive experience all around." Brooke remained silent, unsure of how to respond. "And don't forget the revelation of my dad's secret life!"

"You *have* enjoyed it!" she teased.

Mitch couldn't help but laugh at her dry sense of humor. "Something I don't think I'll ever forget, even if I wanted to." They sat laughing uncomfortably while Mitch gathered his courage to speak his heart's desire. Turning to face her, his voice turned gentle. "I never stopped loving you. There hasn't been anyone since you, and I'm not convinced there could ever be."

Brooke felt the impulse to pull over and have him hold her in his arms. She imagined it in her mind a million times since the day she stepped on the plane. There was nothing she wanted more, but her rational mind prevailed, thinking that if he was capable of allowing her to leave his life once, he might be capable of doing it again. She worked too hard in safeguarding her emotions to allow a single encounter to destroy her efforts, but she knew that this admission was no small feat for Mitch Brody. Rather than destroy him at a critical juncture in his trip, she allowed her vulnerability to shine through her tough exterior. "Me too."

Her answer stunned him. He was sure that she had abandoned all feelings for him long ago. Feeling quite daring all of a sudden, he asked, "You too, what?"

Allowing herself to speak the truth about her feelings for the first time since her dramatic departure, Brooke let her tears flow down her cheeks. "I never stopped loving you either!" she shouted, forcing Kodiak to rise up and witness the scene.

Mitch felt his fear mingle with the overwhelming joy of the moment. He had ached for her for so long that the pain had become second nature. Once and for all, he needed to face the consequence of her shoving rejection back down his throat.

"If I still love you and you still love me, where do we go from here?" he asked quietly, injecting a bit of humor to break the tension. "Besides Oban."

Brooke jerked the car onto the shoulder of the highway. It wasn't a good idea for her to be operating a vehicle, considering her decreased visibility through swollen, tear-filled eyelids. Putting the car into park, she turned to face the man who stole her heart all those years ago. "I think we date," she whispered.

Mitch laughed at the simplistic nature of her thought process. "I don't want to date you. I did that once and don't feel the need to waste time."

Using the back of her sleeve to wipe the tears, Brooke felt as if they needed to reintroduce themselves to each other, since they had become different people. Mitch scowled at her naïve explanation. "What if you're still in love with the Brooke you remember and can't love the Brooke sitting in front of you?" Trying to convince herself as well, she finished her argument with, "We're not kids anymore. We're adults with experiences that could change the dynamic of how we relate to each other."

Mitch turned away to stare at his shoes. She was wrong on every account. But he couldn't help but admire her rational thinking, which was one thing that had not changed. In a bold declaration of his intentions, he unbuckled his seatbelt and leaned over, placing his right hand above her heart.

He gently took her hand and placed it on his heart. She felt it pound wildly. "We know each other *here,* and that's all that matters." Locking eyes, Mitch saw the longing within her to be with him. He added, "I safeguarded your memory in my heart all these years, and if this doesn't work out a second time, it will remain there as a monument to you. There could never be anyone else."

The gesture was far too great for Brooke to ignore. Wrapping her arms around his neck, she kissed him with reckless abandon. All of her defensive alarms sounded loudly in her head as she ignored all her inner demons and followed her heart. While their embrace lasted a few minutes, the large dog crept toward the front seat. Catching a glimpse of her treasured companion, Brooke laughed as Kodiak licked Mitch's face. "I guess you get us both!" she exclaimed as Mitch looked bewildered. With Kodiak retreating to her designated space in the car, Brooke took a Kleenex from the glove compartment to wipe her eyes. Drawing the mirror down from the visor, she checked her makeup and gawked at the puffiness of her eyelids.

"I'm a mess!" she exclaimed. "A big pile of girly mess."

Mitch dabbed mascara away from her cheeks. "Where do we go from here?"

"We continue on to Oban Cathedral. What do you think we should do, just pack it all in because we shared an intimate moment?" she replied sarcastically.

"I meant with us, dingbat."

Returning the visor to its upright position, she sighed, "Oh, that." She rolled the Kleenex into a tiny ball. "It's not like we can leave everything that we've worked for to date each other. I have the dig site to complete, which could take two more years, and then the research data has to be compiled, written up, and presented to the university committees. You can't leave your practice in the States. Do we date long distance, sharing the burden of travel arrangements to have a couple stolen weekends here and there?" She placed her hand gently onto his knee. "I don't know how this could work with all the hurdles."

Placing his hand over hers, Mitch gathered the remainder of his courage, and without looking, he took the leap of faith over the edge of the cliff. "I can move my practice here. I'll do whatever it takes to get the proper license to practice in the UK. And if I can't, then I'll come be some lowly intern at your dig site, learning all about the history business." He squeezed her hand tightly. "I intend on *not* repeating the pain of my mistakes."

Brooke recognized the tremendous offer. She knew his medical career was a priority that he sacrificed for many times through the years. It was the point she wished he had been at when she left after graduate school. Now that he was willing to sacrifice everything, she could too. "You don't have to. We'll work this out, but not today. Today we move forward together." She leaned over, kissing him once more before pulling back onto the highway. "Oh, Pip is going to freak out! I can see her face all lit up and taking credit for this happening."

Mitch felt a twinge of guilt for the feelings he developed for Pip during this trip. If Brooke hadn't been one of the teachers and Pip had not been engaged, he would have considered a romantic relationship with Pip. Coming to his senses immediately, he realized that Pip would have been a quick fix. Seeing her again placed him where he needed to be, in her life and in her arms. A snicker out of the corner of Brooke's mouth begged for a question of her thoughts.

"I was picturing the look on Graham's face when you tell him that we're back together." Slapping her hands onto the steering wheel, she added, "Can I be there when you tell him? His expression will be priceless!"

With all of the commotion after Southwark Cathedral, Mitch completely forgot about Graham. "Holy Crap!" he shouted, pounding the window with his fist. "Do you have a phone on you? I think I left mine at Pip's."

Brooke rifled through her purse and handed him a phone.

"Dr. Wellington," he answered after just one ring.

"Graham!" Mitch shouted through the receiver. "It's me!"

"Mitch?" Graham asked, clearly confused by the phone number that popped up as caller identification. "Where the hell are you calling me from? Where is your phone? Are you OK?" he blurted out without taking a breath.

"Calm down, buddy. I'm fine. I have had a hell of a time due to some unforeseen circumstances. Get me up to speed on Tamara's condition." Silence filled the phone line. "Graham? You still there, buddy?"

"You have some nerve, Brody," he spat. "You dump me here on this case for you, take off to the UK, and disappear without as much as an emergency contact number. Now you call me like nothing has happened, wanting a status report on *my* patient." Clearing his throat, he added, "You must have grown quite a pair of testicles over the last week."

Mitch took a deep breath before answering. He was right; he abandoned him without any information and expected Graham to clean up Tamara's medical mess. Hell, he didn't expect him to clean it up, he demanded it be done. "Sorry is the best I can say at the moment."

Graham snickered. "My mistake, you grew a vagina rather than testicles."

Mitch laughed at the sexist joke. It was like Graham to be mad, make a big deal out of a situation, and then just as quickly pretend that it never happened. Few people could forgive and forget like Graham. "Before I ask you some questions, I'm here with an old friend. Can I put you on speaker?" Graham agreed as Brooke giggled in anticipation of his reaction. Mitch switched over to speaker, asking Graham if he was able to hear his voice.

"Yeah, I hear you. If you tell me that Kingman is with you, I'm hanging up," he warned.

"Oh, it's not Kingman." Mitch motioned for Brooke to say hello. His reaction was instantaneous profanity spilling from lips. "Tame it down buddy, there's a lady present."

"You're kidding me!" Graham exclaimed. "That can't possibly be Brooke!"

Brooke continued to laugh, satisfied with his reaction. "In the flesh, Wellington!" she shouted into the speaker. "How do you like that?"

"I do not like it if you're the reason he left so quickly, leaving me with a mess, just so he could go and get some tail." Graham added quickly, "No offense, Brooke."

"No offense taken, Wellington. I'm honored that you still think so highly of my tail that Mitch would travel all this way just to get a piece of it."

Graham beamed proudly at her bravado. "God, I've missed you. Hope you guys have hooked up, so Mitch can stop his charade of attempting to date while still secretly being in love with you. You did tell her that when you saw her, right, Mitchy?"

Mitch nodded his head. "Sure did. Thanks for the reminder."

"My pleasure," Graham replied. "Now, what the hell has been keeping you from calling me, other than the obvious distraction sitting beside you?"

Mitch kept the tale of his adventures to a minimum, hitting on the key points since they had last spoken on the train to London. He knew Graham's concentration level was intense, due to the fact that he didn't try to interrupt once with a witty remark. After ten minutes of explanation, Mitch caught his breath, allowing Graham an opportunity to speak.

"After I warned you about the level of Kingman's weasellike attributes, you still thought it would be a good idea to invite him along on your appointment in some vain attempt to repay an invisible debt?" Graham asked.

"I guess so," Mitch admitted openly.

"You're dumber than I thought!" Graham shouted. "When are you going to wake up and realize that what I say is golden, my friend?"

"How about today?" Mitch asked. "All you gleaned from the story was that I trusted Kingman? He shot me! Did you not hear that?"

"Yeah, I heard. But unlike you, I don't get caught up in mundane details. I venture straight into the heart of the matter, which is your absolute blind trust of people who are stupid," Graham replied sternly.

Before Mitch could utter a rebuttal, Brooke halted the argument, telling them to get on with what was important, which was Tamara.

"Catch me up," Mitch repeated.

"For starters, she stabilized in a miraculous turn of events. According to labs that I ordered drawn every twelve hours, her organ function is returning, though on a small scale. I'm still not completely sure *why* it is returning, but I never look a gift horse in the mouth, which is something my grandmother used to say and I never knew why." Mitch reminded Graham to halt the rambling. "Sorry, long shift. OK, the second thing you should know is that I added Bradley to the case. She needed a project, and let's face it, that's what Tamara is, plus I thought an extra pair of eyes with a specialty in a different pediatric field than my own would be beneficial."

"You also find her attractive," Mitch added.

"True, but not necessary to point that out at the moment, Brody."

Mitch apologized with a small burst of laughter.

"Moving on." Graham continued, "Bradley has been a remarkable help on this case, and I'm sure that you'll find her work most satisfactory. She's running new labs with the help of her little pathology friend, Dr. Ansilar. I'm confident that she will discover what has caused Tamara's condition."

Mitch applauded. "Nicely done, Graham."

"I thought so, thank you. Lastly, I checked into your new best friend, Kingman, while you were being whisked away to your ass-whooping in some church. I asked the brothers to conduct some light research into his background and discovered that not only did the guy lie in medical school, but he has made deception some kind of sick career decision. He gains membership into organizations that he has no business joining."

"Like what?" Brooke asked, intrigued by the conversation. She remembered Julian Kingman as a wimpy type of guy. She felt sorry for him in school.

"He has quite the reputation for not being proficient in his medical practice. Seems he has a dozen malpractice lawsuits against him, as well as some inquiries into his medical treatments and practices. Questions about his credentials have cropped up, with some even questioning his graduation from medical school. I couldn't get a definitive on whether or not he *did* graduate. The jury is still out on that one."

"He didn't graduate?" Brooke blurted out.

"Hold on, it gets better. He holds three arrest records for domestic batteries against girlfriends. Our dear Kingman has quite the raging temper. Kind of kinky, if you ask me." Mitch recalled the sick way Julian taunted him as well as the way he disposed of Bridget without a second thought. A temper was describing it nicely. "He wasn't formally charged. Seems he settled out of court with monetary gain on the girlfriend's end. He's a real winner."

Mitch couldn't stop from asking, "Anything else?"

"Yeah, one more. He tried to purchase a membership ring from *our* brotherhood a year after they rejected his application. He even stated that he was our longtime friend to secure a position. When he was rejected, he offered the interview committee a rather obscene amount of cash for a ring, regardless of his initiation. He got a little irate at one of the committee members and threw a chair or something, and they called the police. He ran off before the officers arrived to question him and had not been heard from until he raised his little snake face on the train to London," Graham said.

"What are you getting at, Graham?" Mitch asked, trying to process the information.

"Don't you think it's kind of weird that this guy tries to purchase a membership ring from our organization and then all of a sudden shows up unannounced with you in London, stating that he was attending a conference? There wasn't any conference in the UK." Graham added, "If I never see him again, it will be too soon."

Silent as he held the phone out in front of him, Mitch asked Brooke a direct question. "Do you think Julian is after Tamara?"

Brooke's initial feeling was that he wasn't, but she couldn't rule out the possibility. "Didn't you tell Pip that he asked you about the Exile Carpet and the Professor?"

"Yes," Mitch replied quietly.

"Only people privy to the inner workings of this organization know about either one of those things. Maybe Julian isn't after Tamara, but he sure as hell is after the two most important things linked to her," Brooke stated.

"Wait a sec!" Graham shouted. "Will the cast of characters ever end?"

Mitch admired the cavalier attitude Graham used when approaching serious situations. He wished he could be more like that, but tended to panic given something new and possibly dangerous. "I think Bradley was a great choice. If anyone can figure out what the hell we've missed, it would be her." He chose his next words carefully, knowing they could trigger a small amount of panic in Graham's demeanor. "I need you to make preparations for Tamara to travel."

"What are you smoking over there? She can't travel; she just barely stabilized twenty-four hours ago. A plane ride would kill her!"

"Then we have to find an alternate means of transportation. She is the most important part of this puzzle, and in order for all the pieces to fit properly; she has to be here in person," Mitch explained calmly. "I need for you to make this happen."

Graham groaned under the weight of the enormous task. "What are you proposing?"

"What about a boat? If Daphne is still with you, she could attend to her," Mitch said casually.

"Man, do not get me started on that debacle!" Graham snorted. "Bradley and Daphne are like oil and water. It's one big soap opera here day in and day out. But for you, I'll ask her."

Mitch tapped his fingers against the window as a way of calming down his racing mind. "See what you can come up with for the crossing. Lillian will need to come with her, and she'll want Earl. Make some calls, and we'll touch base this evening, OK? I'd also like to hear the results of the labs."

"You never make things easy, Brody," Graham stated with irritation in his voice. "I assume you would prefer protection from the brothers"

"After all I've seen over this trip, hell yeah!" Mitch exclaimed. The flashing battery light halted their conversation. "Battery is dying, Graham. I'll call you this evening, if not tomorrow, but you'll probably have it all figured out by then anyway."

"Hey, Brooke!" Graham shouted. "Take good care of my boy!"

Brooke smiled, raising her voice. "Don't I always?"

Graham's laugh could be heard as the phone clicked off. He passed the cell phone back to Brooke, who placed it within the center console, attaching the car adapter for charging.

"It's great that you and Graham are still close," she said. "Friendships like that are rare."

"Graham is certainly someone you can't get rid of, even if you tried." Mitch laughed. "I'm lucky he still wants to be my friend after all the crap I've put him through over the years." Mitch turned his head toward the window, fearful that Brooke would spot the tiny tears developing in his eyes. It was the one relationship in his life he worked hard at keeping. Attempting to change the subject, he asked, "I never could get the name of this organization you guys work for out of anyone involved. Why is that?"

Brooke's cheeks blushed. "The name of an organization isn't what's important. It's the people in it. If the people are virtuous and honest, then the name benefits from their actions, not the other way around."

Accepting that she wasn't about to divulge details without permission, Mitch dropped the subject. His first view of Oban Harbor was a postcard. Small fishing boats aligned the rock walls of the harbor, a few buoyed off the coast with fishermen daring the early morning chill to tend to their nets. Brightly colored hulls peeked out of the water, bobbing and swaying with the rolling tide. Historic construction combined with modern facades within the town, while larger stone homes and hotels dotted the surrounding hills, giving residents a spectacular view of the harbor. An old distillery housed in its original building from the Middle Ages mingled close to the Edinburgh Woolen Mill with its bright white-washed walls. Visitors pressed their faces against the windowpanes to glimpse the fine array of sweaters, scarves, and hats. He liked seeing the hustle and bustle of the town as tourists mingled with locals. The Scottish people were certainly accommodating, with each new visitor receiving a genuine smile from a local resident. Caught up in the steady pace of movement from people around him, Mitch failed to recognize that Brooke had parked the car.

"William Street!" she stated excitedly.

Mitch looked a little closer, but saw nothing but a buzz of people walking up and down the busy street.

"I don't see a church."

Brooke nudged Kodiak awake, as she attached a leash to her collar. "It's further down the street at the corner of William and George. George is the main drag of town, but I stopped here because our favorite bakery is a block down on the right. They make the best blueberry scones, and the owner always has a treat for Kodiak," she boasted.

Mitch stepped out of the vehicle, grabbing a long black tote from behind his seat. He traded his briefcase for the worn tote, under orders from Pip that it would be easier to carry with the spear and sword being less identifiable. Brooke nodded in the direction they were headed, leading the way through the crowded streets. Kodiak kept her eyes straight and tail aloft, creating a stir on the street with her wolflike appearance. The animal's calm behavior was astonishing, given all the chaos.

Walking along the sidewalk, aromas from restaurants, bakeries, distilleries, and vehicle exhaust mingled into a delectable concoction. Every storefront displayed the wares of each owner, with meats hanging in the butcher's window, breads tempting from the baker, trinkets of china, decorative items, and antiques daring to be purchased. Glancing into the window of an antique shop, a black-marble mantle clock caught Mitch's eye. He stopped for a closer look, as Kodiak and Brooke continued their walk. He yelled out his intention to visit the shop, with Brooke nodding as she headed off to the bakery. She and Kodiak would gather their treats and come back in a few minutes. She didn't see any danger in allowing him some personal time.

The bakery's entrance hadn't changed since her first visit ten years ago. The original owners continued the tradition of scratch baking every morsel each morning, establishing a loyal customer base that reached as far away as the city of Perth. A long wait was never out of the question. Brooke viewed the five people ahead of her as nothing short of a miracle for a busy week day. Two men dressed in dark suits stood at the counter, along with a third, who was far more casual in dirty jeans and a ragged jacket. The owner had been summoned to speak to them by a young counter clerk, who stepped aside to help another patron. As the owner approached, he caught a glimpse of Brooke as a photo was thrust into his hands. Unable to hear the conversation, Brooke watched the owner shake his head, mouthing words that he didn't know what they were talking about. The second man pulled out an additional photo for the owner, who received it with trembling hands. Terror swept over his face as he recognized the individual in the photo as Brooke. His eyes darted back and forth as the two men leaned farther over the counter. Unnerved by the scene, Brooke reached for her phone to call the authorities, forgetting that she had left it in the car, still charging its battery.

Fear escalated as the first man opened his suit jacket to reveal a weapon, causing the owner to gasp as he raised his face toward Brooke. "Run!" he screamed. The three men turned to see Brooke and Kodiak standing with their eyes locked on the owner. The second man drew a gun from his suit jacket as she yanked Kodiak out of the shop. Shots rang out from behind while they sprinted down the street. They quickly approached Mitch sitting calmly on a wooden bench outside the shop. Brooke called out his name, grabbed his tote, and forced him to join her in a flight down the street.

Two more shots fired as angry footsteps pounded the pavement. Brooke stretched her left hand behind her, meeting Mitch's, as they darted onto a small side street. With the men approaching at a faster pace, Brooke made a quick turn into an alleyway. Mitch blindly followed, hoping that she knew where she was going. Kodiak galloped alongside, completely confident in her owner's abilities. Before the three men found the alley, Brooke abruptly opened a weathered door on the right side, turning the unlocked metal doorknob as quickly as she could. "Thank God," she muttered, pushing Kodiak and Mitch over the threshold.

"What is going on, Brooke?" Mitch asked between breaths.

"We've been followed," Brooke said, searching around in the dark room for something to barricade against the door. "We don't have much time," she muttered, locating a dresser to push against the door. "Come with me."

Mitch followed Brooke and Kodiak through a storeroom of furniture into a brightly lit shop. Brooke scanned the room for any other people. Seeing no one, she loosened her grip on Kodiak's leash and turned to explain, when a female voice interrupted.

"Brooke?" the woman questioned enthusiastically. "Is it really you?"

She reached the place where Brooke stood and threw her arms around her in a tight embrace. "I can't believe you are back in Oban." Holding her at arm's length, a barrage of questions launched in Brooke's direction. "How's the dig going? Did you get the post I sent you about the watch? Clarence has a friend who located one that is similar, but not exact. Oh, he'll have to ask you about it; I don't know all the particulars. Clarence does all the business dealings; I'm merely the pretty thing they come to chat with, or so he says," she said, laughing. "I haven't let you breathe! First things first, what occasion are we celebrating to have our Brooke back for a visit, and most importantly, who is this adorable man you have with you?" The woman beamed at Mitch.

"This is Dr. Mitch Brody. I'm accompanying him on a visit to the cathedral."

The woman walked toward Mitch with the intent to hug him just as tightly, which she did the instant she locked eyes with him.

"So good to meet you, Dr. Brody! I am afraid our Brooke has never mentioned you before. I would think that if she had a handsome doctor in her life, such as you, she would see fit to mention your name every now and then. But maybe you will be a happy coincidence in future conversations." Completing her salutary hug, she extended her right hand in a surprisingly strong handshake. "My name is Sophie Stuart, but you can call me Fi." Mitch watched as Brooke's cheeks seemed to flush with pride at the two of them. Meanwhile a gentleman presented himself from the darkened corners, tapping Brooke on the shoulder.

"Never mind all that nonsense, Dr. Brody. I prefer to call her Old Woman, because she hobbles around here as if she has one foot in the grave, but then again, who doesn't?" Brooke laughed as she embraced the man. He patted her on the back, stating, "Saw the dog rush past me for a biscuit and knew you had to be here. Unless you taught her how to drive." He chuckled. "How are you, kid?"

"Slightly petrified," Brooke replied, introducing the man as Clarence Stuart. He used his opportunity to shake hands with Mitch to pull him into a corner of the shop. With the area being less bright than the main floor of the shop, he sat Mitch in a butler's chair, shielding him from prying eyes through the front window. "Don't need anyone else poking their head in the window, so sit here while we do the dirty work." He turned to walk back toward Brooke, but then he whipped back around to Mitch's eye level. "Keep the tote bag close." He took five steps back to Brooke, convening a small conference that only he, Brooke, and Sophie were allowed to attend.

Clarence and Sophie Stuart stood in stark contrast to each other, while complimenting each other harmoniously. His serious nature blended with her soft nurturing side, making their bond undeniable. They were a formidable team, with each one knowing the role they occupied, satisfied with that choice, and performing it without question. Both in their midsixties, they were almost identical in height and slim stature; even the glasses they wore were just a little different. Besides the obvious gender difference, in the darkened corner, Mitch could tell them apart due to the watches that graced each wrist. Clarence wore Mickey Mouse, while Sophie wore Minnie. After a few minutes of hushed whispers, Brooke joined Mitch as the Stuarts retreated to different parts of the store.

Crouching down beside his chair, Brooke explained that they were in the Stuart's antique store, poignantly named "The Rampant," after the National Flag of Scotland. They sold estate- and heirloom-quality objects as well as rare historical finds. Brooke met them during her first trip to the area, fell in love with them as well as their store, and became an adopted daughter. Along with the store, Clarence was a high-standing member of their organization and carried the prestigious title of one of Duncan's closest advisors.

"When the men began to chase me, this was the first place to pop into my brain. Clarence won't let anything happen to us," she stated with a slight tremble.

Mitch understood her fear, having faced it in Southwark. He knew that when she accepted this assignment, the chance of running into people who were out to hurt her had to have been explained, and knowing Brooke, she would have brushed it off without a second thought. However, when the cold, hard truth hits someone square on the jaw, it becomes a different story.

"You OK?" he asked, stroking her shoulder.

"I wish I knew who those men are!" she whispered. "It's a lot easier to create a strategy when you know your enemy and his strengths."

Clarence returned from the back of the shop. "Door is secure. If they barge in, it will have to be the front door, and I doubt that they'd want to take on a tough old German and his Polish wife." He jabbed his fists in the air in a mock fight. "She's scrappy, you know," he added, teasing Sophie, who returned quietly from behind.

She planted a kiss on his cheek. "You old goat," she teased. "I saw to the pup, Brooke. She's all snuggled upstairs with a bone from last night's stew. She loves coming to Nana's house!"

"Would it be OK if she stayed with you for a few hours? I don't want her in any kind of danger," Brooke asked timidly.

"Of course!" Sophie gushed. "Take all the time you need, sweetie. Although, we weren't expecting you until tomorrow."

Brooke stood. "I know this is an unexpected turn of events. Hope this is OK."

Clarence put his hand on her shoulder in a sign of solidarity. "Its more than fine, kid, it was the best split-second decision you made. Don't worry; we've been through worse than this before." He turned to address Sophie. "Fi, remember that estate sale we had on the Isle of Skye? Now that was an unexpected fight! It took me all day to convince that man to sell us that armoire after he had paid an obscene amount of money for it. Good thing you had the truck running. I weaseled my offer low, but he was too flustered to think about it till we were long gone."

Mitch didn't see the connection between men with guns and an old armoire. Instead he watched with great interest as the conversation turned from their immediate danger to the weather.

"I do hope it doesn't rain tomorrow. I had a lovely lunch planned on the roof deck. Rain would be such a disappointment," Sophie whined.

"You're awful quiet in your little corner there, Doctor. What is your take on all of this?" Clarence asked.

"I'm afraid I don't have one. I'm as clueless as Brooke," Mitch replied.

"Oh, Brooke isn't clueless," Clarence rebutted. "On the contrary, she is quite aware of everything that is going on and more. She doesn't let on as a safety measure. You, on the other hand, wear everything on your sleeve. Your fear, your strength, your weakness, your courage. You need a little course in bluffing."

"Thank you?" Mitch responded, unsure of where the conversation was headed. But he wasn't in any mood for another person to read into his character. On this trip alone he had had enough analysis to last a lifetime.

"Sure thing," Clarence said, stepping back toward the cashier counter. "You think you could come out here and try your hand at identifying these weirdoes, should they happen to walk by?"

Standing up from his chair, his hesitation in leaving the secure, darkened corner was obvious. "I guess I could, but even I'm not sure who they could be." As he peered out the front windows of the store, a familiar face peeked through the pane of glass. "Holy shit!" Mitch yelled, and ducked behind the counter.

"I guess that means you recognize the guy," Clarence stated in a cavalier manner. "Does he have a name?"

Mitch forced the lump inside his throat back down into his stomach. "Julian Kingman."

Slapping Mitch hard on the back, Clarence whispered, "That's the guy who shot you? Doesn't look too tough to me."

Looking up at Clarence, who seemed hell-bent on tormenting Mitch's delicate memory of the attack, his response was simple. "Thanks, Clarence."

The bell at the front door signaled Julian's entrance. Clarence whispered to Mitch, "Now watch and learn, Doctor." He stepped around to address his newest patrons, while Mitch peeked around the desk to the three men standing in the middle of the shop. Julian stood with his usual grimace, displaying his general distaste for those around him. The large second man wasn't someone Mitch knew, but the third man in ratty jeans was John, the valet from the Ritz.

"Gentlemen, welcome to The Rampant! What genuine article are we in search for today?" Clarence boldly inquired.

Julian whipped pictures of Mitch and Brooke in front of his face. "Do you have any of these in your shop, old man?"

Clarence leaned closer to the photos. "Don't have the right spectacles on today, sonny. Are they supposed to be in porcelain or full-wall portraits?"

Julian pushed Clarence away from the photographs. "Don't play smart with me, old man. I can make you an antique, if you try my patience."

Clarence laughed directly into Julian's face, causing his temper to flare as he presented his gun. "You can try all you want, youngster, but I doubt that your employer would think too kindly of your threats to superior members of the operation. What makes you think I would be hiding them for their protection from you? If I'm hiding them, maybe it's to hand them off *to* you." At the utterance of his last sentence, Julian's ears pricked up with interest. "On the other hand, why should you get all the glory? Maybe I'll hide them from you, turn them in, and reap all the benefits, while you and your friends crawl back under the rock from which you came."

Annoyed by Clarence's ramblings, Julian called his bluff. "Where are they?"

Clarence pointed to a large armoire standing against the wall on the other side of the shop. "Safest place to keep someone who you don't want getting away is to lock him or her in an armoire. They can kick and yell all they want, but since hardly anyone even visits our little shop, their fight is futile." Julian motioned for the large man to follow Clarence as he stood watch in the middle. The man followed Clarence to the armoire, where he presented an old key from his pocket. "Small key, big lock." he stated casually as the large man breathed heavily. John stood off to the right a few feet from Julian in the center, keeping his attention on an antique book about world events from the nineteenth century. While Clarence fiddled with the lock, Brooke slid next to Mitch behind the counter, whispering their plan of escape. He signaled his understanding with a casual nod, slid the tote bag over his shoulders, and prepared for a run. After a few minutes of fiddling with the lock, Clarence slowly opened the armoire's door. Creaking from age and a lack of oil, the door swung open to reveal its emptiness. The large man took a step toward Clarence with his hand balled up into a fist.

"You're obviously not familiar with the rarity of this piece. This armoire has a hidden chamber off the main storage space, in order to hide various items that you don't wish to parade past authorities. This actual piece came from an estate where a soldier hid to avoid the English during the Jacobite revolution. As you can see from the bullet holes that remain at the back of the piece, they found him without having to look. He died in this armoire." The man looked bewildered. "Sad indeed." Swinging the door open even further, he extended his hand in a manner of invitation for the man to investigate. As the man entered the darkness of the armoire, Clarence forced the door closed, swiftly locking it. John took advantage of the chaos and darted out the front door as Julian withdrew his weapon. Before he got a chance to use it, Clarence shouted out, "Hit it, Fi!"

Sophie Stuart burst from the shadows, striking Julian with a substantial blow from the glass shade of a Tiffany lamp.

"That's for chasing my girl, scumbag!" she spat at him as Julian crumpled to the floor. Brooke and Mitch popped their heads above the counter to watch Julian go down. Unfortunately, Sophie's small stature caused her aim to hit slightly below its intended mark. The blow hit him more on the shoulders than the head. Julian groaned from discomfort as well as from the shards of glass embedded in his skin. Sophie yelled, "Sorry kids, *run!*"

Mitch and Brooke took off at breakneck speed through the shop and out onto the street, where they began to weave their way through the pedestrian traffic on the sidewalk. The safety of the church was blocks away, and Brooke knew that if they could make it, they stood a fighting chance against anything Julian might have up his sleeve.

Fighting their way toward William Street, Mitch saw Julian emerge from the crowd. With shoulders hunched over in pain, he pushed through the crowd, gaining ground with each step. Mitch continued running while glancing back every few feet to check on Julian's progress, which slowed him down considerably. This fatal mistake allowed Julian to catch up with Mitch while Brooke ran ahead without looking behind.

A final glance over his shoulder resulted in Mitch's right shoulder hitting a lamp post, sending a searing pain into his body. The plastic clip on the shoulder strap of his tote bag broke away. Julian shouted more things as he tried to regain his advantage. He searched frantically for Brooke, fearing she had turned a corner without his knowledge. She emerged from the crowd, waving her arms madly for him to follow. After he had seen her, she took off like a bullet, dodging people on the street as she ran. Mitch tried to follow as closely as possible, but the number of people on the street increased, making it harder to maintain a safe distance from Julian. Turning onto the same street as Brooke, he bumped into a young man with his nose buried in a book. The force of their collision knocked the remaining strap of Mitch's tote loose, and it fell to the ground. Feeling the weight of the tote gone from his shoulder, he searched the gutters, doorways, and feet of the people walking around him. He searched in vain, as Julian's voice echoed above the heads of the commuters.

"Missing something, Mitchy?" he said, sneering and holding the battered tote bag above his head.

Mitch started to retrieve the lost article when Brooke grabbed him by the shoulder, yanking him back. "Don't," she whispered.

Continuing his taunting, Julian kept the tote above his head. "You know I was supposed to bring both you and your precious objects to my employer, but I guess today, just the objects will be good enough." He threw his head back in laughter. "Round two will have to be another day. Pity, I so wanted to finish this, but I'm a patient man."

Rage filled Mitch. "You can't get away with anything, Julian!"

"That's what every wimpy hero says right before they are killed," he shouted back. "I look forward to our next meeting, Brody. Hope it'll be soon." He sauntered away from Mitch, swinging the tote onto his back.

Mitch began to follow him. Brooke once again held him back. "I said don't. We have an appointment to keep, and if he thinks he won, then it will make our lives that much easier."

"How are you so calm? We just lost all the objects to that sniveling ass!" Mitch exclaimed.

"Let's get going before he decides that your life really is worth more than what he carries in the bag," she stated calmly, pulling him back down the street.

The Cathedral of St. John the Divine resided on the corner of William Street and George Street. Gothic masonry enticed visitors to ponder what surprises lay inside. Its dignity and spiritual presence was exceptional, given its incomplete structure. The first congregation had gathered at the location in 1846 when open fields surrounded the tiny village of Oban, and a lack of funding resulted in a halting of construction. But it remained a solid fixture within the community as well as in the parishioners' hearts.

Brooke entwined their fingers as they entered the building. Their footsteps echoed from the hardwood floors beneath. Simple yet graceful, the cathedral welcomed them without incident from outside forces. They walked past solid wooden chairs and a pulpit that was moved from St. Columba's Church on the Isle of Skye. Mitch's eyebrows rose at the mention of the Saint's name as Brooke nodded her head at his recognition. Approaching the altar, Brooke pointed out two windows on the west wall. One, depicting the dream of Jacob with his head on a stone pillow, was traditionally supposed to be the Coronation Stone housed in Edinburgh Castle. The other showed the vision of St. John the Divine, where the elders cast their crowns on a sea of glass. Having been through enough symbology over the last few weeks, Mitch formulated his own interpretations.

The altar was an impressive piece of wood. On the front, two saints met face-to-face with hills in the background. Behind the altar, angelic faces looked upon them, with the three center faces as the representation of heaven and earth uniting in perfect harmony. Pointing to a carving on the left side, Brooke stated, "Here we are." Mitch followed the direction of her finger to a wolf head, tilted slightly askew on the altar. She gently turned the head back toward the center of gravity. A small click reverberated against the Italian marble on the walls, as the altar slowly began to slide away, revealing a staircase bathed in candlelight.

"You expect me to go down there?" Mitch asked.

Brooke stepped in front of him. "Where's your sense of adventure?"

"My sense of adventure gets me shot," he blurted out.

"I'll make it worth your while!" she teased, shaking her hips in silent rhythm.

Mitch snickered as she swayed further down the stairs. "What the hell," he muttered.

When he had approached the fifth stair, the altar pulled back into its original position. Mitch panicked. He ran back up into the cramped space, pounding on the solid wood above his head for help.

"You're fine, Brody!" She waved, enticing him to meet her at the bottom. "I promise you'll get out of here."

Slowly making his way down the stone stairs, the walls next to him were moist from the dark and damp of ages. Brooke gave him a sarcastic pat on the head and grabbed his hand for moral support.

They walked side by side down the narrow corridor, leading to a room carved out of the same rock. The room was bright with candlelight as it spilled into the corridor, adding warmth to the subterranean vault. Brooke seemed confident in her steps, with a familiarity about the space. Approaching the room, Brooke let go of his hand, placed the torch into a soffit carved into the wall, and nudged him forward.

"Now, you will be given two things. First, the final piece to the puzzle. And two, the shock of your life," she stated.

"I thought *you* were the shock of my life," he confessed.

"I was just the warm-up," she replied, shoving him farther into the room.

Lit solely by candles, the ancient room held a white marble altar in the center. A single man stood guard behind it. Mitch walked forward, heart pounding, as the man laid both hands upon the cranium of a skull resting on a silver pedestal with a blue stone in the center. Next to it, a large silver box completed the picture. Mitch burst into laughter.

"Tom?" He scoffed in disbelief. "What are you doing here?"

Retaining a professional demeanor, Tom replied, "Trying to save my daughter."

ACKNOWLEDGEMENTS:

With Immense gratitude to.........

My little bears, who show me the essence of love, faith and strength each day I look into their eyes. Without them in my life, I would not be complete.

My husband Todd, who never questioned why, just accepted my theories and research as wonderful tales to write down. Thanks for being my guardian.

My mom, who led me by the hand while at the same time pushing me out of the nest, allowing me to fly on my own. My wings are spread wide because of your example.

The childhood friend, who touched my life and led me to this journey. May your light shine in the tale of your twin, as your soul remains immortal in my heart.

A beautiful malamute named Yeepa, who walks with me in my dreams.

Larry and Paula Sydow, who are unconditional love in human form.

Dr. Norma L. Goodrich, who illuminated my path to Iona.

Dr. Janet Leezer, who held the tiniest part of me in her hands, looked me in the eyes and said "everything will be fine." Your daily battle for the most fragile lives leaves me speechless. I stand in awe.

Dr. Rene Arcellana, the living example of the lesson that fortitude walks hand in hand with faith. You showed me that hope exists and if you dare to grasp it, all things are possible.

To Duncan, Jennifer and Emma Fox Smith, who opened my adolescent eyes to a larger world, including the amazing nation of Scotland. Without you, the backdrop of this book would not have been as brilliantly painted. Thank you for your friendship and memories.

To Jenny Chandler, my Create Space consultant and patch of blue sky.

The brilliant team at Create Space, without you the words would still be imprisoned on a hard drive begging for release. Thank you for making my dream come true.

Keith Dickson, whose artistic talent turned imagination into reality.

The journey continues in………

THE EXILE CARPET

Restoration

E.R. Blake

**Turn the page for a preview of what awaits
Tamara and Dr. Mitchell Brody.**

1

Rigid from head to toe, each man waited for the other to speak. Brooke positioned herself between the two men and the tunnel back to the world above. If Mitch did make a run for it, she would have one last chance to stop him with bodily force. Since no words escaped either man, Brooke took it upon herself to get the ball rolling.

"We're all on the same team, with the same goal." She announced, nervously wringing her hands. "Let's keep that focus and continue with what Tom has to teach." She peeked at Mitch's face as she cautiously asked, "That ok with you, Mitch?"

Mitch didn't think he could handle any more surprises. Tom was the final straw. Their friendship spanned a lifetime. The fact that Tom kept a secret this huge seemed ludicrous. Each time Mitch had broached the subject of Tom's frequent absences, his responses were identical and rehearsed. Overseas business called him away. His business dealings remained vague, but Mitch never questioned Tom's actions. Today, a doubt surfaced which didn't have an easy remedy.

Unable to take the higher ground, Mitch lashed out. "Is this what you meant by overseas business?"

Tom slowed his breathing. He expected a warmer greeting, but understood after all he had gone through. Putting his hands out in front of him, he made a silent surrender to defuse the tension.

"I know you're angry, but this about Tamara. We need to put anger or confusion we have aside for her sake." Lowering his head, Tom added, "Can you do that?"

Mitch felt exasperated by another person asking him to blindly follow into the maze of confusion. Each and every so-called Teacher began their lesson with the identical lecture about abandoning his prejudice, his questions, and his beliefs in order to enter their world of faith. At every step he towed the line, but not this time. This time with two people standing beside him who knew him better than anyone else in the world, he couldn't place who he was aside to follow them into a darkened cave without a flashlight. This time, he needed, he wanted and he would demand answers before taking the leap off the cliff.

"I don't think so Tom." Shoving his hands inside his pockets to avoid the temptation of throwing a punch, Mitch continued. "You see, throughout this trip I have been asked to do that same thing each time I turn around, but from you, I expect a little more. We're friends, Brothers and the closest thing to family without a blood relation. So, I think some answers are necessary before we move forward." Glancing back at Brooke, who looked nervous at his answer, his last comment was for her. "I don't care about any time crunch or schedule to keep." He turned back to face Tom. "You ok with that?" He asked.

Tom folded his arms across his chest; fulfilling the request. If it were anyone else, he would stand firm in his position within the organization and exercise his authority, but for Mitch he would make multiple exceptions. Pointing to chairs lining the wall, he asked Mitch to have a seat. Brooke remained standing as the two men sat down in the well-worn leather chairs with an empty space between them.

A thousand questions filled Mitch's brain, all screaming to be heard. Clarity is harder to find amidst heat from candles and stale air. Taking a deep breath, he found an easy one to start with. "Why me?"

Tom answered with a question of his own. "Can you think of anyone else better?"

"Lots of people." Mitch replied.

"I can't." Tom admitted quietly. "You were the logical choice from the day Tamara was born and we had to choose a Godfather. Lillian and I knew that it would result in a future escapade, although in our defense, we didn't think the situation would be this dire. There were a few considered for the job, but no one like you. You were the obvious choice."

"Come on Tom." Mitch blurted out. "You and Lillian have other friends who are better equipped to handle all of this than me, regardless of our family history. What makes me obvious?"

Tom's facial expression softened. "The way my daughter looked into your eyes the day you held her for the first time." His eyes misted up with the memory. "She was three weeks old, and you had come back from a conference in Europe, bursting at the seams to tell me about a mentor you met." Mitch smirked at his own memory. "You came through the door, sprinted across the room with an armful of pink roses for Lillian and a tiny princess tiara for Tamara, announcing that she was the most beautiful thing you had ever seen. Before Lillian could even object, you scooped her up out of her bassinet and began to sing. I watched Tamara become mesmerized by your presence. Her eyes emanated pure love and trust as she lay in your arms. The two of you knew each other on a deeper level and at that precise moment, Lillian and I saw you as her Godfather. It was Tamara's choice, and she chose you."

Humility was all Mitch felt, recalling the way that sweet bundle cooed as he rocked her back and forth. She was precious, tender and vulnerable to the world then and now. Something Mitch had forgotten during her medical treatment. He had lost her humanity and simply looked at her as a case. Guilt swept over him in one large, painful wave. "I'm sorry, Tom."

It was Tom's turn for bewilderment. "For what?"

"Promise me that after this is over, we can sit and have a beer so I can spill my guts." Mitch asked.

Tom extended his hand, solidifying the deal. "That can't be the only question."

Seizing the opportunity for further clarification, Mitch could no longer contain the myriad of questions flying from his lips. They included Tamara's future, his marriage to Lillian, his relationship to Duncan in the organization, his business dealings and how he managed to keep all of this from the men he called "Brothers" back home.

"Some of them knew." Tom stated, while Mitch gasped at his answer. "Only the upper levels of leadership, mind you, but they had to keep my family safe."

"You couldn't trust ME?" He asked candidly.

"I trust you with the only thing on this earth more precious than any secret. You hold her life in your hands, delivering it back to her time and time again. I needed you to remain focused on her and not on what I was doing." The corner of Tom's mouth turned slightly upwards. "You can't handle too much at one time." He teased.

"Don't I know it." Mitch muttered under his breath. "How did you manage to keep both lives separate?"

Tom admitted honestly. "I know you don't like to mention your father, but like him, I hide out in the open. Not many people question your business contacts when you're the head of an import/export company that specializes in historical antiques." Tom quickly glanced at Brooke blocking the exit to the hallway. "The position makes international travel necessary as well as perfectly logical."

"What is it you do?" Mitch asked, raising his level of frustration from the vague information.

"I scour the globe for hard to find artifacts pertaining to different periods of history and sell them to a private buyer. For Duncan, I use connections within the antiquities market to locate the objects you have been given for the ceremony."

Brooke beat Mitch to the next question, "How did you do that?"

"Duncan contacts me with the needed artifact, Clarence gives me tips on where to look and who to contact and I secure the finances required for the transaction. Once I complete the purchase, I fly back to Oban, hand deliver the item to Clarence for safe keeping until they are reunited with Tamara. Her illness sped up our timeline."

Mitch reclaimed his position as lead inquisitor. "And the organization? What do you do for them, other than purchase items from the black market?"

Tom snickered at Mitch's frank interviewing manner. "I am the High Priest of Oannes. I am second in command, should anything happen to the Master. I am the keeper of the most precious object other than my daughter." He turned his head towards the altar, staring at the skull positioned on the pedestal. "I am the Keeper of the Skull."

36638377R00210

Made in the USA
Middletown, DE
06 November 2016